*Are pharmaceutical companies controlled
by the same powers that control the
world's resources?*

The Trinity Conspiracy

Roger Quinn

Pp
PROSEPRESS
prosepress.biz

Published by Prose Press
Pawleys Island, South Carolina

www.prosepress.biz

ACKNOWLEDGMENTS:

This book would not have been possible without the support of my wonderfully patient wife, Barbara. Thank you from the bottom of my heart.

I owe a deep sense of gratitude to my friends and classmates at Coastal Carolina University's Osher Lifelong Learning Institute for their encouragement.

I am especially grateful to the following:

The staff at the North Myrtle Beach Library.

Elsie Schrage, who initially encouraged my journey into writing fiction.

Kelli Quinn Clark, for critiquing portions of the manuscript.

Annie Pott, editor and master of subtlety.

Bob O'Brien, publisher and friend.

Darlene Eichler, mentor. Thank you for honing my innate ability to weave a story with fabrication, embellishment, and lies.

AUTHOR'S NOTE:

Any reference to real people or historical events or places is coincidental. All the characters in this book are fictional.
The events I describe are based upon my research; government documents, published accounts, interviews and personal experience.

Virology is a topic of great interest as discussions of infectious disease spread from the scientific realm to the political arena.

I have attempted to present these diverse perspectives in this work of fiction.

Cast of Characters - page 303

INTRODUCTION

In June 2004, the Plum Island Animal Disease Research Center (PIADC) celebrated its 50th Anniversary. It was a multimedia event. Officials from local and national agencies mingled with the press and the Island's employees. The occasion served as a public relations opportunity to showcase the transition of this top-secret facility from the Department of Agriculture to the Department of Homeland Security.

The goal was to demonstrate the heightened security on Plum Island. Police cars from the Town of Southold patrolled the road leading past the Orient Ferry Depot to the gates of the Plum Island Animal Disease Center. Federal agents from a number of agencies worked their way among the maze of remote broadcast satellite trucks: CBS, ABC, NBC, Fox.

"This is Karen Walker, reporting live from the North Fork, Long Island, ferry dock at Plum Island Animal Research Center. Armed security guards patrol this facility. Department of Homeland Security agents meticulously follow a security checklist, issuing identification badges to the guests.

"Once known as a quiet fishing and farming community, Greenport and its neighboring towns are experiencing a rapid population growth of year-round residents. Plum Island was once a leading local employer. Nearly every North Fork family either had a relative or knew someone employed on the Island. Docked right behind me is the new Plum Island ferry, named for its long-time and now retired director, Dr. Jerry Callis. The ferry ride will take about 30 minutes, followed by another security check. A major contractor for federal facilities here and abroad, handles Island security. This is Karen Walker, Cable News12, reporting live."

"Karen, this is Scott, back in the newsroom."

"Yes, Scott, I hear you."

"Karen, any sign of protesters?"

"No, Scott, that's interesting, too. There were several protests here in the late 1970's and '80's. We expected some type of demonstration, but nothing at all today."

"Karen, do you think we are seeing a new chapter in the Plum

Island story? Will people be able to sleep better knowing security on the Island has been improved?"

"Environmental groups are questioning the Island's mission and safety. One source close to the North Fork Environmental Group called this the same old dog and pony show. The media, politicians, and agency officials turn out, make promises and then go home until the next crisis."

"Thanks, Karen. We'll see you again with your live report from Plum Island."

"Thanks Scott. And now back to you in our newsroom."

Matt Nagle tuned into WBRU Radio, Providence. He caught the tail end of the morning news.

"*Today's media tour of Plum Island appears to be an effort to offset concerns about the Island's safety record. Located off Long Island's North Fork, the Animal Disease Research Center has been clouded in secrecy and controversy. Author Michael Carroll's book, Lab 257, argues that West Nile Virus most likely originated from a research accident on Plum Island. An Island official declined comment on Carrol's book, noting he hadn't read it.*"

Nagle turned off the radio and searched for a parking space. He found one at the far end of the road. Nagle was an invited guest without VIP parking.

"Name?" asked the guard.

"Matt Nagle. I should be listed under Deputy County Executive Forman's party."

"Yes, sir, Mr. Nagle. Here's your temporary credential. Please proceed through our security check."

It was a rainy day over twenty years ago when Nagle made his first visit to Plum Island. The facility was a closely guarded asset. Until the mid-'70's, few Long Islanders knew it existed. Only a handful knew its mission. For Matt Nagle, the Island was a curiosity, not quite an obsession. Like an itch that wouldn't go away.

The terminal had a fresh coat of paint. Even the old S.S. Shahan had been replaced. A new ferry carried employees and visitors to and from the Island. *Things have certainly changed,* Nagle thought. Or had they?

"If the Government becomes a lawbreaker, it breeds contempt
for law; it invites every man to become a law unto himself;
it invites anarchy."
Justice Louis Brandeis (1928)

"In a political sense, there is one problem that currently
underlies all the others. That problem is making government
sufficiently responsive to the people. If we don't make
government responsive to the people, we don't make
government believable. And we must make government
believable if we are to have a functioning democracy."
Rep. Gerald Ford (1971)

"The United States is so vulnerable to terrorism precisely
because terrorists recognize the high value this country places
on the lives of each of its citizens."
Newsday, June 20, 1985

The Nazi regime and their collaborators performed biological
and chemical research on prisoners. Is it morally and ethically
correct to allow those collaborators to
profit from the research?
R. Gale (2004)

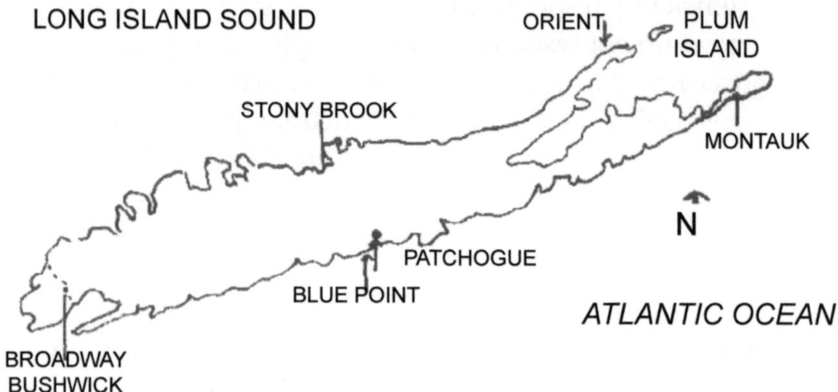

LONG ISLAND SOUND
ORIENT
PLUM ISLAND
STONY BROOK
MONTAUK
N
PATCHOGUE
BLUE POINT
ATLANTIC OCEAN
BROADWAY BUSHWICK

Chapter 1

It all started simply enough. Tony Portavani, Matt Nagle's neighbor, stopped by for wine and cheese, a regular ritual for Tony and Matt. They'd spend hours discussing politics. Matt called it "waxing philosophical." Tony said it was plain and simple bullshitting. In any case, the Portavanis and the Nagles were more than neighbors, they were close friends. Tony's electrical business was expanding. With three full-time employees on the payroll, Tony decided to chance a bid on a government contract. On this day, Tony was agitated and angry. His disheveled appearance puzzled Matt.

"I'm in trouble." Tony confessed.

"What's wrong?"

"About a year ago I bid on this job on Plum Island."

"Isn't that where they do all that secret stuff with germs and animal diseases? That place is so secret the Island doesn't show on a map of Long Island."

"Secret? Maybe. The only secret out there is the mess that place is in. Everything is falling about. And the new contract bids are a mess. If they don't get things going soon, I'm going to default on my bond. I haven't been paid a penny. The Department of Agriculture is holding up the work. Supposedly, there are problems in the Confinement Lab. I don't believe them. I don't trust them. I don't know what's going on. I don't know what I'll do."

Tony rarely talked about his business, so Matt knew the situation was serious.

"Hey, guys." Just then, Matt's wife, Liz, came into the kitchen struggling with two large bags of groceries. "Matt, there's two more bags in the trunk of my car. Bring them in for me. So Tony, where's Joan?"

"Uh…she took the kids to visit her mother and sister in Florida," Tony said.

"Took them out of school?"

"Yes; her Mom's having an operation."

"I'm sorry. Must have been a quick decision. Joan didn't say a thing about it. Want to have supper with us?" asked Liz.

"No, thanks. I was just about to ask your old man if he'd take a ride with me. Maybe take him to dinner. How about it, Matt?"

"Liz?"

"Sure, but I planned on making eggplant. It's your favorite."

"We won't stay long. I'll grab something to eat while we're out."

Anthony Portavani was ten when his mother ran off with her husband's best friend. Tony's father, Nick, a New York Times pressman, sank into a depression. He started hitting the bottle. In July, the summer Tony graduated high school, his father died. "My old man did the best he could for me and my sister," he told the handful of folks who attended the funeral. The insurance money was soon exhausted. After that, Marie, Tony's older sister, left college and worked two jobs to pay the rent on the dilapidated apartment in Astoria, Queens.

After high school, Tony tried to get into the electrical trades. He didn't have a union connection. With nowhere else to turn, Tony joined the Army in 1958.

During basic training, his sergeant discovered Tony could type. By 1958, the military was changing. The Korean conflict reached a stalemate. The Cold War was heating up. Eventually, PFC Anthony Portavani found himself in West Germany. Army Intelligence occupied several converted German Army barracks on Rhein-Main Air Base in Frankfurt. Tony worked as a clerk in a processing center. He rarely talked about those years in Germany. When asked about his military service, Tony would reply, "I stamped forms. It was boring as hell."

Tony was discharged in 1960, about the time the East Germans began constructing what would become the Berlin Wall. "I wanted no part of it. I'd done my time. An Army buddy got me an apprenticeship with Local Three. I finally got my union ticket." Tony worked hard. He was a calculator, always living in the future. Anthony and Joan Portavani purchased their Patchogue home in 1970. In need of repair, it still cost almost more than they could afford. Patchogue's Main Street was a few blocks away. Joan could walk to the stores. She worked part time. Tony walked to the railroad station each morning at 5:30.

In the late '60's, Tony started moonlighting on weekends for local contractors. As business increased, Tony took the risk and started his own business. It was a struggle, but what start-up isn't? "I never want to be poor again."

Tony dreamed of landing a corporate contract like the big shots he worked for. Eventually he landed the bid for repairs on the Plum Island laboratory.

"Government contract bids are complicated," Joan said.

"I checked with the accountant. We can use our home to secure the credit and security bonds."

"I remember contractors coming into the bank," Joan replied. "They were desperate. You may have to wait for months or years for payments."

"We have to take the risk, Joan."

"It's a complex process, Tony. I am really uncomfortable. Suppose something goes wrong?"

"Everything is going to work out."

That was six months ago. Over the last month, Joan's doubts turned into Tony's nightmare. A strange series of events led to Tony's despair. Earlier in the day, Tony received a certified letter from their home mortgage holder. The Portavanis had fallen into arrears on their mortgage payments. They faced foreclosure. Tony needed to confide in a friend.

"See you later, Liz," Matt called as the two friends walked to Tony's black Caddy sedan.

"Where to?" asked Tony as he took a right on Main Street.

"How about the Snapper Inn in Oakdale?"

"You got it."

"I love this car," Tony said, reaching into his shirt pocket for a toothpick.

Matt glanced around. "You're a compulsive neat freak. What's with the mess? The ashtray is stuffed with half-smoked Lucky Strikes and toothpicks. Clothes and junk are on the back seat. Are you living out of your car?"

"The last week's been crazy. It's either chew toothpicks or smoke or…" Tony hesitated. He struggled for an explanation. "I haven't been home in a couple of days. I'm living in my car or at the office. Joan's gone. She took the kids. They're safe, but only for now. A lot's happened."

Matt was confused by his friend's sudden revelation. What catastrophe could so overwhelm his friend? He sensed something had gone terribly wrong in Tony's life.

"I need your help, Matt. You're the only one I can trust. I've got some stuff on the back seat; blueprints, two drawings and a box of documents. Please… I need you to put them someplace safe…out of the way."

"Okay. I'm not going to get into any trouble, am I?"

Tony avoided Matt's question. "I'll show you the stuff later. Right now I need a stiff scotch. I haven't slept for days. I keep telling myself everything will work out, but I'm scared. This Plum Island job has turned to shit. I'm bankrupt."

"How did you get involved with Plum Island?"

Tony drove west towards Oakdale. "Let's take the long way along the Montauk Highway, okay? It's a long story."

"Sure," said Matt.

"Believe me, Matt. I never wanted to jeopardize Joan and the kids. I dreamed of landing a corporate contract like the big shots I worked for. Government contract bids are complicated and require established credit and security bonds. I underestimated the risk. Joan was against it from the start. She kept the books. It's all my fault."

Matt listened. Tony was frenzied. *Tony's going crazy.* His friend jumped from one topic to the other. Matt couldn't hold on to the context. "Slow down, buddy," Matt said. "You're losing me."

Tony grew increasingly agitated. "Remember when we talked about my stint in Germany? Well, I left some stuff out."

They drove south toward the Great South Bay and then west again toward the river. The Snapper Inn was just over the bridge.

Thank God.

Tony choked the life out of the steering wheel. "I need to talk. I trust you. I can't handle this. How do I tell Joan?"

She's probably figured it out by now. What have I gotten into? I could be home with Liz, enjoying eggplant parmesan.

"It was an overwhelming task."

"What?"

"My group processed German nationals. They needed visas and visa renewals to enter the United States. There were rows of card files containing the names of suspected war criminals and SS members. I ran checks on applications and requests for files, and visa renewals. It was a no-brainer. I stamped papers 'approved,' 'denied,' or 'review.' That's it. It was a joke. Another office handled initial visa applications. "

"Sounds pretty simple to me," Matt agreed.

"Seemed like it to me. There was one complication. Intelligence groups were still searching for Nazi war criminals. Nazi war criminals were using false identities. They were traveling in and out of Germany using multiple passports and visas. Do you think a Nazi fugitive was going to use his real name?"

"It must have been a task. Did you have a computer?"

"Not back then. It was an impossible task. There were thousands of applications and requests for records. We had a daily quota. By the end of the day, we'd just sample them. Nobody seemed to care."

"That sounds awfully cynical coming from you," said Matt. "I've read about the Nuremberg trials."

"We had all sorts of intelligence types coming through the office. They called our files the CROWCASS Registry. Other documents were stored in a Luftwaffe barracks. They were classified. Our Registry was intended to locate men and sometimes women who committed war crimes at the camps and prisons."

"Atrocities?" asked Matt.

"Yes. As each card was reviewed, a small red or green dot was placed in the upper left corner. 'Be careful with the green dots,' the civilian supervisor told me. He was always looking over my shoulder. One day I asked him, 'Why the colored dots?'"

"And what did he tell you?"

"He said, 'That's for me to know…not you.' Each time a green dot card was pulled, the supervisor cross-referenced the name to double check if the folder was stored in the Luftwaffe barracks."

Tony's story intrigued Matt. "Anything else?" asked Matt.

"I filed the pulled cards. I recognized a pattern. The intelligence agencies were searching for veterinarians, doctors, chemists, biologists."

"Why would the U.S. government be interested in veterinarians?"

"The Navy Department seemed to take a special interest in veterinarians. Like I said, the top secret files were kept in the Luftwaffe barracks."

Matt looked perplexed. "Did you ever go there?"

"No."

"You make it sound like something sinister was going on."

"I keep thinking about those intelligence types. They scoured the CROWCASS Registry. The Registry cards. I'm telling you there was a pattern."

"Hold on, buddy. Why is all this so important now? My God, man, get hold of yourself."

"Don't you see? They were recruiting scientists. Nazi specialists."

"Who is they?" *Tony is headed for a nervous breakdown.*

"Matt, it's crazy. I think there are still Nazis on the government payroll."

Tony unfolded his handkerchief and wiped away the perspiration on his face.

"I recall reading those allegations a few years ago. The CIA and the Department of Defense denied the charges. There were Nazis in the rocket program. Guys like von Braun. The State Department assured Congress they were not war criminals. Germans were forced to join the Nazi party to keep their jobs."

"Bullshit. You don't believe that. Do you? What's happening to me is…" Tony stopped in mid-sentence. "I skipped over something important," he insisted.

"Take it easy, man. I'm listening. What did you leave out?"

"Back in Germany…one weekend a month, I pulled duty. Three weekends a month I spent in town. Hilda Koch was her name. She was a clerk-typist on the base."

Tony sensed Matt's disbelief. "You don't believe me."

"Tony, quite honestly, it sounds like a spy novel. I want to believe you," said Matt.

"I started to tell you about Hilda. She was some piece of ass, beautiful. Reminded me of the women in old newsreels. Hitler's guests at Berchtesgaden. I like big-ass woman. Hilda was a little plump, but gorgeous. And passionate. One night she nearly killed me."

A vague smile crossed Tony's face. He fidgeted with the car radio. Matt sensed his friend's mind was wandering.

"How is all this related to the job? What happened?" Matt persisted.

"Man, I'm sorry. I can't stay focused. I'm a wreck."

"Get back to your story."

"I was a stupid kid. I bragged about Hilda. One of the guys made a smart remark. I clocked him. He reported me.

"The CO, Captain Kelley, threatened me. 'Love or sex. Call it what you want, Portavani. As far as I'm concerned, these German broads are strictly for fun,' Kelley shouted. 'You're getting off easy this time. Around here we have two rules. Don't get V.D. Don't get 'em pregnant. For you, I'm adding one more rule: Don't get involved. You are her ticket to the U.S. This is your first and last warning. Just test me. I'll bust you.'

"'Fine by me,' I told him.

'Now, get your ass out of here,' Kelley ordered.'

❧

It was a clear, warm summer evening as they arrived at The Snapper Inn. A gentle breeze came across Fire Island and up the river. Tony and Matt talked as they crossed the parking lot and walked along the lawn to the dock.

"Let's get a drink," said Tony. They headed inside. The hostess seated them at a table with a river view. Tony ordered a Johnny Walker Black. Matt rarely drank on weeknights. *Tonight I need a drink.*

Matt ordered an Absolut Martini straight up with three olives. "So what happened with the fraulein?"

"Well, things turned weird. I thought we were having fun. Hilda felt differently. She was falling in love. And me…I disregarded Kelley's warning. I continued to see her. The relationship grew."

"I'm not following you."

"Hold on. One day an inquiry came across my desk from the Navy. They were requesting documents for a Karl Peter Koch, including a folder stored at the Luftwaffe barracks. I couldn't find a CROWCASS Registry card for Karl Peter Koch."

"There were thousands of cards. Maybe his was misplaced," said Matt.

"I checked the 'deceased and missing' catalog. There were hundreds of Koch's, but only two Karl's. Two names came up: Karl Otto Koch and Karl Peter Koch. Both were listed as deceased. Karl Otto Koch was an SS concentration camp commandant. He was executed by firing squad in 1944. The charge was embezzlement. The second card listed Karl Peter Koch. The odd part…no date of death was listed. He was a virologist. His record included the Berlin Institute and Dachau Prison."

"Dachau? Are you certain? Dachau was a prison camp."

"I'm absolutely certain."

"Why?"

"From the last known address. It was the same as Hilda's."

"Your Hilda?"

Their conversation was interrupted. "Your drinks, gentlemen," said the petite waitress.

"Thanks, honey." Tony winked. She smiled. Matt felt awkward.

"Cheers," said Tony, gulping the scotch.

"Tell me. What's the connection between Koch and Hilda?"

"I told Hilda. That was a mistake. She told me her father, Kurt Koch, was a Luftwaffe aviator. He was killed in a bombing raid over London. Hilda's mother, Frieda, never remarried. A widow's pension didn't pay the rent. Life became difficult as the German populace made increasing sacrifices to help the Fatherland's war effort. Uncle Peter, Kurt's brother, came to the rescue.

"Hilda told me, 'Without Uncle Peter, mother and I would have been captured by the Russians. We could not have survived the war. When Germany surrendered we fled to the American Zone.'"

"I've read stories about the Russian reprisals," said Matt.

"Karl Peter Koch had connections."

"Perhaps a stash of stolen diamonds or gold," guessed Matt.

"I double checked. No CROWCASS Registry card for a Karl Peter Koch.

"I hesitated on the Navy's request. I stamped it 'for review.' I notified my civilian supervisor. Within days the Navy's request bounced back. It was 'green tagged' along with several other official inquiries I wanted my supervisor to review."

"In other words, you were covering your ass."

"The supervisor told me to expedite the requests."

"What did you do?"

"What do you think? I told Hilda. She was baffled and angry.

"She said, 'My uncle worked at the Berlin Institute. During the war he worked at Dachau Prison. He is not a war criminal. He left Dachau long before the Americans captured it.'

"Then I made a big mistake. I went over the supervisor's head and informed my CO."

"Kelley? The guy who threatened to bust you?"

"I know. Stupid. I told him I suspected a problem."

"Did he ask about Hilda?"

"Nope. Never batted an eye. But he was interested in my concerns about Koch."

"And?"

"We have a name for altered records…sanitized. I told him Koch's registry card had been sanitized."

"What did he say?"

"There was a long silence. He assured me he would overlook my violation of procedure, you know, dating Hilda. He warned me not to discuss my suspicions with anyone, not even Hilda. I could still face a hearing or even a court martial."

"Just like that?"

"Yes. I was confused. I gave Kelley the CROWCASS cards."

"Besides Koch's name, do you remember the other names?" asked Matt impatiently.

"I'm trying to remember. I recall one, an Otto Bruns. I took a second look at his card."

"Why?" asked Matt.

"Bruns' card was a later entry in the CROWCASS Registry."

"How so?"

"The newer cards included a photograph. After 1943, the Nazis included photos. Bruns had distinct features. For one he had a facial scar, a dueling scar. Give me time and I'll remember the third name."

"So what happened to you and the fraulein?" prodded Matt.

"Frieda? Frau Koch disapproved of Hilda dating an American soldier, but I knew my biggest stumbling block was Uncle Peter. I met him once after the CROWCASS episode. My gut told me he was a Nazi to the core. He didn't like me."

"Did Koch connect you with the visa application?"

"Yes. Of course. Someone inside the unit must have tipped him off. Koch was putting pressure on Hilda to stop seeing me."

'Uncle Peter dislikes you,' Hilda told me. She said to him, 'I don't mean to hurt my mother. For the first time I feel I am enjoying life.'

"Peter told her, 'This affair between you and the American is scandalous. This business must stop.'"

"Did you stop seeing her?"

"No. We found a flat…two rooms with a bath. It was more her idea than mine. Housing was scarce and expensive. Friends cautioned me it was an unsafe neighborhood for uniformed Americans.

"Late one evening, I returned home. Hilda wasn't there, but two goons were. I walked right into it. One guy held me. The other guy, six two, a gorilla, slapped the shit out of me. They tied me to a kitchen chair. Gave me a Gestapo-like interrogation: 'Aufenthalt weg von Hilda. Verstehen Sie?'

"'I don't understand,' I pleaded.

"'Stay away!' the other guy whispered. The big guy rolled up his shirt sleeves. He laughed and turned to his accomplice. I'll never forget his tattoo. An SS blood tattoo on the inside of his upper arm. He swung his arm and punched me in the solar plexus. He laughed and punched me again."

"A blood tattoo?"

"SS members are known to have had their blood type tattooed on their arm. His was bold Gothic 'A-.' Maybe a death camp guard."

"And then what happened?" *This is an unbelievable mystery story.*

"They trashed everything. I woke up in the base hospital. Two MPs were standing guard. I spent the next five days confined to barracks. Protesting was useless. An anonymous caller tipped the Military Police.

"The civil authorities and the military ruled out robbery. Rumors spread that Hilda had a German boyfriend. They chalked up my beating to jealous revenge.

"Kelley came to the hospital. I was confined to barracks."

"'Don't try to contact Hilda Koch or her family. That's an order,' he said.

"I didn't trust him. I was set up. There was something phony going on. Too many coincidences.

"Kelley visited me one last time. He was a changed man. He offered to help me.

"He said, 'I talked with CID. They'll make a few concessions, reduce charges. Everything will be OK.'"

"What? Why the sudden change?" asked Matt.

"Kelley told me, 'You're lucky. You'll be confined to barracks until further notice. You'll need to sign some papers. Simple as that.'

"I was denied telephone privileges. When my confinement ended, I tried to telephone Hilda. Her phone was disconnected. The Koch's apartment was vacant. I never saw Hilda or her family again."

"That was suspicious. You mean she just disappeared?"

"Uncle Peter hired those goons. I know it. It didn't matter. Orders came through shipping me home. Someone wanted me out of there. I spent three months in Kentucky and got an honorable discharge six months early."

"Sounds strange," said Matt.

"Back then I didn't think about it. I just wanted out of Germany and the Army. It took over a year for my ribs to heal. What a beating. Those bastards." Tony took another swallow of scotch.

"Hey, slow down. You're drinking scotch like it's water."

"I worked my ass off to own my own business. Be my own boss." Tony slurred his words. "This whole mess is unfair," Tony protested.

Matt gestured for Tony to calm down. "You've worked hard." He nodded in agreement.

"I've been busting my ass. I've finally got something. I can't let them take it away."

The little brunette waitress returned. She smiled at Tony.

"You're looking good," said Tony.

"She knows she's in for a big tip," Matt whispered.

"Try the baked clams. Most places just open the clams and throw on bread crumbs, but not here," said the waitress. "I've seen the chef at work."

"I bet you have," said Tony, on his third scotch. Music drifted in from the dock. Nearly two hours had passed. Tony rambled on about Plum Island. He wasn't making much sense. The Plum Island debacle would have to wait.

"Okay, okay." *I've had it.*

❦

Matt groped the nightstand for the ringing alarm clock. It was 5:30 a.m. He turned toward Liz. Burying her head beneath a pillow she asked, "What time did you get home? I waited until nearly midnight. I was getting worried. What happened?"

"Nothing," said Matt

"What do you mean, nothing?"

"All we talked about was Tony's time in the Army."

"The Army? He looked like the world was coming to an end. The Army?" Liz turned toward Matt as he fell back onto the bed.

"You know who you remind me of?" he said, sliding his hand under her nightgown. He caressed her buttocks.

"I know," said Liz. She had heard Matt's teasing a thousand times before.

Matt rolled on top of her.

"You know, mister…we have to go to work. The kids need to get ready for school. There's no…. Okay, just a quickie."

Chapter 2

The old man struggled with his suitcase, pushing it with his foot, as the seemingly endless line of passengers waited to clear customs at London's Gatwick Airport. He had been sick since leaving South Africa. The Caledonia flight had stopped for a layover in Ghana, West Africa, one of the few West African nations allowing flights from South Africa to land. Since departing Ghana, he had spent most of the flight in the lavatory stricken with diarrhea and vomiting. Only once before Johannesburg had he felt so ill. He was certain it was malaria.

"Professor Koch, are you sure you will be all right?" asked the sympathetic woman seated beside him.

"Oh yes. Quite sure. Quite sure. I do appreciate your concern." He managed a faint smile, then a grimace.

Alice Thatcher, a British Overseas Volunteer, was returning from a tour of service in Ghana.

"This is my address. Actually, it's my parent's home, but I'll be staying there for the next few weeks. Please, ring me up, if I can help."

The British Caledonian flight landed at Gatwick Airport in London's suburbs. The air-stairs lowered and the passengers disembarked. Koch welcomed the overcast chilly London morning. It was a welcome change from Ghana's humidity.

Koch proceeded through Customs and Immigration. He answered the routine questions, mustering all his strength to avoid suspicion.

"Have you been ill within the last twenty four hours or are you now suffering from an illness contracted while in Africa?"

questioned the agent.

"No." Koch had traveled through customs in more than a dozen countries. He practiced his facial expressions over and over. One wrong body move would reveal him to the experienced agent. His answers must be concise, not abrupt, and always accompanied by a condescending smile.

"This yellow card is a health identification credential. Carry it with your passport. If you become ill, follow the instructions on the reverse side."

"Thank you," said Koch. He tucked the card inside his U.S. passport and moved along. Ms. Thatcher waited for Koch at the exit.

"Ms. Thatcher, thank you again for your kindness."

"Are you certain I can't assist you?"

"Yes, of course." Koch's English was impeccable. His mannerisms would not betray him. Koch rather enjoyed changing the nuances of his voice. The American commentator, William Buckley, and the Brit, Arthur Treacher, were his favorite impersonations. Rod Steiger was his favorite actor. But this wasn't the time. He searched for the airport lavatory. Nevertheless, assuming a new identity was arduous.

Once inside, Koch moved the "wet floors" caution sign and locked himself in the end stall. Unscrewing his watch casing, Koch removed two tablets and swallowed. They immediately began to ease the severe intestinal cramps. When the pain subsided, Koch left the lavatory and followed the directory to the currency exchange window. From there it was a short distance to the South Terminal and the shuttle to Victoria Station. Karl Peter Koch was on schedule.

Victoria Station's bustling crowds made Karl Peter Koch invisible. Koch's destination was the Belgravia Hotel. Before World War I, the Belgravia district represented London's wealth and sophistication. The nightly Luftwaffe's bombings during World War II changed Belgravia and England. Only the building's facades echoed the past. The grand homes had been turned into what Americans call "bed and breakfast" accommodations.

Koch registered. He looked up the winding staircase. The Belgravia did not have a lift. The old man struggled on the last few steps. His third floor accommodations were clean, modest, and inconspicuous. Koch inspected the room then unzipped his battered suitcase.

Koch was exhausted. The medication was wearing off. His body demanded rest. He was reaching his pain threshold. He resisted increasing the morphine dose. *The drug weakens my determination. My mind wanders to the dark days of the war.* Koch rarely thought of his sister-in-law, Frieda, or his niece, Hilda. The last months of the war and the unconditional surrender were a nightmare.

"We are not Nazis," Frieda had protested. "Your brother was not a Nazi. This war has taken my husband and now it has claimed you.

"The Nazis are bent on Germany's destruction. Your brother fought because it was his duty."

"I warn you, Frieda. That's treason. Stop! I forbid it. If Germany is defeated it will be because the German people are unworthy of the Fuehrer's plans. Then they deserve to lose everything."

In the final days of the Third Reich, March 1945, Karl Peter Koch fled to Munich from Dachau and on to Berlin. Koch was constantly on the run. Berlin was a city in chaos. Rumors of surrender and the Russian advance on Berlin convinced Koch he had to flee to the Americans. Germany was in the process of surrendering. Koch and several colleagues began planning an escape route from the ravaged city. Koch knew if the Russians caught him, it would mean execution or deportation to the East. Frau Koch prayed the Americans would occupy Berlin first. She recognized the fear in Koch's eyes.

It was too late. In early April 1945, Peter Koch, along with every able man and boy, was rounded up and sent to the eastern outskirts of Berlin. Malingerers were shot. The directive also mobilized the Hitler Youth and Home Guard. The Russians surrounded Berlin. General Eisenhower, the Supreme Allied Commander, halted the other Allied armies. Berlin was given to the Russians. The street fighting was a ferocious onslaught. Koch managed to escape the Russian assault, but not Frieda and Hilda. They were trapped in the house-to-house fighting. Thousands of women and children were raped and killed by marauding Russian soldiers. Few defenders were spared the "take no prisoners" order.

At first, the Russian officers tried to stop their men, but their fury was too great. They commanded angry peasants, their villages burned and families slaughtered. The officers could do nothing. Fearing their men might kill them, the officers fled. Mother and daughter were left to die. They hid in a basement storage closet of their apartment building. Hilda was battered and in shock. There were no clinics. No medical help. Frieda neglected her injuries, her pain numbed by the sight of young Hilda. Only Hilda's survival kept Frieda from suicide. Koch relived his sister's suffering over and over in his sleep. Koch forced the memories from his mind. *I must focus my energy on the task at hand.*

Time was cruel to Koch. His once taut handsome figure had withered into that of an old man. His eyelids drooped. Wisps of grey flecked his bald head. He avoided mirrors. Koch was physically and emotionally drained. But, he was driven.

Koch's flu-like symptoms first appeared as he departed South Africa. He felt cold and clammy. Koch fumbled with a small Swiss Army knife he carried. He carefully cut a few inches of the stitching of his suit jacket pocket, feeling for one of six pills, an antibiotic he requisitioned in South Africa. It was an experimental drug, yet to be tested on a larger population. Koch swallowed the pill. It was risky. Koch was desperate.

Koch closed the drapes and tried to sleep. He feared sleep, even a nap. He was haunted by a recurring dream. Its intensity frightened him. He never told anyone. He was convinced the haunting vision reflected his sexual impotency. A young, faceless woman twisted and turned. She heaved with excitement, then tumbled into a deep sleep.

Impotency scared Koch. *It is a weakness. My mission relies on strength and virility.* Koch would not betray his immediate task. He had a contract to discharge. No time to sleep. Someday, I will help punish our enemies for destroying Hitler's dream.

Koch paced the room. He glanced at his watch. It was 2:00 p.m. He was due at Harrods in thirty minutes. *My timetable. I must stay on schedule.*

Chapter 3

Descending the steps of the Belgravia Hotel, Koch debated walking to Harrods. This time last year his brisk pace would have covered the distance to Knightsbridge in less than twenty minutes. I'm a tired old man, he thought, climbing into the waiting black cab. Peter Koch much preferred the exclusiveness of Savile Row. For today, Harrods would do. Koch had one, perhaps two, purchases in mind. He suspected this would be his last visit to London. The taxi dropped him opposite Harrods. The old man paused and then turned away. Before indulging himself in Harrods, Koch had an important task. Pacing himself, Koch slowly walked east towards Knightsbridge and Sloan Street, where he entered a small shop. He glanced around and spotted the listing for menswear on the lower ground. Again, he was careful to appear the casual shopper. A collection of ties caught his eye. He ran his fingers along their silk linings. *I never liked silk.* Koch dropped the tie and proceeded to the lower level.

Always cautious, Koch surveyed his surroundings, counting the number of shoppers and clerks. He passed the luxury accessories and stopped at a display of watches. Two male clerks of contrasting physical appearance restocked shoes. The heavier of the two, the one with the slicked down hair, greeted Koch. "May I help you, sir? Do you have something special in mind?"

"I'm looking for a special Irish walking cap. I misplaced mine a while back. As though on cue, the second clerk stepped forward. "Ah, I may have just such a hat in mind. Allow me." Almost as though he had been anticipating Koch's visit, the young man pointed to a cap he had placed on display a few minutes earlier.

"Not much call for Donegal Tweed these days," said the clerk turning toward the display.

"And why's that?" inquired Koch.

"The IRA, Sir. They placed a bomb in a litter bin at the top of an escalator at the exhibition hall, Earl's Court. It was a home show. The blast injured seventy people. Arms, legs, body parts all over the place."

"Awful," replied Koch.

"Yes it was. And just this past week, an off-duty police officer with the Met and a civilian were shot dead. It's been on the news every day. They'll catch them soon and when they do…" the clerk drew his index finger across his throat. "There'll be no mercy."

Koch took quick note of the clerk's trim physical appearance and mannerism. He was an Arab with closely cropped hair and socially acceptable facial hair. Definitely from a military background, Koch concluded.

"Sir, this cap is pure wool," said the clerk.

"Not Chinese, is it"? Koch smiled.

"No, sir. I'm confident you will be pleased."

The label read "Joy and health to you who wear this hat." *Exactly what I need: joy and health.*

"Excellent. What a coincidence. You must have been expecting me. I'll take it," said Koch.

"Care to try it on, sir?"

"I don't think that will be necessary. Do you?"

The clerk and Koch exchanged a knowing smile. Koch paid with a credit card.

"Your card, Mr. Bruns." As Koch signed the receipt, the clerk reached under the counter. With sleight of hand, he placed a plastic box, no larger than a pack of Players Number Six, into a small shopping bag along with the cap.

The clerk handed Koch the shopping bag. "Thank you, sir."

Pleased with his purchase, Koch ignored further pleasantries and returned to the street. Koch was fatigued. *Assuming another identity is draining. I am losing my stamina. No time to rest. I have to be at the Post Office.* He glanced at his watch. *4:05 p.m.*

Koch crossed to Brompton Road via Harrods. *There is still time for one last walk through the store.* Koch stopped on the sidewalk.

One last look around. An elderly couple walked by. Koch felt a momentary longing. *What would life have been with Anna?* Koch entered the ground level through the revolving door. *Ah. Just as I recall.* His eye caught the Fine Jewelry Room. *Perhaps a token?* His mind wondered to a distant time of brief happiness. *Would she understand my intention?* Nothing caught his eye.

The store was crowded. A sudden shove from behind startled Koch. A young woman with two children in tow tripped and stumbled forward into him. Koch lost his balance. *What's happening? The shopping bag.* Koch reached for a countertop to break his fall. His elbow smashed the counter's edge. Koch winced. The pain amplified through his body. Instinctively, Koch turned and scolded the two ruffians: "Stoppen!"

"I am so sorry," said the woman. She hurriedly gathered her packages.

"Get back, you two." The two boys disappeared down the crowded aisle.

A careless mistake. I lapsed into German. Hopefully in the excitement, no one noticed. He checked the shopping bag's contents. The unpleasant incident brought him back to the moment and mission at hand. Koch took a deep breath, exhaled. He exited Harrods onto Brompton Road. The Knightsbridge Post Office was a block away.

Koch arrived at the post office and looked for a telephone kiosk. Inside the kiosk, Koch paused. A sly boyish smile briefly revealed the professor was playing one of his mind games. Koch was fluent in four languages. He also took pride in his ability to mimic dialects within each. *Ah! Shall we try Midlands English? It has that special touch of upper social class.* At precisely 5:00 p.m., he made his first call. The number rang through.

"Hello." Koch immediately recognized the timeless voice. He hesitated. The scientist's reason fought a long-lost passion.

"Good afternoon. Is this the residence of Mrs. Anna Mueller?" inquired Koch.

There was a short pause. "Yes. Who is this, please?" Anna Mueller spoke with a distinct German accent.

"Mrs. Mueller, this is Selfridge's calling. The tea set you ordered has arrived."

"Oh," replied Anna, a bit surprised to have received the call so soon.

"You'll be coming in?"

"Yes. Thank you," said Anna. She gazed out the kitchen window. *Why, after all these years?*

Koch kept to his timetable. He reentered the phone kiosk at 5:15 p.m. He removed the small box from the shopping bag. He had used a similar device only once before. It reminded the professor of the small tape recorder he used for dictation. This device was far more sophisticated. Koch dialed a number on the kiosk phone. He listened intently for the call to the States to go through. An answering machine responded. Quickly, Koch placed the device near the phone's mouthpiece, activating the transmitter. In a split second, the coded message was delivered. *Mission accomplished.* He smiled with a sense of satisfaction and relief.

By seven o'clock, Koch returned to the Belgravia Hotel. "Good evening, Herr Koch."

"Any messages for me?" inquired Koch. He knew there wouldn't be any, but guests always ask for messages.

"No, sir. Perhaps you will join us in the library for a brandy?"

"Not tonight, thanks." Koch turned toward the winding staircase.

"Your usual morning reminder?"

"Yes. Thank you." *I feel a bit unsteady.* He hesitated. He stumbled and dropped the shopping bag.

"Herr Koch, may I assist you?"

"Very kind of you, but no, I will manage. How unfortunate your lift is out of order." *The incident at Harrods was enough anger for today.*

The evening manager sensed Koch's displeasure. He tactfully responded, "Yes, sir. I was assured it will be repaired by tomorrow evening."

Koch nodded, grimaced and climbed the daunting steps to his room. With each step, he reviewed the day's events. All was proceeding according to his plan. He regretted the call to Anna Mueller. Koch had an ulterior motive. The telephone call to the States was the imperative. The burst transmission signaled Phase One had begun.

All things considered, the tired old man was pleased with his efforts. Koch slowly, painfully undressed. He meticulously placed his overcoat on a hanger, then his pants and suit jacket. He draped his tie over the valet. His shirt hung near the bathroom shower. Koch had followed the same ritual since childhood. He discarded evening prayers. He was no longer a child. Koch avoided his reflection as he splashed water on his face. *Will I recognize Anna after all these years? How will she react, seeing an old man? Forget this nonsense.* He was disciplined not to feel.

The Allies labeled Koch a war criminal. *I am no villain. I did what I was required to do for the Fatherland.* I became a party member to secure my university position.

Koch might still be languishing in Spandau had it not been for a trick of fate. Koch owed his freedom to another Koch, Karl Otto Koch, the first commandant of Buchenwald. He was a villain. Prisoners were stripped naked. Their recycled possessions added to Himmler's accounts. An audit revealed Karl Otto Koch and his wife siphoned SS funds for personal use. The Nazis were superior record keepers. Shoes, teeth, clothing, personal possessions of every prisoner, had to be recorded. The SS executed Karl Otto Koch by firing squad before Germany surrendered. Karl Otto Koch's execution granted Karl Peter Koch his freedom. After the war, thousands of pages of statistics were found. Perhaps the most significant find was the card catalog the Americans seized. Row upon row of cabinets stored meticulous records of military personnel and civil servants. Therein lay Koch's salvation. Somehow, some way, when Karl Otto Koch's personnel index card was pulled, Karl Peter Koch's card was pulled as well. Both were refiled in the section labeled "deceased." A "coincidence" Koch well understood.

No! I am no villain. I am a patriot. I am a scientist. The world needs a powerful antibiotic more than ever. My research will save lives. Koch's fingers tightened into fists. He recalled the so-called notable acquittals. They collaborated with the Allies in return for their freedom. Some now worked in the United States. They were granted entry permits and citizenship. Two of Koch's colleagues were smuggled into the States by submarine. *Enough!* Koch swallowed two sleeping pills. His hands trembled. Koch slumped on the bed.

The sleeping pills and antibiotic didn't help Koch sleep. He grew restless. He rolled off the bed and managed to walk to a chair. His labored breathing was a new symptom. Koch's mind raced. *Project Naomi is straightforward. It has to work.* He recalled his meeting with the Black Knight's directors. Koch anticipated resistance from at least one director. Koch was not a unanimous choice to manage Project Naomi. Berg, one of the directors, resented his control of the project.

Koch likened the cartel to a pack of wolves. "Outside the closed circle there is no one." The ruthless and cunning directors imagined themselves Teutonic knights. Profit displaced chivalry. They were a new breed, driven by flowcharts and technology. Espionage and viruses replaced swords and shields. Sophisticated laboratories replaced concentration camp holding cells. Government contracts replaced monthly payments to the SS for a guaranteed number of test subjects. Nevertheless, the directors were powerful men with the ability to reach into governments and forge destinies. The new world order ruled through powerful economic alliances that controlled world markets. The cartel thrived on subtle international conspiracy. Anonymity underscored their power. Violence was still in Black Knight's arsenal, but only as a last resort.

Koch scorned their frivolous pageantry. Ever the realist, there was one thing of which he was certain. *This will be my final mission.* He contemplated his future when this contract ended. He much preferred a small secluded villa in Argentina rather than an assassin's bullet, or perhaps a remote controlled weapon, that would mark his demise.

Ah, yes, technology. Koch knew little about these giant computers and their so-called printouts. Two plus two no longer equaled four without an algorithm. So, to bolster his presentation, Koch had reams of paper run through those noisy printers. He imagined the Fuehrer would have expected such intricacy. Did it matter? Koch had lost all awe for Hitler. Koch considered Hitler the architect of Germany's demise. Hitler used suicide to avoid accountability for the final mania. Koch could not grasp Black Knight's obsession with a mythical order of Teutonic dark warriors not unlike the Nazi leaders who brought ruin to the fatherland.

Koch's London mission was top priority on Black Knight's agenda. Timing was critical. The order gathered for only the most important matters. Using an international corporation as cover, Black Knight purchased a secluded estate on the bluffs overlooking Long Island Sound.

The North Shore stone mansion might well have been a Bavarian hideaway. Perhaps nostalgia of the glory days motivated the cartel to purchase the estate. In the late '40's and early '50's, the walled estate served as a safe-house for SS and fellow travelers along the "rat lines" through the U.S. to South American sanctuaries. Later, it became a touchstone for the Knights. From the balcony of the huge second floor hall hung a banner with the order's insignia; a medieval black shield emblazoned with an inverted cross.

In the center of the hall was a great round walnut table. Inscribed on each chair was the name of a Black Knight. Each Knight wore a unique black tunic trimmed with red and white insignias, indicating his rank. Standing at attention, Walther Liechtenauer, the Grand Master, turned and faced the north wall. On cue, the gathering recited their oath:

"Through death we find life.

"Struggle is our blood, our mission, our destiny."

The pall of Himmler's spirit shrouded the room. Surely, the Reichsfuhrer's conjured spirit was present. "Seig Heil!" the Knights shouted in unison.

"And now, gentlemen, to the business at hand."

These men are possessed. Koch stepped away from the table to begin his presentation.

"Project Naomi has begun, Gentlemen."

"And how can you be so sure the operation will succeed?" demanded Albert Berg, Black Knight's Keeper.

"Our operatives are in place."

"All is ready? Are you sure, Koch?

"Yes. In 1972, the super powers agreed to a treaty banning germ warfare research. They agreed to outlaw the stockpiling of biological agents. Our intelligence reveals the United States and the Soviet Union continue to conduct experiments."

The Directors, nurtured on conspiracies and secret reports,

were intrigued with Koch's presentation. He sensed he held their attention.

"How credible is our information?" Berg demanded. He challenged Koch's reputation for detail.

Koch grew edgy. "We know from our agent in Sverdlovsk the Soviets are experimenting with pulmonary anthrax in a lab outside the city. He has traveled to the Urals several times over the last year. He is now in place."

"Do your assets have knowledge or contact with one another?" asked another Director.

"No," said Koch. "The threat of a double agent is always a reality. A KGB intercept, even torture, will not betray our plan. The same is true in the States."

"And Ansgar?" asked Berg.

"Ansgar is in a London safe house," said Dr. Liechtenauer. "No one needs to know his location. Attend to the matters at hand."

Koch was surprised at Liechtenauer's remark. The others could see Koch had been caught off-guard. *I thought I shared the key details with Liechtenauer.*

Koch continued with his presentation. From his briefcase, Koch withdrew blue-covered copies of a document for each Director. The report was titled "Project Naomi"

"Gentlemen, your copies are numbered. I will personally collect them. Liebling is our most trusted operative in the United States. Nothing must happen to this agent." Koch always spoke of his assets in the singular, never revealing if Liebling were a man, woman, or even a committed cell. Anonymity helped assure his assets' safety.

Koch waited. The Directors took a quick look at the four page document. "According to Liebling, the Americans are researching a 'doomsday bug.'"

"Is his report credible?" asked Liechtenauer.

"We know the United States Army offered political asylum to many of our scientists," interjected one of the Directors.

"The Americans captured Japanese scientists instrumental in germ warfare experiments," added Kurt Strauss.

Berg interrupted. "I directed Von Leer to research several small pharmaceutical companies. Several Japanese firms are also shopping."

"Berg, you try my patience. Never mention Von Leer's name again. He represents our financiers. I never authorized you to contact him." Liechtenauer's admonishment disturbed the others.

Berg stammered the next comment. "I've learned the General Accounting Office has been making inquiries as to recent pharmaceutical patents; specific inquiries regarding research at Plum Island and Fort Detrick."

"Berg, you are a fool. What will happen if Von Leer falls under suspicion? All our efforts could be ruined. Our personal fortunes, perhaps our lives, could be placed in danger should our financiers become alarmed." Liechtenauer was livid. "What else do you know?"

"Our man at the FDA reports test trials. The government has prioritized Rift Valley Disease. They are focusing on the work of Sato Yamada."

"Who is Yamada?" asked Liechtenauer.

"A former government consultant. Von Leer insists Yamada was connected with Unit 731."

"He may be one of the Japanese researchers granted immunity from prosecution. The U.S. government denies Americans were test subjects for Japanese biological experiments."

"We all know that, Berg."

Liechtenauer turned to Koch. "Yes, I know of their aerosol anthrax weapon."

Koch referred the Directors to a footnote in his report. "Our agent, Leibling, reports the Americans have moved major research from Detrick to the DOA facility on Plum Island. One of my former associates, Erich Traub, has been working there."

"Traub's expertise is with ticks, vectors and viruses. The United States Navy brought Traub into the country," said Fritz Schmidt.

"And where is Traub now?" asked Liechtenauer?

"West Germany." said Fritz Schmidt.

"He has been traveling in the Middle East," said Koch.

"Reiter, here is a task for you. Why the emphasis on Rift Valley Disease? Was Traub conducting research in Egypt? He's a virologist."

"Yes, Dr. Liechtenauer. I start my inquiries in the morning."

Where is Liechtenauer going with this? Koch turned on a projector and on the far wall displayed photographs of Plum Island.

"Ah, these photos show striking similarities between the Soviet's Urals facility and the American complex," noted Kurt Strauss, the Knight's Treasurer. A patch covered his right eye. Three Heidelberg dueling scars cut across his face.

"Gentlemen, notice the similarities." Another photograph was projected on the wall.

"It's Himmler's complex: Reims Island. I worked there in 1942," said Eric Reiter.

"Why all this detail, Koch?" asked Berg.

"The Soviets' facility at Sverdlovsk sits right in the middle of a closed industrial city with a population of over one million.

"While the American facility is located on an island, viruses and bacteria are shipped from Fort Detrick several times a week. The courier uses an unmarked van. Still quite a dangerous procedure."

Berg interrupted. "Where are you taking us with all this information, Koch?"

Fritz Schmidt listened patiently to the presentation. He had served on the defense council for the scientists at the Dachau military trials. "Koch, how is it that you are able to manage such a diverse project?"

"When my initial application to work in the States was rejected, I asked Doctor Liechtenauer for help. The Americans found him to be a credible resource. They were searching for research scientists. In turn, Dr. Liechtenauer recommended me to the Allies.

"To this day, I do not consider myself a criminal," Koch proudly declared. "Had Germany won the war, I might have been a revered scientist. I was forced to reveal my role at Dachau."

"You confessed to the Americans you assisted Klaus Schilling with the malaria experiments?"

"Yes. And other experiments as well. They were particularly interested in my knowledge of anthrax and antibiotics. Within days, my interrogators had a list of questions. The Americans were fascinated with Schilling's work."

"Why Schilling's work? The Americans had Schilling and executed him."

"Schilling's notebooks disappeared. Schilling's last request was to have his research published."

"Enough of the trivia, Koch. Get on with it!" Berg was antagonizing Koch.

Koch nervously began to pace.

Schmidt pressed Koch, "Why would the Americans place you in a position of authority? They granted you a security clearance. You travel freely."

"Exactly." Koch looked directly at Doctor Liechtenauer. Liechtenauer's influence reached deep inside the U.S. intelligence and scientific community. Dr. Liechtenauer was the mastermind behind Black Knight and the newly formed Trinity PharmoDynamics Group.

Walther Liechtenauer founded WL Pharmaceuticals in 1940. After World War II, the company was banned from operating inside the United States. It was too closely tied to IG Farben, the chemical conglomerate. IG Farben had a notorious reputation dating back before World War II. Farben and the Nazis worked on a number of chemical research projects involving prisoners.

Doctor Walther Liechtenauer devised a threefold plan to gain U.S. accreditation. Liechtenauer turned to an international group so powerful few dared mention their name. Herr Doctor referred to his backers as the Circle of Twelve. With their blessing, Liechtenauer created Trinity PharmoDynamics Group. Trinity's existence depended upon a complex plan. Liechtenauer deposited funds into three distinct offshore funding corporations located in the Bahamas. He named the umbrella corporation The Trinity Fund. The first Fund paid for lobbyists. The second bought influence within the walls of Congress. The third Fund was the most critical; its mission was to mold American public opinion. Trinity needed a huge public relations campaign. No expense was spared. Trinity purchased a major Madison Avenue advertising agency.

With the purchase of two independently owned pharmaceutical laboratories, Trinity PharmoDynamics, USA was born. These laboratories held FDA certificates. Before long,

Trinity bid on small government supply contracts. Eventually, they turned to pharmaceutical sales. A massive advertising campaign was launched. Trinity purchased television and radio ads. They purchased multipage advertisements in local and national newspaper and magazines. Every available means of communication was employed. Trinity's brands became household names. Now was the time to expand their horizons. Karl Peter Koch was well-suited for Liechtenauer's next endeavor.

"Continue with your story, Koch." Liechtenauer was growing impatient with the constant questions and interruptions.

"Within six months, I was recruited by an intelligence agent. My papers were processed. When I arrived in the United States, the Army assigned me to Project 63," Koch said.

Liechtenauer became impatient with Koch's tale.

"Koch, please," said Liechtenauer. His scowl signaled to Koch, 'stop'. "You have revealed enough. Move on with the subject at hand."

Koch definitely sensed Liechtenauer's mood swing. *Something is wrong.*

Koch's intuition was correct. Unknown to Koch and the others, Liechtenauer had made a decision to change Black Knight's immediate mission.

"One last question, please. Were the Americans researching such a weapon, a virus?" Fritz Schmidt asked.

"Yes. And they continue to do so. Keep in mind, our early studies used prisoners for experiments with malaria. We were searching for a vaccine. The Americans have divided their continuing research into teams. Our focus deals with anthrax, the other Rift Valley Disease."

"Koch, I suspect they are continuing their vector research with ticks and mosquitoes, also," said Reiter.

"International treaties allow biological research to develop antibiotics. However, the Americans trouble me. Bioresearch has a flip side. As we create a mutant, we also discover ways that may destroy it," Doctor Liechtenauer added.

"And what does our Argentinean lab conclude?" asked Koch.

"The Americans may have stumbled on to something unique. They have a research and development team, code name Project

Naomi."

"And what would that be?" asked Schmidt.

"Perhaps a new antibiotic."

Koch was visibly stressed. "What about antibiotics?"

"The Americans continue to research additional infectious and less treatable strains of malaria. They may have discovered an antibiotic variant."

"We must be sure. Imagine the value of possessing a powerful multi-purpose antibiotic. It would be worth untold billions. We must get our hands on that research."

"We are already testing a formula. A small quantity has been manufactured in South Africa. Your lab in Argentina will soon receive a shipment," Koch answered.

"We need a large population study," said Schmidt.

"Exactly!" There was urgency in Koch's voice. "My plan, gentlemen, is to act quickly on two fronts. Two disasters. Our own Armageddon."

Koch grew more enthusiastic. The tempo of his presentation increased. Koch's hands trembled and he dripped perspiration. "Once we control this new antibiotic, the potential is unlimited. Two disasters will create world-wide fear. Can you imagine the demand? Trinity must control the manufacture and distribution of a wonder drug. I believe we have such a medication. For now it is called 'andraxicon.'"

"We will control the marketplace," said Doctor Liechtenauer. The Doctor rose from his chair. Leaning over the table, he shouted, "Koch, you are brilliant!"

"Will our first test be in the Urals?" asked Director Berg. Berg had tempered his sarcasm, sensing the other Directors were growing impatient with his attacks on Koch.

"Time and opportunity will determine our path." Koch pointed to a map of the Urals.

"Congratulations, Koch. Well done," exclaimed Doctor Liechtenauer.

∾

The knock on Koch's door awakened him. "Professor Koch," came a quiet voice from the hallway. "Professor."

"Yes, yes. I am up. Thank you." Koch's bed linen was soaked with perspiration. His joints ached. Each morning it became increasingly difficult for Koch to discern his dreams from reality. His mind and body were preparing Koch to die.

Chapter 4

Wiping steam from the mirror, Koch examined his face. Each day, the telltale signs were more deeply etched. Perhaps today would be different. Not having been visited by nightmares was a good omen. Yes, today was going to be memorable.

In the far corner of the room was a sink with a mirror and several fresh towels. Koch leaned against the basin, staring at his reflection. Anguish and time had taken their toll. *Old and tired.*

It was the beard. The beard had to go. He soaked his face with a hot towel. He lathered and began drawing a straight razor meticulously across his face. Each razor stroke drew him into the past.

At the same time, Anna Mueller was finishing the breakfast dishes. Her husband had left for work just as he had done for the last 28 years. Anna could hear the usual bustle in the kitchen directly above. The Muellers shared their home with their daughter, her husband, and their six-year-old son.

The Muellers lived in Brentwood on the outskirts of London, part of the commuter beltway. It was a growing community struggling to keep its historic identity. Brentwood had been a refuge for Crusaders going to the Holy Land. Author Robert Graves claims Brentwood was the site where the Romans defeated the Ancient Britons.

George Mueller worked for Thermos Limited during the war. The British military's demand for Thermos bottles during the war pushed Thermos production to its limits. Popular mythology had it that every time a thousand bombers went out on a raid, 10,000 to 12,000 Thermos vacuum flasks went with them. After the war ended in 1945, Thermos plants were reconverted to civilian and peacetime uses. George Mueller was promoted to Overseas Representative. Mueller traveled to the United States and Germany, meeting with corporate representatives and government officials. Thermos was expanding and one of its major clients was the Atomic Energy Commission. In turn, the Department of Agriculture showed a keen interest in Thermos vacuum bottles for biological containment and transport.

In 1948, George Mueller met Anna Bruns through mutual friends while on a trip to Germany. Thermos corporate headquarters made a few inquiries and, with some official intervention, Anna was granted a passport and permission to move to Brentwood, England.

After a brief courtship they were married. Mueller was a good man, and a devoted husband. His only vice was a bit too much ale on payday. Now, after all those years, Peter Koch was back in her life. Anna Mueller finished wrapping the tiny parcel with brown paper, placing it on the kitchen table. Glancing around her newly decorated kitchen, Anna felt a sense of accomplishment. She remembered the final days of the war. Everything was in ruins. Life in England was good.

There was a time far in the past when the young Anna and Karl Peter Koch were lovers. Anna remembered those days in Germany before the war. They met at a Hitler Youth rally. They were both enthusiastic senior members. Anna's parents, Otto and Edna Bruns, were loyal party members. Otto Bruns was a middle level bureaucrat in the transportation ministry. Anna's membership in Hitler Youth strengthened the image of a family loyal to the Fuehrer.

Otto told Edna about the whispered rumors circulating at work. He suspected the gossip was fact. New German civil service laws, the first anti-Semitic regulations, were enacted. Colleagues at work were dismissed. Germans of "non-Aryan" descent were denied public employment. Anna was a loyal German, but questioned the fear and distrust that seemed to be engulfing the new Germany. Such talk would be considered disloyalty. Otto also feared Anna would discuss her concerns with friends. His job might be jeopardized. In the new Germany, everyone was a suspect. Anna might be reported to the authorities.

One day, an official visited the Bruns' home. The SS Officer's formality frightened Edna.

"I'm here to meet with your daughter, Anna." He took some documents from his leather case.

Edna struggled to maintain her composure.

"You should feel honored," said the official. "We have completed a thorough investigation of your family's genealogy. At this point Anna has been found *racially pure*. Anna will serve the Fatherland and our Fuehrer by conceiving a child for the new order."

As Otto Bruns entered the room, he heard the conversation. Edna turned to Otto. She was pale. "I don't believe this, Frederic. You can't let this happen."

Otto was fearful and said nothing.

"You're sending my daughter to a breeding ground?"

"Silence, woman!" Otto instinctively shouted.

The SS officer stiffened. "Frau Bruns, please. Surely your daughter has discussed this with you. This is an honor. Not a punishment." The officer handed Edna several forms.

Edna pushed the papers aside.

"Your daughter will receive excellent medical attention. The doctors will carefully select a compatible male. Your daughter has been deemed racially pure. Once the child is born, both mother and child will continue to receive the best care."

"And then what? The child will be taken?"

The officer stiffened. "I am growing impatient with you, Frau Bruns. My courtesy is giving way to your intolerant insistence. Herr Bruns. Surely you understand."

"Lebensborn!" But what of love?" pleaded Edna.

"Love, Frau Bruns, is no longer a private matter for your daughter. It is the business of the Fatherland. The Jews, the communists, even the Catholics, all of our enemies, have weakened Germany. It is our duty to create a nation to endure for a thousand years. It is Anna's honor to bear a racially pure child."

"And your job is to replace love with future SS leaders."

Otto was panicky. He knew Edna had gone too far.

The officer stepped forward, then turned and glared at Edna. Otto mustered enough courage to step between the officer and his wife.

"We must secure our race, Frau Bruns. The decision has been made. The papers are in order. Read them. You must present Anna for an examination ten days after menstruation. Both of you must be there. Heil Hitler."

Otto returned the salute. The officer left.

"Our daughter is to be sent to a selection camp. Young girls used by the SS men," Anna raged at Otto. "And you. You coward! How can you allow this?"

"We are powerless to stop this." Bruns grabbed his wife's shoulders. She shook free and turned.

"Stop this. Do you understand? Stop this!" she shouted.

The news of Anna's selection stunned Koch.

How could this be? Only days before, the University awarded him a research fellowship. Medical research grants were difficult to receive. The University faculties were in turmoil. The purge wasn't limited to Jews. Christian critics and intellectuals of all sorts were being dismissed. Many were fired after years of service. Their pensions were denied. Some were sent to prison.

Koch was fortunate. His grant provided an income for the next two years. The work involved travel and the promise of a faculty position. Koch suspected there would be a number of future openings at the University as the purges continued.

The faculty newsletter declared, "The Fuehrer Himself Is The German Reality."

A nick from his straight razor returned Koch into the present moment.

The past is a luxury I can no longer afford. Sentimentality is a weakness.

Chapter 5

The black Opel sedan stopped in front of the Belgravia Hotel. Anna Mueller had no sooner arrived when Koch opened the car door and painfully scrambled to get in.

"Drive!" he ordered. "Drive to the intersection. Then turn left."

Anna drove towards Knightsbridge.

"Quickly. Another left."

"After all these years, not a 'hello'…no warm greeting?" she exclaimed. Anna's mind raced in confusion. *Karl Peter Koch…I never…you've grown so old.* She avoided her own reflection in the rear view mirror.

"Watch out!"

Anna burst back into the moment, avoiding a collision with an oncoming truck.

"We must stop. You owe me an explanation."

"Not now. Pay attention to the traffic."

"Peter, you are frightening me."

"Not now." His eyes fixed on the wing mirror.

"What is going on?" Anna's voice bristled with confusion and anger. Anna glanced at Koch.

"Keep your eyes on the road."

She squeezed the steering wheel. "I demand an explanation! Are you insane?"

"We can't risk being followed. Did you bring the package?

"Yes, I have it." Anna pointed to the glove box. "What danger?"

"Did you open it?"

"No. Of course not. For the last time…what danger?"

"As I left the hotel lobby, I sensed someone was watching me. A Land Rover was parked across the street."

"Peter, you don't look well. Your imagination is playing tricks." Anna took a quick look in the review mirror. "No one is following us. I'll pull over."

"No. Not yet. We are almost there."

"Where are you taking me?"

"To a parking garage just up the road." Koch pointed. "There, beyond the petrol station. Take the second entrance ramp."

Anna made an abrupt turn up the ramp. The Opel bottomed out on the incline and stopped inches from the entrance booth.

The attendant left the booth and ordered her to stop. "Slow down, lady. Have you gone completely bonkers?"

Anna scowled, reached out for the parking ticket, and drove off.

The angry attendant turned and shouted, "Blimey, I thought you were going to drive right into me."

"Drive to the far side and park."

"I'm sick of your orders, Peter. What now?"

Koch opened the glove box.

"There's your precious parcel and I didn't open it. I have no idea what's inside"

Koch got out of the car and walked to the driver's side. As Anna opened the door, Koch grasped her arm.

"Peter, you're hurting me. Let go."

Koch loosened his grip. They walked to the other side of the parking garage.

"What's this?"

"A rental." He unlocked the driver's side door of the Ford Cortina. "Get in. You drive."

"And your package?"

Koch placed it in the Cortina's glove box, and Anna drove out of the garage. A few minutes later the Cortina entered West Hampstead's main round-about.

"Go north toward Danbury." Koch's frantic demeanor slowly transformed. Neither party spoke.

Koch spoke into the eerie silence. "I am so sorry, Anna."

"Not as sorry as I am."

"Thank you for delivering the package."

"I hope it is worth this madness."

"I can't tell you what the package contains. Your life would be in danger."

"You haven't endangered me already?"

"I would never hurt you."

"Peter. Time has been unkind to you."

"Yes, in many ways. I live for my work. And you, Anna…how has it been?"

Anna looked away. *You are a dispassionate bastard,* she wanted to scream. A pain deep in her chest stifled the words. Tears rolled down her checks. "I have fantasized about this moment over and over. Now look at us. Why have you done this to me?"

"Forgive me, Anna. I planned this moment to be special. I am an old man incapable of compassion."

"Stop, Peter. You make me feel ashamed. George loves me. I shouldn't be here…should never have come. I still don't understand your suspicions."

"Please trust me. Drive. I will explain. Time changes us. We have no control over our lives. Our destiny has been predetermined."

"Still the loyal Nazi. Possessed. You haven't changed. You're selfish."

Anna is so wrong. I have changed. I no longer know who I am.

The car slowed. The approach to Market Hill followed the river with its sharp winding curves. Passing Abbey Church, they came to a small inn on the outskirts of Coggeshall. "We only have a brief time. Shall we stop for lunch?"

Anna turned and looked at Koch. *No. Why rekindle feelings. I am an old foolish woman.* "Yes, that will be fine. I must be home by six. George will worry. Six at the latest."

The Canterbury was a small country inn. The proprietors refurbished the interior true to its simple, yet elegant, atmosphere. Koch glanced around, searching for a secluded table.

"Good afternoon. A table for two?"

"Yes, please." Koch attempted a smile.

"The patio looks alluring, Peter."

"Ah, yes. The owners call it their Greek atrium." The young woman directed them to a secluded corner of the enclosure.

"I've always dreamed of having my own garden room," Anna sighed. "They have such lovely gardens in York. Have you visited

York, Peter?"

"No."

"It is the most beautiful spot. George and I spent a week in York last spring."

"Why don't you have a garden?"

Anna looked away without answering. *His question sounds almost genuine. I don't trust him.* "Peter, I feel very uncomfortable."

"Please, forgive me. Once again I've exercised poor judgment. I agree it is a mistake for us to meet after all these years." Koch lapsed into German. "I should never have asked you to…"

Anna interrupted. "Please, speak English. You'll draw attention to us."

Koch paused and looked across the room. Two men entered the inn. They requested a table out of earshot, settled in with their pints.

"So far from London? I doubt someone will recognize you."

Anna frowned. Koch failed to reassure her.

"Aren't you curious to know about my life here in England?"

"Of course I am."

"I am blessed with a wonderful husband. We share our home with our daughter and her husband. I have a six-year-old grandson. They are saving to buy their own place. George is very special. After all these years, George never once pressured me to talk about the war." Anna rolled her eyes and fought back the tears.

"Why did you agree to meet me?"

She smiled. "You know why. How else would you have gotten your precious package? You exploited an old woman with foolish daydreams."

"Never."

"Protest all you want. You will never feel as I do. I prayed you were alive. I never lost hope. Selfishly, I imagined one day you would find me."

"I did search for you. I was hiding from the Allies. They hunted me like an animal. Soon it became impossible."

Anna made a great effort to regain her composure. "How did you escape?"

"Friends."

Anna understood the ambiguity. Rumors abounded in

Brentwood's German community. For the inexperienced ear, it was a vague phrase. Anna knew better. She pushed the word away.

'Friends.' The invisible network. The safe houses. The escape routes for war criminals. The unspoken truths.

"Are you feeling ill?"

"Oh. This whole affair, today's events, have gotten the best of me."

"For a moment you appeared to have difficulty breathing."

I'm afraid of what more you may reveal. I don't want to know.

Anna's hands trembled. She barely managed a sip of water.

"What happened to your family, Peter?"

"My brother, Kurt, was killed at Normandy." Koch looked sad. "My sister never recovered from the Berlin bombings and the Russian atrocities. She was institutionalized and died several years ago. It is just as well. She was tormented."

"And your niece"?

Peter shrugged his shoulders. "Hilda. That one lost her dignity. She went from one American soldier to the next. I tried to discourage such relationships, but in the end she married an officer stationed at the base where she worked."

"Do you hear from her?"

"No. I don't wish to. My last contact with her was years ago. They were living on Tortola in the British Virgin Islands. Running a charter boat business. As you can tell, I have no one."

"After all these years, why did you want to see me? How did you find me?"

"A friend of a friend at the embassy. They were very persistent. You would be surprised at the records they maintain. They know everything about us. We Germans are meticulous record keepers. Unfortunately, most of us can't alter the past."

"I never gave up thinking about you, Peter. The horror of war drained my soul. I longed for happiness. George loves me. I betrayed his love with a memory. Your memory."

"My love for you did exist, Anna, if only for a brief moment in time. I loved you. I have no reason to lie. Believe me. I am an old dying man." Koch looked away.

"We all have our illusions, don't we?" Anna added.

Koch's eyes glistened. The Dachau professor was slipping out of character.

"I want to leave, Peter. It's time. "

"Perhaps a cognac for old times." he suggested.

"There is something you must know," Anna tensed.

"As you wish, but wait one moment, please." Koch walked into the far room. The two men were gone. Koch requested two cognacs and returned to the table. Anna was crying.

After a few sips of cognac, Anna and Koch appeared a bit calmer. Anna resolved to tell Peter her secret.

"We have a child, Peter. We have a daughter." The dreaded moment was over.

"How can that be? The SS selected you. I don't understand. They would have punished you."

"I fully expected to be rebuked, or worse. I loved you more than my own life. I risked everything for that one night we shared."

"Please stop. No more," Koch pleaded.

"Hear me out." She demanded.

Peter pushed back in his chair and braced.

"I did not tell my parents. How could I? My father would have ordered me out of the house. Unwed mothers were shunned. A friend told me, 'Himmler has a program for unwed mothers.' I sent a letter to Munich. I visited a clinic. Then, an official came to my home."

"Didn't you know the child would be taken from you?"

"I was frightened. I needed you. You abandoned me. What choice did I have?"

Koch turned away in silence.

"Once again, I went to the local SS clinic for a final physical. An attendant handed me an examination robe. She was gentle but firm, almost kind."

"'You must submit to the exam,' the attendant insisted.

"Why? I've signed the papers. I have my certificate of racial purity for three generations.

"'Nevertheless, we have rules,' she insisted."

Koch fought being drawn into Anna's story. He swallowed the cognac too quickly. His throat burned—or was it his anger? He avoided Anna's eyes.

"The examination room was cold. The antiseptic smell still

haunts me." Anna's voice grew deep and raspy with fear and anger. "I have never told anyone what happened." She trembled. "An SS doctor entered the room. He had dark, deep, penetrating eyes. His pale complexion blended into his white surgical gown. His voice was hypnotic. He was evil."

"'Lie back, child,' he whispered."

Koch reached across the table.

"Don't touch me." Anna pulled away from Koch's gesture. "I begged the doctor.

"The doctor assumed I must be pregnant." Anna wept. "Believe me. It is so difficult to tell you. All these years I've kept our secret."

"I begged him, 'Please don't hurt my baby.'"

Koch lowered his head. Shame brought pain. He swallowed the last drop of cognac. "You don't have to tell me more."

"Believe me. You were my only lover. I was never with another man."

"The doctor continued to probe. His smile slowly grew colder than the room. He was so evil. I started to scream. He covered my mouth. 'Be quiet. Don't be frightened, child.' At that moment, I knew...."

Anna paused. After a long breath, "I pleaded. He held my wrists against the table. In one frenzy, it was over."

Suddenly, Anna reached across the table. Her arms shook with fury. "No one helped me. And you, Peter...you abandoned me." Anna was consumed by anger.

"'Get dressed, child,' the monster told me as though nothing had happened. I was bleeding. I feared for our unborn child.

"'I warn you, child. Say nothing of this episode,' he warned me. I hate that fiend. Oddly, when the SS attendant returned, I sensed she knew what had happened. In her own way, the woman tried to comfort me."

Koch tried to touch Anna. She pulled away.

"Don't touch me, Peter. It's too late."

"What can I do, Anna?"

"Nothing. Just listen."

Anna said she never saw the SS doctor again. Out of fear she never reported him. All she wanted was sleep and isolation.

It was Himmler's plan for women to give birth away from

their families. Anna was sent to a small town near Munich to give birth. She worked at the clinic; first in the nursery and then in the administrative office.

"Those were awful days. I thought of you through sleepless nights. My only comfort was our daughter. The SS authorities forbade me to name the baby. I called her Nadine. She would need courage. I lived each day never knowing when Nadine would be taken."

"I am so sorry," said Koch. *I remember our night together.*

"I continued to work in the nursery. I was allowed to visit Nadine twice a day.

"There were other young women, many unwed. Steinheoring was Himmler's first Lebensborn. Years later, I read a newspaper story. The writer claimed the same doctors who delivered our baby performed hideous experiments on the children of Dachau."

Koch's expression betrayed the truth he wanted to deny.

"And the child? What happened?"

"They took Nadine away. A Naval officer and his wife. I was frantic. Our child, gone forever."

"You were never warned?"

"I hated you."

The inn's hostess, sensing something was wrong, approached the couple. "May I assist you? Perhaps another cognac?"

"Yes, two more. We are recalling old times." Koch regretted the remark.

The interruption increased Anna's resolve to finish her story.

"No chance to hold my daughter one last time. No farewell kiss. I hurried to the office window only to watch the couple drive away with our daughter."

Anna returned to the office only to find the letter and documents were gone. An index card waited to be filed. The card listed a registration number. She took the card.

She knew the number by heart: SS 1-3128.

"Who were they? Did you ever discover their name?"

"No."

"What did you do?" Koch persisted.

Anna cupped hands over her eyes. Her voice lowered to a whisper. Her words were muffled. "Life as I knew it ended that day. Still I had to survive. I applied to remain at Steinheoring as a clerical worker. I couldn't return home. My mother may have welcomed me home, but not my father."

For the next few minutes, silenced prevailed. Anna seemed to be in a different place in time, as though she were experiencing a great relief. They faced each other in total silence. It was time to leave. Koch sensed Anna's story was unfinished.

"What happened to Nadine?"

"It's time to leave," Anna said, breaking the unbearable silence.

Koch signaled for the check.

As the couple approached their hired car, something out of the ordinary caught Koch's attention. The two men from the inn - the two who had left earlier - stood next to a Land Rover 109. They appeared startled. They flicked their cigarettes to the pavement, climbed into the idling Land Rover, and drove away. The incident unsettled Koch. A Land Rover 109. *That Land Rover was parked outside the Belgravia yesterday and again this morning. We were followed.*

"What is it, Peter"?

"Nothing. My mind is failing. Nothing."

The return trip to West Hampstead was uneventful. Koch drove.

"Peter, I asked about your family, but you never inquired about mine. Is that because your 'friends' at the embassy have informed you?"

"Anna, I seem to have filled this occasion with sadness and apologies. Of course, I am interested. You shared only a bit about your life here."

"Then you also know my mother and father were killed in Berlin during a night bombing raid. I saw them only once before they died. From a distance. Unwed mothers were abhorred, Himmler's constant pronouncements to the contrary. They made no difference. I couldn't bring myself to burden my family."

Anna related her experience following Germany's surrender. She was one of the fortunate Lebensborn mothers. She had escaped to the American Zone when Germany surrendered. The Americans confined her, along with many displaced women, in a former army barracks. The other prisoners did not know

Anna's background. Women in countries formerly under Nazi occupation were less fortunate. Their heads were shaven. They were sometimes marched through the streets in shame. Spat upon, taunted, and often beaten, they were eventually abandoned.

Thousands of children were kidnapped from Poland and other occupied countries. They were given to SS families and others. At the war's end, many were never returned to their birth parents. Others were too 'Germanized' to be returned.

"I'm certain you already know the rest, Peter," Anna said.

And he did.

Soon they arrived at the West Hampstead garage where Anna's car was parked. Their farewell was brief and unsentimental. Sadly, their brief rendezvous never quite became reconciliation. With a few parting words, Peter and Anna drove off in different directions.

It began to rain, not hard but enough to cover the windscreen. Anna drove cautiously. She was worried about being delayed. About five miles from West Hampstead, Anna saw a flashing blue and orange light reflected in the rearview mirror. She gave way, allowing the police vehicle passing room. Its two tone horns sounded. The Range Rover 109 raced ahead and abruptly stopped, blocking Anna's car. She was shaken. *What have I done?* A tall man exited the police vehicle and approached. *He looks familiar.* The man raised his arm shoulder high. He waved what appeared to be a police badge.

"Remain in your auto, please," called the man. "Don't be alarmed."

Anna rolled down the window, anticipating the officer's request for her driving license and registration. The man smiled as he approached the open window.

"Officer, what's wrong?" she asked.

The tall man never answered. With one swift motion, his task was complete. The Beretta Model 70 .22 caliber pistol was modified for low-powered ammunition. A silencer was not necessary. The bullet penetrated Anna's forehead, ricocheted and halted in her lower jaw. Anna's bulging eyes revealed the sudden agonizing pain. A perverse smile never left the assassin's face.

Ever so casually, he returned the pistol to his waistband. He reached into his left raincoat pocket to find a small leather case. From it, he removed a tattered tiny piece of cloth and whispered "Vriend." The tall man casually returned to the Land Rover. *I wonder what Koch told her? Whatever. No one will ever know.* Without exchanging a word, the pair disappeared into the misty dark night.

It was time for Ansgar to leave the London safe house. Everything had gone according to Dr. Liechtenauer's plan. Dr. Liechtenauer will be pleased. No need to worry about tracing the abandoned brass bullet casing. The armorer supplied West German ammunition to confuse the police. Dr. Liechtenauer will have to deal with Professor Koch.

◦§◦

Winter/Spring 1942 – A home in the suburbs of Amsterdam, The Netherlands.

Ansgar had vague memories of his childhood. He never knew his parents, though they visited him each day…in visions, that is. Sometimes they brought a loaf of bread, a square of cheese, and always his favorite, chocolate. Their visits were brief. His parents never met the stooped, grey-haired woman. At first she frightened Ansgar, though he welcomed the morsels she brought. The old grey-haired woman christened the boy, "Ansgar."

The old woman called the second-floor room Ansgar's "speelkamer," his playroom. Light from the playroom's two opaque windows reflected off the mirrors. Only the old woman was allowed to switch on the overhead globe; a rare luxury. The four-legged tub occupied most of the room. The commode and washbasin were fitted against the outside wall. A cast-iron grille covered the duct from the furnace below. The room was always cold. A vanity with a unique clothes hamper stretched along the far interior wall. Each evening, the old woman would slide the hamper aside, revealing a cubbyhole-sized storage closet. "Goede nacht, kind" (Good night, child), she whispered, handing the boy a cloth doll fashioned from a man's sock. The boy tucked the sock doll under his shirt. The old woman tucked the blankets up around Ansgar's shoulders, then slid the hamper back in place. At first light, the old woman would return. Over time, the fear of darkness and cold Ansgar associated with the cubicle slowly dissipated. "Never leave this room without me, Ansgar," the old woman warned. She bent over with a pained expression and pointed a gnarled finger at him. "Do you understand, child?" Ansgar did not reply.

There were no colorfully illustrated children's books to occupy his time. No toy trucks, cars or toy soldiers. Only the sock doll he named "Vriend". The bathroom's black and white tiled floor embellished Ansgar's visions. It was his imaginary playground where friends gathered. Ansgar taught Vriend to play checkers. Together, Ansgar and Vriend imagined a world beyond the forbidden door.

One morning, Ansgar and his companion quietly opened the door and crawled unnoticed to the railing. Looking around, he saw a winding staircase leading to an immense hallway below. He heard people talking. It was the grey-haired woman. Peering below, he watched a baldheaded man slowly limp behind the woman. He used a cane to keep from falling. The woman embraced the man. He opened the front door and departed. As she turned, she caught a glimpse of the boy on the second floor. Without a word she climbed the stairs. Reaching down, she took hold of Ansgar's arm and dragged him back into his playroom. "I warned you never, never to leave your room!" She gave the boy a severe spanking. Tears filled her eyes.

"Now will you listen?" she demanded. Ansgar nodded and forced a pained smile. He rarely spoke. "Be silent. The man will hear you. Never let the man hear you, Ansgar. He will take you away."

Gestures and expressions replaced words. The days passed. Time lost its meaning. Ansgar's visions marked life's dimensions. The cubicle's sleeping quarters grew smaller with each passing year. The gray-haired woman's visits brought brief respite. Then, one day, it all came to a frantic end.

The grey-haired woman had no time to bang a warning on the water pipe. She protested, than screamed loudly in horror. Ansgar disregarded the woman's admonishment to hide in his cubbyhole. Instead, he returned to the railing. The old man with the bald head was being dragged across the hallway floor. One man pulled the old man, while another kicked and cursed him. Ansgar was confused and scared. The woman pleaded for mercy.

"Please stop. Don't hurt him," she screamed one last time. A short fat woman dressed in a uniform struck the woman's head with a wooden baton. The two men returned and dragged the woman over the entrance threshold. Ansgar ran back into the bathroom. It was too late. The short fat woman had spotted Ansgar. Two days later, he was sent to a transport camp to await his destiny.

The warm July sun prior to roll call betrayed the ugliness of the day's events. Ansgar, along with about one hundred children and teenagers, assembled in front of their barracks at Westerbork Transport Camp. One by one, they were separated into three groups. At the end of the day, the healthy teenage boys departed for forced labor camps. All but a few of the remaining children were destined for the killing center at Auschwitz. Many died during systematic medical experiments. Ansgar had no way of knowing his destination.

The following morning, a naked Ansgar stood in judgment before the detention center's tribunal; a physician, a matron and a government official. The doctor conferred with the man in a black suit. The man's face had fish-like gills and a mouth that curled into an odd smile. It was a new smile Ansgar filed away. The Dutch boy did not comprehend German. It did not matter. Ansgar had become a body language linguist; a shrug, a nod, and of course, the "smile." Ansgar was an observer of the human condition. Ansgar studied the man in the black suit like a virologist viewing a specimen in a Petri dish. For a moment, Ansgar recalled the grey-haired woman's admonition "Be silent." The man in the black suit smiled and motioned for Ansgar to go with the matron.

Ansgar knew little of the events surrounding his arrival at Dr. Walther Liechtenauer's country farm in Germany. He arrived carrying a small bundle and an ID card listing the Liechtenauer farm as his address. Liechtenauer's contributions to the Nazi war effort kept him away from the rural estate. The boy lived with the property manager and his wife. Ansgar worked hard cleaning the barns and feeding the few remaining animals. He learned to speak German. One morning, Herr Liechtenauer came across Ansgar and the manager. Liechtenauer exchanged few niceties, then immediately turned to the impending Russian advance. With only a cursory look at Ansgar, Liechtenauer left. Within days, the Russians arrived. The property manager was killed. His wife was carried off along with the horses, cows, a few chickens, and loot from the main house. From his hiding place, Ansgar remembered the old grey-haired woman's warning: "Be silent, Ansgar. Say nothing. Don't let the man find you. He will take you away."

The boy wandered the countryside until he was found by an American Army patrol. Days later, Ansgar was dispatched to a displaced persons camp in the American Zone. The American authorities recognized Dr. Liechtenauer's name on Ansgar's identity card. In spite of his pending war crimes trial Walther Liechtenauer was becoming a person of influence with the Americans.

On July 7, 1945, while U.S. Supreme Court Justice Robert Jackson inspected Nuremberg's Palace of Justice as a location for the forthcoming war crimes trials, Dr. Walther Liechtenauer accepted guardianship for Ansgar. In the spring of 1946, Walther Liechtenauer was tried and convicted for crimes against humanity. He was sentenced to five years in prison. He served three. During Liechtenhauer's absence Ansgar was left in the care of Dr. Heinrich Franz, a colleague of the infamous Dr. Josef Mengele. Franz's specialty was mind control and behavior modification including the use of hallucinogenic drugs. The young Ansgar became Franz's first test subject.

And so it was with Ansgar – he grew numb to pain and his own humanity. Over time, Vriend, the fabric doll, disintegrated into shreds, as did Ansgar's recollections. Ansgar kept a remnant in a leather pocket case. It was his talisman. After each kill, he rubbed Vriend's fabric between his fingers. The distant voice warned, "Say nothing, Ansgar."

Chapter 6

Two days had passed since Koch sent the encrypted message from the Post Office. He hid in the shadows, carefully watching a West Hampstead building. Most shops were closed. The alley next to the building was dark. The building's outside light had been broken for months. Still, Koch could see the outline of the staircase leading to the second floor flat. After thirty minutes, Koch crossed the street and climbed the exposed staircase. He knocked. With the door slightly ajar, a voice inquired, "Herr Bruns?"

Koch nodded and entered. At a table on the far side of the room, Koch recognized a familiar face.

"Here are the passports, Professor Bruns," said the seated man without formality. "You may call me Abid." The man spoke English with only a faint Middle Eastern accent.

"These U.S. passports appear authentic," said Koch. He held each one under a light. "Quite good." Both passports were issued to Otto Bruns. The first also included Koch's photograph. The second described a different man. The space for a photograph was empty.

"They are quite authentic, Herr Bruns," said a second man. "I am Rajid." The man's pencil-thin beard and deeply-set eyes deceptively aged the Iranian.

"These passports are excellent," assured Abid. He stepped from behind the table. Abid easily passed for any department store employee. Koch nodded his head in recognition. Abid was the clerk at Dunhill's where Koch had purchased his Irish walking cap. The initial contact flashed through Koch's mind.

"Your American Express card, Herr Bruns." Abid smiled and nodded. Karl Peter Koch's new identity as Otto Bruns was authenticated. Uncomplicated. Simple. The contact was made. The purchase cleared. The exchange made.

Nevertheless, Koch was uncomfortable. Why had Doctor Liechtenauer been so insistent Koch re-enter the United States with a new identity? The always suspicious Koch couldn't push the question to the back of his mind.

Abid and Rajid were no more Abid and Rajid than Koch was Otto Bruns. *All the better.*

"And the third passport.? There are only two?"

"South Africa is very unpopular in the UK, and Africa second only to Israel these days."

"Where is the passport?"

Abid and Rajid looked at each other and then at Koch.

"Surely you know," said Abid.

Rajid added, "Your compatriot arrived earlier in the day."

"Odd. I received no such change in my instructions," responded Koch, apprehensively.

"We received a call. The password and the code matched the document your compatriot presented. It was his photograph on the passport."

My compatriot? "Are you certain?"

"Absolutely. The passport was issued to an 'Ansgar.'"

Koch never met the man. Walther Liechtenauer presented Ansgar's name. Koch contracted Ansgar's services via mail. Advance payment was made through South African channels. *Why is Liechtenauer circumventing me? I will lose contact with Ansgar.*

Ansgar's deviation from Koch's timetable was alarming. Why had Ansgar failed to rendezvous that morning? Ansgar would never renege on a contract. His reputation would be tarnished. Koch returned to the matters at hand.

"Are the other cells in place?" Koch asked Rajid.

"Yes, Herr Bruns. Each cell is independent. We know there are others. Where? Their mission? We know nothing. The dragon, Ladon, had fifty heads. For each head cut off, a thousand foes die. Eventually all of Ladon's foes will be vanquished."

Of course, Koch knew quite a different story. *There are no other cells.* It was an illusion. Convinced they were part of a larger plot, Abid and Rajid waited to make their mark on London. They mapped Belgravia Station and accounted for its vulnerable location. They were growing impatient.

"Remember," Koch warned. "You must not be captured. Your failure will betray the revolution."

"We will not dishonor our families," Abid answered. He reached to the small of his back drawing a Walther PPK pistol. Koch stepped back. *The pistol makes me remember the Berlin Home Guard.* Koch was well-acquainted with death. *Ironic, after all my time at Dachau, why feel squeamish around firearms?*

"Your families will be well provided for."

"We are prepared to die, but not without a fight," said Rajid. His eyes grew colder. "We are ready." Abid glanced around the room as if to imply they were prepared for a final battle.

Koch departed with even less formality than when he entered. *Assuming an identity is exhausting. Who am I now, Koch or Bruns?* Crossing the street he walked to the rented Opel parked nearby and drove away. He grappled with Ansgar's disappearance. Koch's next stop was Knightsbridge.

Entering the Knightsbridge Post Office, Koch walked directly to the telephone kiosk. He dialed a number in Hamburg, Germany. A young woman answered the phone.

"Are there any messages for Herr Bruns?" Koch placed the small burst transceiver to the phone. The red light flashed. Message received. Koch left the post office and returned to the Belgravia Hotel. A hotel employee returned the rented auto.

"Good evening, Herr Koch," greeted the assistant manager.

Tonight there was little time for pleasantries. Koch nodded without smiling and climbed the stairs to his room.

There was an urgency to decode the message Koch had received. Perhaps it would reveal Ansgar's location. It did not. Instead, the message read:

'Six C-130 transport planes. Unusual troop movements in Sinai.'

So, at last, the Americans have decided to make their move in the Sinai. Six planes meant three hundred paratroopers. A Special Forces mission, Koch conjectured. He walked to the commode and flushed the paper. Now, Koch understood the

Americans' need for a vaccine. They need a vaccine against Rift Valley Disease. North Americans did not have an immunity to the sickness. Mosquitoes carried the blood-borne vector. The disease could vanquish an army. Project Naomi was the name given to the joint government venture to develop a Rift Valley vaccine. It was a complex task involving the DOD, DOA, CDC, INS, NSA and CIA. Project Naomi was a maze. All the components were under pressure from the State Department. There are too many cooks involved in Project Naomi. Regardless of events in the Sinai, Koch's objective was anthrax and a vaccine.

Back in Washington, the Secretary of State telephoned General Mark Webster, a longtime friend. The next morning over coffee, the Secretary explained the request.

"Mark, I need your help."

"How can I help?"

"I'm certain we face an information and coordination gap on a top secret development program at Fort Detrick."

"That's the biological warfare center."

"We are bound by law to limit our work to specific sites. In this case, Detrick and the Animal Disease Research Center on Plum Island, off the coast of Long Island."

"Those labs deal with dangerous and highly contagious diseases. We have treaties preventing bio warfare research."

"We have an alphabetical list of agencies involved. I trust you, Mark, for a special role."

"What would that be?"

"Deconfliction."

"Deconfliction, Mr. Secretary?"

"I need a strong, no bullshit personality for a special mission. Your job will be to minimize conflicts between the agencies, insure the sharing of information, and above all, keeping me in the loop. Are you up to it?"

"Sounds like a challenge. Beats sitting behind my desk marking time until retirement. Yes, sir. I'm on board."

"We have three scientists heading the research. Intelligence refers to them as the Wizards. Contact Professor Karl Peter Koch. I've read his file. Horrible background. Koch was an SS researcher at Dachau. He deserved a five- or ten-year prison term in Spandau.

I would have hanged him. Now, our government needs him." The Secretary frowned.

"The CIA, FBI, DOD…Koch must be important, but why?" asked Webster.

"This is a joint operation, Mark. When the Russians captured Berlin, they got their hands on a number of top scientists. They grabbed twenty or more chemical and nuclear scientists. They disappeared. More important, the Berlin University library contained hundreds of reports and research notes."

"I can understand why Western powers would be concerned," Webster said.

"The Joint Command was frantic. Then, sometime in July 1945, a German prisoner was cleaning the toilets in a barracks. Hidden in the toilet's water closet was a list of Germany's top chemical, nuclear, and rocket scientists."

"And he turned the list over to us?" asked Webster in amazement.

"The Army rounded up Werner von Braun and his gang. 'Bingo!' In spite of the Geneva Convention, we have a secret prison right at our back door in Virginia. The military called it 'Operation Paper Clip'. I surmised that's how we got Karl Peter Koch. His Nazi file was sanitized."

The Secretary waved Koch's dossier in the air. "Sounds outrageous."

"How is that possible?" Webster asked.

"Cold war politics, Mark. President Eisenhower warned America, 'Beware of the military-industrial complex'. Americans didn't listen.

"Can you imagine the public outrage, if word leaked we had Nazi scientists on our payroll?" Webster answered.

"The world is changing, Mark. These guys helped to kill millions. Now they are valued professionals. Why?"

"To keep them from the Russians. My gut tells me there's more to this. When do I start?" asked Webster.

"Immediately. Your first stop – Fort Detrick."

⮑

Several months later, Professor Karl Peter Koch became

General Mark Webster's "go-to man." The cold war formatted extremes in secrecy and strange bedfellows. For the experienced inquirer, secrets were usually inadvertently revealed.

In truth, the Black Knight organization discovered Project MKNaomi by accident. The cartel owned extensive land and cattle holdings in Argentina, Brazil, and Chile. The DOA published bulletins and updates dealing with animal diseases. Imported beef had to pass rigid DOA health inspections. Argentina, Brazil, and Chile wanted larger shares of the market. The cartel routinely compiled and summarized bulletins. Professor Koch was alerted. Koch soon fashioned his own scenario. His personal diabolical Project Naomi was born.

Now, Koch found himself in London carrying out his most difficult, and hopefully final, mission. *Life changes in a moment and today's events proved it.* Koch was tired of world travel and living out of a suitcase. *My health is failing. I long to retire.*

Amid and Rajid, the young radicals in search of a cause, would soon find their work rewarded. The two Iranians met while studying electrical engineering at Cologne's university. They were recruited for Muammar al-Gaddafi's terrorist training school. Trained deep in the desert, the program's graduates were a new breed for the coming technological age. Base 21 consisted of three large hangars. Hangar One, the largest building, housed scale models of buildings. Beyond small arms instruction and bomb building, the curricula included communications and remote controlled devices. Interrogations were physical and sometimes violent. Disguises were selected. No detail was too small.

"You're working with the best," bragged one American expatriate instructor. "By the time you leave here you'll be experts in any form of barrier penetration. No alarm, no surveillance system, will be too sophisticated." The hard-nosed American mercenary was right. Surely any one of the graduates could paralyze New York City with a few grenades. When the cartel needed two operatives, they called upon Gaddafi. Abid and Rajid were selected. In late spring, the pair was inserted into the United Kingdom.

Suddenly, a shock of pain drove Koch against the wall. He felt the throbbing in his joints. Each day, the illness was robbing more of his vitality. His facial muscles twinged. Each step was agony. From behind the dresser mirror, Koch retrieved Anna's parcel. He struggled to break the string. He examined the parcel's precious contents: three vials and a package containing six blue pills. Koch had depleted his initial cache. He broke the seal on one of the vials and swallowed its contents. The six tablets would suffice until he arrived in the States. Koch opened his briefcase. A small slit in the lining would conceal the remaining vials. He placed the pills in his shaving kit.

Along with the vials, the package contained a small envelope. Koch was surprised. His vision was blurred. Removing the shade from the nightstand lamp, he opened the envelope. "No. It can't be!" he said aloud. The envelope contained a locket of hair. A piece of paper fell to the floor. Koch bent forward, picking up what appeared to be a tattered card. *The card. Anna's precious index card: SS 1 – 3128 – SS Lebensborn – Steinheoring. It was Nadine's identity card. Anna had kept it all these years.*

The old man's mind peeled away the layers of convoluted reality. Koch struggled to overcome the dulling effects of the drugs.

"You are quite insane, you know," spoke the invisible voice.

The old man was startled. He was alone. *The mind plays cruel tricks.*

"Don't ignore me, Karl Peter Koch."

Koch's eyes darted about the room. *I am going blind and mad.*

"You are going blind and mad," echoed the voice.

"No crazier than you. No more insane than the rest of the world," retorted the old man. He stepped backward, groping for the chair, almost falling over it.

"You're growing weak and exhausted, Peter Koch. Soon you will die." The voice came from the recesses of Koch's mind.

Koch tore at his tie and buttoned collar, his hand shaking in frenzy. The ritual had worked before.

"Not this time. I'll not be driven away. Not by drugs, not by sleep, not by pain."

"You will!" Koch furiously punched the air.

"You are the desperate one. You think you have succeeded. You are all alone in this world. Now you will never know," taunted the invisible voice.

"Goddamn you. Never know what?" Koch clawed his face.

"They murdered her this evening. You knew they would. You exploited her. Anna trusted you."

Gasping for breath, he fell to the floor. "Never know what?" he gasped.

"Your daughter. You will never know if Anna was telling the truth. You'll never know if you have a daughter. Anna was the key."

Koch's head fell against the floor. He struggled to pull himself on to the bed. With a loud gasp he collapsed and fell back onto the floor.

Hours later Koch awoke in a pool of perspiration and urine. The medication no longer helped. His condition seemed worse since consuming the vial's contents. Eventually, he showered and packed his suitcase. He policed the room for any misplaced items. He wiped the surfaces to remove telltale signs of his presence. Koch paid his account, retrieved his passport and quickly departed the Belgravia. On his way to Heathrow Airport, Koch requested the driver to pull over. He entered a pub searching for a public phone. *One last call.* Koch dialed the West Hampstead police station. The call set off a chain reaction.

Acting on a tip from an unknown caller, the police notified Scotland Yard, The Metropolitan Police and MI-5. Two IRA terrorists were hiding in a West Hampstead flat.

"They are armed. I've seen the explosives," the caller warned. Officers from Special Branch, including sharpshooters from the anti-terrorist unit, were also dispatched. The week prior, a London police officer had been killed. The execution was attributed to the IRA, although no group claimed credit.

"I've never seen anything like it," Martin Brown told a BBC reporter. Brown was working unusually late in a nearby office building when officers rushed in and ordered him out. "Then all bloody hell broke loose."

In the second floor flat across the street, Amid and Rajid were awakened by the owner's barking dog. Startled and half asleep,

Amid peered at the street below. Rajid opened the outside door.

"Someone is down there," he whispered. Amid removed his pistol from his bedside drawer.

"Quickly! Get the grenades and the Uzi." Amid grabbed the satchel with the explosives and Uzi magazines. The two men pushed the heavy table toward the door and flipped it to make a barricade. Descending the staircase leading to the street would surely mean disaster. The rear windows opened to the roof of the garage. Their only escape route meant jumping from the second story window to the roof below. Rajid rushed across the room, pushing furniture against the front windows. A crowd of onlookers stood behind the police barrier. An officer ordered them to leave. Only a few left.

"We have time," said Amid, kneeling by the exposed window. "The police have said nothing. No demands. No request for surrender." There wouldn't be any warnings or demands for surrender. This was an opportunity to settle scores for last week's senseless killing of the London officer.

Suddenly, a tear gas grenade crashed through the front window.

"Quickly! The fragmentation grenades," Rajid shouted. Abid smashed the window with a chair and tossed a grenade to the street. Then a second. The satchel held an assortment of phosphorous and fragmentation hand grenades, twelve 32-round Uzi magazines, and two gas masks. The Iranians' eyes burned, but they were able to put on the gas masks. Rajid began firing his Uzi randomly, sweeping both the police and the crowd. There was screaming. Another explosion. Ever-intensifying cries for help.

A barrage of gunfire was returned. Bullets from below penetrated the floor. One bullet hit a gas line. A severed electric wire provided the spark.

"Fire," shouted Amid.

Rajid pointed to the rear window. "I'll jump first. Cover me!" A hail of bullets sprayed Rajid, suspending him in midair. His limp body hit the roof, rolled and tumbled to the ground. An officer fired four more rounds into Rajid's lifeless corpse.

Calling upon all his reserves, Amid crawled to the front window. The police were smashing the door. He emptied the

Uzi's magazine at the door. The pounding stopped. Reloading, he moved to the opposite window and fired into the alley below. He knew there would be no surrender. Amid had prepared for this final moment. He fired a burst into the assault below. There were intense screams. Pleas for help echoed from the narrow alley. There were calls for a mother's comfort. Amid dropped another white phosphorous grenade. Phosphorous engulfs. Water increases the chemical's intensity. The victims ignite. A rising stench filled the air.

"Cease fire! Hold your fire!" shouted the West Hampstead police inspector. "We need them alive." The firing continued.

Tear gas engulfed the flat. Smoke rose from below. The sickening smell of burning flesh drifted over the police sharpshooters. Their anger intensified.

For Amid, the end came quickly. The 5.56mm bullet crashed through Amid's shoulder diverting into his thoracic cavity. With one final thrust, Amid pulled the grenade's pin and fell forward.

The following morning, the BBC News reported: "Two Terrorists Die In Fire. Evidence links pair to the Irish Republican Army". British Intelligence needed a quick cover story. Forensic evidence pointed to a different conclusion. The men were Islamic fundamentalists with UK passports.

Pan American flight 5017 departed London's Heathrow Airport at 1930 hours (8:00 p.m.), an overnight flight to the United States. On board jumbo jet N750 PA was economy class passenger Otto Bruns.

It was an uneventful flight. Traveling with a new identity carried risks. Koch had cleared his first hurdle. He still wondered why Liechtenauer insisted on the cover.

"May I offer you a beverage?" asked the attractive stewardess.

"Yes. Thank you." Koch turned toward the young woman and reached for the glass. His eyes seemed to fix on a point over her right shoulder. She turned her head and glanced back as though to see what captured the man's attention. The aisle was empty. Koch's glass fell into the aisle. He slumped forward. His eyes remained open.

The stewardess called for help. A man two rows forward responded. He was a physician. Another stewardess rushed to help with an emergency medical pack. They applied oxygen and desperately worked to revive Koch.

The plane was beyond a point of return. The physician checked Koch's pulse, his airway. A minute, perhaps two passed. Karl Peter Koch, aka Otto Bruns, was dead.

The physician exchanged a few hushed words with the Captain. Captain Elliot returned to the cockpit. Each plane carried a World Health Organization Guide For International Flights. He reviewed the regulations.

As quickly and discreetly as she could manage, a stewardess returned carrying a black body bag. Across the dead man's forehead, the stewardess printed the date and time of death with a black marker. A passenger volunteered to help the struggling physician and stewardess place the body bag under Koch's legs and pull it up and over. Next came the zipper and an incident report tag.

One elderly woman began admonishing the crew as they dragged the bag forward. "Have some respect for the dead," she scolded. A stewardess, sensing the woman might start a disruption, offered a prayer.

Koch's travel documents were placed into a pouch attached to the front of the bag. A bright yellow seal was affixed to the body bag. The oversized "Q" was the symbol for "quarantined". The bag was secured in the rear lavatory.

Surprisingly, the passengers remained relatively calm. The chief stewardess deserved praise. Her professional demeanor and reassurance soothed most of the passengers.

The captain radioed Kennedy International Airport of the situation.

"Flight 5017. Stand by."

It took nearly five minutes for a response.

"Pan Am Flight 5017, this is JFK calling."

"Go ahead JFK."

"Pan Am Flight 5017… request you refer to page 101 of your WHO guide." Elliot expected the tower's instructions. Aircraft buffs monitor these frequencies. The slightest mention of "quarantine" would be on every media broadcast within minutes.

Elliot handed the guide to his co-pilot. "Dave, you read the check sheet and protocol aloud."

"Captain, ever dealt with this before?" asked Dave Pierce, Elliot's new co-pilot.

"Just once. On a flight from India. Our job is to keep things calm. We may have a real emergency on our hands. Then again, it may be nothing. Until we know, we treat it like the plague."

Pierce swallowed hard. His expression turned grim. He read the protocols aloud. It was the responsibility of the flight crew to assure the passengers that this was a routine procedure when there is a death onboard an international flight.

Under no circumstances will the terms disease, quarantine or references to medical inspections be used. Avoid medical terms. Use commonly accepted lay terms.

The plane and its passengers followed an alternate landing and deplaning procedure. Immigration officials and medical personnel for the Centers for Disease Control would board the plane. A Quarantine Official would assess the situation.

First, the corpse would be transported to an isolation area within Hanger 80.

Then, medical personnel would provisionally screen the passengers and shuttle them to Hanger 80 for a debriefing and further screening. The manual called it 'patient surveillance'.

"JFK, Pan Am Flight 5017 calling."

"Go ahead Pan Am Flight 5017."

"Protocol check complete."

"Affirmative, Pan Am Flight 5017."

"Pan Am Flight 5017 out."

As Flight 5017 made its final approach to JFK Airport, Dr. Liechtenauer was meeting with Black Knight's directors at its Long Island headquarters. The grounds were cluttered with trucks and workers. As usual, Albert Berg was the first to arrive. The electronic gates weren't working. Two armed security guards stood at the entrance. The guard with the captain's bars asked for Berg's identification. He checked with the main desk and cleared Berg.

"Stay to the right," he said and waved Berg on to a temporary parking space.

Kurt Strauss was next to arrive. Berg paced the entrance foyer waiting for Strauss.

"What's going on here?" Berg demanded. "No one told me the estate was being renovated. Have you seen the inside?"

"I have," said Strauss. "I authorized the funds."

Berg was infuriated. "Why wasn't I informed?"

"There was no need, my dear Berg. Once the construction is completed, I'll turn the facility management over to you. I wouldn't let Liechtenauer learn of your consternation. My advice…regain your composure. I have no idea why Liechtenauer has called this meeting. I suspect there are a number of changes coming."

"Gentlemen." It was Fritz Schmidt.

"You're dressed rather casual today," said Berg.

"Playing golf this afternoon with an important client. Nine holes, mind you, but enough to feel him out. I think Liechtenauer personally arranged the round for us."

"Something big must be up," said Berg.

Strauss and Schmidt both knew Berg was fishing for information.

One of Liechtenauer's many assistants entered the library to inform the three the meeting would begin shortly in an anteroom off the main meeting hall.

The assistant led them around several piles of construction materials. Scaffolding blocked the doors to the main hall. The second floor was no longer open. Large pieces of plate glass were being fitted in place.

Eric Reiter was the last to arrive. His flight from Argentina had been delayed. He hadn't slept in two days. Reiter was nervous. The others attributed Reiter's behavior to fatigue.

The anteroom was bare, with the exception of a long mahogany conference table, chairs and a display board sitting on an artist's easel.

The directors hadn't gathered since the night Koch made his presentation. They were stunned to see Liechtenauer sitting in a wheelchair. He was wearing a nasal cannula. The thin plastic tube was connected to an oxygen bottle. An intravenous bag suspended from an apparatus next to the wheelchair was connected to

Liechtenauer's right arm.

There was no need to say anything about the doctor's appearance; he saw the shocked expressions on their faces. An attendant stood next to Liechtenauer.

"Gentlemen. Let's get directly to business, shall we?" Liechtenauer's voice was weak. He tried to control his trembling left arm.

Berg looked at the doctor in disbelief. *My God. He's lost so much weight.*

Liechtenauer struggled to stand. He did not have the strength. Over the last year, he began to feel a loss of muscle strength. Routine tasks such as getting out of a chair sometimes proved impossible. *I must gather my strength. I need to remain in control.*

Liechtenauer continued, "I have determined to make several strategic changes for our organization. Thanks to Strauss' unquestioning loyalty and service, Black Knight will turn in a new direction."

"What?" demanded Berg.

"Albert. Be cautious. I warn you," replied Liechtenauer. "Don't interrupt me again."

"Professor Koch's blueprint for anthrax and the antibiotic will be placed on hold. I recognize the profit an anthrax vaccine will bring. The project must wait."

The others looked at one another. Even the loyal Strauss was unaware.

"I'm dismayed, Walther," said Kurt Strauss. He was the only director who called the doctor by his first name. "I'm certain that the others are just as surprised as I am to see you in such poor health. And now you are about to present a new mission statement. This is a bit much all at one time."

"I understand your feelings. Koch's plans will be implemented. Our financial investments will not be lost. His work in South Africa remains a priority. We are still in search of a wonder drug. However, allow me to outline several important points."

Liechtenauer explained his new plan. "Several months ago while Koch was visiting a research facility in Egypt, he filed a report with you, Reiter."

"Yes, he did. Koch alerted me Rift Valley Disease was an

increasing concern for the Egyptian government. Thousands of animals were diseased and dying. Then, a regional hospital in Zagazig, Egypt, reported two humans contracted and died from the disease. How is RVD connected with our search for an anthrax vaccine?"

"In time, Reiter," said Liechtenauer. He sensed the tension. "Please place the first chart on the easel."

"Black Knight will no longer exist after today. Walk the halls. Gather your memories. Nothing will remain. In another six months, the interior will be completely changed and modernized to fit our new image. Destroy anything connecting you to Black Knight or our Nazi past."

"New image? Destroy the past? Impossible," said Berg.

Liechtenauer scowled. "I have received information from a highly placed source inside the State Department. Anwar Sadat is in deep trouble. Egypt is deep in debt. There are increasing threats of terrorism from the Muslim Brotherhood. And there is an outbreak of Rift Valley Disease. A virulent strain; thousands, perhaps hundreds of thousands, of people will be affected. Egypt's domestic food supply could be jeopardized. Sadat's popularity is at a low point. The CIA speculates a coup may be in the works. Sadat needs to do something to regain his power."

Liechtenauer again turned to Eric Reiter.

"We are working on a response to RVD," replied Reiter.

Kurt Strauss turned in his chair. "And what of our investments in Egypt? Sadat owes us a huge debt."

"And the Israelis? How are they responding?" asked Fritz Schmidt.

"Stop! One at a time. Look at the chart. Both the CIA and MI-6 have supplied these statistics. Sadat's popularity was decreasing with each increase in Rift Valley Disease."

Liechtenauer went on. "I have confirmed both Sadat and Menachem Begin will arrive at Camp David, soon. The date is a closely guarded secret. The Americans are proposing a summit of sorts at Camp David. Carter wants to strike a deal over the Sinai. My sources tell me all sorts of activity is taking place in preparation for the meeting."

"It won't work," said Berg. "Not without the Palestinians."

"Tell me again, Reiter, where we are with RVD research," said Kurt Strauss.

"We are nearly ready, thanks to Koch's work in South Africa and Egypt. We need to deal with the animals first. A vaccine. We have an element we did not have with the anthrax project."

"And what is that?" asked Berg.

"A large population of humans for test subjects."

The assistant who escorted the directors to the anteroom returned. He whispered to Liechtenauer.

"Put up chart two, please," Liechtenauer said.

"This is the new organizational structure for Trinity PharmoDynamics Group. Reiter and Strauss will meet with me later in the week to formalize the new conglomerate. One last point, gentlemen. I want to introduce my successor."

"Your successor?" asked Berg. "Outrageous. How could you pick a successor without consulting with the directors?"

Liechtenauer paused. The doctor had made two very difficult decisions since learning he suffered from ALS. He recalled his first decision, Ansgar's secret adoption. The doctor's wife died during childbirth. Their daughter died a few weeks later. Both were buried in the Liechtenhauer family plot near Leipzig.

"Mother, do we really need such a large cemetery plot?" he asked.

"Walther, I appreciate your concern. Don't be concerned. All the plots will be filled soon enough."

Several days later, his mother's physician called. "It's time," he said.

Walther sat beside his mother throughout the night and into the next evening, praying the Rosary. Walther hated the Rosary. He disdained religion. Nevertheless, it was his duty to pray.

He opened the small guide of Christian promises and began fingering the beads. Liechtenauer hated Jews. He disliked women. American women and the Jews were fueling the civil disobedience and social unrest the Negroes started. His mother hated Jews.

And still he prayed. His mother died as Liechtenauer adjusted the blinds. The setting sun cast a shadow across his mother's face. Walther was his mother's sole heir. Now there was Ansgar. *Mother would never have approved.* In the furthest recesses of

Liechtenauer's mind, he suspected Ansgar was a Jew.

It was his decision. He stood firm.

"Liechtenauer, tell us how you came to this decision," demanded Berg.

"Berg, you are a fool. Liechtenauer has selected his man. You will pay for your antics," whispered Fritz Schmidt.

Schmidt was correct. Liechtenauer was determined to stand firm. Early in 1974, Liechtenauer informed the Alliance of his progressive illness. The twelve expressed continued confidence in Liechtenauer's leadership of Black Knight. During that summer, the Alliance presented two candidates: Jules Smylee and Ashton Pickering. Liechtenauer would pick his successor. Neither candidate was a Black Knight director. The successor would be secretly groomed. The Alliance would give the final approval for the transition.

The doctor spent hours searching through their dossiers for hidden clues to their weaknesses. Trinity PharmoDynamics Group required a strong-willed leader. Jules Smylee was Liechtenauer's favored candidate. The senior partner in the firm of Richardson, Deckmann, and Smylee caught the eye of the Twelve as they began recouping and reorganizing their World War II investments. In the positive column, Mr. Smylee had a knack for dealing with marginal characters that lurked in the shadows of death. Smylee was the go-to man for contacts in the Grand Caymans and Switzerland. In the negative column, Smylee had failed to acquire Wesfield Laboratory for the Alliance.

It was time for the Alliance to move from manufacturing household detergents, chemicals and insecticides to their goal: pharmaceuticals. Jules Smylee was charged with purchasing small US laboratories. In 1972, Smylee made the first attempt to purchase a small Michigan company. Wesfield Laboratory was a family-owned and managed company. Mr. Smylee hired Hermann von Leer, an Austrian-born, Washington-based lobbyist, to negotiate the purchase of Wesfield Laboratory. Joseph Westerfield, the 72-year-old president, refused to sell. Westerfield suspected the acquisition amounted to a scam. *The new owners would bleed Wesfield Laboratory's assets, fire loyal personnel.* The privately owned airport was going through extensive renovations.

Several storage buildings were under construction. The entire facility was surrounded by a chain link fence. Security guards were posted at the entrance.

Why all this activity? All Smylee wants is Wesfield's FDA license and patents. Smylee began acquiring a dozen or more FDA approved firms. Seven companies owned drug patents and registered marketing names. Owning a brand name…a trusted household name…was worth millions, maybe billions, of dollars. It didn't take long for Joseph Westerfield to discover the offshore Trinity PharmoDynamics Group was looking for a legitimate brand name in the United States. Westerfield refused to sell. Smylee, and in turn, von Leer, raised the ante.

On one occasion, the elder Westerfield warned his grandson, "Jeff, trust no one. Trinity is trying to get a foothold in the United States. Trinity is a spinoff of IG Farben. IG Farben and the Nazis worked hand in hand. The people involved with IG Farben will stop at nothing…not even murder. Wesfield Laboratory isn't falling for their scheme. I may be getting old, but I can still put up a fight."

In 1974, Smylee became desperate. The unholy Twelve directed Smylee to acquire Wesfield Laboratory at any cost. Smylee directed von Leer to once again approach Joseph Westerfield. This was the final offer. The offer failed. Smylee's dossier tells the full tragic story.

Jules Smylee committed suicide rather than face the Alliance's wrath. Hermann von Leer managed to avoid reprisal, but his time was coming to an end.

The remaining candidate became Liechtenauer's tentative successor. His name was Ashton Pickering, the great grandson of an Alliance charter member. Pickering was a Harvard graduate. Unlike Jules Smylee, Pickering was not an attorney. His earned graduate business degrees were from Harvard, then Stanford, and finally, the Wharton School of the University of Pennsylvania. Pickering was driven, but overtly mild-mannered. He preferred to manage from behind the scenes. When his father suggested a position on the Federal Reserve Board, Ashton declined. He enjoyed marketing and then perhaps a stint with John Foster Dulles or his brother Allen.

"Out of the question," Ridgeway Pickering declared. "Use your talents where our country most needs them." Ashton admired his father and followed his advice. He reluctantly accepted a position with the Office of Special Operations at the National Security Agency. The OSO protected the NSA's image. Ashton Pickering made it his business to know everyone else's business. Pickering took great pleasure following the machinations of the General Accounting Office and the Department of Justice. Ashton snickered at newspaper reports following J. Edgar Hoover's death. Dakota Putnam, a writer with the *Washington Post*, claimed the Attorney General had personally ordered a top to bottom search of the FBI building upon learning Hoover had died. The Attorney General wanted Hoover's secret files.

Too late. I've got them, Mr. Attorney General. And I've got you, too. Just step out of line once and I'll release your file. Those bathroom photos will make great fodder.

"We are still waiting for your answer, Liechtenauer." Berg was now shouting.

Fritz Schmidt looked at Berg. *Berg has signed his own death warrant.*

Finally, Liechtenauer raised his left arm and signaled for silence. The doctor motioned for his two assistants to leave the room. The anteroom door re-opened. In an almost theatrical fashion, a man entered.

"Gentlemen. Allow me to introduce Ashton Pickering."

Not another word was spoken. The room was filled with tension. Even Berg was afraid to speak.

"Remember our history. We represent the most powerful people in the world. Their interests come before any one of us. We are tools. Nothing more. Each of you swore an oath; a life commitment. You have profited from your work and loyalty. Make no mistake. The new Trinity cartel will be in place. All traces of Black Knight will be expunged. A single error will be costly. Good day, Gentlemen."

Pickering remained silent. His thin, pale face was expressionless. *It's time to go.* Pickering carefully pushed Liechtenauer's wheelchair in the direction of his private elevator. No one followed them. They had never been invited to Liechtenauer's quarters.

Liechtenauer's decision was firm. Walther Liechtenhauer would soon fade away. The four remaining directors looked at one another. None had the courage to challenge Liechtenhauer's selection. Now it was too late.

"With Liechtenhauer gone, what will become of us?" asked Berg. The once fierce adversary trembled with fear.

Fritz Schmidt stifled his response. *After your performance today, Berg, I sense what will become of you. The Alliance distains memorial services.* He said, "Gentlemen, my recommendation is simple. Insure your niche within Trinity. As for me…I plan to offer a toast to our new leader, Ashton Pickering. Shall we retire to the library? I know where Walther stashed his prized Scotch."

Chapter 7

The fog began to lift along the Potomac River. A light mix of snow and rain left the streets with a slippery sheen. The telltale remains of a late March snowstorm were slowly melting away.

Northern Virginia was experiencing its worst winter in two hundred years. President Jimmy Carter's inauguration was overshadowed by headline reports of severe cold weather gripping the Northeastern United States. The Potomac tidal basin froze solid. Skaters could be seen near the Memorial Bridge. Every few days, several more inches of snow were added to the piles accumulating along the streets and in parking lots. As March came to a close the weekend called for temperatures in the high 40's. The promise of warmer weather ensured tourists would be returning to Washington, D.C.'s National Mall for the first time in four days.

Early morning joggers were the harbingers of spring. Anticipating warmer temperatures, many had shed their winter sweats, favoring T-shirts and shorts. Mark Webster hated jogging. That's why he could be spotted most workday mornings jogging the circuit from the Capitol to the Lincoln Memorial and back. Jogging, like most other things in Webster's life, reflected his personality. The General was certain that if he disliked physical exercise, it had to be good for him. Webster was a contradiction in terms. He disliked arbitrary rules, yet chose to spend his adult life in the military. Webster's unpretentious office was a short walk from the Capitol. General Webster directed a complex network so secret and sensitive few within the incoming Carter administration had been briefed on its existence. Each component operating under Webster's purview was compartmentalized on a "need to know basis." Webster reasoned the simplicity of his work could be masked by complexity, and so it was.

On this particular Friday morning, Webster looked forward to a weekend with friends in nearby Fredericksburg. He wanted to be out of Washington before noon. A quick trip to his office and he'd be on his way for an extended weekend. Webster headed off on a clockwise circuit that included his ritual dash up the eighty-seven steps leading to Lincoln's statue.

Piles of snow forced the General to weave his way along the Mall. He trailed a jogger timing his strides with hers. Webster sensed one or two runners close behind. A quick glance confirmed they would soon pass him. Directly to his left, on the opposite side of the Mall, was the Hirschhorn Museum.

The first of the trailing joggers passed Webster. The blonde ponytail caught Webster's attention, then her shorts. They accented the tight ass of a woman in top condition. She had a great body, Webster mused. Accelerating ahead, she gave Webster a knowing smile. The General's momentary distraction ended as the second jogger ran closer. The pavement was wet and slippery as they approached the 9th Street intersection. Suddenly, the second jogger appeared to be losing her balance. Falling forward, the runner reached out as though to fend off the impending collision and break the impact of her fall. Webster felt a momentary sting as her left hand brushed the back of his leg. Webster stopped and turned to help. In one continuous motion, the runner regained her momentum and sprinted north toward the National Portrait Gallery.

The General stopped and felt the back of his thigh. There was a tiny red welt. Webster continued his run for a few hundred feet then changed his mind and headed back to his office. He felt light headed. His body temperature was rising. Webster's pace slowed to a walk. He stumbled and fell. A police officer radioed for an ambulance.

At 11:35 p.m. on Friday, April 1, 1977, General Mark Webster, United States Army, died. Doctors at Walter Reed Hospital were baffled. Controversy surrounding Webster's death continued. The cause of death was checked "inconclusive" pending an autopsy. The medical examiner was directed to wait for a DOD team due in on Monday morning. Until then the cause of death would be attributed to cardiac arrest.

✦

Saturday, April 2, 1977

The unusually cold spring slowed work on the addition to the Controller General's D.C. administrative headquarters. The absence of North West G Street's congested traffic gave it a strange feeling. Sam Beverly rarely came to work on a weekend, a promise he made to his wife when he accepted President Ford's nomination.

"I finished reading the preliminary report late last night. General Webster has some explaining to do," said Sam Beverly, looking out on Washington, D.C.'s deserted G Street below.

"That would be simple enough," responded David Clayton. "But we have one problem." The lines in Beverly's face deepened.

"Webster is dead. He collapsed Friday while jogging. Died last night at Walter Reed."

"Dead? What? How do you know?"

"A buddy at the Pentagon called." David Clayton's name had become closely connected with the House Subcommittee on Immigration and Naturalization. General Webster was scheduled to appear before the Committee. CIA wanted Webster to testify behind closed doors. The White House was asking for more time, too."

"Now that's ironic. General Webster. A U.S. Army combat hero in Vietnam. The poor bastard dies jogging," said Beverly.

"General Webster's been under a lot of pressure the last few weeks."

Clayton handed Beverly a heavy brown folder. "What's this?"

"I put together anything I could on the General. A lot of paper. A lot of smoke. Strange. Everything goes blank about a year ago."

The weight of Clayton's folder amplified the unwanted burden Beverly felt. *Why me?*

Sam Beverly's title, Deputy Inspector General for the General Accounting Office, carried no glamour, no chauffer, no perks. Simply put, Beverly regretted his decision to remain at the GAO. Sam Beverly's Senate confirmation created controversy within the GAO. The agency's bureaucracy had its own unwritten code. Fordham graduate or not, Beverly's Jewish heritage often closed doors. Nevertheless, the prior administration staunchly backed Beverly's appointment, more from pride than principle. When Senate support wavered, the President turned up the heat. It was in the last year of his first fully-elected term. From Sam Beverly's perspective, accepting the nomination meant days of public and private scrutiny. His law partners weren't keen on Sam taking a one-year appointment at the GAO. It wasn't a high profile appointment that brought business into the firm.

Sam Beverly's nomination stalled in committee. Then, at an early morning breakfast with the Senate Majority Leader, the President let slip his carefully controlled composure. Smashing his fists on the table, he declared, "By God! Beverly gets that job or else I'll be calling in a few IOU's!" Sam was finally confirmed.

Privately, Sam was becoming ambivalent about his life. Sam's wife, Grace, was disillusioned with Washington life. Sam's job meant increased time away from home. Grace, a successful editor, reluctantly moved from Manhattan to the D.C. suburbs. Grace was unhappy working at a distance. It wasn't long before Grace began extended business trips to the New York office. On those occasions, Sam couldn't sleep. He had no reason to distrust his wife. Still, when Grace was away, Sam found himself restless and unable to sleep. Grace was an independent, beautiful, high-spirited woman. That she enjoyed New York nightlife added ambiance to a successful career. It was a frenetic pace, but exciting. Washington was different. Grace knew how to use her deep brown eyes and smile. Life along the Washington Beltway amounted to petty politics, repetitive committee meetings, and gossip. *There has to be more to life than driving the kids to sports and music lessons.* When Sam agreed to stay on with the new administration, Grace returned to their Manhattan apartment.

"We have to talk," she blurted one evening after a vodka Martini.

Sam braced. *I know what's next.*

"I need my space…time…I just don't fit in here. I'm not asking for a separation."

"And?".

"We'll have to work it out. You'll have to take care of it. Maybe you'll be home more."

Sam's eyes were downcast.

Grace swirled the last few drops of vodka and sighed. *Please don't say anything else, Sam. I don't want to hear it.*

Sam knew the discussion was over. *Grace will twist my comments. An argument will surely follow, all for nothing.* "Whatever!" He raised his glass and whispered "Cheers."

Sam rarely met in person with the Inspector General. The 'IG' avoided staff meetings these days. He announced his resignation, effective July first. At this point, the IG was preoccupied with his pending divorce. The IG sent Sam a three-sentence memo. Until further notice Sam was to cooperate fully with the New York Congressional Delegation. It was quite unusual, but the IG assigned Sam to personally supervise GAO's participation.

∾

David Clayton was stunned to learn he would be working with Beverly. While attending New York University's law school, Clayton served as a volunteer and speechwriter for candidate Elisabeth Harrington's campaign. When he passed the New York Bar exam, Clayton followed the Congresswoman to Washington. Clayton's staff position belied his hopes for an official title within the delegation. Writing press releases and briefs for the New York State Congressional delegation proved boring. Even though Clayton's current assignment provided free time other staffers didn't enjoy, Clayton saw himself in a "dead end" job. *It's time to return to Manhattan.* Though he found his day job monotonous, Clayton's extracurricular life was exciting and frequently exhausting. Among the Congressional staffers, Clayton earned a playboy reputation. Clayton's shenanigans enlivened the water cooler gossip.

"You're wrong," said the petite blonde, unconsciously holding the water cooler as though fondling a lover. "He didn't come on to me. It was me. Does it matter?"

"He's not serious with any woman. He's having too much fun," replied the intern. She had slept with Clayton after a late night staffing.

In a nearby office, Clayton waited impatiently to meet with Congresswoman Harrington.

"I'm sorry, David. David?" Harrington's secretary repeated. "Are you okay?"

"Yes. Thanks for asking." Clayton was deep in thought, fantasizing about a petite brunette *Washington Post* reporter. Then again, Harrington's secretary had a tantalizing shape that stirred him.

"David, Ms. Harrington just called. She's still in committee. She'll get back to you. Oh, she did say to keep your eye out for a letter. She sent it by courier earlier this morning."

"That's it?" he asked.

"One more…ah…one personal note. I go to lunch at one o'clock."

Clayton winked and gave a halfhearted smile. *On any other occasion, lunch would have been a pleasure.*

Clayton thought about his initial request to meet with Harrington. He wanted her recommendation for an opening at a Wall Street firm. Life can change in a moment, as David Clayton would discover.

On his desk, Clayton found a letter from the New York delegation. He was being assigned as liaison with the General Accounting Office. The New York delegation was investigating allegations Axis war criminals were on federal payrolls. The charges weren't new. A journalist presented the latest claim.

"CIA Funnels Collaborators Through 'Rat Lines' In Southern Europe," read one headline. The story went on to quote an anonymous source; a former DOJ official. He asserted U.S. agencies helped Nazi scientists escape justice by relocating them incognito in South America. Were Nazis brought to the United States?

The source assured the writer Nazis were living with impunity in the United States. Two subsequent articles created a furor. The controversy sparked the interest of a young *Washington Post* reporter, Dakota Putnam.

The intelligent and vivacious Putnam had a reputation for being relentless when it came to uncovering a story. The rumors had been around for years. It was an election year. Beltway politics followed a strict unwritten rule. Statesmen debated issues in Congress. Politics was left to the golf course. Talk of Nazis and Cold War politics was the stuff for secret rooms and guarded exchanges. Republicans and Democrats were uncomfortable.

A young New York Congresswoman named Elizabeth Harrington opened an inquiry. She demanded to know if government agencies had indeed helped war criminals enter the United States. Were the reports simply a fishing expedition?

Dakota Putnam was convinced the stories weren't fabricated.

"Did the Immigration and Naturalization Service expedite the entrance of Nazis and other war criminals into the U.S.? It's a simple straight-forward question. No one will give me a simple 'Yes or No.'"

"It's not quite that easy, Ms. Putnam. Congress held hearings in the late '60's. The intelligence community assured us there were no war criminals in the country."

Dakota's persistent inquiries drew Congresswoman Harrington's attention. The House Committee on Naturalization and Immigration delayed an official inquiry until the spring of 1977. Committee staffers were conducting inquiries and cultivating their own sources.

The General Accounting Office was officially asked to review these allegations. "Let the GAO trace intelligence agency expenditures."

"Now that's a joke," laughed one member of the Oversight Committee. "CIA and the rest of them have discretionary funds. How can GAO track those expenditures?"

At first, it appeared that government agencies were fully cooperating with Harrington's inquiry. There was the usual window dressing; press releases, photo ops, and brief hearings. Harrington requested a series of unpublished Executive Orders from the Truman and Eisenhower archives. The President's chief counsel asked for additional time. He could invoke executive privilege.

David Clayton welcomed the new GAO assignment until he received a disturbing telephone call.

"Mr. Clayton, I understand you are searching for a rat line."

"What rat line? Who is this?" demanded Clayton.

"Listen carefully, Mr. Clayton. The oversight committee isn't getting the real story. The testimony is disinformation. A fabrication. The documents have so much expunged material they're useless. I personally handled three priority packages from Germany."

"What is a priority package?"

"Three Wizards."

"Wizards?"

"Three scientists. We brought them in for a top secret research project."

"Listen. Before you tell me anything else, I'm not in charge of the General Accounting Office investigation. I'm an assistant counsel for the New York State Delegation," Clayton protested.

"Come now, Mr. Clayton, I know you're investigating war criminals living in the U.S. Aren't you curious how I acquired your unlisted telephone number?"

Clayton didn't acknowledge the caller. He squeezed his Styrofoam coffee cup spilling black coffee across his desk.

"How many people know your private telephone number? It's nine o'clock. I know you're already at work. The drive in from Manassas can be grueling." The mysterious caller's sarcastic tone revealed a bit of pleasure.

This guy is antagonizing me. "Damn it. You've been following me?"

"Your phone number, your daily routine and, well…I'll leave the rest to your imagination. So…if you're not interested?"

"I'm not into covert spy stuff," Clayton replied.

"You are now."

"Let's meet. We can talk about this."

"Too risky."

"How can I trust you, then?" Clayton asked.

"Remember Deep Throat? He led Woodward and Bernstein to the Oval Office. Deep Throat was their guardian angel."

"Maybe Deep Throat never existed. Maybe Woodward and Bernstein knew Deep Throat and the whole thing was a cover," Clayton retorted.

"No meeting, Mr. Clayton. That would involve great risk. We would both be in jeopardy."

"How serious?" Clayton asked, fearing the answer.

"Mr. Clayton, it is too late to turn back. Your adversaries fear what you may uncover."

"I haven't uncovered anything. I told you. I'm an assistant counsel. A liaison with the GAO. That's it."

"David, David. Calm down. Be cautious."

"Who are these adversaries? How do I know you're telling the truth?" Clayton asked.

"I will call again. I'll set up a dead drop. A secret location. I'll leave an envelope for you. Its contents will establish my bona fides."

Clayton struggled to gather his thoughts.

"No need to put a trace on your phone, Mr. Clayton."

"Wait. What's your name?"

"Ah, I thought you understood, Mr. Clayton. No names. But if you must, call me…Robert." The line went dead.

A week passed. No call from Robert. Clayton suspected the anonymous caller was a member of the New York Congressional delegation. *Someone is testing my loyalty. Politics.* Clayton's first instinct was to turn the matter over to the FBI. That would prejudice the GAO's report. After all, the FBI was one of the organizations under review. If his source was credible, Clayton had a duty to protect him. Several more days passed. Clayton made a critical decision. *I'll tell Sam tomorrow. I trust Beverly.*

"Of course I believe it's possible. Mysterious phone calls are old hat in Washington politics. Come on over. I'll wait for you."

"Thanks for meeting me on such brief notice, Sam."

"Brief notice? Nonsense. I've been thinking about assigning you some work space in the building. Give me a few days. Now what did this 'Robert' have to say?"

David related the mysterious call. "It troubled me. After Robert's call, I started digging a little deeper."

"You didn't go beyond our mandate, did you? Our job is data…numbers. We aren't hunting for individual Nazis."

"That was before Robert's contact."

"I don't want to be involved in a Cold War controversy."

"I know; we have to maintain our credibility."

Sam grimaced. "General Webster's death throws everything off. Let's review what we have."

"One or more government agencies is stonewalling us. I'm sure of it."

Beverly looked puzzled. The traces of worry lines deepened on his crinkled face. He tossed his jacket over a chair and loosened his tie.

"David, do you recall when the inquiry became official in late January?"

David nodded.

"At the time, you were confident everything was on the up and up. Federal agencies were fully cooperating with the oversight committee."

"I thought they were."

"You thought, David? So where does this leave us? Are you telling me there's evidence of a cover-up?"

"I'm no longer certain. Robert's call…I feel uneasy. We aren't getting the whole story."

"Uneasy, David? What about our reputations? Our credibility? Our careers are on the line."

"Robert's call. This guy is more than a whistleblower. Robert insists there's a cover-up," David replied.

"We're talking about obstruction of justice, my friend. You aren't a Hollywood tabloid reporter. You better get your act together."

"I'm exhausted." *I wish had taken Harrington's secretary's offer for lunch.*

"Go home. Sleep in. You need it." Sam needed a break, too. *All this bullshit. I haven't spoken with my daughter in days.* "Got tickets for tonight's game. The Bullets are playing Cleveland."

"Bullets got it." David smiled to ease the tension.

Beverly put on his jacket and straightened his tie. "The drive in was miserable. Damn fog." Holding the doorknob, Sam turned to David. "You know, buddy, this thing could blow back at us."

"I've thought about it. So much time has passed since World War II."

Sam shrugged. "Even if we had access to records, they're sure to be sanitized. Sometimes I wish it would all go away, but I know it won't."

Clayton frowned. "FBI said they gave us all the documents. Insist we have everything."

"Anyone can see there are gaps."

"I'm not certain where all this is leading." Clayton rubbed his chin. *What am I getting into?*

The next morning, Sam reluctantly telephoned the Attorney General. Anticipating an uneasy conversation, Sam jotted a few notes on a pad. The Attorney General had a reputation for being a savvy political animal. In Washington parlance, that meant "watch your back with the son of a bitch."

"Who else knows of David Clayton's suspicions?" the Attorney General asked. The absence of inflection in the Attorney General's voice troubled Sam.

"Clayton assures me that I am the only person in whom he's confided." Sam was being less than candid. He did not reveal the call from Robert and the possibility of an insider's testimony.

"Your boy's suspicions trouble me. I hope the FBI and CIA aren't involved in a cover-up. Concealing information in an investigation is serious business."

"I felt you should be informed."

"I understand your concern, Sam. This is sensitive shit, to say the least. Keep this among the three of us. Nice work, Sam. I'll get back to you."

Sam pictured the Attorney General flicking cigar ash in a Churchill fashion. *I don't like the sound of the Attorney General's good old boy – 'Nice work Sam.'*

Sam knew the meaning of "sensitive." *If Clayton's suspicions didn't fly...if Robert was a hoax...so many "ifs." I dread the consequences.*

Sam recalled growing up with bullies and bigots. The anti-Semites. Sam recalled the viciousness of his Senate confirmation hearings. *I am gun-shy.* Sam removed his reading glasses and nervously tapped them on his desk. *Am I being set up?* He wiped perspiration from his face.

The Attorney General did not return his call. One of his assistants did.

"Mr. Beverly, the Attorney General has scheduled an appointment for you at Justice. He urges the greatest discretion. He requests you keep your conversations on a need to know basis."

The following Tuesday, Sam Beverly and David Clayton met in the lobby of the Justice Department.

"David, if word of our *sub rosa* investigation leaks, it could mean the end of our careers in Washington. I have a family to think about. There's time to distance ourselves. Turn the investigation completely over to the Justice Department."

"You raised this before, Sam. You're the boss." Clayton looked away, avoiding eye contact.

"Boss?" What's that supposed to mean?"

They stepped into the elevator and rode to the fourth floor. Room 408 was at the end of a corridor lined with stacks of file boxes.

"What a dump."

Sam grabbed Clayton's right arm. "You didn't answer my question."

"What question?" Clayton glared at Sam. "We have a responsibility not to let this thing sit on a shelf at The National Archives. Selective amnesia. You know…out of sight, out of mind."

"Nazi Germany was defeated. It's over. A decision was made to allow war criminals to go free. We didn't make that judgment. Think about it. Who really cares?" Sam's voice grew louder.

"I care. We both care."

"The Cold War breeds strange bargains. Suppose we really did need Nazi scientists. They may have possessed special knowledge."

"I've heard the argument before. The Russians had them and we needed them, too. Right? Like you said, it's the Cold War."

"Then let's stop right here and not go any further. I don't have a wife and kid to put through college. The last thing I want is a career in politics."

"What happens if we uncover some real dirty business?"

Clayton stopped. "You want to end it right here? Then don't go through that door. I'm out of here. No hard feelings. I'll have a life again. I haven't been to the Crazy Horse in weeks."

Sam turned his back to the door.

"Sam, you've had me locked away reading about Nazis and concentration camps. You want to stop, I'll stop." Clayton was furious.

Sam Beverly's face was turned red with anger. "You're pissing me off, Clayton. I know my responsibilities. I'm no lackey."

"I know. That's why I'm here."

Sam turned back toward Room 408 and opened the door.

"This can't be some guy's office. It's a mess."

"Just like the mess we're in," Sam snickered.

Room 408 was a windowless converted storage room. A small fan failed to dispel the odor of paint. The back wall remained unpainted. A single light hung from the drop ceiling. Four chairs, a worn metal desk, and a dented filing cabinet completed the furniture. A single line telephone sat on the floor. Its cord was too short to reach the desk.

"Be with you in a minute." The man tossed the contents of a cardboard box on the concrete floor. A cup crashed.

"Damn it. No carpeting."

"Mr. Thompson?"

"I'm Thompson." The man continued sorting items. He paid little attention to the visitors. Using a chair for support, Thompson stood. "Yup, I'm Thompson."

Beverly and Clayton looked at each other in surprise. They were expecting a Justice Department blue suit, not a Lieutenant Colombo caricature. His wrinkled white shirt was covered with dust. Its frayed collar revealed more than years of wear. His baggy trousers were shiny. The man's sunken eyes and pale complexion hinted an untold story.

Thompson looked around the room and laughed. "Excuse the mess, gentlemen. Yesterday, I was retrieving documents from the basement archives. Today, I have my own office. Very strange."

Sam stared at Thompson for a moment. *Strange. This office is strange. You're strange.*

Clayton scratched his right ear, wondering how this guy could assist them.

"Last week, I considered resigning. Then, presto! Never expected this." With one wide gesture, Thompson threw open his arms and asked, "Why me?"

When Jack Thompson arrived at the Justice Department, he was an aspiring attorney with a bright future. Straight out of law school, Thompson had all the credentials. He worked on a number of high profile civil rights cases. Then came Watergate. The insiders at Justice needed someone dependable, yet expendable. Thompson still pondered how he became the man.

In 1973, Thompson was assigned to Sam Dash, Chief Counsel for the Senate Watergate Committee. Thompson remembered a strategic error. On several occasions, he was seen sitting next to Dash during the televised hearings. The late night calls began.

"Lower your profile, Thompson. Just go with the flow."

Regrettably, Thompson failed to heed the warning.

"Stay out of it. You're there for looks."

Then it happened. Thompson encouraged Dash to call White House aide Alexander Butterfield to testify. Butterfield revealed the devastating news. Nixon had been secretly recording Oval Office conversations. The President refused to turn over the tapes. He ordered the Attorney General to stonewall the investigation. The Attorney General refused. The so-called "Saturday Night Massacre" followed. On Monday morning, there was a new Attorney General. Thompson found himself in the Justice Department's basement. They called it the archives. There was little to do but read a novel or Playboy. No one cared about the extended lunch breaks at the Old Ebbitt Grille. One martini led to the next. Thompson was drowning in alcohol and despair.

"So, gentlemen, I have a question for you. Why, after years in exile, has Jack Thompson been elevated to Room 408? On the other hand, don't answer that."

"Your question troubles me." Sam rarely used sarcasm. *Was the Attorney General trying to sabotage the investigation by assigning this fool?*

"From what little I've gleaned, the GAO is up to its ass in Nazis." Thompson casually turned his back.

Clayton removed two files from his briefcase. He dropped them on Thompson's desk. "We need you to read these files."

Thompson paid little attention.

"Listen, Thompson. Cut the bullshit. This isn't a game." Sam's temper flared.

Thompson avoided eye contact. *So this is why I'm here. I'm being set up again. If I go through with this briefing, there'll be no turning back. At least I get out of the basement.*

Thompson brushed the dust from his shirt sleeves and trousers. "Gentlemen, you have my full attention."

Over the weekend, GAO requested a crosscheck on The National Security Agency's data banks.

"They have new computers. It would take days for our office to research the task."

"Leave it up to the feds to want to know everything about everything," said Thompson.

"It would seem so," replied Sam.

"The original database came from health insurance records."

"It's a great way to cover your ass. Beats 'I don't remember,'" Thompson added.

"The Congressional Oversight Committee scheduled General Mark Webster to testify. His dossier is in the top folder. Read it," Sam ordered.

"Why is Webster so important?" Thompson glanced at the folder.

"Webster was supervising several top secret biological research projects. Sam already told you…do your homework, Thompson."

"The General's dead. Heart attack on Friday, April first," Sam added.

"And where was Webster before April 1, 1977?"

"Webster's project was classified and unattached. He wasn't accountable to a specific agency or department," said Clayton.

Clayton handed Thompson a photograph. "This is a recent identification photo of General Webster."

"GAO accessed those documents under protest. We had to go to the top."

"The documents you're holding reveal General Webster's people had been pushing a so-called 'biogap'. Nothing new. Intelligence knew Soviets were outpacing our research into biological warfare. Webster had the authority to foster his own budget line using cross-agency funds. Clayton and I have reason to suspect General Webster was diverting funds into another research project."

"Or maybe a Swiss account?" Thompson had dealt with a few Swiss diversions.

"Weren't you guys at GAO aware of this?" Thompson started leafing through the pages of the red-jacketed folder. "You guys are supposed to be safeguarding taxpayers' money."

"Right. CIA, Defense, National Security Agency…those budgets are classified. We only see the vapor trails from the high fliers. They're spending billions and most of it goes unchecked…no audits," Sam said.

"Last year the CIA withheld its budget figures. The intelligence community's budget is classified."

"We suspect…and I emphasize 'suspect'…few knew of General Webster's pet project," said Clayton.

"So Webster can start a rogue project and GAO doesn't know about it?"

"Sure, until something unexpected happens…like Webster's death. And then we 'may' stumble over it."

"How can it happen?" Thompson returned to his boxes.

"Perhaps…just imagine, it might have happened this way," Sam stepped behind the desk. On a legal pad he sketched a flow chart.

"Picture this, there's a national defense matter - top secret - high priority. DOD, the CIA, State…who knows? They need an all-out effort to send troops someplace, say, Africa or the Middle East. And for argument's sake, that force could be exposed to, say, some kind of bioagent…a virus. Those troops need to be vaccinated. They need drugs to fight the disease."

"Where does Webster fit in?"

"Envision this scenario: The NIH and the DOA are conducting a joint research project under a high-pressure schedule. It might be simple to have a rogue venture."

"Or maybe feeding information to a private party, like a pharmaceutical company."

"Gentlemen, may I remind you that you're mixing with America's most secret agencies? They employ thousands." Thompson started to close the folder.

Thompson's telephone rang. "By God, someone's calling me? The phone was just installed. I don't even know the number.

Thompson here." His expression changed to a frown. Thompson muffled the receiver and whispered. "It's for you, Clayton."

"This is Clayton."

"Mr. Clayton, this is Robert. Did you read today's *Post*?"

"How did you find me here?"

"Never mind that, Mr. Clayton. You will be interested to know that today's *Post* shares your concern."

"My concern? How do you know what I'm concerned about?"

"Please, Mr. Clayton, we have so little time. The *Post* story… General Webster had a stock account. The *Post* claims the account has over four million dollars. Now, we know better. Don't we?"

"The money. Where's the money coming from?" Clayton shouted into the phone. "You're toying with me."

"Temper, temper, David. You wanted my bona fides. Check out the *Washington Post*."

"The dead drop. You never…"

"Ah, so now you are starting to take me seriously," said Robert.

"The dead drop. Where? When?" Clayton impatiently protested.

"All in good time." The caller was gone.

Clayton turned to Sam: "It was Robert."

"Who is this guy?" Sam looked befuddled.

Thompson looked at the ceiling for a second. *Perhaps I should retire now before they send me back to the basement. Why bother unpacking?*

"Robert? Who in hell is Robert?" asked Thompson.

"Clayton's guardian angel," Sam replied.

"Robert tipped the Washington *Post*. Robert's stirring the pot. The *Post* is working on a story. Robert told them General Webster had access to millions of dollars. Robert also told them Webster may have been using government money to buy and sell securities," said Clayton.

"Where was the money coming from?" Sam asked.

"That's what we have to find out."

"We? What we? I haven't agreed to anything," Thompson protested. *This has to be a cruel joke. A payback. Some prick is getting even with me for Watergate. They just can't let go.*

Then Thompson's posture stiffened. "Do you two know what

you are getting into? You're talking about Nazis and the intelligence community. Are you looking to get yourselves killed?"

"Take it easy, Thompson," said Sam.

"You see this?" Thompson pointed to a miniature brass pelican perched on the corner of his desk. "My wife left. Had an affair with our accountant. Get the picture? She took the kids, the parakeet…everything but that pelican. I got screwed. I got shit! Nothing. And now something tells me I'm about to get screwed again."

Chapter 8

A man's face flashed across the conference room screen. "Gentlemen. Meet Professor Karl Peter Koch, aka Peter Koch, aka Otto Bruns. This is our most current photo of Herr Koch. It's his DOD photo ID." Sam Beverly had worked through the night, preparing this morning's briefing. "Koch was born and educated in Germany. At this point, what little I know suggests Koch was involved in a research project at Dachau Prison during the war. Sometime in the late '50's or early '60's, he mysteriously turned up at Fort Detrick, Maryland. He became a naturalized American citizen in 1966."

"Naturalized American citizen? How the hell did that happen?" David Clayton asked in disbelief.

"Hold on. Let me finish"

"This is a passport photo for Otto Bruns. Otto Bruns died last week on a Pan American flight from London to New York."

"Except for the beard, it's the same guy," said Jack Thompson.

"So who is he? Koch or Bruns?"

"At this point, I suspect the dead man is Karl Peter Koch, our DOD scientist," Beverly responded.

"You mean DOD Nazi scientist," interjected David.

"Hold on. Let's not jump to conclusions." Sam was cautious. "The FBI ran the dead man's prints. They belong to Karl Peter Koch."

"Why was Koch traveling under the name Bruns?" asked Jack.

"Get this. Koch was also carrying a South African passport issued to Otto Bruns. INS ran a check. The real Otto Bruns worked for the Berlin Ministry of Transportation. Otto Bruns died in Germany during a bombing raid on Berlin." Sam pointed to the photographs again.

"So Koch was carrying forged passports," said Jack.

"An interesting point, Jack. The answer is 'Yes' and 'No'. INS and DOD both vouch for Karl Peter Koch's passport. He had a top security clearance code imbedded into his photo. The other passports were not forged. They are the real McCoy. It had to be an inside job involving the South African and West German embassies. Now, how was that accomplished?" asked Sam.

"It's my guess there may be another Bruns living here in the States."

"That makes sense, David. Somehow a Nazi scientist winds up in the States under an assumed name – Otto Bruns."

"Why would Koch be carrying Bruns' passport?"

"That's what we need to find out. I trust you're keeping good notes." Jack's casual demeanor annoyed Sam. Jack poured his third cup of coffee and then nibbled on a doughnut.

"This is all very interesting, but how does Koch's death connect with the GAO's assignment?" asked David.

"There is a connection between Koch and General Webster. At the time of his death, General Webster was directing several interagency ventures. His mission was to coordinate the different departments and agencies. It was Webster's responsibility to make sure all the parties were pooling research. Above all else, Webster had to guard against any rogue operations," said Sam.

"Rogue?" Jack returned to the conference table.

"No unauthorized projects…rogue projects…siphoning appropriations. There was some concern personnel might sell secret research to a third party," said Sam.

"There's one reference to a Project 63, but that's it."

"I didn't come across a Project 63 in the stuff you gave me, Sam." Jack scanned his notes.

"It's top secret stuff." replied Sam.

"So is just about everything in Washington," said Thompson.

"The intelligence community doesn't release its budget figures. GAO tracks categories. From what I can tell, Project 63, Webster's baby, was buried in one of the research and development categories."

"Research and Development? What the hell is that?" asked

David.

"Who knows?" said Sam. "Given what little we know it may be a cover. Webster had a small office here in D.C. As the program expanded, the operational center moved to Fort Detrick."

"Interesting. Webster and Koch were connected?"

Sam moved to the next slide. "This is a list of DOD personnel cleared for Fort Detrick. The first name on the civilian list is Karl Peter Koch."

"Excuse me, Sam. Could we turn up the lights? I spilled coffee on my shirt."

"Jack, how could anyone tell? Looks like you've worn that shirt for days."

"With all these files you asked me to read, I have little time for ironing shirts."

"Could we get back to business?" *You two act like eighth graders.*

"Sorry, Sam," said Jack with a smirk.

"Jack, I want you to learn everything about Karl Peter Koch… his habits, friends, acquaintances. Better yet, I want you to become Koch. Did a government agent help Koch into this country?"

"I smell a cover-up," said David. "Koch didn't follow the usual Naturalization procedures. Whoever brought him in had to have the tacit approval of the DOD and the Department of Justice."

"Ah, very interesting…advanced research and technology… secret fluoride studies, mein Fuehrer?"

"Stop the Doctor Strangelove shit, Jack. David's not the only one who's tiring of your humor," Sam frowned.

Jack's smile turned to a scowl. "We're looking for a paper trail, misappropriations, not real Nazis. You're out of your mind if you think I'm hunting Nazis. That's dangerous."

"Jack may be right, Sam. We have no idea where this investigation is headed. We are tracking payroll. The FBI and INS are charged with weeding out Nazis," said Clayton.

"Leave that work to the Israelis. I'm looking forward to moving south and playing golf. No thank you, Sam. I'm not looking to get killed."

"Think about it, Sam. General Webster died just before a closed-door hearing. Next, Karl Peter Koch died on a flight from

London. Koch turns out to be an alleged Nazi scientist with a top secret clearance. Koch and Webster were collaborating on Project 63. Too many coincidences, Sam." David echoed Jack's concern.

"And don't forget those mysterious calls from the so-called Robert," Jack added.

Jack drew a triangle on his legal pad. He scribbled Koch on one angle and Webster on the other. Then he said, "Something doesn't work. There's a piece missing.

"I keep looking for the connection between Webster and Koch, Sam."

David reached across the table for Thompson's legal pad. "We could be looking at this from the wrong perspective. Let's call your triangle the apparent view. And here we have a parallel view." Clayton drew three parallel lines.

"Where are you going with this?" Jack asked.

"Give him a chance, Jack."

"The information we have. It's too simple. We submit our findings. The subcommittee publishes a summary. A tight package buried in the Library of Congress, subbasement five. That's all they're looking for."

"Odd coming from you, David. Your assignment was to write a report for the New York delegation. Do you think they would be satisfied?" asked Sam.

"Here's my point: I'm not satisfied. It's all too simple. I could put a report together tomorrow. On the other hand, suppose DOD brought Koch in with INS help. That means Federal laws were broken. We can't overlook that," David insisted.

Sam reminded David, "The DOD, have a responsibility to defend our nation. No easy task. Look at it from the Defense Department's perspective. We are involved in the Cold War. Fear of another world war…this time closer to home."

"The Nazis might be able to help us against the Russians. The Russians have Nazi scientists, too," Jack insisted.

"There's another angle to our mystery," said David.

"What angle?"

"Hold on, Jack. Let's hear him out."

"For now, let's simply call it my parallel view. It's a long shot. Maybe it's an oddball perspective, but here goes."

Both Sam and Jack nodded in agreement.

"Let's hear it," Jack insisted.

"Imagine this. Suppose some big company was behind this whole episode. We know big companies like IG Farben were involved in chemical and biological research with the Nazis. Maybe some international company was paying Webster and Koch. Paying them to pass on information. Better yet, imagine a pharmaceutical company getting their hands on research from one of Webster's projects."

"Why not? Perhaps whatever Webster's Project 63 was researching," Jack was intrigued.

"That's crazy, David. Would our government risk breaking international treaties and violating federal laws?" Sam wasn't convinced.

"You need proof; hard facts," said Jack.

"The Nazis' research, international patents; the bundle could be worth millions. A powerful pharmaceutical company could easily embellish trials, and publish the data." David's speculation made sense.

"There's one problem," said Sam. "A pharmaceutical company needs research labs."

"And they need a manufacturing facility here in the United States," said Jack.

"Or buy one or two small existing pharmaceutical laboratories," added David. "Can you picture an international cartel controlling a 'silver bullet' antibiotic or vaccine? Now we're talking billions and billions of dollars." David was excited.

"Then again, all those experiments could be worthless. It's crazy science. Hitler's scientists were mad. Maybe that stuff's worthless," said Jack.

"You may be on to something, David. I recall Warner von Braun. We captured von Braun and his research along with several V-2 rockets, too. How quickly we forget. Remember the bombing raids on London?"

"That's true. The U.S. couldn't match von Braun and the work his team accomplished for Germany. So we brought that gang here. We 'rehabilitated' them, so to speak. We needed them to compete against the Russians," agreed David.

"We may have something, David."

"Help me. Is it possible the Immigration and Naturalization Service isn't the culprit? INS may be taking a fall for the intelligence community?"

"INS may have collaborated. From where I'm standing, we're missing a big piece of the puzzle. I'm saying we need to rethink our approach." David pointed to his diagram.

"A parallel view?" asked Sam.

"Exactly. Start over, change perspective. Rethink our assumptions. Allow the possibility of another player," said David.

"You've drawn three parallels." Jack pointed to David's legal pad.

David paused, then said, "My gut tells me the third parallel holds the answer."

"And that is…?" asked Sam.

"I suspect some big industrial complex is behind the deaths of Karl Peter Koch and General Webster. Some kind of a plot."

"Not another conspiracy theory, Clayton," said Jack. "Don't we have enough to deal with?"

David recoiled from Jack's off-hand remark. All three men felt an uneasy tension. Sam picked up the pad.

Jack gathered the other files and handed them to Sam.

Sam walked to a wall safe. "I'll lock these in here. No one else has the combination."

"Good idea," Jack agreed. "If someone else saw those notes, they might have all three of us committed. The whole idea of some international cartel killing people to gain control of a wonder drug…well it's hard to swallow," Jack added.

"I'm exhausted. Too much information." Sam glanced at his watch. "Damn! I forgot to call home. I'm supposed to do something…can't remember. The stress is getting me. There's a ton of paper sitting on my desk. This case is eating me alive."

"Let's call it quits for now," said David

Jack agreed. "We have our assignments."

"Oh. Not quite. There's one last thing. The DOA forwarded a copy of this Freedom of Information request." Sam handed the letter to David. "Here's something for you. It's a response to the DOA from Senator Javits' office. Of course it's a 'handoff' to me.

So, now I'm passing it to you."

"And?" asked David.

"It's a Freedom of Information request from a college professor, Matthew Nagle. Lives on Long Island. Mr. Nagle has stumbled into our investigation. I want to know what's behind the inquiry. He's in way over his head. Go through the usual channels. Check him out. Stonewall him. Remember, get back to me ASAP."

"Long Island?" asked Clayton, reluctantly. "I have to interview the guy? Fly to New York? This case is swallowing me alive, Sam."

"The request may not be a coincidence. Yes, I want the guy interviewed." Sam was adamant.

"Jack, didn't you live on Long Island? Why don't you go?"

"Cut out the bickering. The work is just beginning. You two better learn to get along," said Sam. "Work it out. Both of you go."

Sam wanted this inquiry finished. "The average Joe wants to put World War II and the Nazis behind."

"For God's sake, Sam, what's next?" Jack asked.

"Don't tell me. I can imagine. Find Japanese war criminals in the U.S." David was tired and exasperated.

"You're right, Sam. Nazis and aliens. Americans are tired of comic book suspense and allegations. Clayton's got a point. Who cares if U.S. submarines or spaceships smuggled Nazis into the country? Think about it. You said it before –'conspiracies'. John Kennedy, Martin Luther King, Bobby Kennedy, all assassinated. Folks have had enough."

"Interesting coming from you, David," Sam rebutted. "You're the one who insisted we stick with the inquiry even before we brought in Jack."

Clayton recognized the all too familiar 'You're pissing me off' expression cover Sam's face.

"What will we discover, if we continue on this path?" asked David.

"I have to be honest with myself. The story is complicated. We all have our stories – our lives – beyond this place. We sacrifice a lot," insisted Sam.

Clayton and Thompson nodded in agreement.

"Suppose the allegations aren't a crazy conspiracy theory. Don't we owe it to the Nazis' victims and the American public to bring this story to light?"

"But at what cost?" asked David.

"Sam's right, David. Those who suffered have a right to be heard. Are we so afraid of the Russians? Are we so paranoid and hysterical? Are Americans willing to accept mass murderers?" Jack slumped on to the couch. "Perhaps we are. Perhaps we are," he conceded.

"I'm convinced the three of us are not going to let that happen," said Sam. There was a prolonged silence. The trio looked at each other with unspoken agreement.

The trip home that evening took longer than expected. Sam was exhausted. The drive was his quiet time out. *Am I truly committed to this investigation?* Sam recognized his work was taking a toll. *When will this road construction along I-95 end?*

The Beverlys moved to Fredericksburg, Virginia, six months after Sam's confirmation as Deputy Inspector General. Initially, they leased a Georgetown apartment. Sam promised Grace his new job was temporary. They would move back to Manhattan at the end of President Ford's first term. When Sam agreed to remain in Washington, it was time to look for a larger residence. Weekend house hunting is stressful. They finally found a home in Fredericksburg, Virginia.

Fredericksburg was a compromise for Grace. The city offered a contrast with life in Manhattan. The pace was slower. The downtown area with its quaint shops offered a Colonial ambiance. Once the summer tourists departed, the locals returned to the restaurants and sidewalk cafes. Mary Washington College was a few minutes' drive from their home. Grace was concerned about the public schools and the underlying racial tension. Hopefully, we'll only be here for a short time, she thought.

Rachel, their daughter, would be attending American University after high school graduation. She'd been awarded a prestigious Presidential Scholarship. Sam and Grace promised to pay Rachel's other expenses. Sam didn't want his daughter facing the financial burden he carried after college and graduate school.

Grace was fortunate. Her parents paid the whole boat.

Growing up, Grace had always enjoyed the finer things in life. Ponies, sailboats, summer camps were taken for granted. She was Daddy's Girl.

Sam loved Grace. At times he would become unsettled, thinking Grace no longer loved him. Grace had a way of making him feel inadequate. Sam pushed those thoughts away, conceding Grace had unspoken regrets about their marriage. They had married too soon. Both held expectations neither could fulfill. Their marriage and lives provided a frenetic distraction from a situation neither wanted to acknowledge.

Grace opposed Sam's decision to take a leave from the law firm. Sam's GAO salary was less than a third of what it was. Sam's financial and legal expertise attracted big ticket clients to the firm. The GAO demanded more and paid less.

Grace missed Manhattan Publishing. Her father, John Bosco, the noted World War II historian, helped launch his daughter's career. Bosco persuaded his editor to give Grace the opportunity. Soon, Grace was recommending acquisitions and dining with leading authors. Life was exciting.

Grace grew lonely and tired of life in Fredericksburg. Sam was preoccupied. When Sam worked at the firm, they would chat about books, their daughter, and the theater. Now, they rarely spoke and when they did, the conversation frequently drifted into bickering.

"Things will get better once I'm settled in at the GAO," Sam assured Grace.

"Fine," she replied.

Sam knew it was time to shut up. *The romance is dwindling. Isn't that what happens at some point in a marriage?*

Chapter 9

David and Jack left Washington early on the morning of April 20, driving north along I-95.

David resented the trip to Long Island. *It was Jack's fault.* Jack had a sister living there. He had the option to fly. David disliked flying, especially on short commuter flights. The night before, David declined a dinner invitation with his friends Tim and Mary Bland. Mary had a girlfriend she wanted David to meet. *Instead, I'm working overtime. Look at me. I'm a chauffeur picking up a car at the motor pool.* The vehicle was a mess. The smell of cigarettes made David nauseous.

David planned to leave D.C. by 6:00 a.m. to beat the traffic. As usual, Jack was late. He finally arrived at 6:30, carrying his briefcase, an overnight bag, and balancing a cup of coffee as he opened the Sedan's rear door, tossing luggage on the back seat.

"Today's the day," said Jack.

"What about it?"

"According to the *Washington Post*, the Senate is voting on a bill to end electronic surveillance without a court order." Jack raised the paper and pointed to the headline.

"You're blocking the view. Put that paper down. Drink your coffee. Just for an hour will you stop talking and let me enjoy some quiet time?"

Jack ignored David's remark. "This new bill could affect our investigation." Jack turned serious. "Suppose we need a wiretap for our case."

"You're unbelievable. One day you're babbling about some sports record and the next you're into court precedents."

Jack made the weirdest face he could imagine to show his

displeasure and said, "Forget it."

"Wiretaps. That's your forte, Jack. I don't know anything about that stuff, and the less I know the better. I think we have enough spy agencies to deal with." David leaned against the door, thinking about the day ahead and bemoaning the missed possibilities of his cancelled dinner engagement.

Dense fog enveloped the New Jersey Turnpike. The constant stop and start traffic made David nervous. He strained to see the brake lights of a semi ahead. Jack fiddled with the radio, searching for a local weather report.

"Turn off the radio, Jack. I'm trying to concentrate on the road."

"David, may I ask you something?" Jack's jovial expression vanished.

"Do you always ask permission to ask a question?"

"David, you don't like me. Do you?"

David's face flushed.

"Well, let's put it this way…I'm not one of your fans."

"You don't know a thing about me," said Jack.

"I know you were exiled to the DOJ basement."

"You got that right," Jack replied.

"I know your wife left you."

"Right, again."

"You are never on time." David rattled off a list of grievances. David also picked up on a rumor: Jack had a reputation as a heavy drinker. David let that tidbit lie.

"Wow. You must have been practicing. That's quite a list." Jack finished the last of his coffee. He rolled down the window and tossed the empty container. Looking back at David he said, "You're right. I just don't give a shit."

"That's exactly what I'm talking about. You do things for effect. You like pissing me off. Close the window."

"And you, David? What brought you on board?"

David started to speak, but Jack interrupted. "You're a bored pretty boy lost in D.C. politics. An occasional night with a senator's wife or congressman's daughter is no longer exciting. I'll wager you were scouting New York City law firms when this gig came along."

"Don't preach to me." The tension was building. *I'd like to smack him.*

"I'm getting ready to turn in my papers. I've had it with Washington. But you…what's in it for you?"

The dense fog made driving increasingly dangerous as they approached the George Washington Bridge.

"We are hunting numbers, not Nazis, for the GAO because a congresswoman asks for a report. And suppose we do stumble onto something. Nothing will be accomplished," Jack added.

"What do you mean?"

"The bad guys always prosper in Washington. They always survive. Once you've been through the mill, you'll get the picture," Jack continued.

"I don't believe it. Not as long as there are guys like Beverly around."

"And at what cost? You think I wanted to end up in the stinking basement at Justice? No!" Jack nearly tore the steering wheel away from David.

"Sure. Something went wrong," said David. A bitter smile crossed his lips, like a taste of revenge. He was taunting Jack. Next came a cross-examination.

"Whatever. You want to be a son of a bitch, fine by me. When this so-called investigation is finished or the power brokers say it's finished, nothing will have been accomplished. They play both sides. The kingmakers keep on doing what they're doing and we keep on getting what we deserve…shit! Nothing will change." Jack grew silent and turned, looking out the window. A pall fell over the car. Neither man spoke or looked at each other for over an hour.

"Once we take care of business on Long Island, we can head to New York on Friday. Did you call the INS for clearance on Friday?" Jack's cavalier attitude didn't sit well on top of David's nausea and aching eardrums.

"All set. I called the U.S. Attorney's office yesterday. We're covered. Koch's luggage is in the property room at the Medical Examiner's. I have the tag numbers for two pieces; an overnight bag and a larger piece."

After a pit stop and cup of coffee, Jack drove. Back on the

highway, he flipped open a small pad.

"Keep your eyes on the road, Jack."

Jack frantically flipped pages searching for the numbers while steering the Ford Victoria. "Here they are." He grinned, nearly driving onto the meridian.

"Koch died on an international flight. INS accepted the body bag and tagged luggage. Strange INS didn't take jurisdiction. The body cleared quarantine."

Reaching into his jacket pocket, David found the list Sam Beverly had given him the other morning.

"We better double check with their forensics lab. Koch's corpse will be shipped to Fort Detrick for an autopsy," David noted.

"DOD must consider Koch a priority," said Jack.

"Sam agrees. He wants copies of the forensics report and anything else the ME's office can share. Remember the luggage."

"I'm not escorting a corpse back to Maryland."

"Of course not, Jack. CDC will handle it. Probably a land transport."

"I have Koch's prints and ID photo. "I brought a fingerprint kit and a camera, just in case," David pointed over his shoulder to the back seat.

"You're reading too many detective novels."

"I've never been involved in a case like this. Can you imagine if we shipped the wrong corpse?" David laughed.

"No way."

They checked in at the South Side Motel just off the Sunrise Highway.

"Are you sure this is the place?"

David double-checked the reservation. "Sam's office booked it. This is it." David started to open the door. "You're wearing one of your weird expressions. What's wrong?" David asked, bracing for Jack's response.

Jack looked back at David. "If I wanted to stay at a place that looked like it promoted prostitution, this is it." Jack turned off the car engine. He shook his head in disbelief, gave one last look at David and got out of the car. The two men grabbed their luggage and entered the hotel lobby. Shortly after that, a tall woman followed by a younger, shorter man entered the lobby. The blonde stood against the far wall.

"I'll check us in," said Jack. David didn't hear him. He was concentrating on the blonde. *Nice body, but an ugly face.*

"Excuse me. I'll only be a minute." The young man pushed ahead of Jack. "I need a room. Pronto!" *This guy's a punk.* He haggled with the desk clerk over the price.

"I need it for a couple of hours." The clerk remained insistent. *This kid is a real oddball. He's intentionally causing a scene.*

"Wait over there," said the clerk, and pointed to the blonde. "Let me take care of the guy behind you," the clerk said, looking directly at Jack.

"You're unreal," the young man said to the clerk.

What kind of a place is this?

"Your room isn't ready, Mr. Thompson." With that the clerk abruptly turned and left the counter.

Jack exploded. He flashed his shield and scowled. "You see this?" Jack shoved his DOJ shield in the clerk's face. "Now tell me the room isn't ready."

The clerk turned white with fear. He scrambled to find a room.

Jack turned and winked at David. Jack's casual Detective Colombo persona had turned into a ferocious street savvy Shaft.

"Second floor. Room 203," said the clerk, handing the key to Jack. The man's hand trembled. He was obviously shaken. "You're an animal," said the clerk under his breath.

"Where's the elevator?" asked David.

"There isn't one," said the clerk.

David and Jack looked at each other, shaking their heads in disbelief. "Sam's going to hear about this." Jack was pissed.

"What a dump," David said as the two started to climb the stairs. "And what's with the shield waving?"

"Hardly ever display my shield," said Jack. "The clerk probably thought I was vice. He's still trembling." Jack laughed.

What's come over Jack? David wondered.

"Have to admit, working on this case has energized me. I wasn't always a passive guy, killing time until retirement. Lighten up, David."

I'm taking this thing too seriously. Jack has a point. David nodded in agreement.

Jack unlocked the door to their room, walked in and tossed his suitcase on one of the beds. "This is the best room GAO could get us?" he said, thinking David was behind him.

David was still in the hallway in the middle of a thought. *Jack has something. What's happening to me?*

He recalled the late evening telephone two nights ago.

"Hi. I needed someone to talk with," she whispered.

The attractive brunette relished calling David at bedtime. "Can you come over?"

"Not tonight." *Am I crazy or what?*

"Wow. Did you just turn me down?"

"I have two meetings and an interview to conduct tomorrow in Maryland."

"What's come over you?" *This is becoming a habit with him. He's taking me for granted.* A bottle of chilled champagne and two glasses were awaiting David's anticipated arrival.

"I'll call. I promise. Rain check?" David knew she was a determined woman. Perhaps there wouldn't be another invitation. He'd have to risk it.

"Rain check?" she asked. "Enjoy your interview."

"Hey, David, are you daydreaming or what?" Jack yelled, pulling open the dusty drapes.

"This isn't the Hilton," David walked in and dropped his suitcase. He reached for the telephone. 'I'll call in."

"Any messages?"

"There's a message from Nagel on my service. Wants to talk right away. From the tone of his voice, I guess he may regret his Freedom of Information request."

"Freedom of Information inquiry…is he crazy?" Jack's comment underscored Nagle's predicament. "Every agency from the FBI to the Internal Revenue will be crawling up his back. A response with black lines running through anything significant. That's all he'll get."

"I'll bet the FBI has already gleaned Nagle's personnel file," David added. "Nagle probably suspects something, but he'll never know who's pulling his strings."

David's hunch was nearly correct. Early the previous Monday morning, two men visited Suffolk County Community College.

Dean Carter, the Director of Personnel, was attending a conference in Manhattan. His secretary, Alice Belle, looked forward to a day without Dean Carter's constant pressure. Miss Belle was just finishing her morning coffee when the pair entered the office.

The taller of the two did most of the talking. He presented his FBI shield and stated his business. Naturally, Miss Belle was more than willing to cooperate with the agents. *This has to be important. Not one agent but two. Of course I'll let them read Matthew Nagle's file.*

"Here's Mr. Nagle's file." She handed the thin folder to the tall agent. "Is Mr. Nagle in some kind of trouble?"

"Not at all," replied the tall agent with a smile. "Simply a routine check."

The tall man has a sinister smile. He frightens me.

The two men walked to a counter on the far side of the room and began leafing through the file. Miss Belle strained to hear their conversation. She could infer from the shorter agent's gestures, they found something of interest. The tall agent closed the folder. He handed Miss Belle two separate pages.

"Please photocopy these two pages," requested the tall man.

Miss Belle hesitated. "I'm sorry. I'm not allowed to do that without Dean Carter's approval."

"Is there a problem with helping us?" The second agent stepped forward. "This is official FBI business."

"I understand." replied the secretary. "Dean Carter will be back tomorrow. He authorizes this type of request. It's College policy."

"I'm certain Dean Carter would not object," the tall agent assured her. The man's smile turned to a threatening sneer.

"Perhaps a call to the President's office?" The other agent insisted.

Alice Belle understood the implied threat. "Anyone who handles a personnel record has to sign," she said. Alice Belle's protest dwindled. In the end, the agents got the copies and left without signing a single form. *I have to be careful. I want to forget the incident.*

The fear of a reprimand or worse haunted her for days. She worried she might be fired.

But that was Monday and today was Wednesday. Neither Jack nor David could have imagined the complexity of the situation.

"We haven't heard from your friend, Robert."

"It's been more than a week and no call. I was thinking about that, too."

"He's playing with us, Jack. Dangling the information. Leading us where he wants us to go."

"By the way, I called my sister. She asked us over for dinner. I told her we'd have to get back to her."

"Call Nagle first." David wanted to meet the teacher as soon as possible. "We've got a lot to accomplish in a few days."

Jack called Nagle and arranged to meet at Suffolk County Community College that same afternoon.

Jack looked around the room one last time before leaving. "Great view of the Sunrise Highway." He frowned.

David nodded his head in agreement and locked the door. The hallway smelled like mold spores.

"You drive, Jack."

"Over there." Jack pointed to the far side of the parking lot.

David turned to see what had caught Jack's attention. "What is it?"

"A 1973 GTO." Jack swung the car around to make a quick stop. "Nice. Brewster green coupe with a white vinyl top."

"What makes you so sure it's a 1973?" challenged David.

"Check out the heavy chrome bumper. It's a '73, all right."

"We can check it out when we get back. Probably belongs to the blonde and her boyfriend. That's one more thing I know about you, Jack. You're a car buff."

Jack didn't reply. He simply put the car in gear, and floored the Crown Vic as he pulled out onto the highway.

"Slow down, buddy. Let's get there in one piece." Wishful thinking on David's part. Jack drove faster than he talked.

Suffolk County Community College is located on the grounds of a former county sanatorium known as the "Infirmary," not far from Selden. There is an odd assortment of stores stretching east and west along Middle Country Road.

"Must be an experience living here." David looked bewildered. "This is it?"

"The most excitement the place sees is the annual firemen's parade and carnival."

"Sure doesn't excite me. Place looks dismal."

"Oops. Damn, this is our turn." Jack hit the brakes and made a quick right without signaling. Suddenly they heard car brakes screech and a crash. David turned around to see what happened.

"Now you've done it. The car behind us got rear-ended, Jack."

"It's not my fault."

Jack pulled off the road. A pickup truck had rear-ended a black sedan. The driver of the pickup truck jumped out and ran to the sedan.

"Enough of this. We're out of here." Jack pulled into traffic and drove to the college.

"Strange," said David. "Thought I saw your '73 GTO a few cars back."

"What? I don't think so. Your imagination."

David let it pass.

"Nagle said he'd meet us in the Student Union building." A security officer directed them to the building.

There were a few cars in the huge parking lot. Jack and David waited in the Student Union.

Looking towards the winding campus road below, they saw a motorcyclist riding up the hill. The rider parked the bike, removed his helmet and entered the building.

Matt Nagle's sport jacket, T-shirt and faded jeans set him apart from the typical biker. He stood about five feet ten inches tall.

"That's Nagle." David nudged Jack.

"Professor Nagle?"

"Yes, I'm Matt Nagle, but I'm no professor. I'm an adjunct."

"I'm David Clayton. This is Jack Thompson. We're with the GAO task force."

Jack pulled out a small pad and pen.

Nagle look bemused. *I'm in for the Mutt and Jeff routine.* "I got it. Good cop, bad cop. Right? Want coffee or something?" He had a dry sense of humor.

"No thanks. We're set. Your call sounded urgent," said David.

"One thing. Under no circumstance is my family involved. My wife will kill me." Nagle led them to a student lounge on the second floor.

"Of course, we will be discreet. We'd suggest you keep our discussion to yourself." Jack didn't share his concerns inherent in a FOI request.

David asked the first question. "Mr. Nagle, what prompted you to write your inquiry?"

"I wrote the DOA after a friend told me about an incident." Nagle watched Jack taking notes. *Should I have talked with a lawyer before I agreed to meet with these guys? I haven't broken the law.* "I called Senator Javits' office. Spoke with an aide. No one got back to me. That troubled me."

David looked at Jack and said, "That's odd. There's no mention of your call in this letter." Jack handed Nagle the letter from Javits.

"Did you get a name?" asked David.

"Might be in my journal."

"What did you tell the aide?" Jack was carefully taking notes.

"Nothing. Like I said, no one returned my call. I suspected someone was checking me out." Nagle leaned across the table and looked directly at Jack.

"Here's a couple of things for starters. My phone had an echo and strange clicks. My wife noticed it, too. I disconnected the bedroom extension. The echo persisted."

"Did you call the phone company?" Jack asked.

"Get this! I called. No reported problems in my area. I told them I saw a guy working on the switch box just down the street. There was no record."

"That's it. Could have been a coincidence," said David. Jack agreed.

"Yesterday, I received a panic call from Alice Belle, the Dean's secretary. Two guys were inquiring about me. Alice claims they bullied her into copying my personnel record. That's contrary to school policy. She could lose her job."

"I requested the FBI background check," said Jack.

"Belle said they wouldn't sign the receipt."

"That's unusual. Did she describe the pair?" David asked.

"She focused on the tall agent. Smiled. The other agent tried the roughshod approach."

"I'll check into it," said David.

"I'm fascinated by your suspicion." David carefully recorded Nagle's comments. *You've gotten yourself into a mess.*

"Now what do you think, David?" Jack was back to good cop bad cop again. He knew damn well he owed it to Nagle to come clean on the interview.

"Seems coincidental to me." A poker-faced David scratched his head. *I'm an awful card player.*

"Where does it fit in?" Nagle asked.

David and Jack shrugged. They had no idea. "It might not be your imagination. Have you written any other FIO requests?" asked David.

Nagle nodded yes. "One other. I inquired about Rift Valley Disease research at Fort Detrick."

"Maybe that's it," David replied. "One letter is a coincidence, but two. You may have triggered something."

"What motivated the inquiry?"

Just then, a man and woman walked through the entrance at the far end of the lounge. Something about the young couple troubled David He couldn't put it out of his mind. The couple tumbled onto a couch against the east wall with their backs to the room.

"Let's get back to your inquiry," David continued.

"There's always been a cloud of secrecy about the Animal Disease Research lab on Plum Island. The place isn't even on a map. A local story speculated the lab was researching Rift Valley Disease, only found in the Middle East." Nagle explained.

"Mr. Nagle, one thing bothers me," said Jack. "Why all this interest in disease research?"

"Give him a chance," David insisted.

Jack made a point of looking at the wall clock. "We have other work to do. We're here at Mr. Nagle's request. No time for small talk," Jack growled.

"In other words, Mr. Nagle, what's the back-story? Once again, what piqued your interest?" asked David.

"After I mailed in the requests, over a month ago, I got a call from the program director on Plum Island. He invited me for a visit. Here's my point: My home phone number is unlisted. I didn't include it in any of my correspondence."

"Are you certain you didn't include it?" *He probably did.*

"How the hell did he get your telephone number if it's unlisted?"

"Did you ask him?"

"No. I only thought about it later."

"Did you go?" Jack and David were now taking copious notes.

"Yes. I called the editor of a local magazine. She encouraged a free-lance story. It's not the money. My wife works. I like writing."

"So, getting back to the Plum Island story," said David. Something about the couple on the couch continued to bother David.

"I visited the Island. Saw little or nothing. They gave me a press package. Had lunch with the Director and his assistant."

"That's it?" asked Jack.

"That's it. I've read there are two labs in separate buildings. I never got a tour."

"Where did you get your information?" asked David.

"A newspaper on the east end, Dan's Papers. From time to time they run a story about the Island." Nagle rummaged through his knapsack and pulled out a file. "Here's some of the stuff I clipped. I also checked microfilmed copies of Newsday."

"A lot of work for one story," said Jack.

"Listen. Take the folder with you. Just return it." Nagle wanted the investigators to have a clearer understanding of the Island's history.

"The Island is surrounded in mystery."

"Yes. And that's when I really became concerned. I spoke with a colonel at Fort Detrick, Maryland. Here are my notes. I don't have copies. I want them back," Nagle insisted.

Nagle recalled the telephone conversation. "I finished the interview with a sense the colonel was waiting for me to ask a final question, like there was something he wanted to tell me, but only if I asked."

"What do you mean?" asked Jack.

"The colonel's responses always seemed to lead me in a different direction. He told me viruses being researched are shipped between a containment lab in Pennsylvania or Fort Detrick and Plum Island."

"They can't ship live virus. It's against the law," said David.

"The specimens are freeze dried. Then shipped," Nagle responded.

"How?" ask Jack.

"You'll love this. By service courier."

"You're kidding. What proof do you have?"

"Just what the colonel told me."

"Did the colonel name the viruses?" Jack was pressing.

"No. He didn't," replied Nagle.

"Why not?" asked David.

"I didn't know the right question to ask. I was hesitant of pushing the colonel," said Nagle.

"Specialist?" asked Jack.

"Deals with anthrax, malaria and Rift Valley Disease," said Nagle.

"You started to tell us about a friend. What about him?" asked David.

"Why don't we take a break? I need some coffee." Jack checked his watch. "I'll call in."

Jack found the phone both near the cafeteria and called Sam Beverly.

"Sam. Our hotel is a dump," Jack complained.

Sam laughed. "Tell Special Services. Where are you?"

"We're at Suffolk County Community College interviewing Nagle. David's with him now." Jack filled Sam in on the day's events. "Did you get the FBI field report?" Jack asked.

"No. Colter, the agent in charge of the Melville field office, called earlier. He apologized for the delay. He assured me he would have someone at the school's personnel office by tomorrow morning."

"What?" There has to be a mistake, Sam. Two agents were here on Monday. They weren't FBI?" Jack was having an "Aha" moment.

"Are you positive?" asked Sam.

"The secretary called Nagle. Do you want me to look into it?" Jack asked.

"No. That's for the FBI. Keep me in the loop," Sam responded.

Jack returned from the cafeteria, doing his usual balancing

act with three Styrofoam cups of coffee. "Ok David. I suggest you check your messages, also." Jack pointed in the direction of the pay phone.

David dialed his home answering machine.

"Mr. Clayton." It was Robert's voice. "I regret having delayed my promised contact. You must be patient. The deaths of General Webster and Professor Koch place me in a precarious position. This fellow Nagle on Long Island and his FOI request…certain people have the jitters, shall we say. Desperate people do desperate things, David. I may have placed all of us in danger. I will get back to you. Be careful."

Reaching the top of the landing, Jack motioned to David to look out the eastern window toward the parking lot. "Over there." He stretched his neck using his nose as a pointer.

David spotted the green and white GTO from the motel parking lot. The one he saw in the rear view mirror. *You can't mistake that chrome front bumper,* he thought.

"Not many students on campus," said David.

"We're on break," said Nagle. "The library, administration building, and snack bar are open. That's about it."

Jack was on to something. He set the coffee on the table, ignoring the cup that flipped. He turned and ran into the parking lot. At that instant, the GTO sped away. He did get the plate number: SQ222. Jack's adrenalin pumped. He bent over, placing his hand on his knees. *I haven't moved that fast in years,* he thought. He joined Nagle and David inside.

"What was that all about?" asked David.

"Are you kidding? We've seen that GTO three times today. I got the plate number. I'll ask Sam to run a check."

The three men sat at the round table and continued the interview. David opened his notepad and reviewed several points. "How does your friend Portavani fit into all of this?"

Nagle related the evening at Snapper Inn when Tony told him about Plum Island. "Tony was upset and frightened. Never saw him like that."

"Did you see him after that night?"

"He dropped by one night around suppertime. He gave me a heavy cardboard box. I hid it on a shelf in my garage."

"Did you hear from him again?" asked Jack.

"No. I called. The phone was disconnected. I went to his house. When no one answered the doorbell, I walked around and looked in the windows. No furniture. Nothing."

"What about the box? Did you open it? What was inside?" asked Jack.

"There was a binder with government bids. A list of contractors. I also found Tony's day planner. A journal. He was working for a company called Tanzanite."

"Tanzanite?" Jack recognized the name.

Nagle nodded in agreement.

Jack and David exchanged looks of recognition. "Tanzanite Corporation is listed in one of the DOA confidential memos I read. I'll have to check again. I think they're a subsidiary of Trinity PharmoDynamics Group. Professor, we need to see the contents of that box. Let's knock off and get together tomorrow."

"I have a few calls to make. No sense just talking about a journal. Let's read it," said Jack.

As David rose to leave, he noticed the couple in the far end of the lounge had left. "Do you think the couple from upstairs was driving the GTO?" he asked Jack.

"Could be. I'll know more once we check the plate."

As the three departed, Nagle agreed to meet them again tomorrow. "Let's meet here," Nagle insisted. "I don't want my family involved." Jack and David agreed. *The fewer people involved the better,* Jack thought.

Jack started the car, then suddenly pulled away even before David closed the passenger door. "There they are," he yelled. "At the bottom of the hill by the entrance." With that, the GTO sped out the gate.

"Looks like they don't want us following. Step on it, Jack!" David was caught up in the excitement.

The Crown Vic raced east along Mooney Pond Road.

"They turned left. Jack, watch out! That car was coming right at us."

"I've got everything under control."

Jack turned the wheel hard left. The Crown Vic raced through the intersection and headed north. Jack ran the next light and sped toward Middle Country Road.

"We got 'em now," shouted Jack.

"Watch the road, Jack. You'll kill us."

With that, the GTO flew recklessly into a Friendly's parking lot. The sidewalk was crowded with pedestrians. Jack followed, but hit the brakes just in time to avoid hitting a couple leaving the restaurant. David wasn't wearing a seat belt. The sudden stop tossed him against the dashboard. The GTO disregarded oncoming traffic and jumped a curb, cutting across the entrance to the parking lot of an adjacent shopping center. The GTO crashed through a line of shopping carts and sideswiped a delivery truck. There was confusion everywhere as frenzied shoppers grabbed their children and scrambled for safety. With one last burst of speed, the GTO jumped another curb and headed north.

Jack and David saw chaos everywhere. The GTO had vanished.

What the hell did we just do? David thought.

"We're nuts, Jack." Perspiration was dripping off David's face. Jack had the oddest look of satisfaction. "Never did something like this before," he said.

A police car, lights and siren blaring, pulled behind the Crown Vic. "Do not get out of the car," came the warning.

"We're not going anyplace," said David.

A motorcycle weaved its way around the parked cars and stopped. Jack rolled down his window. It was Nagle. "I couldn't keep up with you. Where'd they go?" he shouted.

Jack pointed. "Across the parking lot and up that road, headed north."

Jack tried to warn Nagle. "Those guys mean business," he shouted.

Nagle revved the Kawasaki 400 and worked his way through the crowd. Nagle wanted to warn Nagle not to pursue the GTO. Even if he caught the car, what would he then do? Too late; Nagle was gone. He headed north on Boyle Road in pursuit of the GTO.

A second blue and white Suffolk County patrol unit soon arrived. Jack stretched his arm out the window, displaying his shield.

"What's going on?" the officer demanded.

"Government business, officer. We were in pursuit of a green and white GTO. I got the plate number – SQ222.

"Are you kidding? You two aren't going anyplace." This was a first for the veteran road sergeant, thought the officer.

"There'll be hell to pay if that car gets away," warned Jack.

It took the bewildered officer over an hour before he finally received the okay to release Jack and David. The GTO was gone and so was Nagle.

While David and Jack were being detained, Nagle had nearly caught the runaway GTO.

Matt Nagle began to overtake the GTO. The car was approaching seventy miles an hour. Nagle hit a patch of sand almost laying the bike down. Somehow, Nagle recovered from the momentum of the near spill. *I'll catch those bastards, yet.* Nagle revved the engine and turned the throttle wide open. Suddenly, the GTO's driver hit the brakes and Nagle passed on the right. Nagle's adrenaline rush overpowered common sense. As the motorcycle came even with car, the passenger door flew open, nearly crashing into Nagle's left leg.

For an instant, Nagle and his adversary came face to face. The guy was laughing hilariously. No, he was snarling. *My God, he looks like a weasel.*

Wedged between the car and a curb, there was no room to maneuver. Nagle tried to regain his balance. It was too late.

The door flew open again. It was him. The "weasel-looking" guy was the guy with the woman at the Student Union. The momentary distraction proved costly for Nagle. All Nagle remembered was the weasel flipping him "the bird." Right where the curb ended, Nagle and the motorcycle tumbled and slid along the grass. The engine rollbar kept the bike from crushing Nagle's leg. The hot exhaust pipe burned him. Nagle never saw his adversary flee north toward Route 347.

Somebody called for an ambulance.

"You're some lucky guy," said the attending EMT. "You'll need a new helmet." The EMT drew his finger along the gouge on Nagle's helmet. "You are one lucky dude."

Oh, no. How am I going to explain this to Liz? What story can I concoct to explain that crazy chase? It better be the same one I tell the cop. My brain is scrambled. I can't think. A vice grip headache scrambled his thoughts. A cloud drifted over his eyes.

Nagle had plenty of time to think. He spent the next five hours in Stony Brook Hospital's emergency room.

"You're a lucky man, Mr. Nagle. Nothing broken, but you'll be hurting for the next few weeks. Keep an eye on the road rash, too. We'll give you something for the pain."

"Mr. Nagle. Your wife is waiting."

Oh boy. Here we go.

The kids were asleep when Matt and Liz arrived home. Matt limped into the kitchen. His jeans were torn and his shredded shirt was blood-stained. The hospital dressing on his right arm was oozing blood.

"Now, let's start over and this time I want the truth. What happened to you?" Liz demanded. "Damn you and that motorcycle." She was both angry and relieved.

"I fell in some sand. That's all. What did the cop tell you?"

"The cop said a passing motorist called in. You were chasing a car. Witnesses said a car ran you off the road. Oh, and your precious motorcycle is totaled."

The hospital painkillers weren't working. He took two more.

"It's like I said. I have no idea why they cut me off. And yes, I lost my cool. I went after them. It's my own damn fault; period, the end."

"That's all? It's another one of your bullshit stories."

Liz's temper was beginning to show. Oddly, Liz's fury always excited Matt. Her pouty lips. The tilt of her head. *Oh, I want her*, he thought. On any other night he would have pulled her to the kitchen floor and made passionate love.

"Matt, what's going on? You've been acting strange. This Plum Island business. Forget your so-called story. This whole thing… Tony's disappearance, the telephone calls. Who needs it? I'm telling you, you're asking for trouble. I can feel something awful will come of this."

"It's important to me." He tried to stand but fell back onto the chair.

"Oh, the editor. She told me your proposal is science fiction. Matt, what did you write? She suggested you send it to a detective magazine. Her readers want happy stories. Wrap your article around something like 'Plum Island research saves pets,' then call her." Liz tossed her car keys on the kitchen table.

"Matt, this whole thing is crazy. Give it up, before something serious happens. If you don't care about yourself, then think of the kids and me."

"Everything will be okay." Matt reached out to hug Liz. She backed away.

"No, it won't be okay. You're a history teacher, Matt. You've worked hard. Why jeopardize everything for the sake of a story? You're not a reporter. Try spending more time at home. Try paying the bills." Liz angrily reached for a pile of mail on the table and threw it at Matt.

"You want me to walk away. Should I forget Tony, Joan, and the kids? Is that what you want, Liz?"

"Maybe Tony and Joan ran into financial problems," Liz began to cry.

"There's more to it. There's got to be."

"I'm going crazy. Teaching is a full-time job. Caring for the family, the housecleaning while you're chasing who knows what? I'm sick of it." With that, Liz ran to the bedroom, locked the door and threw herself on the bed. *Why did I have to fall in love with a crazy bastard?*

Chapter 10

"Damn if that wasn't some adventure. I feel like I'm back in high school."

"You drove like it, too. You're a maniac, Jack. What got into you? It's nearly six and we're just getting back to the motel."

"I got you here, didn't I?"

"I'll send you my doctor's bill."

"Let me talk with the clerk. Maybe I can learn something about the couple in the GTO. You pissed off the guy when we registered."

"I'll head on up to the room."

David approached the desk clerk. "Excuse me. When you checked us in earlier, there was a couple…a little guy…kind of obnoxious. He was arguing with you."

"Yes, I checked the guy in. What about it?" The clerk was defensive. "You guys are cops."

"Sorry about my partner's behavior. He likes throwing his weight around." David avoided a direct answer.

"Come on. You recall the guy. He was with the tall blonde. Are they still checked in?"

"No. They left right after you. We only checked in a few people. I'm telling you, I thought they were cops. We're a 'legit' motel."

"Right."

"Folks want to pay for a room for a couple of hours. That's their business."

"What made you think they were cops?" David asked.

"The little guy. He was packing."

"Carrying a gun? What made you think so?"

"Are you kidding? I saw it when he reached across the counter."

The clerk turned cocky again. "Thought they were plainclothes."

The clerk smirked as though he had the upper hand.

"Thanks." *They weren't here for a matinee. They were following us. Why? They must have followed us from the airport. They're clever. Maybe too smart for their own good.*

Jack was on the phone when David entered their room.

"I understand, Sam. It won't happen again. Yes, it was a crazy stunt on our part. We'll finish the interview with Nagle tomorrow and head into Manhattan. No more hot pursuits. I promise. We'll check in tomorrow." Jack hung up the phone. He looked like a reprimanded schoolboy.

"What was that about?" asked David.

"Sam is ticked off."

"And?"

"Remember the cop wrote us up? Sam said the Deputy Police Commissioner called him."

"Are you kidding? Sam doesn't know the half of it."

"Sam warned me, another incident and the cops will lock us up."

David tossed his briefcase and jacket on the bed, loosened his tie and walked into the bathroom. "This is my fault, Jack. I should have stopped you. Hot pursuit. We're not cops."

David slammed the bathroom door. From inside, he called out, "That GTO followed us from the airport. And the clerk is sure the guy was carrying a handgun.

"Did Nagle call?"

"No. My sister called a couple of times. She said to bring a pizza. It's too late for her to plan dinner."

"Why don't you go? Look at the time. I don't want to impose."

"It's my sister. We aren't imposing."

"Okay, but let's go now."

On the way downstairs, David filled Jack in about the desk clerk's remarks.

"Where are you going?"

"Give me one second." Jack sauntered over to the registration desk. The seated clerk looked up. Jack held out his shield, curled his lip and snarled. The man was taken aback.

"Jack, please. Let's get going." David looked around the lot, wondering if another car might follow them.

A few minutes later, they drove to a shopping center and picked up a pizza and a six pack. While in route to Elaine Wade's Blue Point home, Jack said, "My sister is a lot like you. You'll like her."

"How so?"

"For starters, she's my younger sister. I was in high school when she was born. My Dad died while she was in elementary school. My mother never remarried. She's from a different generation. We used to argue a lot. Not such much now."

David pretended to be listening, but he didn't want to. He had already made up his mind about Jack. Jack's casual revelations were too personal. David didn't want to like the man.

Jack rambled on, "Elaine appears very straight and bookish on the surface, but she isn't. She's very bright, street savvy with a cryptic sense of humor. She's single, or rather, divorced. Elaine married her college sweet heart, Butch Wade. Things happen. Next thing you know, she was pregnant. After Vietnam, Butch joined the Suffolk County Police Department. Never got over the war. He became a loner. I never questioned his love for my sister. Sadly, Butch had two loves, Elaine and the Great South Bay. The Bay won out."

David found himself listening intently as Jack talked on about his sister.

"Clamming."

"I don't understand."

"He preferred digging clams rather than riding in a sector car."

"What happened?"

"One day… no explanation, Butch packed his clothes and left. Moved to a houseboat on Corey Creek."

"Just like that? No warning?"

"I'm certain there were signs. Love blinds us. Look at me. I didn't see it coming."

"Then what happened?" asked David.

"Elaine went a bit crazy, too. One night the cops found her. She'd wrapped her Morgan around a tree. Lost the baby and…," Jack stopped talking.

"Her husband still around?"

"Yes. He went bonkers after the accident. Blamed himself. He's not a bad guy. Just different. Spent a few months in Pilgrim State Psychiatric Hospital. The County put him on disability. Still living on the houseboat. They still love each other."

"That's an awful story. Is your sister okay now?"

"Pretty much. Elaine has her days…Christmas… their wedding anniversary. She's a third grade teacher. Third grade teachers are tough. Enough about Elaine."

"I hope this isn't an imposition. It's almost seven o'clock."

"We have the pizza. Elaine is anxious to see me. I'm not sure about meeting you."

As they pulled into the driveway, David remarked, "Nice place."

They followed the winding brick path to the front door. It was a cottage-style home. A dog yapped, sensing their approach. *Probably one of those annoying toy dogs.*

A woman stepped outside, hugging a barking miniature schnauzer. "I'll put her down in a minute. Dusty, calm down," said the woman. "Jack, what took you so long?"

"Nice greeting," Jack called back.

"Hi. I'm Elaine. My brother is always late."

"I've noticed." David stepped aside. Jack gave his sister a quick hug.

Elaine whispered, "Happy Anniversary."

Happy Anniversary? Jack's anniversary?

Elaine pointed to the door. "Come on in. I'm starving."

Elaine struggled with the little dog. "Calm down, Dusty. This little girl is too much. She's spoiled. Dusty and I are roommates. She's my constant companion. I love her."

David gave brief attention to the dog. He was captivated by Elaine. *She looks so much like Dakota. Gorgeous.* Elaine wore a white spring dress fashioned with a bit of tantalizing modesty.

Jack was already checking out the refrigerator. Elaine closed the front door and led David into the kitchen.

A double-sided fireplace separated the living room from the kitchen. The room conveyed and warm ambiance.

"Beautiful home."

Elaine smiled. "Thank you, Mr. Clayton. The kitchen is my

favorite spot. I enjoy cooking. I love a country kitchen," Elaine caught David's quick look at her brother.

"Jack told me."

"Damn it, Jackie. You've been talking about me. I hate that."

"Sorry, Sis."

"When Jackie and I were growing up, my parents practically lived in the kitchen. People were coming and going. Dad always kept a pot of coffee on the stove. Once upon a time we... I... entertained a lot." Elaine's voice drifted to happier times.

I can't stop comparing Elaine and Dakota. Elaine tilted her head ever so slightly. Her long brunette hair fell to one side, revealing a deep scar.

Jack grabbed a bottled water from the fridge, opened the pizza box and asked, "Hey, you two, one slice or two?"

"Boys? Beer, wine, soda?"

"Beer, thanks. No glass. The bottle is fine."

"No beer for you, Jack?"

"Bottled water, my favorite." He folded a slice and stuffed the cheese pie into his mouth.

You are disgusting, Jack.

Elaine caught David's momentary frown. "Forgive Jack. He is so uncouth. Jack, you have no manners."

"Not when it comes to pizza. I'm famished. What a day."

Once they finished eating, Elaine showed David the rest of her home.

"You have great taste. Elegant. One day, I would like a home like this."

Elaine's face turned a light pink.

"May I ask you a personal question?"

"You can ask whatever you like. I may not answer...keep you guessing."

"Fair enough." David paused as his gaze followed Elaine. *This woman is alluring. Her smile is mysterious. She makes me feel good.*

"You wished Jack a 'Happy Anniversary' when we arrived. What was that about?"

Elaine turned and looked up at David. "You don't know?"

"Know what?" asked David.

"How long have you two been working together?"

"A short time. We're not exactly buddies."

"Jack told me you're hard to get along with. To answer your question, Jack is a recovering alcoholic."

Elaine read David's surprise; she could see David was caught off-guard.

"Jack has been sober for two years. Please, let him tell you."

David felt a bit uncomfortable. *It's time to change the subject.* They returned to the kitchen.

Jack was talking on the phone. The phone cord was stretched to its limit. David only heard the muffled, "I'll check into it and get back to you in the morning." He ended the call with an abrupt "We're on it, Sam." Elaine and David both looked puzzled.

"What was that about?" David asked.

"I called Sam. He's positive those two so-called FBI agents were phonies. The local agents plan to interview Alice Belle, 'ASAP'. The plates on the GTO were reported stolen and so was the car."

"But why use a conspicuous car? We spotted it immediately."

Hearing their exchange, Elaine interrupted. "Did you say GTO?"

"Yeah," said Jack. "We had a run-in with a couple driving a GTO."

"A two tone green and white?"

"Yes," said David.

"Day before yesterday, a green and white GTO was parked across the street. I noticed it when I put the garbage can to the curb. Two people inside. I'm sure one was a woman. They drove away when they saw me."

"Are you positive?"

"Hey, Butch had one. I remember the payments," she answered, walking to the refrigerator. She opened the door and retrieved a bottle of beer. "Think I'll have one after all."

"Elaine, believe me. I have no idea what today's GTO encounter is all about, but it's serious business."

David nodded his head in agreement. "I'm not trying to frighten you, but it's best to be vigilant. Keep your doors locked."

"Dusty will look after me. You're a great guard dog." Elaine leaned over and picked up the schnauzer.

"I think it's time for us to head back. We have homework and a few calls to make," said David. Jack nodded agreement.

"I'll call you in the morning, kid," Jack said to his sister. Elaine saw the worried look on her brother's face. As the two men left, Jack listened for the bolt on the front door to lock. Jack turned back and waited.

"What's wrong?"

Jack looked worried. "This thing is getting out of hand." He hesitated. "Maybe it's me. I'm worried my sister is being dragged into our investigation. Somebody is pulling our chain and I don't like it."

"You could be on to something. What else?"

"I think Sam's a straight shooter. Still, I sense he's withholding information. He knows something we don't."

David climbed into the car. "Not Sam. I trust him."

Jack looked straight ahead, deep in thought.

Jack's silence troubles me.

Jack turned on to Montauk Highway and headed back to the motel.

Silence underscored their ride back to the motel. Jack was uncharacteristically quiet.

David was also preoccupied with the events of the day.

Jack broke the silence. "So, what did you think?"

"Think?"

"My sister is pretty special."

"Yes, she is. You're lucky to have her in your corner."

Jack smiled.

Opening the door to their motel room, Jack saw the "message waiting" light flashing.

"That's odd. No message."

"I'll check my home answering machine. With all the excitement, I never checked for messages." David dialed his Manassas number and waited for the messages to begin.

"David. What's going on? You haven't called. Give me a call." It was Dakota. David was ambivalent about returning her call. He liked Dakota more than he wanted to admit, but she was the consummate reporter. She grasped his vulnerability; especially in bed. *I can't help myself. The taste of her lips. She smells so good. She's incredibly passionate. I trust myself less than I trust you. Sorry,*

Dakota. I can't call. Not just yet. It's too complicated.

David crashed back into reality with the second message. It was ominous.

"David. Be careful. You and your colleagues have stirred the pot. They will begin to apply pressure to discourage your inquiry."

David dropped the phone to its cradle and slowly walked to the motel window. *They? Who the hell are they?* He peeked through the dusty blinds to the parking lot.

"Everything okay?"

"What the hell have we gotten into, Jack?"

"Robert. The message was from your friend Robert."

"What could be so vital that its discovery could put us in jeopardy?"

"I've been thinking the same thing. Today's episode was insane."

Jack stretched out on the bed. "I'm bushed."

"Maybe Sam was right. Who cares about Nazis and germs?" He remembered his conversation with Sam before they met Jack. David had a chance to back out then. Now, the decision to stay on gave him a pounding headache.

"One more day like today, I'll go bonkers."

David turned around. Jack was fast asleep. His snoring grew increasingly louder.

Jack snored all night. David counted sheep. He even tried remembering the Rosary from his childhood. He couldn't fall asleep. It seemed like he just fell asleep when there was a pounding on the door. David looked at his watch. "Jack. Jack. Wake up. Someone's at the door. Damn it. Get up."

Jack leaned on his elbow and twisted out of bed. He slipped on his pants and walked to the door. "Who is it?"

"Suffolk County Police. Open up."

Jack looked through the security peephole. A tall, heavyset uniformed man paced outside the door. "What do you want?" Jack demanded. Actually, Jack was still half asleep. He didn't ask for the cop's ID.

"Are you Clayton or Thompson?" The cop kicked the door again.

That was enough for Jack. He unlocked the door.

"I'm Thompson and that's Clayton."

In walked a cop with three cups of coffee in a cardboard carrier. A gold shield and insignias were pinned to his heavily-starched white uniform shirt. A snub-nose revolver took the place of the standard service revolver. *This is the Suffolk cop who reported us to the Deputy Police Commissioner.*

"Morning, boys. I'm Tom Briggs. You don't know me, but I know you. We need to talk. Hopefully, this will be the last time we meet."

David slipped on a pair of pants. "You get right to the point. Was it your idea to have the Deputy Commissioner call Washington?"

"That's me. You're lucky I didn't bust your balls. I could still have you locked up. On the other hand, the best way to deal with a crisis is just let it brew."

And one day you'll be Police Commissioner or County Supervisor.

Briggs must have read Jack's mind. "Let's have our coffee and talk about this," said Briggs. He pulled a chair out and dropped into it.

"Boys, let's begin with this dump. Why here? This place is notorious," he laughed. Briggs sipped his coffee. "Your little joy ride yesterday caused a lot of disruption in Selden. Our emergency switchboard was overloaded with calls." Captain Briggs removed his cover and placed it on the desk. He opened four packets of sugar and stirred them into his black coffee. "I know all about your friend on the Kawasaki."

"You do?" David's face reflected disbelief.

"Yes. He chased that GTO. They ran him off the road. He spent hours at Stony Brook Hospital. His bike was totaled."

Jack looked shocked. "No. We had no idea. He didn't contact us last night as promised. Figured he had family stuff." Jack rubbed his eyes and yawned.

"Is Nagle okay?" David picked up one of the cups of coffee and returned to the window, just as he had the night before.

"Nagle's lucky he wasn't killed. He's got a wife and two kids. What's wrong with you Feds? Why get Nagle involved in your antics?"

Jack and David gave one another an incredulous look.

"We got him involved? You got it all wrong." *You don't know as much as you claim.* David decided not to relate how Nagle became entangled in the investigation. *And that's the way it was going to stay.*

"What's going on, boys?" Briggs was playing "good cop."

"You said you knew the whole story. You tell us." David was starting to wake up. David turned from the window and sat in a stained chair on the far side of the room. He ran both hands through his hair. Jack let David take the lead. "We're here on a routine GAO audit."

Jack added, "Neither my partner nor I have any idea what led to yesterday's megillah."

"Megillah, you say?" Briggs laughed. "Nice way to put it. I'd call it chaos." Briggs' pale complexion was slowly turning red as he grew impatient with Jack and David. "The GTO was stolen. The plates were, too. The driver and his accomplice vanished. All we have are you two would-be cops and a teacher who thinks he's riding with CHiPS."

"You're kidding. That's all you have to go on?" David's question brought a quick reaction.

Captain Briggs went on the defensive. "We found the GTO. Abandoned and torched near Port Jefferson. The perps bungled it. The fire department got there in the nick of time. Forensics is on the scene."

"And the plates?" David had the upper hand. Captain Briggs' face was brighter red.

"The plates were gone. Jack, you must have gotten the numbers wrong." Captain Briggs pulled out his leather covered notebook. "You told the officer SQ222."

Jack got up and walked to the closet. He pulled a crumpled wire notepad from his suit jacket. "There's no mistake. The plate was a New York state plate, SQ222. So what's the problem?"

A rash was becoming apparent on Captain Briggs' neck. He looked at both men and said, "That plate was reported stolen from a vehicle owned by Trinity PharmoDynamics, USA."

"Trinity," Jack exclaimed. "Not Trinity PharmoDynamics Group?"

"Yes. One and the same. PharmoDynamics Group is the

parent company. They carry a lot of weight here."

This guy knows an awful lot about Trinity. "You seem to know a lot about them."

"I ought to. They're a huge contributor to our youth programs. I've attended several of their fundraisers. They're good people."

David gave Jack one of those "I don't believe this" looks.

Briggs continued, "Listen carefully, boys. As far as the Deputy Commissioner is concerned, you guys are not part of any joint task force. Like you said, you're doing an audit. A word to the wise; finish your work and head back to D.C." Briggs dropped his unfinished coffee into the wastebasket next to the desk. It fell with a thud as if to make his point. He held his cover under his left arm. His smile turned sour.

"Captain Briggs, one point you may find interesting. My sister, Elaine Wade, lives in Blue Point. We were with her last evening. She saw a green and white GTO parked across the street from her home. Fits the description."

"Did she get the plate number? It might be a lead."

Jack wrote his sister's name, address and telephone number on a piece of paper and handed it to Captain Briggs.

"I'll check into it." Briggs gave one last menacing look. "Stay away from Trinity. Got it?"

Jack and David didn't like Briggs, but they sensed he could be trusted.

After Briggs left, the two men decided to skip breakfast and meet with Matt Nagle. "As long as I get some coffee, fine by me."

Jack's cooperative attitude caught David off guard.

David opened his memo pad. "I'll call Nagle."

"Not sure Nagle wants us to do that.

David squeezed the phone between his left shoulder and ear. He turned to Jack. "It's not Nagle's choice. He didn't check in. Let's get finished and vacate this dump."

Nagle's home phone rang several times. A woman answered.

"Good morning. I apologize for calling so early. Is Mr. Nagle home?" David tried to be as casual as possible.

"May I say who is calling?"

"David Clayton." The woman's voice suddenly grew loud and angry. "You're one of those government men. Matt met with you yesterday." She shouted into the phone.

"And your name?"

The woman's voice dropped several decimals, but burned with rage. "Do you know Matt was nearly killed yesterday? What the hell are you putting him up to? He's a teacher."

Jack mouthed the name "Elizabeth…'Liz.'"

David paid no attention. "I regret what happened to your husband, Mrs. Nagle, and I'm certain this is Mrs. Nagle. We'd like to share some information we gathered. An arrest may be pending. We need to clarify a couple of points. It could be helpful when you file your insurance claim."

What? I can't believe what David's telling her.

"He'll be home for a couple of days until his legs heal. He needs a physician's clearance to return to work. We're home. He's still sleeping."

"Thank you, Mrs. Nagle. We'll be dropping by this morning before noon."

Jack laughed. He grabbed a towel from behind the bathroom door and turned on the shower. "Let's get there by ten. I'll shave tonight," he said and headed for the bathroom. Leave a message for Sam; we'll call from Nagle's."

"I hate this constant phone call in bullshit." David was frustrated.

By nine o'clock, both men had showered and dressed. "Take your briefcase and anything of importance with you."

"Guess you're right. I'd like to pack and get the hell out of here."

They locked the motel room door and headed downstairs to the lobby. Jack stopped at the registration desk.

"Where's Wolfman?"

The receptionist continued to read her magazine. "Who?"

She eventually looked up at Jack. "Yeah. What's up?"

Couldn't get any more gum in your mouth could you, sweetheart?

"The kid with the bush beard. He's been here the last few days," David added.

"He didn't call in. Bruno's never done this before. I don't know nothing else."

Jack turned to David. "Another mystery."

It was less than five miles from the motel to Matt Nagle's Oak

Street home in Patchogue.

Jack saw flashing headlights a few houses away. "What's that?"

"Take a look. I think they're for us."

David pointed toward a grey sedan about two hundred feet away on the opposite side of the street. As their car approached, the headlights flashed again. The driver rolled down the window. It was Captain Briggs, in an unmarked car.

"Pull over there. I want to speak with you." Briggs got out of his car and walked to their car.

Jack pulled across the street, turned off the car, and was about to get out when Captain Briggs signaled to roll down his window.

"Why didn't you tell me you were Butch Wade's brother-in-law?" His question sounded ominous.

"I told you my sister's name." *What's next?*

"Your sister, Elaine Wade, called dispatch about two hours ago and reported a break-in at her home. She was hysterical."

Jack turned the key in the ignition and started the engine.

"Hold on, Jack." Briggs frowned as though there was more bad news.

"A sector car responded. Seems your sister was out for her morning run. The patio door lock was forced. She found the door open. Your sister called from a neighbor's."

"Is she okay?"

By now, David was leaning over, trying to look around Jack and get a better view of Briggs.

"It's the dog," Briggs said.

"Dusty? What happened?" asked David.

"Your sister thought the dog had run off. The responding officer found the dog. The pool cover had a lot of water at one end. The dog appears to have drowned."

"I better get over there. We can talk with Nagle later." David agreed.

There were two sector cars in front of Elaine's when they arrived. A run-down Ford pickup truck blocked the driveway. Jack recognized the truck "That's Butch's rust bucket."

Crossing the street, David saw three men talking on the front stoop. David guessed the guy in the jeans and tattered jacket was Elaine's ex. The three men stopped talking as he approached.

"Morning, Butch."

"Didn't know you were in town, Jack. Business or pleasure? "

Butch greeted his ex-brother-in-law as though they had just talked yesterday.

"Elaine's inside. I guess Briggs told you what happened."

Jack nodded and walked into the house. David waited outside with Captain Briggs. "Excuse us, Mr. Clayton. I need a private pow-wow."

David nodded and walked to the back of the house. The yard was enclosed by a black chain link fence with self-closing child-proof gates. Then he walked over to the pool. The blue winter pool cover sagged. Water had accumulated on the far left side, covering what he assumed were stairs. *That's probably where Dusty drowned.* A blue and white towel covered the dead Schnauzer. David lifted the towel. *Can't imagine how she fell in.*

"What do you think?" Captain Briggs called out. Butch Wade was with him.

"Who knows? You're the cop." David's voice revealed a sincere deference.

Butch Wade was thin, tanned and self-assured. *Could this be the guy who spent months in a nut house?*

"Didn't get a chance to talk a few minutes ago." Butch smiled and extended his hand. They shook hands. Wade's prematurely grey, unkempt beard added to the clammer's weathered appearance. *A bayman's life must be tough.*

Captain Briggs walked to Dusty's body. "I go along with you, Butch. Whoever broke into the house killed Dusty."

"That pup was a yapper," said Wade.

"Jack is with Elaine. I'll call her later today. Give her some time." Wade gave a casual salute to Briggs. David sensed they were old friends. "Hope to see you again, Mr. Clayton." *So that's Butch Wade.*

"Butch." Butch turned at Briggs' call. "Butch, you're not a cop anymore. Keep that in mind."

Butch smiled, turned and walked away.

He won't listen to me. Briggs looked down at the towel covering the dog's body. "God help the person who killed Dusty, if Butch gets to him first." Briggs walked through the open patio door into the house. "Coming, David?"

Entering the kitchen, both men could hear Elaine crying. Jack was trying to comfort his sister.

"Excuse me, Elaine. I apologize, but I need to speak with you."

"Of course. Tom, thank you for helping. Have you met my brother, Jack?"

"I met the Captain earlier this morning. Official business. What happened to your assurance a patrol car would check out my sister's home?" Jack approached Briggs.

Briggs towered over Jack, but stepped back. "Listen, I was driving to work when it hit me. Wade? Blue Point? I've known Butch for years. I checked the slip of paper you gave me. What's your point, Jack?"

"My point? Look around; nothing's been touched. The dog's dead."

"A forensics team is on its way. We don't know the dog was killed. Maybe Dusty got too close to the pool, fell in, and drowned. Let's not jump to conclusions."

David walked over to Elaine. "I'm sorry, Elaine. I know how much Dusty meant to you." While they were talking, Jack and Briggs walked into the kitchen.

David comforted Elaine. "You're in safe hands with Captain Briggs."

"Oh, I know. I don't want to believe someone would kill Dusty. Why break in, then simply leave?"

The telephone rang. Jack answered in the kitchen.

"What time? The forensics unit is winding up. Sure, I'll stay here. Yeah, that sounds like a smart move. See you then." Jack replaced the phone in the wall cradle

"Captain Briggs."

"Out here."

"Butch knows a veterinarian. He agreed to autopsy Dusty."

"I'll clear it with Forensics. We'll get to the bottom of this."

"That's it, Captain. We've finished. This place is clean as a whistle. Too clean." Briggs followed the detective to where Dusty's corpse lay. He knelt over the dog, lifted the towel and said, "Captain, my gut tells me this wasn't an ordinary break-in. There's something else. Has to be."

Briggs agreed.

"One last request. Butch Wade called. Is it okay to let him have the dog autopsied?"

"Sure, Captain. Have Butch ask the vet to keep the dog on ice until I receive a copy of his report."

David walked out to the patio. "Jack, Elaine is asking for you."

"Excuse me, Captain."

It's important for Jack to be with his sister. Still, Sam needs us to finish the Nagle interview. David approached Briggs.

"Captain Briggs, I need your help."

"What's wrong?"

"I'm in a jam. Jack and I have to finish our interview with Nagle. I feel like a heel. I don't know how to pull him away from his sister."

"Back to Nagle's? Sure. I'll speak with Jack and Elaine. Butch will be back soon. I can hang around for another hour or so."

"I sound heartless, but we have to wind things up. We're expected in Washington on Monday morning."

Briggs left David on the patio and walked inside. He coughed and said, "Jack. Your partner needs to speak with you. He's on the patio."

"Thanks. The Nagle interview. Right?" Jack looked worried.

On the patio, David expressed concern. "We'll miss our appointment at the ME's office unless we complete the Nagle interview today."

"I agree. Butch and Briggs will look after my sister." Jack clenched his fists as though he were about to box an unseen opponent. "I keep thinking that this mess is somehow connected to me.

"This incident may be a bizarre warning. Someone is warning us, 'We can get to you any time and any way we choose.'" Jack punched the palm of his hand.

"I'm starting to think you may be on to something. I thought we were following a paper trail. Why all the muscle?"

Both men returned to the living room. Jack hugged his sister.

"Thanks for your help, Briggs. I'm sorry we got off on the wrong foot."

"I'll give you a call once we find something substantial," said

Briggs.

Jack and David left via the patio. Both men paused at the gate, looked back at the towel covering Elaine's beloved Dusty. "Briggs will come up with something," David said.

Jack looked at the rearview mirror. Butch Wade's pickup truck was pulling into Elaine's driveway.

Butch parked his truck and entered the house. "I'm here to take Dusty's remains to the animal hospital."

"Up to you, Butch." Briggs shrugged his shoulders as though to say "whatever". "Butch…I warned you. This is a police matter."

"Gotcha!"

I know damn well Butch won't let go.

"I'm warning you, Butch. I appreciate your help. Don't take matters into your own hands."

Butch winked and repeated, "Gotcha!" Butch returned a few minutes later and carried Dusty's remains to the pickup. *I'll get the son of a bitch who did this.*

Elaine followed Butch to the truck. "Thank you for helping me. There's only so much you can do. Please don't get into any trouble on my behalf."

"I promise. Briggs knows I'm not a crazy cop. I'm going on a hunch."

"What hunch?" Elaine stepped back.

Butch walked around the truck and was about to get in. "Later."

The pickup started with a puff of black smoke. "Time to get rid of this thing."

Elaine walked back into the house.

"I have to head over to the Fifth Precinct. Please call me as soon as you hear from Butch."

Elaine smiled to hold back the tears.

"I'll keep in touch," said Tom.

Briggs was about to call it a day when Butch called the Fifth Precinct.

"Tom, I'm with the vet."

"Okay, Butch, but slow down. Catch your breath. What'd you find out?" Briggs reached for a pad and pen.

"Dusty did not drown. The vet is positive. There's no water in Dusty's lungs."

"What? What does the vet think?"

"Tom, the vet, Bob Lewis, is standing right across from me. Bob is certain Dusty was killed. Dusty's neck was broken."

"Let me speak with Dr. Lewis."

"Hello. This is Bob Lewis."

"Doctor Lewis, are you absolutely sure the dog's neck was broken?"

"Yes."

"Before it hit the water?"

"No doubt in my mind. I checked both lungs for fluids. None. I sent the bloodwork and stomach contents to a lab. I'm confident the report will confirm my findings. The dog was dead before she hit the water."

Butch took the phone from Dr. Lewis. "Tom. This is scary. Dusty was a friendly dog. A monster killed Dusty."

"This case gets more involved by the hour." Briggs grew impatient. "Butch, you've done enough. Stay out of it. I'll lock your ass up if you interfere with this investigation."

"I understand." Butch didn't mean it.

Briggs' other line flashed. "Got another call."

"Captain. The Deputy Commissioner's secretary called. You're scheduled to meet at his office."

"When?"

"0900 hours."

"Any agenda?"

"Yes, sir. Bring your notes on the case involving the stolen plates from the Trinity vehicle."

Trinity? Here goes my promotion to Inspector down the drain.

After leaving Elaine's home, Jack convinced David it was time for lunch. "Hungry?"

"Yes. We haven't eaten since last night." David rubbed his stomach. "I don't know how you live on coffee."

"Got someplace in mind?"

Jack thought for a minute. "I have the perfect spot."

Jack made a quick turn off Montauk Highway and headed for the Sunrise Highway. "David, I think we should compare notes before we meet with Nagle."

"He may not be there. His wife was hostile."

"I propose we make a checklist."

"Does that include the break-in at Elaine's?"

Jack paused. "Let's set that aside and see what we come up with." Jack made a quick left and drove to the Sunrise Diner's parking lot.

The diner's owner greeted the pair.

"Coffee, gentlemen?"

"Yes. We'll be here for a while."

The waitress returned with the coffees. "Take your time, gentlemen." She smiled.

"This damn case is turning into a nightmare." Jack took out his notepad.

"I've been expanding on my notes a bit," said David. He reached into his briefcase and removed a spiral notebook. Across the top of a blank page, he printed "What We Know."

"So what do we know for sure?"

David took a sip of coffee. "Koch and General Webster are dead. They were both connected to the same research projects at Fort Detrick. We still have two more Nazis we haven't identified."

"Both Trinity PharmoDynamics Group and Trinity PharmoDynamics, USA are connected to some degree."

"Their names keep coming up."

"Trinity wheels a lot of influence. Even Briggs warned us to stay away. I think he's an honest cop."

Jack reviewed his notes.

"Jack, are you okay?"

"Sure, why?"

"The expression on your face. You look like you could kill."

"It's frustrating to know we're onto something, but don't know what it is."

"What do you mean?"

"Are you shitting me? We've been tailed since we arrived on Long Island. Nagle is nearly killed. And my sister's dog…" Jack's voice began to break. He choked a bit as he rehashed the incident at Elaine's home.

"We'll learn more once we examine the stuff Portavani left with Nagle."

After lunch they drove directly to Nagle's home.

Jack rang the doorbell.

Liz Nagle opened the door. "You two again. He's in the kitchen. I'm warning you now, keep him out of this."

Jack looked directly at Liz. "I'm afraid it's a bit too late for that and you know it, Mrs. Nagle."

Liz directed the two men to the kitchen. Nagle was sitting at the table. His right leg was stretched across another chair.

"Don't get up," said Jack.

"Dark humor, Mr. Thompson." Nagle flinched from pain as he straightened himself on the chair.

"Nagle, were you out of your mind?" asked David.

"I got carried away. The son of a bitch opened the passenger side door into my bike and the rest is history."

"You got a good look at him?" asked David.

"Yeah, I did. I'll never forget his face. Looked just like a weasel. I'm certain the driver was the blonde from the Student Union building.

"Sit down. Let's make this quick. Liz doesn't want me talking with you."

Jack said, "The police are doing all they can to find the couple. It's going to be tough. They found the GTO…burned out…over in Port Jefferson. The plates were stolen."

"I can't help you. Look at me. It's my own fault." Nagle struggled to get to his feet. "Hand me the crutches."

"We need to go through the stuff Portavani left."

"Yes." Nagle winced again. "This damned ankle. Follow me."

They entered Nagle's garage through the kitchen. He pointed to a box and a long mailing tube on a shelf. Jack put the box on Nagle's workbench.

"Nothing much in here. A journal. Receipts. Stuff like that."

Jack handed the box to David.

"These binders may be helpful."

Clustered with the binders was a leather-bound journal.

"You read this?" David hand the journal to Nagle.

"No."

David opened the journal. "Portavani's recorded mileage and random expenses." David continued to flip through the pages. "I found it!"

"Found what?" asked Jack.

"The so-called incident on Plum Island."

David read the notation. "Unknown accident in the main lab. Work stopped. We were directed to the Ferry Platform. Security told me there was a power outage in the pressurized lock. Air pressure fell. Allowed air to rush out of the lab."

"How does that help us?" asked Nagle.

"Let me finish." David continued to read: "I saw the German at the dock. One of the big shots was with him. And an Asian man, too."

"Asian guy?" asked Nagle. "Tony never mentioned any Asian guy."

David turned to Portavani's final entry: "Saw the Asian and the German from Plum Island at the Smithhaven Mall. Followed them. The Asian's name: Kumori"

"Japanese, maybe?" asked Nagle.

"Who knows? I don't have any information about an Asian or a Kumori. Damn it! Why can't things be simple?" groused David.

Jack reached for the document tube. He unrolled its contents onto Nagle's workbench. It was a map of Plum Island. "Portavani must have drawn this. Rand McNally doesn't show Plum Island."

"That's odd," said Nagle, pointing to the left portion of the map. "I read a Newsday article about the lab accident. The DOA spokesman said there was little chance a virus or bacteria could leave the Island. He noted there were no natural habitats for birds or water fowl. Portavani's map shows wetlands and a pond."

"Birds, mosquitoes," said Jack. "Deer and strays that swim to the Island can be shot by security. How do they control migrating birds, ticks and mosquitoes?"

"I have no idea, Jack. We're not here to investigate Plum Island."

"I'll wager Karl Peter Koch is connected to the Island."

"Who is Koch?" asked Nagle.

Before Jack could answer, Liz Nagle walked into the garage. "You guys have been here almost an hour. It's time you cleared out."

Jack and David agreed.

"I want you guys out of here. My husband is a teacher, not a cop. He's in enough trouble. We have two kids and a big mortgage. You want excitement, Matt? Get a part-time job at ShopRite." She turned and left.

"We need to take this stuff with us. There may be more here than we can tell," said David.

"Take it," said Nagle.

Jack printed and signed a receipt.

David gathered Portavani's papers and carried the box and map to the car. Jack handed Nagle a crude receipt.

"Matt, your wife is right," said Jack. "Leave the investigative reporting to Newsday. Cops and reporters get paid for that stuff. You don't."

Nagle frowned and glanced toward the doorway his wife had gone through in a huff. "Perhaps you're right," Nagle said.

Jack turned to Nagle. "This entire situation seems to get worse by the day. No sense hurting your family, either physically or financially."

"Take care of yourself."

Chapter 11

Jack and David drove into New York City around seven Friday morning. The smartass desk clerk was still missing. Traffic on the Long Island Expressway was unusually light for a Friday until they hit Queens. Sam left a message on their hotel phone. Koch's body had been moved to the ME's new headquarters in Manhattan. Traffic crawled through the Mid-Town Tunnel, but eventually they arrived at their destination.

"Odd," said Jack. "Why would CDC move Koch's body from the Queens morgue to the Chief Medical Examiner's headquarters?"

"I was thinking the same thing. Sam told us the CDC would have the body shipped to Detrick for the autopsy. I'll take the next exit and look for a pay phone."

David double parked while Jack called Sam.

"Damn it. Sam didn't answer. I left a message on his machine. Asked him to contact us at the ME's office in Manhattan," said Jack.

"I'm stumped," said David. "Leaving the Mid-Town Tunnel, they drove to 520 First Avenue, the ME's headquarters.

The ME's headquarters houses the executive offices, the mortuary, autopsy rooms and the toxicology laboratories. David and Jack headed directly to the ME's office. After a brief wait, a deputy medical examiner entered the waiting area.

"Good morning, Gentlemen," said the thin, raspy voiced man wearing wrinkled purple scrubs. "I'm Doctor Bob Johnson."

Johnson led the pair to a small office. It smelled of cigarette smoke.

"Strange, you two still need more information? I turned

everything over to the FBI yesterday morning," said Johnson, going to a filing cabinet with unfiled reports sitting on top. "Hmm…here it is. Koch, isn't it? Just thinking out loud. Don't be alarmed. Of course it is. Karl Peter Koch." Johnson returned to his desk with the file.

"Two FBI agents were here yesterday?" asked Jack.

"Exactly. Around this time. I met them downstairs. They had a release for Koch's body and effects. Koch's brother and sister were with them."

"Brother and sister?" asked David.

"Yes. A tall blonde woman and a short man. They were a strange pair," said Johnson.

"Did you see credentials? Authorizations?" asked David.

"Of course. In fact, since this was a deviation from the original instructions, I called the CDC regional office. They faxed a copy of the authorization."

"You called the telephone number on the authorization?"

Johnson stepped back. "Oh, no."

"Whoever sent the fax also had someone waiting for your call and it wasn't CDC. May I see the file?" asked David.

Johnson handed the heavy folder to David. There was a brief pause.

Jack tapped David on the shoulder. "Excuse me, David. I tried calling that phone number. No one answered. It has to be phony."

"Doctor Johnson, your summary sheet notes the autopsy report is incomplete, or at least it was yesterday morning," said David.

"Correct. Let me check this morning's incoming correspondence. I was concerned with the manner in which Koch died, international flight and all. Ah, here it is," said Johnson. He opened a brown routing envelope and began reading the toxicology report. His smile faded.

"Something the matter?" asked David.

"I'm not sure," said Johnson. "Our lab is holding out on the final report. We've run tests, but rather simple ones. I'll give a call."

Johnson called the chief of toxicology. After a brief conversation he looked perplexed. "Toxicology called in a specialist in Mideast diseases. An Egyptian," said Johnson. "His findings…Koch died from Rift Valley Fever."

"Never heard of it," said David.

"No. Not many North Americans have. It's a disease and a bad one, found in the Middle East. From what I've read Egypt is dealing with an epidemic…maybe two hundred thousand. It affects animals and can be transmitted to humans. North Americans have no immunity to it," said Johnson.

David and Jack looked at one another. They both sensed panic in Johnson's voice. "What's wrong?" asked Jack.

"Bluntly? I screwed up. With all this FBI and CDC pressure, I released all the paperwork and Koch's body prematurely. There's a major problem," said Johnson. His voice sounded weaker and raspier. "I need a cigarette," he said.

"We better get to Sam with this new information," said David.

"Not yet. Let's see where this is taking us," said Jack.

"Dr. Johnson. It's important we review yesterday's events and today's report with you. Describe the FBI agents," said David.

"A Mutt and Jeff duo…Dumb and Dumber. It was probably an act. The tall one, early 50's. Military type. The other agent was short, stubby looking. Can't imagine him passing a law enforcement physical."

"To whom was the body released?" asked David.

"The brother and sister signed. I signed an authorization for a Queens funeral home – it's in the folder – to transport to their facility. The woman informed me the family planned a cremation. They were in a hurry to return home to Wisconsin."

"Sounds like our couple from the motel, Jack," said David.

"Dr. Johnson, have one of your staff give the funeral home a call and see if the cremation took place."

Johnson left his office for several minutes. He returned smoking a cigarette. He had changed into his street clothes, including a blue linen sport coat and a stained blue tie. "I called one of our specialists, Dr. Youssef Massri. Massri is an Egyptian-American. He worked at a hospital in Cairo for several years. Let's talk with him," said Johnson.

The three men walked to the elevators. Along the way they encountered Johnson's secretary. "Dr. Johnson, I spoke with the director at the Petty Funeral Home in Queens. They never issued any certificate to transport. They have no clients dealing with Karl Peter Koch."

Johnson looked stunned. "My God, things are going from bad to worse," he said. His voice now trembled.

They rode the elevator into the sub-basement where Dr. Massri was waiting outside the morgue. After a brief introduction, Massri requested the three put on paper surgical gowns and masks before entering room 101 of the mortuary. An attendant was washing a body. He glanced their way and quickly returned to the task at hand. Room 101 was cold. Massri led them to a glass-enclosed room. "We keep the specimens here. Yesterday, I received the organs and body fluid samples taken from Koch. The liver specimen raised concern. Luckily, we discovered it."

"Discovered what?" asked David.

"Rift Valley Virus. It's known by several variants, RVFV or RFVD. In any case, it's a major concern in Egypt." Massri's voice underscored the magnitude of the finding.

"How does someone get it.?" Jack asked.

"The prevalent way? A mosquito carried a microscopic vector. It bites an animal. The mosquito bites a human. The vector is transferred."

"I can tell you are still puzzled, David."

"Dr. Massri, what is the impact?"

"In Egypt, for example, there is an epidemic. Not everyone dies, however. An outbreak in the U.S. would be a catastrophe. Most Americans do not have a natural immunity. I suspect from the number of scientific articles published recently, the government and the private sector are close to finding a vaccine."

Dr. Johnson stepped forward. "When a case arrives, as Koch's did, particularly when the body has not been fully identified, we store the corpse at between fourteen and minus 60 degrees Fahrenheit. In other words, frozen, to decrease decomposition. Koch's body was shipped from the Queens morgue to us."

"Any idea why?" asked David.

"I reviewed the folder. Seems a number of federal agencies were interested in Koch. Interesting, the first directive from CDC requested they perform the autopsy. The following day, a second authorization came through official channels for us to handle it.

You have all the paperwork. Correct, Dr. Johnson?" Massri looked to Johnson for his response.

Johnson merely nodded.

"Herein lies our challenge," said Massri. "As I noted previously, the virus vector is transported by a mosquito. Humans are a dead end, with perhaps one exception."

"And what's that, doctor?" asked Jack.

"There have been several rare cases of disease dispersal. International air travel might be one way the disease could be spread. How the disease operates remains poorly understood."

Jack asked again, "At this point you are certain there is no vaccine?"

"No. There is another issue." He turned to Dr. Johnson.

"I contacted CDC with our findings." Johnson and Massri looked at one another.

"And?"

Johnson continued. "I recommended all the passengers on Koch's flight be contacted. Within an hour, the CDC returned my call. I was instructed not to release the information. Several minutes later we received a faxed directive."

Johnson handed the copy to David. The three-sentence directive ordered Johnson, "Do not release report to airlines. Your report has been classified by the State Department."

"This is a highly classified investigation, Dr. Massri. We aren't authorized to take any action without authorization," said David.

"We have a responsibility. We are required by law to follow through on this," said Johnson.

"I'd hold off, Doctor Johnson. You may be in trouble now, but things could get much worse if you start revealing classified information," warned Jack.

Both doctors began to protest. "In 1976, it took government agencies over seven months to isolate Legionnaires' disease bacterium. We simply don't have the resources to act overnight," said Massri.

"We have no early warning systems for an exotic disease like RVFV," protested Johnson.

Over the next thirty minutes, Massri shared his experience with RVFV in Egypt. "Egypt's president, Sadat, would give a fortune to come up with a vaccine for the virus. Sadat's popularity has fallen drastically. I met several researchers from the United States – DOA and CDC personnel – working with Egyptian and Jordanian counterparts. I have reason to believe federal labs are at work on a vaccine," Massri concluded.

It was nearly noon when Johnson, Jack and David returned to the ME's office. A message from Beverly was waiting. It read, *"Call me as soon as you get this message; home or work. SB"*

Johnson directed David and Jack to a vacant office to telephone Washington.

"You two guys have stirred the pot. I sent you on a quick trip to Long Island to tie up loose ends. What have you two done? I got a call from the FBI's special agent in charge in Suffolk County."

"Hold on, Sam. There's something very important. The two phony FBI agents showed up at the ME's office. Koch's body is gone. They secured copies of all the documents. The death certificate is provisional, but everyone's vanished." David spoke slowly with intent.

"Anyone form CDC show up?"

"No. The documents look authentic, Sam."

"Let me speak with Jack."

"Jack, you're an experienced lawyer. What's happening? I expected this would be a simple in and out."

"Sit down, Sam. There's more," said Jack. He pictured Sam growing more inpatient. "Koch probably died from the complications of an exotic disease called Rift Valley Fever. The medical examiner wants to issue a public alert."

"What?" Sam shouted. "No alerts! We are bound to violate some law. Tell those guys to sit tight."

David and Jack returned to Johnson's office. "Doctor Johnson, Sam Beverly the Deputy Inspector General at the GAO, cautioned against issuing any public announcement," said Jack.

"Any idea what happens to the passengers on Koch's flight?" he asked.

"We'll have to take this one step at a time," said Jack.

"Doctor Johnson, I see from this receipt, so-called FBI agents left a piece of luggage behind."

"Yes. The Evidence Unit received all of Koch's personal

belongings. Normally we turn them over to the NYPD. Since a federal agency was involved, we stored four pieces. The clerk discovered the agents in their haste signed for three pieces, a suitcase, overnight bag, and carryon. A small leather briefcase was left behind. You're holding the ticket."

"We'll take it," said Jack.

Johnson called the evidence room and requested the briefcase be sent to his office. After a few minutes, a clerk knocked on Johnson's door. He brought the case, a small leather brief folio. Jack signed the receipt and took the folder. He looked inside. "It's best if we examine the contents back in Washington. We have enough to do for the moment." They all agreed.

A quick glance and David said, "It's time we head back to Washington." They left a bewildered Johnson with a final warning: "Not a word, Dr. Johnson. This goes way beyond fear of losing your job. This is a national security issue now." Johnson turned into milquetoast.

The pair left the building and headed back to D.C.

The return trip to D.C. took nearly eight hours. The two men rarely spoke, with the exception of a brief stop in Delaware for gas and coffee. They were both preoccupied with recent events. David appeared oblivious to the stop and go traffic outside Baltimore. Jack paid little attention. He doodled on in his notebook, then ripped the page from the spiral binding, rolling the paper into a ball. He was careful to place the paper into his sport jacket pocket.

"That's so annoying," said David.

"What?"

"Writing a note, tearing the paper from your notebook, then rolling it into a ball. If you have something to tell me…get on with it," said David. A look of disgust briefly crossed his face.

Jack didn't respond. He returned to his notebook.

Sometime after 9:30 that evening, David dropped Jack near the Washington monument. Without a word, simply a gesture, Jack grabbed his briefcase and suitcase. After several failed attempts, Jack finally hailed a cab and headed to his apartment. David returned the car to the motor pool. The attendant pointed to the rear quarter panel.

"Where's this thing been?" he asked.

David didn't respond.

In turn, the attendant made a few notes to cover his ass. He walked to the time clock to record the return time. David paid little attention.

"Your car is parked in spot twenty-seven on the far side," said the attendant. He seemed annoyed David wasn't taking this whole business seriously.

"Thanks," said David. He placed his briefcase strap over his left shoulder and dragged the overnight pack with his right hand. The parking spot was dark and David mistakenly placed the ignition key in the door lock. It jammed. Without warning, suddenly and uncontrollably, David turned and shouted, "Damn it." He kicked his suitcase into the garage wall. He gave it a second kick for good measure, but the suitcase didn't budge. Instead, a pain surged from his right knee to his brain. "Shit," was all he could manage as he stumbled back and fell onto the concrete garage floor. David sat there for several minutes. Then he struggled to his feet and carefully removed the ignition key from the door lock. A disheveled David started the car and drove to Manassas. All he wanted was a Jameson's and a good night's rest. He wasn't looking forward to Monday's meeting with Sam.

Unbeknownst to Jack and David, Beverly was still in his office. The Deputy Inspector General was bending over, focused on a dozen or more index cards scattered on the desktop. He kept moving the cards as though he might be assembling a jigsaw puzzle. Beverly had one more complication to cap off his day.

"Sorry to drop in unannounced, Sam," said the Inspector General.

Sam stood as though he was a military adjutant saluting his commanding officer. "Colonel," said Sam. The IG cherished his former military rank and kept the title after entering civilian life.

"Relax, Sam," said John Evans. "I was on my way home from the club and thought I would drop by."

"Nice day for a round of golf," said Sam. He struggled to overcome his apprehension. Sam hadn't seen the IG in a couple of weeks. Evans was on the brink of retirement from the GAO. He telephoned Sam from time to time. Never any small talk. The calls decreased with Sam's increased involvement in the GOA inquiry.

Evans, the once handsome Air Force colonel, was a caricature of his former self. He'd grown fat, gray and old, an Eighth Air Force relic. His complexion was ruddy from sun and alcohol. Sam knew this was no random visit.

Sam walked around his desk to shake hands with Evans. The stale cigar breath and whiskey smell were strong.

"Something is troubling me, Sam," said Evans.

"And what's that, John?"

Evans looked around then slumped into a leather wing-back chair. "The duration of this inquiry of yours," said Evans. "What's the problem here?"

Sam started to answer, but Evans interrupted.

"Sam, why do you think we assigned you to Congresswoman Harrington's pet project?"

"Because you didn't want to be involved," said Sam.

"Ah. Just the answer I expected. You must be feeling quite secure in your job, Sam."

"Forgive me, John. I was being juvenile."

"No need, Sam. You are correct. I didn't want to be involved. I, or better yet, 'we,' handed it to you because – and I mean this seriously - we think you are savvy enough to handle it. Are we wrong?"

"John, I'm not sure where you're going with this."

"There are a half dozen or more agencies involved in a special project. You know that." Evans' tone was sarcastic.

"Do you believe I'm stalling or delaying this inquiry? We've been working on nothing else but the inquiry."

"Exactly, Sam. Let's just put some numbers together…a spreadsheet or two, and get on with it. We all know Nazis have been on the payroll. Operation Paper Clip is old hat."

"This may be an entirely different situation, John. My team is tracking definitely two, possibly three, Nazi war criminals working on highly sensitive biological research at three government labs. One's a mere stone's throw from here: Detrick." Sam walked behind his desk and unlocked the top drawer from which he took a key. He walked to the far wall, opened a closet door and there stood a large safe. It required both the key and a combination to unlock. Sam took his time to withdraw a folder to emphasize the importance of the documents he was about to reveal. "Here; this is what we're working on."

Evans lit a cigarette and began leafing through the folder. "Makes no sense to me. A bunch of spy stuff. We're not the FBI or NSA. Be real, Sam. Leave the detective work to them."

Sam looked astonished.

"My last ten years in the Air Force, I moved into procurement. Ball bearings, Sam. Ball bearings! Ball bearings reduce friction, Sam. The government buys them for a buck apiece. They go for twenty cents in a local hardware store."

"I'm lost. What's your point?" Sam said.

"My point - here's my point - nobody gives a shit. That goes for your damn inquiry, Sam. All I want is a report. Get me the numbers. Let Congress and the public draw their own conclusions."

The conversation grew heated.

"I birdied the fourth hole today," said Evans. "I bought a round of drinks for the boys to celebrate. Right in the middle of my moment of glory, I got an urgent phone call. Guess who, Sam?" Evans' face was flushed. He crushed his cigarette butt into the ashtray with such force the ashes flew onto Sam's desk and the carpet.

Sam shrugged.

"The Under Secretary of Defense for special research, Buster Kennedy, that's who. That little shit worked on my staff and never rose above the rank of major. And now that mother's calling me on the phone. He put the screws to me. 'What's going on with your inquiry?' Holding me accountable for your investigation, Sam. Not mine." Evans' hands shook as he attempted to light another cigarette. "You have no idea what you're getting into."

"I thought I did."

"You're messing with guys who are way out of our league. This thing goes way beyond national security. You're involved with multinational corporations older than both of us combined. Who do you think your germ scientists worked for in Germany? They worked for powerful corporations. Money, Sam. Big money stood behind Hitler. Hitler is gone. The big money, the power brokers, live on. Ball bearings, Sam. Are you blind?" Evans waved his arms as though possessed.

"How do you know this, John? You barely skimmed these documents and my team hasn't scratched the surface. What's going on?"

It had to be the booze. Evans was starting to ramble. Multinational corporations. National security. Out of my league. Evans should go home and sleep it off.

Evans looked around the room as though he suspected someone was eavesdropping. He lowered his voice to a whisper and tried to regain his composure. "I've told you too much already. I hope you know what you're doing, Sam." Evans struggled to extricate himself from the chair. Sam stepped forward to steady his boss. Evans waved him off. He tossed his cigarette towards the ashtray. It hit the carpet. Sam picked it up and held it briefly in front of Evans as one would hold a pointer.

"John, what the hell is going on?"

"Ball bearings, Sam. It's your career. Take my advice and submit your report before Harrington's committee comes back in session. Six months from now, nobody will give a shit about Nazi war criminals. You'll be out of a job." Evans tossed the folder on to Sam's desk.

"Are you okay to drive home?"

"Don't worry about me. You should start thinking about your career," said Evans. He turned and walked to the door. Holding on to the doorknob, with a look of disgust, Evans added, "By the way - word on the street has it your marriage has gone south. Can't say I blame her. You must be a difficult guy to live with, let alone love."

Sam's body tensed. He wanted to lunge at Evans. Too late. Evans left without closing the door. Sam walked over to the open door and kicked it closed. "You son of a bitch," he said aloud, again too late. Evans was already in the elevator.

Sam walked into the small bathroom attached to his office. He splashed water on his face and ran his fingers through his thinning hair. He'd slept on his office couch last night, or at least tried to sleep. Tonight, he wanted to sleep in his own bed. The empty house accentuated Sam's loneliness, but it provided sanctuary.

Grace moved back to Manhattan. Rachael decided to enroll at nearby Mary Washington College. She moved into a dorm. Sam took one last look at the index cards. He slumped into his desk chair and cupped his face in his hands. Evans' warning troubled him. He gathered the project file and returned it to his office safe. It was the only file without a distinct label. He scribbled "Project Naomi" on the edge.

Returning to his desk, Sam made two telephone calls. The messages were cryptic: "Nine o'clock Monday morning. My office. Bring everything you have. Plan on a long day."

Sam sensed the inquiry had reached a turning point. Evans' visit was ominous. Was Evans threatening or warning me?

Jack and David may also be facing an uncertain future. Sam knew he had to tell them. We are on a dangerous path.

Chapter 12

Dakota Putnam first met David Clayton at a "welcome back" cocktail party sponsored by the New York Delegation in January, 1973. She was recovering from an affair that had ended without warning Christmas Eve.

"This isn't working," was all she remembered him saying. Dakota cried through the holiday. How could she tell her father? He warned her to go slow.

Dakota was experienced at picking up the pieces from an affair. Bob Doyle, Senator Javits' aide, was different. Dakota had an awful track record of poor choices, and Bob Doyle was no exception. Reluctantly, Dakota pulled herself together.

When she first started horseback riding, her father told her, "You fall off your horse, you get back on. Otherwise, he has you licked. The same is true in life."

I can't stay home forever. I have to face the crowd at some point. It might as well be at the delegation party. She purchased a low-cut dress. It cost a week's salary. The spike heels cost more. She felt foolish and betrayed. Why am I doing this? "Damn you, Bob Doyle."

The party was in full swing when Dakota arrived at the Washington Hilton. Gulping her first champagne, Dakota left the empty flute on the bar.

"Gin and tonic, please. Extra gin." she said.

The bartender winked and poured more gin than tonic. 'Good luck," he said. Naturally, Dakota didn't have to wait long to see her "ex" on the far side of the room. Dakota still felt a sense of longing. Look at him. So damn smug. Dakota watched Doyle's nervous habit of stroking his long dark hair as he slowly beguiled a new

Congressional intern. Doyle had a passion for short brunettes. Touching her own dark shoulder length hair, she could still feel her ex-lover's insatiable appetite. A forced smile disguised her contempt for Doyle. Dakota's predicament wasn't all Doyle's fault. Dakota fell in love too easily. She had rushed into the affair. Doyle represented everything a newcomer expected from the fast life in D.C.; parties, intrigue, and excitement. The sex was great.

Doyle glanced across the room and spotted Dakota. He smiled and nodded. Doyle and the intern put down their drinks and left the party. *She'll learn. I remember…* Suddenly, her fantasy was interrupted.

"My God, man," she exclaimed, stepping back.

"Sorry, I was reaching for a champagne."

"Oh, stop stammering." This outfit cost me a week's salary."

"I am sorry. My name's David Clayton. Please…wait…here's my card. Send me the bill. I didn't bump into you on purpose."

"Forget it!" she fired back. "This entire evening has been a disaster."

Dakota glared at David.

"Honestly, I wanted to meet you, but not this way. It was an accident."

"I'm just venting. You're the nearest target. Don't call me." Dakota clutched her coat and left. The incident made it an even colder and lonelier night. And that's how Dakota Putnam met David Clayton.

Dakota's brief affair with Doyle provided a new taste for D.C.'s insider politics. The New York delegation epitomized the D.C. lifestyle. Dakota had an investigative reporter's instinct. She understood critical issues weren't debated in Congress. They were bantered about at cocktail parties. There was an abundance of parties. Her favorite parties were thrown by the pharmaceutical companies; tons of shrimp and magnums of champagne. Scantily clad waitresses flirted with politicos. With few exceptions, Dakota's skepticism of Washington politicians grew.

Dakota admired New York's Republican senator, Jacob Javits. Javits' liberal position rankled party bosses. Despite her unhappiness with President Nixon's handling of the Vietnam War, Dakota respected Jack Javits' judicious response to the Watergate scandal. Putnam agreed with Javits' position – Nixon was innocent until proven guilty.

Dakota respected Bob Woodward and Carl Bernstein. The pair helped break the Watergate story. Their persistence eventually led to the Oval Office.

After Dakota's love affair with Doyle fell to pieces, her life centered around her work. Dakota was a cub reporter at the Washington Post.

"Focus. Stay focused," her father told her. "You want to be an investigative reporter? Stay focused on your work. Nothing else matters."

Day after day, Dakota managed to find excuses for remaining at work, hoping to catch the ever-increasing rumors. Did the Watergate cover-up reach into the FBI and the Justice Department? Initially, Dakota doubted the allegations. How long would Woodward and Bernstein rely on the credibility of a faceless whisper or a shadow in a parking garage? Dakota overheard a water cooler exchange attributing the Post's leads to the so-called "Deep Throat." Who the hell is this mysterious Deep Throat?

Sunday, July 15, 1973, the hottest day of the year, found Dakota Putnam working the weekend desk. She pushed back from her cluttered desk and glanced at the clock. Dakota was bored. Nothing was happening. I need to stretch my legs, walk around a bit. That's when line two on her phone flashed. The events of the following hour changed Dakota's life.

"Putnam," said Dakota, answering the incoming call.

"With whom am I speaking?" the caller asked.

"This is Dakota Putnam. May I help you?"

"No, but perhaps I can help you. Miss Putnam…it is Miss, correct?"

Dakota walked around her desk, sat down and began searching for the pencil she just tossed aside.

"I have a message for Bradlee," said the caller. "Are you ready, Miss Putnam?"

"Yes," replied Dakota scrambling to find another pencil. "Okay. What's the message?"

"Alexander P. Butterfield, an official with the Federal Aviation Administration, will be testifying before the Senate committee on

Monday."

"Who is Butterfield and what's his connection with the Senate committee?"

"Please, Miss Putnam, no questions. Just leave the message for your editor. By the way, Ms. Putnam, Butterfield knows Nixon has been recording conversations in the Oval Office." There was an abrupt click. The line went dead.

Suddenly, Dakota Putnam became an insider to one of the biggest stories of the century. Dakota worked the phones for the remainder of the day, asking "Who is Butterfield?" All she got were "no comment" and "can't help you." Dakota's final call was a long shot. Dakota telephoned Harry Dash's office. Jack Thompson answered the phone. Dakota couldn't believe her luck. Thompson confirmed Butterfield was listed to testify on Monday morning. The story broke in the Post on Tuesday, July 17, 1973. Dakota was credited with contributing to the story.

On August 9, 1974, Richard Milhous Nixon, the 37th President of the United States, resigned in the face of almost certain impeachment and subsequent removal from office. Gerald Rudolph "Jerry" Ford became the 38th President. Dakota watched the coverage of Nixon's departure. One day I will be an accomplished investigative reporter akin to Woodward and Bernstein. On Tuesday, September 8, 1974, Dakota Putnam shared her first byline: "President Ford To Pardon Former President Nixon." Indeed, President Ford did grant Richard Nixon an unconditional pardon.

The following morning, September 9, Jack Thompson, along with two cardboard boxes, quietly vacated his fifth floor office at the Department of Justice. He was bitter. He blamed himself for his zealous participation on the Senate Watergate Committee. Thompson decided not to confront Dakota Putnam. What good would it do?

In the end, Thompson shrugged and sighed "whatever," accepting the Attorney General's reprimand. Only two of the building's twenty-five elevators descended to the damp, unventilated basement. Accompanied by Mac, a security guard, the pair descended into the bowels of the building.

The elevator doors slid open. Immediately, the pair was struck by a terrible stench. "What is that odor?" Jack gagged.

"The stink is making me nauseous. I think I'm going to…" Too late, Mac turned and vomited on the elevator floor.

"It's okay, Mac. I can manage from here."

"I'm sorry, Mr. Thompson. I can't believe they're sticking you down here. I know that smell. Forty-three years of mold spores. It ain't fair to you, Mr. Thompson. And I'm not the only one who feels that way."

"Thanks, Mac. I can find my way. One question."

"Yes, sir."

"I see the hallway leading to my new quarters is partially blocked by boxes."

"The brown cardboard boxes are archived records. The white boxes arrived a few at a time over the last six to ten months. They're labeled 'Trinity'. I imagine someone in Justice is investigating Trinity PharmoDynamics Group. I've heard of them, but that's all I know.

April, 1977 - Manassas, Virginia

David Clayton's one-bedroom second floor apartment was located just off Route 66 on Sudley Road in Manassas, Virginia. The unpretentious apartment complex suited Clayton's bachelor lifestyle. A peek in his refrigerator said the rest: a few bottles of beer, a pint of milk, and some rotting tomatoes. After the monotonous car ride from Long Island, Clayton's body ached. He unlocked the apartment door. The bedroom light was on. Without closing the door, he cautiously approached the bedroom and peered in.

"What?"

"I thought I'd surprise you," said Dakota. She turned and sat up against the headboard. Her clothes were draped over a chair. She was wearing one of David's T-shirts. Dakota brushed back her long brunette hair into a ponytail. "Aren't you happy to see me?" Dakota asked. She kicked the comforter away, revealing the extent of her invitation.

"Yes, I'm happy to see you, but I'm exhausted. It's been an awful week."

"Come to bed and I'll put you to sleep," said Dakota.

David undressed, showered, and soon they were making love.

They hadn't been together since their weekend at the Homestead two weeks ago. Dakota was especially passionate this evening. Dakota climaxed and drifted to sleep. Even Dakota's passion failed to block the kaleidoscope of events replaying in his brain. David tossed and turned, and finally fell asleep.

Awakened by his ringing phone, Clayton reached for the handset.

His fumbling fingers knocked the cradle to the floor, startling Dakota. The alarm clock glowed 1:30 a.m.

"Hello," Clayton answered in a hushed, slightly confused voice.

"David, who in the hell is calling at this hour?"

He shrugged, but Dakota couldn't see him.

"Hello," he repeated, a bit louder.

"Ah, David. I apologize for calling at this hour."

"You're damn straight."

Dakota rolled over in the opposite direction and turned on the bedside lamp.

"This is absurd."

David motioned for her to be quiet.

"Please give Ms. Putnam my apology, David. I will be brief."

David turned back and looked at Dakota.

"What do you want, Robert?"

"Listen carefully. I suspect I have been followed. The dead drop.

"Remember your request?"

"Yes," David replied. He frantically opened the nightstand drawer, searching for a pencil and paper.

"The Mayflower Hotel." There was a long pause.

"Are you still there?" David asked.

"Go to the Mayflower Hotel for lunch tomorrow, at noon precisely."

David could hear the nervous tension building in Robert's voice.

"Place your order. Consider the scallops. They're my favorite. The place has lost a bit of its ambiance since Mr. Hoover died. The menu needs luster."

David felt certain Robert's sarcasm was a cover. Was Robert in grave danger?

"Order a cocktail, then your meal. At 12:15, go to the men's room. The bathrooms are being renovated. Workers are constantly coming and going. Their lunch break starts at noon. There will be a notice directing patrons to use the lobby facility. Ignore it. At the far end of the bathroom entrance is a service closet. It will be unlocked. You will find a brown envelope on the top shelf. Presto, David. Your new dead drop. Any questions?"

"No. I've got it."

"I feel certain more eyes are following you than mine. We will not use this drop box location again."

"Please be casual leaving the hotel."

"I understand."

"Ms. Putnam is a beautiful woman. You have excellent taste. Nevertheless, Senator Avery's wife is far too old for you, David. Stick with Ms. Putnam."

"Wait. Don't hang up." David glanced over his shoulder. Dakota was taking in every word. He got out of bed and stretched the telephone cord to its breaking point.

David whispered into the phone, "You told me you handled three Nazi scientists. You never mentioned a fourth. An Asian."

"Harrington is searching for Nazi war criminals. That delivery did include a fourth person. He was Japanese. Never charged. The records were expunged."

He knew all along. The staccato response clinches it. David felt angry and frustrated.

"I must guard my own identity. Do you understand the risk I am taking? Your life may be in jeopardy, also. I must be careful. These people are powerful. They may not go after you directly. They never do. They send subtle warnings. I fear for my family. David, any attempt to discover my identity and our contact will end."

"I understand."

There was a moment of silence. Robert was gone. David walked back to the bed and placed the phone on the nightstand. *That cryptic s.o.b.*

"Who the hell is Robert?"

"I can't talk about it. You've been around Washington long enough to understand." *Oops. I should never have said that.*

Dakota's eyes opened wide. She sat up in bed. "Come on, David. You can tell me."

"No, I can't. This is classified."

"Stop talking. Listen to me. Do you think you may have been followed here this evening?"

"How would I know?"

"The caller knew you were here."

"Forget it. No more questions." Dakota slid under the comforter.

David sat next to Dakota. "You're not going to get any anonymous source quotes out of me," he whispered. "Sam Beverly warned me about you, Ms. Putnam."

"What?" Dakota pulled away from David.

"I'm working with the Deputy Inspector General at the GAO. You must have known that. Beverly mentioned a story you worked on. I told him I knew you."

"Out of the clear blue sky, Beverly brought up my name?"

"Something like that. He cautioned me."

"About what?"

"You must know you've made enemies. Some call your paper the 'Pravda of the Republic'. That's your Watergate inheritance, I imagine."

"He really means watch out for Putnam. She's an 'uppity bitch'. One of those 'libbers'. If that's the price I have to pay, so be it."

"Beverly never said that. He doesn't want the GAO's credibility questioned or our work compromised."

Dakota kicked off the comforter. "That's a lot of crap and you know it. Everyone knows you're hunting Nazis for Harrington's committee. You don't trust me."

"David climbed out of bed and embraced Dakota. He hated moments like this. "It's not a matter of trust. Don't manipulate me."

"Then what is it?"

"I have my job to do. You have yours. If we can't keep the two separate…better we find out now." David turned and walked toward the kitchen.

Dakota had pressed the wrong button. She hadn't reached a point of declaring her 'love' for David, but she was pretty damn close. *I'm not going to sacrifice my career for him.* She gazed into the bathroom mirror. *What's happening to me? Another love affair gone bad? Stop this childish nonsense.* "Stop it!"

"Stop what?" called David. "Please. Let's go back to bed. We can talk about this in the morning."

Dakota was determined to discover the importance of the call. *Who is this mysterious Robert?* She sensed a story. *David can't tell me what I can do.* Dakota returned to bed. The love-making was over, at least for tonight.

Early the next morning, David reached across the bed for Dakota's warm body. Wiping his eyes, David called for her. No answer. He stretched and slipped into his boxer shorts. On the kitchen table was a note:

"Hi: Have some stuff to do. See you soon. D."

She was gone. *Work? She's on her way to the office. I should have listened to Sam.*

David Clayton wasn't the only one to receive a mysterious call that evening. When Jack Thompson arrived home, there were two messages on his machine. The first message was from Jack's "ex." Kathleen was a determined woman.

"Jack. You've fallen behind with your support payments. I don't want to call my attorney."

Bullshit. She was antagonizing. You emptied our joint bank account. Now you want my pride. His credit cards were nearly maxed out. Kathleen continued to live in their Maryland home. Apartments in and around Virginia are expensive. Jack rented a one-bedroom apartment at Eaton Square in Alexandria. *It's unfair. I'm thankful for my sobriety. After our assignment on Long Island, I'll be happy to just hang out.*

The second message on his answering machine was from Sam Beverly.

Jack walked into the bedroom. He tossed his sport coat over a chair and placed his overnight bag and briefcase on the bed. Sam's message finished playing.

Yes, Sam. I'll be on time for Monday's meeting. Yes, Sam. I will have my report ready for nine AM sharp. Yes. Yes. Yes. Jack looked around the bedroom. He felt angst. He wanted a drink. Loneliness began to overtake him. He walked to the kitchen. He grabbed a

Coke. He telephoned his sponsor. No answer.

He fell asleep watching television. The phone rang. At first he thought he was dreaming. *Who the hell is calling at this time of night? Damn it.* Jack didn't answer the call. The caller didn't wait to leave a message on the answering machine. The phone rang again. "Oh, hell." He picked up the phone.

"Who is this?"

"My name is Eric Peterson. I regret calling so late, but this is rather urgent business."

"Have we met before, Mr. Peterson? How did you get my phone number?"

"No. We've never met. You'll have to ask my secretary how she acquired your number. She's quite efficient."

"No time for small talk, Mr. Peterson. How can I help you?"

"Perhaps we may be able to help each other, Mr. Thompson. It's late. Would it be possible to meet with me? I promise I will be brief."

"You still haven't explained why you want to meet with me." Jack was growing impatient.

"I represent several international business interests. My employers are anxious to expand their interest in Virginia. This growth requires experienced personnel."

"That leaves me out," said Jack.

"There's a small garden on the left side of the old Smithsonian. Do you know it?"

"No. But I'm sure I can find it," said Jack.

"Sunday morning. Ten o'clock. I'll be sitting on one of the benches in the garden, reading the Sunday New York Times Book Review. Please be on time and come alone. This is very important and beneficial for both of us," said Peterson.

"I don't know…and what if it rains?"

"It will be a very pleasant day, Mr. Thompson."

"Good night, Mr. Peterson."

Jack waited until seven o'clock the next morning before telephoning Sam.

"Sorry to bother you, Sam."

"What's up?"

"I received a late night call from an Eric Peterson. I have no idea how he tracked me down."

"What did Peterson want?"

"He said he represents clients interested in bringing me on board a project."

"That's it?" asked Beverly.

"Not quite. Peterson asked to meet with me tomorrow morning."

"I don't know, Jack. Sounds odd. Why you? Why now?"

"Exactly."

"I'd think about it, Jack. Suppose it's a ploy? Entrapment." Sam paced the kitchen.

"That's why I'm calling you. I don't want to compromise our investigation."

"On the other hand, it might be interesting to find out what Peterson is up to."

"What are you telling me, Sam?"

"Okay. Meet Peterson. But be careful. It's the weekend. My FBI contact won't be in. I'll ask the weekend staff to do a background search."

"No. I'm uncomfortable. Too many coincidences."

"One last thing... Jack paused in mid-sentence. *Not a smart idea over the phone.* "Oh, forget it. I'll speak with you on Monday morning." *How did Peterson get Sam's unlisted telephone number? He probably knows where I live. The Justice Department doesn't.*

Then he realized a grave possibility. *Our calls to Beverly from Long Island. Our home phones. Any of our telephone conversations… someone might be listening?* "The phones are tapped." Jack recalled his meeting with Nagle. Nagle insisted his home telephone was tapped.

"My wife is sure our calls and mail are being monitored," Nagle insisted.

Jack felt an urgency to inform David.

A few hours later, Jack was pulling into the parking lot of David's Manassas apartment complex. Jack took a deep breath and knocked on the apartment door.

"This is a surprise," said David.

Jack held his index finger to his lips, motioning for David to be quiet. Then he motioned for David to step outside.

"What's going on?" asked David.

"I suspect our phones are tapped and perhaps our homes, as well."

"Are you crazy? Why would anyone be so intent on us?" asked David. "Have you told Sam?"

"No. Why tip anyone off? I'll talk with him on Monday."

"You drove here to tell me this?"

"I couldn't call."

"I'd invite you in for coffee, but like you said…we can't talk."

Jack didn't deserve that. I'm tired and angry. Dakota, you are driving me nuts.

"Fine by me. Don't say I didn't give you a heads up." Jack walked back to his car. His next thought was not to wait until Monday to speak with Sam. As Jack headed for Route 28, he changed his mind. He made a U-turn and headed back to Alexandria.

Sam Beverly decided to drive to Sammy T's on Caroline Street in downtown Fredericksburg. Sammy T's was always crowded on Saturday morning, and this was no exception. He waited at the bar for Diane, his favorite waitress, to find him a booth.

"Miss 'B' in the big city again?" Diane was Rachael's classmate at Mary Washington College.

Sam nodded and smiled, but continued to browse the paper. He was trying to forget how lonely he felt, especially on the weekends. Grace hadn't returned home for a month or more. She had called once or twice, but only out of necessity.

"Could you mail my passport? I'll be going to London on business."

"How are you? Will you be coming home soon?"

"Sam, dear…I just told you I'll be in London for a bit. Let's not go through this again. I'll be home when I'm home."

"Mr. B, your booth is ready. Sweet tea and a burger? Maybe some chips?"

"Thanks, Diane. Hold the chips."

And that's how Sam's weekends went; Sammy T's, long walks through town. Tomorrow, he might walk through the Federal cemetery.

Sam Beverly and Jack Thompson were casualties. They'd worked hard, but not smart. The country was going through a social revolution, and they seemed to be left behind by the women they loved. David Clayton, in contrast, was enjoying bachelorhood to its fullest, or so he thought. Finding Dakota in his bed last night was a pleasant surprise. He hoped she'd stay one more night. *I am taking life too seriously. This job doesn't pay enough.* All three men were experiencing changes in their personal lives.

Jack Thompson's alarm clock was set for six a.m., but Jack didn't need it. He'd spent a sleepless night. His mind was scrambled. His thoughts jumped from rumination to expectation. *Why was Kathleen pressuring me for money? She never had in the past. Who was this mysterious Peterson? Should I meet him? Was it a trap?*

Jack slipped into his gym shorts, T-shirt and sneakers. He worked out in the residents' gym, returned to his apartment and poured a cup of coffee.

It was time to meet the mysterious Mr. Peterson. Jack would have to hurry to beat Peterson to the Smithsonian. Jack found the winding path by the main entrance and followed it to a small garden. All three benches were vacant. Not a soul in sight. Jack felt a bit uncomfortable, but sat down on the wooden bench on the far side, next to several rosebushes. The cherry trees were late blooming after the exceptionally cold winter. After a few minutes, a woman walked down the winding path and sat opposite Jack. She smiled and began reading a book. Soon after, a man wearing a trench coat sat down on the third bench. From the pile of papers, he selected the NY Times book review. He held the paper nearly face-high and casually turned left, then right. The woman paid no attention. Jack recognized the signal. The man lowered the paper and walked toward Jack.

"Excuse me," said the man. "I've finished reading my paper. Rather than tossing it, would you like to read it?"

"Yes. Thank you," said Jack. With that, the meeting was initiated.

Peterson introduced himself. Both men spoke in whispers. The woman on the far side of the garden appeared deeply engrossed with her book.

"How can I help you, Mr. Peterson?" asked Jack.

"We may be helping each other, Mr. Thompson. Would you be open to joining our enterprise?"

"How soon would you expect me to start work?" asked Jack.

"My employers suggest September. We would have to begin the transition no later than mid-August."

"Why me? What would I bring to the table?"

"Initially, you would be our liaison with the Department of Justice," said Peterson.

"Are you aware my office is in the Justice Department's basement? I've been there since Nixon resigned."

"Of course. But you aren't now. You are part of a significant inquiry."

"And how do you know that?"

"My staff is very thorough, Mr. Thompson."

"Why would I leave now?"

"My employers are prepared to triple your government salary. There will be other incentives. Would you be willing to consider the offer?"

Jack pressed Peterson. "Liaison with Justice? Seems vague to me."

"I am not at liberty to reveal specifics. Should you decide to accept, you would be working with a group of international investors. I assure you, they are very powerful and influential people with many investments. They are keen on expanding into pharmaceutical research. Such a project requires a considerable effort."

"In other words, you want a base for operations in the United States?"

Peterson's expression changed, as though he were weighing Jack's question. "Not exactly. We…they…need to acquire several manufacturing plants and research facilities. Of course, we also have to gather a competent research team," said Peterson.

"And that's where I fit in?"

"Yes. Over the next year, we will be seeking several pieces of legislation from Congress. We will also need to coordinate efforts with the FDA. Our work will be highly guarded, especially with regard to the research."

"The law is complex; you'll need a team of attorneys. You'll need lobbyists, sympathetic politicians, and more."

"I am not at liberty to elaborate. I hesitate to create a conflict of interest for you, Mr. Thompson. I know you're gathering information on several ongoing research projects."

"I can't confirm that."

"Allow me. The government is conducting classified research. As we speak, the DOA has undertaken several projects of interest to my employers."

Jack looked perplexed. "How do you know this?"

"Biological research into disease prevention can quickly turn into biological warfare experiments."

"That's outlawed by international treaties."

"Nevertheless, the government has been researching a number of potential weapons…anthrax…malaria…West Nile Disease… and others, I'm certain."

"I'm no scientist."

"We know you and your colleagues at the GAO are involved to some extent. Please, no need to confirm or deny it. I'll accept you are unaware the DOA and CDC are under pressure to develop a vaccine for Rift Valley Fever Disease."

"And…?" Jack paused. The woman on the far side of the garden was leaving. *Odd, all this time she's been reading, she only turned a few pages of her book.* The woman was sitting too far away to hear their conversation. She smiled at the two men. Jack returned the smile. She glanced at Peterson. He did not acknowledge her.

"Congratulations, Mr. Thompson. You've gotten more information from me than I intended to share."

"Excellent." Peterson stood. "I will be in touch."

Jack watched Peterson walk to the edge of the garden. He dumped his newspaper into a trash can. Looking back over his shoulder, Peterson smiled and continued walking out of the garden.

Chapter 13

"The boss in?" asked Jack.

"Not yet, Mr. Thompson," said Sam's secretary. "There's coffee."

"Thanks, Lynn. I'll get it." *She's still calling me Mr. Thompson.*

"I'm surprised Sam isn't here already."

"Oh, he is. He's down the hall. Things are becoming very mysterious around here," said Lynn.

Jack didn't respond.

"Mr. Beverly had the typing pool's room vacated. It's moved downstairs."

"What's that about?" asked Jack, as he opened the door and looked down the hall to where the typing pool had been.

"Mr. Beverly laughingly calls it a situation room. Security is being updated. He's the only one with a key and the combination."

Jack's interest was piqued, but he knew better than to pressure Lynn for more information. It would come in time. Jack finished his coffee. The bank of windows behind Lynn's desk offered one of the best views of the Capitol.

Jack was about to refill his coffee cup when David walked in. He was carrying the box of Portavani's records. Koch's briefcase hung from a strap.

"Get a chance to go through anything?" asked Jack.

"Unusual to see you early for a meeting," said David. He avoided Jack's question.

Jack's face tightened with anger. *Kiss my ass.* This wasn't the time or place for a confrontation with Clayton, but it was coming.

Jack Thompson was anxious to meet with Sam and David. He had come to respect both men professionally. Personally, he disliked David Clayton. *He thinks I'm a washed-up drunk. David is flashy, smart…a bit too smart for his own good…and a womanizer.*

Jack's take on Sam was different. Sure, Sam knew all the right people. Sam's career had advanced rapidly, thanks in part to his wife, Grace. Nevertheless, Sam was paying the price for hard work and ambition.

Lynn answered the intercom. "Excuse me. Sam wants you to join him in the situation room. Down the hall on the left, third door," Lynn said.

The newly stenciled letters on the door's opaque glass window read, "Closed Archives." "Archives," said Clayton. "Welcome home, Jack."

"What's that supposed to mean?"

"The Archives…your former home before Sam rescued you." David pressed an electronic buzzer. It took a minute or two before the door was unlocked. Sam greeted the pair.

The two quickly realized why Sam referred to the location as the situation room. Sam's new headquarters consisted of two rooms. They were standing in an outer office with a phone and conference table. David placed the box on the table, and gave the briefcase to Jack. Sam led them into a second larger room. Tacked on the far wall were photographs of people, locations, and things. Above the array Sam posted MKNAOMI.

"Sam, how long did this take you to put together? Don't you sleep?" Jack placed Koch's briefcase on a long table.

David nodded in agreement. He scratched his head and walked closer for a better look. Under each photograph was an anecdotal card. Some were blank; others already had a second card taped to it. "A lot of work went in to piece this together, Sam. And MKNAOMI, what's that about?

"The CIA uses a coding and encryption system. From what I can tell the MK must refer to their technical division."

"Like gadgets and disguises?" Jack placed his pocket comb under his nose.

"Get serious, Jack. What else did you find out? David asked.

"I think we are dealing with some aspect of the Agency's effort with the DOD to experiment with biological weapons."

"And NAOMI?" David looked puzzled.

"I'm guessing it's a cryptonym. In this case a reference to a specific program and location."

"Perhaps it's General Webster's program at Fort Detrick," David added.

"Do you have any proof, Sam?" Jack suddenly turned serious. "I thought President Nixon ordered biological research stopped several years back."

"And to answer your question, I sleep, but not well," said Sam, responding to David's earlier remark. The buzzer sounded. Someone was at the door. Jack turned.

"No. I'll take care of this. The fewer people involved, the better," insisted Sam. All three walked back into the smaller room. Sam motioned for Jack to close the inner office door. Sam looked through a peephole and unlocked the door. A woman attired in a blue skirt, white blouse and jacket walked in.

"Good morning," said Sam

"Gentlemen." The woman acknowledged Sam and the other two with a smile.

Jack did a double take. *I've seen her before. Where?*

"Jack Thompson, David Clayton, this is Special Agent Lou-Ann Stokes, FBI. Of course you remember, Agent Stokes, don't you Jack?" asked Sam with a smile.

"Yesterday…the garden at the Smithsonian," said Jack. "You were sitting on the far side of the garden."

"I'm afraid you've found me out," said Stokes.

"I requested a backup for you, Jack. I felt it best not to tell you. I was concerned for your safety. The Long Island trip was more than we expected. I wanted you to meet Agent Stokes in person."

"Yes. I appreciate your help even if I didn't know about it at the time."

"I suggested Sam not tell you. I didn't want to throw your timing off."

"Pleased to meet you, officially," Jack nodded.

"I asked Agent Stokes to come by this morning simply to meet you, Jack."

"Thank you for coming by, Agent Stokes," said Sam.

Clayton stepped back, taking it all in. "You're the first female field agent I've met," said David.

"I've been in the field for several years, in Milwaukee. I'm stationed in Washington now, working white-collar crime."

"Will you be joining our investigation? It's getting a bit crowded."

Agent Stokes and Sam looked at one another.

"Not at this point, Mr. Clayton. That's about all I can share."

Jack caught the exchange between Stokes and Sam. *Sam's holding out on us.*

"Gentlemen, nice meeting you. I'm off. I have another meeting this morning."

"Lou-Ann, may I have a moment of your time before you leave?"

"Of course, Sam."

"Excuse us one moment." Lou-Ann and Sam walked into the other office.

"She's nice looking, Sam. And did you get her comment, 'On call for Mr. Beverly?'" David winked.

"Let's not go there, David. You've got a dirty mind. I advise you to restrain your prurient drives."

"What kind of drives?"

"I know Sam warned you about Dakota Putnam. Does he know you've disregarded his advice?"

"Not that's it's any of your business, but I planned to meet with Sam. Privately."

"I wouldn't mess with her, David."

Anger flashed across David's face "Mind your business."

Their argument was interrupted as Sam and Lou-Ann walked out of the inner room.

"Thanks again, Agent Stokes." Jack smiled and gave a casual salute as Stokes left.

Sam looked at David and Jack. "Something wrong, men?" Sam sensed they had been bickering again.

They walked back into the larger room. "From now on, this is where we will meet for briefings and strategy. Refer to it as the situation room. Let me show you what I have." Sam walked to the far wall. From now on I'll refer to the inquiry as 'Project Naomi.'"

"So you agree? General Webster is our man?" asked David.

"Almost. Webster's project was MKNAOMI. I suspect there was a spin-off."

"Espionage or sabotage?"

"Be patient, David. Follow me here." Sam pointed to the colored yarn connecting Koch and Webster.

"What's the larger blank card on the top of the flowchart designate?" asked David.

"I'm waiting for you guys to tell me. Koch and Webster weren't acting alone. My guess, a foreign power or even a corporation, is involved."

"Really? How did you come to that conclusion?"

"We checked Webster's credit cards. He owed thousands in Vegas. Someone was paying for his frequent trips to the Bahamas."

"And Koch?" asked David.

"Koch is an enigma. We know he was sending money from here to Germany. There are frequent wire transfers to two Swiss banks. Still, I can't piece it all together. So what did you bring me?"

"We have a box of Portavani's records and a map."

"And the ME's report?"

"I have them. There's something I need to cover. It's bothering me. I suspect our phone lines are tapped. There may be listening devices in our homes, even our offices."

"A federal agency would need a warrant. Even the NSA needs approval," replied Sam. "Tell me more."

"Eric Peterson's call, for one. He knows too much. Nagle insisted his home phone was tapped. Robert is a mystery. I suggest we check for listening devices in our homes."

"I'll call the FBI. I am a bit paranoid about contacting other agencies," said Sam.

"As long as we're straying from the topic, Robert called over the weekend."

"And?"

"He told me to go to the Mayflower Hotel today at noon. He set up a drop."

"I think you should keep to Robert's schedule. Jack and I will go through Portavani's records. Did you complete your summary?"

"Yes," said David.

Jack opened the documents from the medical examiner and handed them to Sam.

"I've gone over them a few times. Koch died from Rift

Valley Fever. Whoever snatched Koch's corpse and personal effects overlooked his briefcase. I found a few random notes and telephone numbers…foreign exchanges. I think Koch was taking something." Jack handed the pieces of note paper to Sam. "Check the times and references to dosage."

"Do you think he was experimenting on himself?" asked Sam.

"Who knows? Koch may have known he was ill. He could have contracted the disease," said David.

"A unique way to get an exotic disease into the country."

"Did you get Webster's autopsy report?" asked David.

"I know he was poisoned. A chemical - Substance 83. We captured it from the Germans. One drop on the skin kills. By the way, the DOD classified the report."

"Anything else about the poison?" asked Jack.

"I did a bit of research." Sam looked through his notebook. "Here it is. Our soldiers found underground factories and storage facilities filled with the shit."

"The Nazis were diabolical." David looked pained.

"The Nazis didn't make it. It was IG Farben's scientists."

"I remember reading something about IG Farben's involvement in chemical and biological research in the Trinity files," Jack added.

"Trinity files?" asked Sam.

"During my exile in the archives at Justice, I came across stacks of boxes marked 'classified', with the designation 'Trinity Files'. I rummaged through a few."

"What did you find?" asked Sam.

"I can't reveal the particulars, but the Department of Justice and the FBI were investigating the connection between Farben and Trinity PharmoDynamics Group. Trinity is an international holding corporation based in the Bahamas."

"Not Trinity PharmoDynamics, USA?" asked Sam in disbelief.

"One and the same. Trinity is part of the Trinity Dynamics Fund, another offshore group. Justice was investigating Trinity's connection to Walther Liechtenauer. Liechtenauer was an associate of Albert Speer's. Liechtenauer spent a brief time in prison for his wartime activities. Received a pardon."

"Where did you get this information, Jack?" asked David.

"When you have nothing to do and all day to do it in…well, the devil got the best of me. That's all I'm saying."

"Where's Liechtenauer now? Is he still alive?" asked Sam.

"Long Island…damn it. He's on Long Island," said David.

Sam looked surprised. "How the hell do you know?"

"I don't. But Trinity's U.S. Headquarters is on the North Shore. The couple who tried to run down Nagle…their car had stolen plates registered to Trinity. Now that's a coincidence," said David.

"Liechtenauer is also chairman of Lansdorf Research in Leipzig. Justice must have been conducting an intensive investigation; suddenly everything was boxed and shipped to the basement. That's all I know," said Jack.

"Who else knows you were snooping around?" asked Sam.

"No one."

"If Eric Peterson knows, others know, too."

Sam tacked new cards to the wall: Trinity PharmoDynamics Group and Trinity PharmoDynamics, USA, Eric Peterson, and Walther Liechtenauer.

It was after eleven AM when David left for the Mayflower Hotel.

When David left, Sam turned to Jack. "We have to talk."

"Isn't that what we've been doing?"

"I'm serious. I didn't want to discuss this in front of David."

"Okay." Jack looked perplexed.

"I'm concerned for your safety."

"My safety?" asked Jack.

"First, we have the incident with Nagle on Long Island. Then your sister's home was broken into. And now, a mysterious Mr. Peterson invites you to join a nameless investment group. Why, Jack?"

"It's a mystery to me. Perhaps the so-called investors are looking for inside information related to our investigation," said Jack. "There's something else. Out of the clear blue sky, my ex-wife is pressuring me for money."

"Blackmail. Maybe you're being led into a trap. Perhaps someone wants you to sell information."

"Why me?"

"Several days after I was placed in charge of this inquiry, I received a memo from the Inspector General and initialed by the Attorney General."

"What about it?"

"Simply put, you were being assigned to the task force. I didn't pick you. I vaguely remembered your name from the Watergate debacle."

"Actually, it did seem a bit strange. Suddenly, I had a real office and title. I didn't know who to thank."

"'Thank' is the wrong word. I don't believe in coincidences. I have no idea who selected you, but one thing is clear. That person figured you were washed up. I knew you were winding up an awful divorce. You were broke. And, you're a recovering alcoholic."

"Did you share this information with Clayton?"

"No."

"So someone thinks I'm a useless bag of shit. Right?" Jack tensed.

"Go easy on yourself. Whoever made that decision forgot what got you in trouble in the first place."

"And what was that?" asked Jack.

"Once you get your claws into something you can't let go. When you think you're right, there's no stopping you."

"When I first met you and David, I didn't give a damn about this investigation. As we started putting the pieces together, my imagination ran wild. Our government sent a task force to Europe to save paintings, statues, and buildings. We sent another invisible team to round up Nazis, not for punishment, but to come to work for us. It's 1977 and we still have them on our payroll. But what the hell are they doing?"

"That's what we need to discover, Jack. But I'm afraid it's going to be dangerous work from now on."

"Let's not discuss this with David."

"That's your call, Jack. Watch your back."

"Who's gonna start my car in the morning"? Jack asked, only half-kidding.

"I'll have a security detail check your apartment."

"Have them sweep my apartment for listening devices. I'm not paranoid. Someone is watching our every move."

"Let's get out of here," said Sam. "I'll meet you in my office at two. We'll spend time going through Portavani's files."

Jack nodded in agreement, but said nothing. *Why is Sam so concerned for my safety?* Jack watched Sam double-check the alarm and lock the outer office door, as though an invisible force was watching.

Chapter 14

The sun was breaking through an overcast sky as David left the GAO building. Three months ago, folks were skating along the Potomac. Today was a perfect opportunity to catch some rays. By car, the ride takes about ten minutes. Walking, the slightly over a mile distance would take Robert thirty minutes. He had plenty of time. He decided to walk from the GAO. Placing his car keys back in his London Fog raincoat pocket, David tossed it over his shoulder. He walked west along G Street. Robert told David to arrive at the hotel precisely at noon. The walk provided an opportunity to clear his head before the two o'clock meeting with Sam and Jack. *The meeting is bound to go on into the late evening.* As David turned on to K Street, he thought he caught a glimpse of two men he had noticed a few minutes ago on Sixth Street. He stopped and looked at his reflection in a shop window. Turning and looking directly down the street, he saw the two. They stopped and the taller of the two headed across K Street in the opposite direction. *I'm imagining things.* David took a deep breath.

David arrived at the Mayflower Hotel exactly at noon. He checked his raincoat and briefcase and followed the receptionist to a table near the bar. She nodded to a waiter.

"Would you care for a cocktail while you're deciding on your order?" the waiter asked.

"Yes, please. I'll have sparkling water with a twist of lemon."

"Yes sir."

"One last thing…where are the restrooms?"

The waiter pointed to the far exit. "Just through the far doorway. The first floor restrooms are being remodeled. There's a sign directing you to either the main lobby or the mezzanine."

David surveyed his surroundings. *I agree with Robert. The place has lost some of its charm.* The service was slow. The restaurant was nearly empty, with the exception of a man at the bar and a couple sitting at a table on the far side of the room. David watched the couple. He pretended to read the menu. *Honeymooners? Cheaters? They aren't interested in me. Perhaps the man at the bar? No. I must remain vigilant. Robert's last call sounded an alarm.*

The waiter returned with David's drink.

"May I take your order?"

"Everything looks good," said David.

"May I suggest the scallops? They aren't on today's menu. They just arrived this morning. Chef has a delightful garnish."

"Yes, the scallops."

"Very nice. They come with asparagus and rice. Perhaps a salad."

"Yes. Fine."

David whispered to the waiter, "I'll be right back."

"Of course, sir."

The doorway on the far side of the room opened onto a hallway. There was David's first cue. "Main Restrooms Closed. Please Use Lobby Restrooms". The lobby was deserted. David was cautious. It was time for another deep breath. *Here goes.*

A service closet was at the far end of the hallway leading to the closed restrooms. As Robert promised, it was unlocked. On the top shelf behind an assortment of cleansers and paper towels, he found a brown envelope. David reached high, almost on his toes, and removed the cans of cleansers. He grabbed the envelope. *Now for the tricky part.*

Holding the precious envelope in his left hand, David used his right to unbutton his suit jacket and reach behind his back. He quickly exchanged the empty envelope for Robert's packet. *Just in case someone was aware of Robert's packet.* David tucked the retrieved envelope into his waistband. He straightened his suit jacket and returned to his table. *Well done, David. All in a few minutes and without a hitch.*

David tried to be as casual as possible. The waiter returned with his scallops. *I've lost my appetite.* He managed to eat most of his meal. He paid the bill, retrieved his raincoat and briefcase, and walked into the main lobby. *So far, so good. My imagination may have gotten the best of me.* He felt relaxed. *Mission accomplished.* He left the hotel.

"Taxi, sir?" asked the doorman.

"Yes, please." It was a short ride by cab to the GAO.

The doorman signaled for a cab. It pulled forward. Just as David was about to step to the curb, he turned to tip the doorman. From the corner of his eye, David saw a short pudgy man rush forward. There was little David could do. The assailant shoved David into the path of the cab.

"Hey, you! I'll take those," he growled. In one swoop he snatched the briefcase and yanked the raincoat from under David's arm.

David flew sideways, landing on his left hand and knee. The spill hurt. David's trousers were torn. His hand was scraped and bleeding. Two or three people rushed to assist him.

"Holy shit." *That guy just stole my raincoat and briefcase.*

"Hey, stop," shouted the doorman. The culprit darted down the sidewalk to a waiting car. The sedan pulled into traffic and sped down Connecticut Avenue.

"You're lucky, man. That guy was trying to kill you," said one of the excited bystanders. Several others helped David to the sidewalk.

A woman consoled David. "I tried to get the license plate numbers, but they were just too quick."

"What the hell was that all about?" David asked aloud. "Did anyone see where he went?"

"Yes, sir," said the doorman. "He took off in a black sedan. It all happened so quickly. Please, let's go inside. I'll call hotel security."

"No need for security," David responded. "I need to clean up."

It took about twenty minutes to wash his hands and apply gauze and tape to his left wrist. *I could have been killed.*

It was after two when David arrived back at Sam's office. A golf ball-sized lump on his forehead ached. *I don't remember hitting my head. God, it aches.*

"What the hell happened to you, David?" asked Sam.

"Yes, David. Looks like you were hit by a bus." Jack couldn't restrain his sarcasm.

"You're a real jerk, Jack. No, it wasn't a bus. A taxi almost got me. I don't understand how it didn't."

David related his lunchtime experience. *My head throbs.*

Lynn brought David an ice pack and two aspirins.

"Did you find the drop?" asked Sam.

"Isn't anyone concerned about me being nearly run over?" David reached behind his back and pulled out the envelope. "Here's the damn package." Then David realized, "Sam, damn it. The son of a bitch who pushed me took my raincoat and briefcase."

"The perp must have known about the dead drop. Probably thought you had something of value in your briefcase or raincoat," Sam speculated.

"Any important papers in your briefcase?" Jack inquired.

"No."

"It was a great decoy. The guy probably figured if you had something important, that's where you'd put it."

At that moment David gasped, "My keys! Car keys…my apartment key. They were on the same ring. Oh, no…"

"What?" asked Sam. "And your ID?" Sam dreaded David's response.

David nodded. "He's got my ID pass for the parking garage."

"Now you're screwed. I wouldn't want to be in your shoes when you request another ID." Jack appeared eager to predict the worst.

"How do you plan to get home?"

At that point, Sam waved his hand. "Knock it off," he ordered. "I'm tired of your antics, Jack. Let's get to work on the dead drop material and Portavani's records."

"Let's stop our wrangling," David said.

"David's right," Sam agreed.

The trio returned to the matters at hand. Sam opened what appeared to be a closet door, revealing a huge steel door.

"Nice. Fort Knox?" Jack said.

"No. But close to it. This safe requires a key and combination to unlock. I'm the only one with access. Not that I don't trust you two. It's simply a matter of security."

"Fine by me," said Jack.

David didn't seem to care, either.

Sam sat down with Jack and David on either side. He opened the dead drop envelope and began placing its contents on the table. The first three pages were reports from a file marked "Operation Paperclip."

"I seem to recall that title. Where did I read about "Operation Paperclip?" asked David.

"It's before your time, buddy." Jack answered. "Refresh the young man, Sam."

"That's my intention, Jack. I might as well do it now." Sam walked to the safe and unlocked it. He returned with a folder. Inside were a number of files. He pulled out the file marked "Operation Paperclip". There were a number of documents, but with so many heavy dark lines covering the contents, it was difficult to read.

"Did you know the U.S. Army formed a team of art specialists to be part of the Normandy invasion? They were supposed to locate stashes of paintings and other art works the Nazis took from Jews and other victims."

"I recall something about it. They had to find the artifacts before the Germans could hide or destroy them," said Jack. "There were millions in precious metals, too."

"Operation Paperclip was part of a subsequent parallel program. The military was determined to get their hands on Nazi scientists before they went into hiding or the Russians got to them first. The British and French wanted them, also," Sam continued.

"That's old news," said Jack. "As I recall, the papers were filled with revelations about Werner von Braun, the Nazi rocket scientist."

"Now I remember. We sent a number of scientists back to Germany when it was discovered they lied about war crimes," said David.

"Not exactly. First, some didn't lie. They were never directly questioned. We wanted their skills. It was the cold war. Our government brought them here. Put them up in hotels, and new homes. In some cases we brought the entire family. No questions asked," Sam confirmed.

"Von Braun was a brilliant scientist. He helped launch America's space program," said Jack.

"Von Braun and his henchmen were responsible for countless deaths and destruction in England," Sam replied.

"During the war, those rockets were being assembled by slave laborers. They were worked to death or killed as examples for others to work harder," said Jack.

"I'm putting you on notice. These documents are classified. We can't even admit to their existence," Sam warned. "These documents must never leave this room." He pulled the third page from the pile of nearly fifty documents. All the pages were 'sanitized' with heavy black lines. Sam placed the paper on the table for David and Jack to read. "It's clear our government was involved in a biological research project so complex that very few individuals could piece it together," Sam asserted.

"According to this report, the project was a joint effort…the military, civilian government agencies, and a number of U.S. corporations were under investigation," said Jack.

David paused, scratched his head and said, "This lists a number of big financial institutions and prominent U.S. citizens. I'm troubled. It's out of context. I doubt leading Americans were tied in with IG Farben right up until we entered the war."

"The same names reappear on the following page. Look!" David's hand trembled.

"This stuff is top secret. We must never tell anyone we know of their existence," Sam warned again. "If you think your Long Island fiasco was dangerous, you ain't seen nothin' yet. It could cost you your lives."

"Could this be an original file copy?" David held the paper to the light.

"These documents aren't supposed to be released until the nineties. For the last time - forget you ever read them. Understand?"

Jack and David looked at one another. "Agreed."

"This list would outrage Congress, especially Congresswoman Harrington and the Oversight Committee," said David.

"Outraged? Who? Something tells me the average American has too much to worry about. We're still licking our wounds from Vietnam. There will be no outrage."

"I agree, David. I can't imagine Elizabeth Harrington doesn't know. How did the GAO get assigned this task? Congresswoman

Harrington. It doesn't matter. It's clear to me the GAO investigation is Congresswoman Harrington's strategy for bringing these documents to light," said Jack.

"There's more to it. A number of government agencies were involved," Sam added. "These files demonstrate where and how IG Farben's top scientists were recruited. The same ones involved with Dachau and Auschwitz."

"So the original testimony from the Justice Department and the other agencies was bogus?" asked David.

"Here it is. These documents substantiate IG Farben worked hand in hand with the Nazis. They used slave labor. The Nazis SS got paid for human guinea pigs," said Jack.

"Never. Our government would never do that. Not in a million years," David argued.

"I know it's hard to believe we picked up where the Nazis left off," Jack added.

"If these files are legit, President Truman was definitely misled. In some cases, the Immigration and Naturalization Service cooperated. On numerous occasions, the State Department went right around the INS. Several of Truman's closest associates came under suspicion for being too soft on the Nazis," Sam conceded.

"Let's be fair. Put this thing in perspective. No sooner did the war in Europe end when the Cold War was thrust upon us. Our government had to act fast or the Russians would snatch all the scientists. We know they dismantled factories in occupied territories and shipped them deep inside Russia," said Jack.

"The military shipped rockets to the U.S., along with the components to make and launch them," Sam reminded David.

"Be realistic," said Jack. "We were still waging a horrific battle in the Pacific. An invasion of Japan offered hundreds of thousands of American casualties. The Japanese would fight us relentlessly. We needed Nazi research… the 'ultimate weapon'. Truman said he never lost a night's sleep about dropping the bombs on Japan. Too many American lives were at stake."

"Biological research gives me the creeps. Who's going to believe any of this?" asked David.

"No one is going to know, at least not from us. Truman and Eisenhower both wanted Nazi war criminals rounded up and sent back to Germany for trial," said Sam.

"According to you, Sam, we can't inform Congress about these documents without breaking the law," Jack added.

Sam walked to the large wallboard. General Mark Webster's name was printed in bold letters. "Webster's job was to keep all the pieces together. Make sure there were no conflicts. I'm convinced Webster was supplying information to someone. He knew every aspect of the secret project, including MK-NAOMI."

"Just suppose Webster was working for…and I'm only speculating…a corporation and not a foreign country."

"Go on, I'm listening," said Sam.

"Eric Peterson told me his employers were interested in independent laboratories."

"And?"

"Perhaps General Webster had outlived his usefulness. The so-called investors had what they wanted. It was time to cut any ties to Webster."

"You may be on to something, Jack," David agreed. "Webster had gambling debts. He may have become a liability."

"In what way?" asked Jack.

"Imagine one of IG Farben's spin-offs wants to rehabilitate themselves so they can move into the States. Once they have what they need, then it's imperative they cut their ties to the past."

"The kid may have something, Sam"

"Okay, David. You continue to follow up on your theory."

Next, David removed the remaining documents from the envelope.

This is Koch's dossier." David began to read the report. "Not much to it. Wait a minute…what's this? Look at this last entry."

There, on the bottom of Koch's file, was an authorization for Koch to deal with a liaison research team from Trinity PharmoDynamics, USA.

"Trinity?" Jack asked. Webster had initialed the authorization.

"That's it! Our military and corporate connection," said David.

"The pieces are falling into place. Webster and Koch are dead. Nagle was nearly killed. My sister's home was broken into. Over the weekend I receive an attractive job offer. Today, David was nearly killed. No shit."

Sam said it first, but the others agreed. "Someone is trying to shut down our investigation."

David walked to the board. He tacked a new card directly in the center.

"Trinity. Trinity is behind this. Trinity has a need for Project Naomi's research," Sam insisted.

"What research were Koch and the rest of them doing?" asked David.

"You said it before. Biological research: germs…disease. Disease prevention can easily be turned into biological warfare's offensive weapons. During the '60's, the papers covered chemical warfare and several accidents. We have so much of that stuff, it would take years to dispose of it." Jack pointed out. "It's imperative we discover what Trinity's intention."

"How? Putting Jack inside Trinity is too obvious," said David.

"We'll come up with something," Sam assured them.

Sam was tired, and he sensed David and Jack were, too.

"David, I'm not sleeping here tonight; I'll drive you to Manassas. I'm exhausted and I'll bet you guys are, too.

"You're a lifesaver, Sam. I appreciate the ride."

"You got it, David. Just wish the traffic along Route 66 wasn't so backed up. I hate stop and go."

It was the usual stop and go traffic along Route 66.

"I've heard nothing but bits and pieces regarding the Long Island episode. I'll go through the reports tonight."

"It was a fiasco. It was a bit scary, Sam. One thing right after another. I'm still troubled about the incident involving Jack's sister."

Chapter 15

Prior to leaving Washington, David called the apartment superintendent. David was in luck. "It's a long story, Bob. I've lost my keys. I'm leaving work now."

"Sure thing, Mr. Clayton, I'll have a key waiting." Bob Fellows, the building super, was a jack-of-all-trades. Fellows led an active life and rarely answered the phone after five o'clock.

"I'll be home after seven. Be sure to ring the doorbell a few times, just in case I have the TV on."

About five miles outside of Manassas, a three-car accident had traffic narrowed to one lane. It was after eight p.m. when they pulled into Building C's parking lot.

David waited in front of Bob Fellows' apartment for several minutes, but Bob never came to the door.

"The superintendent isn't home."

"I guess we'll have to wait."

Finally, David spotted Bob Fellows walking towards their car. Fellows waved.

"Thanks, Sam. Why don't you leave? I know you're beat."

"Sorry for making you wait, Mr. Clayton. Around here, I'm the sales agent, the super and now I'm turning into the security guard, as well."

"I understand, Bob. I wouldn't want your job."

"You sounded pretty down when you called."

"It was a crazy day. All I want is some shut-eye."

"Me, too."

"This might interest you. The reason I wasn't home, I got a call from a tenant in your complex."

"What was wrong?" asked David.

"The tenant saw two men walking around the complex, like they were casing the place."

"Casing the place? Sounds suspicious. Did the tenant call the police?"

"Some folks are funny when it comes to calling the cops. They call me first. Then it becomes my problem."

"I walked the entire complex…found nobody walking around, but I saw two guys in a car. They spent a few minutes sitting outside your building. Then they drove away."

Sam overheard their conversation. He got out of the car and joined the two men.

"Did the tenant give you a description?" Sam was curious. Bob shook his head.

Sam and David looked at each other. The superintendent handed David the duplicate key.

David thanked Bob. "We'll take a quick look for ourselves."

Sam motioned for David to get back into the car.

They circled the entire four-building complex, but found nothing.

"No news is good news," Sam made a feeble attempt to downplay the superintendent's concern. "Nevertheless, it may have been the same pair that attacked you outside the Mayflower."

"It was probably nothing. Thanks for the ride. Hit the road. You still have a drive to Fredericksburg."

Sam agreed. "Be cautious."

He waited until David climbed the outside staircase to his second floor apartment. Once David was inside, Sam left.

Since Grace returned to Manhattan, Sam's life had changed. Sam entered the house through the garage Sam remembered the mail. *It can wait. I just want to get a snack and go to bed.* Sam opened the refrigerator. An odor reminiscent of a dead animal rushed out. *I've got to clean this thing. The Chinese takeout was a week old.* Sam gagged. A bottle of Grey Goose lay on the bottom shelf. Sam grabbed it. He walked to the counter and poured a few ounces of vodka into a tumbler and swallowed.

What's happening to me? I'm turning into an alcoholic. Can't sleep.

A jar of peanut butter and a box of saltines sat on the kitchen table from this morning's breakfast. Sam's last meal. Just as he sat down, the phone rang.

Damn phones. Who the hell would be calling now? He walked to the wall phone.

"Hello," he said. No response. Sam sipped the last drop of vodka in the tumbler.

"Hello," he said again.

"Look in your mailbox. I will call back tomorrow night," said the voice on the other end. The line went dead.

Oddly enough, on his drive home Sam had been thinking about the sequence of events since his team started their inquiry. David had been the first to receive mysterious calls. Then Jack was offered a position with a yet-to-be disclosed corporation. Sam felt certain that David's caller and the attorney seemed to be coming from different angles.

Robert, David's source, appeared to want the Nazi scientists exposed. Sam wasn't quite sure about Eric Peterson. *Why would an international investment venture be interested in Jack? Peterson was looking to buy an insider, someone who would feed the so-called investors information.* Sam pondered the events to the point of rumination. Then a thought struck home. *This is more than a hunt for three Nazi scientists. Operation Paperclip was old news back in the '60's. There was little or no interest in Nazi hunting. No; there had to be more. They had stumbled on to something of significance, but what is it?*

Sam hesitated for a moment. He walked through the foyer and opened the front door. Along with the mail, a large brown envelope was stuffed into the mailbox. No stamps. No address. Sam's hands began to shake. He took the mail and envelope back inside. He tossed the mail on the kitchen table. *What have I gotten myself into?* Sam took a kitchen knife and carefully slit open the envelope and removed its contents. There were five photographs. Sam's face flushed with shock.

The photos showed two naked women having sex. Not just two women. It was Sam's wife, Grace, and Vikki Ambrose, Grace's so-called best friend. The five photos were sequenced. The first photo showed the two on a bed. Each shot a bit more explicit. The fifth shot revealed the couple on the carpet. Sam crumpled the photo and tossed it on the floor. He picked up the empty tumbler and threw it across the room. It hit the far wall and smashed on the tile floor. "No!" he sobbed. The sobs turned into a moaning chant. "Why, God? Why?"

There was no mistaking the two women. It was Grace and Vikki. Sam recognized the location from the first shot. *It's the bedroom of our Manhattan apartment. Has it been going on all these years since college? How did the caller get hold of these photographs? This is insane. I'm losing my mind. It can't be. Why Grace? Who sent these? Why?*

Someone had dug deeply into Sam's past and discovered Grace and Vikki had been in a relationship since they were roommates in college. It was true. When Grace announced she was going to marry Sam, Vikki raged with jealousy and anger. She felt betrayed. Grace tried to reassure Vikki their relationship would continue. Grace still loved Vikki. Six months passed. Vikki's torment grew. Within days after Grace's wedding, Vikki moved to San Francisco. Sam never understood the suddenness or the reason for Vikki's departure. Several years later, Vikki wrote to Grace. Vikki had met Tom Ambrose, an Army Officer stationed at the Presidio. They were getting married. Another year went by. Grace and Sam flew to San Francisco for a vacation. Grace convinced Vikki to return to New York. Tom left the Army and completed his master's degree. He found a position teaching on Long Island. Grace's dad helped Vikki secure a position with a Long Island daily.

As the years passed, Tom and Vikki Ambrose became the closest friends of the Beverlys. Both women gave birth to girls. Soon, the families were going on camping trips and vacations together. They practically raised their families together.

Near collapse, Sam sat at the kitchen table and rested his head in his cupped hands. *What should I do now? Should I warn Grace? No. What will I say?* Over and over, these thoughts ran through his mind. Finally, he called Grace in Manhattan.

"Hello," said the voice, awakened from a wine-induced sleep.

"Grace, it's Sam. We have to talk. No. We have to meet."

"Meet? Why?"

"I got an anonymous phone call."

"When?" Grace sounded troubled, almost desperate. Her

breathing a bit labored.

"About thirty minutes ago. I'm upset. Please stop the questions."

"Anonymous? Was it a man? A woman?"

Grace's questions and tone stoked Sam's anger. "It sounded like a man. He told me to check my mailbox. There were five…" Sam paused. His mind began to race again. Perhaps the vodka was kicking in. *Did Grace anticipate my call? Grace knows already. Why didn't she call me? Wasn't she concerned how Rachael might react? Of course not. Grace. Grace. Grace. It's all about Grace. What a bitch. And I'm a jerk.*

"Five what, Sam?" Grace interrupted. "Let me guess. There were five photographs of Vikki and me getting it on. Is that why you're calling? Of course it is."

"Yes, but there's more," said Sam.

"More? What more could there be at this hour?"

"Are you alone right now?"

"Yes."

"Have you been drinking? You sound like you're drunk."

"Get to the point, Sam. I've had an awful evening."

"The photos…"

"Yes. If we're talking about the same photos, I've seen them."

"Grace, please. We have to talk."

"Not tonight, Sam."

"Stop. For once, will you let me talk? Your phone is probably tapped. Someone may be listening."

"Brilliant, Sam. Just brilliant. Some criminal has access to our apartment. He manages to hide a camera in my bedroom. He sent copies to you and Tom Ambrose."

"Tom has them? All five?"

"There are only four and Vikki has them. Tom ripped one to shreds during his confrontation with Vikki. He demanded she leave or he would show the photos to April."

"No. Show them to his daughter? What good would that do?"

"Shit. You don't think this guy would send photos to Rachael?"

"Who knows? Whoever is behind this is ruthless and wants to hurt us.

"Where are the photos Tom got?"

"Vikki. She came here. That's how I saw them. She has them."

"Where is Vikki?"

"I have no idea. We had an argument about what we should do."

"And?"

"Vikki left. I got drunk on Pinot Grigio. Unusual taste. No one is sorrier about the photos than me. You and Tom are so stupid. You didn't have a clue about us. Vikki said Tom raged. He broke the kitchen chair. She threatened to call the police."

"And what would she tell the cops? Oh, I know…my husband has gone apeshit over pictures of me and my best friend having sex? Yeah, sure."

"Get real, Sam. Those photos are setting us up for something… maybe extortion. Tom, Vikki, you and me are beyond embarrassment. What other motive could there be?"

"The photographs. This guy or whoever, he's not after you and Vikki. He's after me. Why did it have to come to this?"

Grace grew silent.

"Are you still there?"

"Yes. It's way too complicated. It would take a lifetime to explain."

"Grace, don't hang up. Listen to me. There's bound to be more than one camera in the apartment. Get out of there. Go to a hotel. Don't call me back. Wait until the morning. Then call me at work. I'll arrange for an electronic sweep tomorrow."

"Good night, Sam." Grace dropped the receiver on the carpet and rolled into a fetal position.

"Grace. Get out of there. Grace."

It was useless. Grace had fallen asleep. The opened bottle of wine she had taken from the refrigerator was spiked. The intruder had no intention of murdering Grace. His employers wanted to send a simple message to Sam: "You are vulnerable."

The apartment on the sixth floor of Grace's building had been leased about a month ago. The tenant was completing major alterations to the bathroom. Grace was annoyed by the intrusive noise at dinnertime, when the board regulations specifically state work would conclude each week day at 6:00 PM. Only emergency work could be completed on weekends. Grace experienced such a weekend the third or fourth day renovations began on apartment

602. During Sunday brunch with Vikki, Grace received a call from the building superintendent. The hot water pipe in 602's master bath burst. The bathroom floor was flooded.

"Isn't that bath directly over your master bedroom?" the superintendent asked.

"Of course it is. You know that. Get up here now," Grace yelled into the phone. With that, Grace and Vikki ran to the master bedroom and hurriedly gathered pictures on the nightstands and dressing table. They quickly returned to pull off the bedspread and blankets. Water was dripping from the light hanging over the foot of the bed. The drip increased to a stream. The plaster could no longer hold the weight of the accumulated water trapped in the ceiling. As the ceiling collapsed, the fixture sparked and the circuit breaker switched off. The bedroom was in ruins.

Within hours, the landlord and a fire and restoration team were on the job working to clean the mess and repair the damage. The tenant in 602 was apologetic to the point where flowers arrived the next day. It took about a week before Grace could return to the master bedroom.

A few nights later, Vikki asked, "Have you met the upstairs tenant?"

"No. Not yet. I think it's a man. Anyway, he certainly is conscientious. All the construction is done while I'm at work. The place is neat as a pin. Never any mess. And, according to the superintendent, he's covering the entire bill. No need to notify the insurance company."

Vikki shrugged and smiled. "Nice. I feel reassured a rival isn't lurking in Apartment 602."

Grace simply let the remark pass. "I'm happy to have the apartment cleaned up so quickly."

Apartment 602's two occupants were very quiet. A stubby man sat at one end of a long folding table. He wore earphones and pressed the left earpiece to his head. He needed to be sure Grace had fallen asleep. There wasn't a sound. The cameras in the master bedroom and bath were working. There hadn't been any activity since the two women argued hours ago. They were both stationary cameras, but the bedroom camera looked directly down at an angle to see that Grace was on the bed. The wine and dissolved lorazepam had taken effect. She appeared to be dead out.

Several minutes passed. Then the stubby man and his tall male companion unlocked the door to apartment 502 and entered. The tall man was Ansgar. He closed the door. Both men slipped paper booties over their shoes. They wore surgical gloves. Neither spoke. They communicated by simple hand signals. Each knew his assigned task. The stubby man entered the master bedroom and walked to Grace's side. Grace never moved. Her breathing was shallow and labored.

Not to worry, Mrs. Beverly. You'll be all right. You'll have an awful headache in the morning or whenever you wake up. The stubby man signaled to Ansgar to enter the bedroom. He had two listening devices to remove, along with the stationary cameras. Then they sanitized the rest of the apartment. The stubby man had listened to Sam Beverly's warning to Grace that the apartment was bugged. The operation needed to be closed down, leaving no telltale clues. Any nicks or splinters could easily be attributed to sloppy work by the water damage crew.

Ansgar took pride in his ability to complete a mission. This one took only a few minutes and they were gone. As they returned to apartment 602, the stubby man finally spoke. Neither Ansgar nor the stubby man remembered the wine bottle on the carpet floor near Grace's fingertips.

"Mrs. Beverly was hardly breathing. I hope I didn't give her too much diasepam."

"I hope so, too," replied Ansgar. He focused on the stubby man and said, "You were cautioned not to kill her."

By 6:00 AM, apartment 602 was thoroughly sanitized. The two men left through the basement service door.

Chapter 16

Sam wandered the house until 2:00 AM. He fell asleep on the living room couch. The vodka induced a restless sleep. The shadows below his eyes revealed the story. The extra-long shower didn't help. Sam dressed and drove to work. *The Beverlys were in deep shit with more to come. From what direction? I'm missing something.*

"Morning, Sam. Coffee's up."

"Thanks, Lynn. I've got an awful headache," Sam said as he rummaged through a mounting pile of correspondence overflowing the "in" basket.

"Sam, if you feel the way you look, your headache must be a doozy."

"Do I look that bad?"

"It looks like you haven't slept in days." Lynn handed Sam his coffee mug.

Lynn Stahl worked at the GAO before Sam came on board. After graduating from a business program, her father, a Post Office employee at the Capitol, encouraged her to take a government job.

"You won't earn much, but you'll get a good retirement if you stick it out," he told her.

Lynn took her father's advice. She accepted a stenographer's position at GAO, eventually working as Sam's secretary. Sam Beverly was different than the other lawyers and accounts she encountered. Lynn admired Sam Beverly, more than she wanted to admit, even to herself. Sam had earned a reputation for honesty and determination. *Sam has his quirks. But don't we all have our eccentricities?* Lynn felt a sense of devotion. Lynn knew enough about her boss's habits to know he wasn't tied to the atmosphere of tacit Washington corruption.

"I'm not sure I can stomach black coffee," Sam said.

"Truthfully, Sam, you look a bit green about the gills. Black is what we got. By the way, Agent Stokes is waiting for you."

"Where?"

"In your office. She's all business this morning. No small talk."

As Sam walked into his office, he found Lou-Ann Stokes standing at the window behind his desk.

"Nice view, Sam."

Sam closed the office door and walked to the window.

"Lynn doesn't know you're helping me on the case," said Sam.

"Are you kidding yourself, Sam? I've seen the way Miss Stahl looks at you. She has a crush on you."

Sam blushed. Lou-Ann liked that quality in a man.

Agent Stokes was Sam's confidential informant at the Washington Bureau. She had access to files Sam wanted.

"I'm in a lot of trouble…well, not me, exactly, but it's bound to blow back on me, and maybe my team and our investigation."

"What's wrong?"

Sam felt himself becoming anxious as he told Lou-Ann about the incident at the Mayflower Hotel. He sat on the edge of his desk.

"You don't look well, Sam. What is it?"

"Last night I received a package of photographs…quite graphic. I'll show them to you when I'm up to it. I called Grace in Manhattan. She had already seen the photos."

"And?"

"I am…well…she has a lover, named Vikki. We've known Vikki and her husband for years."

"Where were the photos taken?" Lou-Ann asked. Just then Lynn knocked at the door.

"Sam. Could I speak with you a moment?" Lynn began to sob. "I have Agent Farrago calling from New York City. He says he's with the Manhattan Task Force. You requested an electronic sweep of your apartment."

"Thanks, Lynn. Hello. This is Sam Beverly."

"Mr. Beverly. This is Special Agent Dennis Farrago."

"Have you been to our apartment already?"

"Well…yes, sir. We arrived a few minutes ago. Mr. Beverly, we need you to come to New York as soon as possible."

Sam tensed. "What's wrong?"

"It's your wife, Mr. Beverly. I called the paramedics as soon as we found her."

"Paramedics?"

"Mr. Beverly, I'm sorry. There was nothing they could do. Mrs. Beverly must have died during the night. A forensics team is on the way. We had to inform NYPD. We need you here."

Sam swayed. Luckily, Lynn was standing next to him as he dropped into a chair.

"I'll get there as soon as I can. I'll call the task force number when I arrive." Sam struggled to get the words out.

"Now what?" Sam said, looking up at Lynn. "What am I going to do?"

At that point, Lou-Ann Stokes walked into the main office. In between sobs, Lynn was trying to comfort Sam, but to no avail. Lynn looked up at Lou-Ann. "Mrs. Beverly died last night."

While Lynn telephoned Mary Washington College to contact Rachael, Lou-Ann helped Sam walk back into his private office. "Let's stay in here until you can catch your breath. No sense having to speak with anyone else."

Lynn walked into Sam's office. "Sam, Rachael is on an overnight field trip. I called the Vice President's office. They'll try to get a message for her to call you, but they don't expect the students until late afternoon tomorrow."

"Thanks. If Rachael calls, please tell her I'm on my way to New York City. I'll call her dormitory room tomorrow. Did you explain the circumstances to the school?"

"No. I told them it was urgent Rachael wait in the dorm until you speak with her."

"Thank you, Lynn."

"Sam, I'm driving you home. You can pack some clothes."

"There isn't enough time. I have a few things at the Manhattan apartment."

"At least allow me to take you to the airport. There's a commuter flight around two this afternoon. I've taken it," said Lou-Ann. "I'll ask Lynn to book a flight."

The drive from the GAO building to Washington National Airport usually takes about 30 minutes. Just before the junction of Route 395 and Maine Avenue, the traffic came to a halt. Sam was lost deep in his sorrow.

"Sam, is there anything I can do here while you're in Manhattan?" Lou-Ann's question drew him back to the investigation.

"You've done enough. You've already put your job in jeopardy by helping me with Thompson's predicament."

"Nonsense," said Lou-Ann.

"Yes. This fellow, Eric Peterson, what do we know about him?"

"That's what brought me to your office this morning," she replied.

"I sensed something was up. You and Lynn are great. I appreciate your help."

Lou-Ann skipped over Sam's remark as though dodging an oncoming truck. "Moving on; I have a lead on Eric Peterson. His real name is Hermann von Leer, an Austrian national. He's a registered lobbyist for Trinity PharmoDynamics, USA. Trinity is part of an international operation with U.S. headquarters on the North Shore of Long Island. I looked into the files. Von Leer has connections to an international company in Leipzig. It was banned from the United States. It was too closely tied to IG Farben, the German chemical conglomerate. Farben and the Nazis collaborated on numerous projects, including Auschwitz. Von Leer has been working with several public relations firms in Maryland. His tracks lead back to Trinity PharmoDynamics' group's headquarters in the Bahamas."

"Where is all this taking us, Lou-Ann?" asked Sam.

"My guess? Trinity PharmoDynamics, USA is a front for Leipzig. Someone is trying to restore Leipzig's reputation. Get U.S. approval. I think it would be simpler for Trinity PharmoDynamics Group to begin purchasing small U.S. pharmaceutical companies."

"Why the push, Lou-Ann?"

"Maybe…and this is speculation…just maybe, something big like a new miracle drug is out there. Trinity needs the facilities and the registered brand names. They need all sorts of agency approvals, including the FDA's."

"To do what, Lou-Ann, manufacture drugs?"

Sam and Lou-Ann were deep in conversation. Traffic began to creep. A horn blast from an impatient limo driver startled them. Lou-Ann tried to focus on the traffic as they approached the airport entrance. She wondered if Grace's death was somehow connected to Trinity PharmoDynamics. *This isn't the time for me to talk about my suspicions. Sam has too much to deal with.*

"Lou-Ann, I'm worried someone will connect the two of us."

"Why, Sam Beverly. I'm surprised at you. You actually believe someone might accuse us of having an affair?"

"The FBI did a thorough background check when I was screened for the GAO position. I answered all questions truthfully."

"And you would have told them about us, Sam."

"They never inquired."

"Relax, Sam."

"We had a brief affair when we were sophomores in college."

"Please, Sam. It wasn't what I would call an affair. We were two kids exploring our freedom. We slept together a few times. It wasn't like we were madly in love." Lou-Ann stared directly ahead.

"I guess that's what you might call it now," said Sam.

"I feel awful we even have to talk about this," said Lou-Ann.

"Please, don't risk your job. That's all I'm saying."

Sam's mind began to drift, again. *Grace is dead. Grace is dead. Why? How? Those photographs. Would Grace kill herself? Never! Who sent the photographs?*

"We're almost at Departures," said Lou-Ann.

"There's just too much going on for me to digest everything," said Sam.

"Watch yourself, Sam. You're too open. Too honest. There are too many coincidences. Someone seems to be tracking your every move. Did you ever think a faction within the Justice Department might be conspiring to hamper your investigation? Maybe someone inside Justice is working for Trinity."

"I'm not big on conspiracy theories, Lou-Ann."

"From my perspective, someone is sabotaging your mission. There are too many coincidences, Sam."

"We don't know who we're dealing with."

"I think some very powerful people are behind Trinity," Lou-

Ann insisted.

Lou-Ann pulled up to the Alleghany departure area and double-parked. Sam got out, opened the back door and grabbed his overnight pack and briefcase.

"Thanks again, Lou-Ann."

"Right, Sam. Take care of yourself. Oh, Sam…one last thing. If you talk with David Clayton…"

"Yes?"

"Tell him I saw his pal Dakota Putnam leaving Anthony Dulles's office at Justice."

"Dulles, with the Office of Planning Coordination?"

"One and the same. He also has his fingers in the Office of Special Investigations."

"What the hell? I warned Clayton to stay away from Putnam. She's hungry."

An airport police officer approached Lou-Ann's car. "Lady, are you planning to set up camp here? Move on. You're blocking traffic."

She reached into her pocketbook and flashed her FBI shield.

"Look, lady. You're still blocking traffic. You want to stay here? Put on your flashers and dash light…if it's official. If not, move on."

This guy is a real ballbuster. Either he dislikes the FBI or women. Maybe both.

"I've got to run. Thanks. You're great," said Sam.

"Thanks, Sam. I am the greatest," she said and then regretted it.

Sam's flight arrived at LaGuardia Airport on time. It was late afternoon. Sam was concerned about catching a cab and going directly to his apartment. "Paging arriving Alleghany passenger Mr. Sam Beverly. Please come to the Alleghany Airlines Service Counter on level one." The page was repeated three times. Sam scrambled for a service phone. "This is Sam Beverly. I heard your page the first time. I'm on my way." He slammed the phone down before the service representative could respond. Sam was unaware FBI Agent Dennis Farrago and a New York City detective would be waiting at the service counter. Sam's internal pendulum swung from sorrow to anger. Sam followed the signs to the baggage area.

The Alleghany service counter was near the airport exit.

"Mr. Beverly?" asked one of the two men waiting at the counter.

"I'm Sam Beverly."

"Agent Dennis Farrago. We spoke this morning," said the taller of the two men dressed in a dark blue suit, white shirt and tie. He looked like an FBI stereotype. "This is New York City Detective Al Napoli."

"I'm assigned to the U.S. Attorney's Office for the Southern New York District, along with Agent Farrago." Napoli looked like a slick used car salesman.

Sam shook hands with both men.

"I'm curious, Detective. What brings you into this case?"

"Quite frankly, Mr. Beverly, I haven't a clue as to why either Farrago or I are involved with this case. Your request for an electronic sweep went directly to Farrago. His team went to your apartment. Farrago found your wife… Mrs. Beverly, dead. Instead of one of the homicide detectives coming on board, I'm directed to meet you."

Farrago gave Napoli a look of disapproval. *What the hell is going on with this guy?*

"We haven't ruled out homicide, Mr. Beverly. You're not a suspect, at least not yet," said Napoli.

"We get involved in some interesting business at the GAO, as I'm sure you two must also find on the job," said Sam.

"Not like this, Mr. Beverly. Farrago investigates violations of federal law. FBI doesn't have any jurisdiction here."

Agent Farrago resembled a spectator following a tennis match. His head turned back and forth between Napoli and Sam as they volleyed.

"Gentlemen, let's carry this conversation to the car. We shouldn't be having this conversation in public."

This guy Napoli has a chip on his shoulder. Sam didn't want to discuss his work.

"No luggage, Mr. Beverly?" asked Napoli.

"I never went home to pack a bag," said Sam.

As they headed back into the city, Napoli said, "I worked homicide. FBI agents are okay at what they do, but they aren't real detectives."

"Bullshit, Napoli. What the hell got you off on this, anyway?" said Farrago.

"I don't like getting assigned to a case and nobody tells me a thing. What do you think, I'm here for my looks?" said Napoli.

"I'm working on an unusual case. The GAO office deals with numbers, accountability. My mission has been expanded," said Sam. "Right now, the most important thing is to determine what happened to Grace."

"He's right, Napoli."

"I can tell you this. I refuse to believe my wife committed suicide. So don't even go there."

"I don't think she did either," said Napoli. "But I'll wait for the autopsy."

"Could we go to the morgue? I want to…you know…see for myself," said Sam.

"The medical examiner asked us to delay until an expedited autopsy has been performed. I know this sounds awful, but do you have any funeral arrangements planned?" asked Farrago.

"No. I haven't spoken to our daughter. I'm Jewish. My wife was born a Catholic. I'm not religious; neither was my wife. My daughter is spiritual, but has no religious affiliation," said Sam.

"New York City has regulations about releasing the deceased, especially if a crime is suspected," said Napoli. Napoli was weaving in and out of traffic almost defiantly. At one point, he let go of the steering wheel to light a Marlboro. The ashtray was filled with cigarette butts. The car smelled of smoke.

"We decided to take you to your apartment. You won't be allowed access without one of us," said Napoli.

Chapter 17

When they arrived at the West Side apartment complex, Farrago said, "Leave your briefcase in the car. You won't be able to stay in your apartment. It's a crime scene until we find out differently."

Sam's shoulders drooped. He began to choke up. "I hadn't planned on staying here."

The three men rode the elevator to the fifth floor where they were met by two NYPD patrolmen. The apartment door was sealed. "Forensics will be back in about an hour," said one of the patrolmen.

Napoli took a switchblade knife from his jacket pocket and cut the official sealing tape. "Let's go in. Don't touch anything. So far, we know the door lock was tampered with. The forensics tech found filings. The lock could have been picked, but more likely a duplicate key was used. It needed to be steel-brushed to fit. The door lock and deadbolt are keyed alike. Convenient, but dangerous," Farrago added, "I still can't figure why Mrs. Beverly didn't have the chain lock in place."

"That is strange," added Sam. "She was always so careful."

"Do you think Mrs. Beverly was expecting a guest?" asked Farrago.

"Perhaps. Grace had moved back here full time. We were living apart. We weren't officially separated and never discussed divorce. My job, I guess. She wanted to explore her freedom, too. It's complicated," Sam searched for the correct words.

Napoli and Sam entered the bedroom. "Were you aware your wife was taking sedatives or sleeping pills?" asked Napoli.

"Yes. I knew she was taking 5 milligrams of diazepam."

"We found a bottle on her nightstand. The prescription was refilled yesterday morning. Thirty pills. There were twenty-nine left. We also found an empty bottle of Pinot Grigio on the floor next to the bed," said Farrago.

"I have some pictures to show you," said Napoli. Sam winced. *What photos? Grace and Vikki?* Napoli removed a stack of crime scene photos from an envelope.

Sam made an effort to regain his composure as Napoli handed him the photographs.

"You okay, Mr. Beverly?" asked Napoli.

Sam nodded. At first, he briefly glanced at the pictures. Then he began to examine each for detail. The wine bottle was on the carpet. The phone receiver lay immediately next to the bottle. "It's difficult to look at the photo of my wife slumped over the side of the bed," he said to Napoli.

Napoli didn't reply.

"Where's the wine bottle, now?" asked Sam.

"The lab. They'll check the contents and prints," said Napoli.

Sam walked back into the living room. "Did anything turn up as far as listening devices or cameras when you guys checked the apartment?"

"Whoever tried to sanitize the place was in a hurry. They weren't the best. Look here," said Farrago. He walked Sam to the living room bookshelf.

"I don't see anything out of the ordinary," said Sam.

"Look closely." There, in the corner, was a small hole. "They splintered the wood pulling out the wire. Room 602, upstairs. It's cleaned out. We're ninety-nine percent sure they were located right over this apartment. No doubt they had cameras here. Those are dummy smoke detectors. Code requires one in each room. These rooms had at least two. I'm surprised Mrs. Beverly didn't suspect something. Women usually notice even the smallest changes," said Farrago.

One of the patrolmen on hall duty came to the door. He whispered something to Napoli. Napoli said, "Time to go. They're waiting for us at the Medical Examiner's office. One other thing, Mr. Beverly," said Napoli as though he were about to spring a surprise. "Are Mr. and Mrs. Ambrose, Vikki and Tom Ambrose, friends of yours?" asked Napoli.

"Yes. They are," said Sam.

"About an hour ago, Mr. and Mrs. Ambrose and their attorney walked into Midtown South. Mrs. Ambrose was hiding in a hotel near Penn Station. She appears to have suffered an emotional breakdown. They're asking for you. Any idea what it's about, Mr. Beverly?" said Napoli. "I hope for your sake you aren't hiding something from us," he added.

Sam looked at Farrago then back to Napoli. He said, "So much is happening. My wife's death. I'm so stressed, I don't know what I may have forgotten. Let's get out of here."

"You want something to eat or drink?" Farrago asked Sam.

"No. I just want to go to bed…to go to sleep, maybe forever."

As they walked to the unmarked car, the detective said, "Hold on."

Farrago and Sam looked at Napoli as though something were about to happen.

"Over there. Dirty water dogs. Want one, Beverly?"

"Oh, come on, Napoli. This guy just told you he didn't want anything to eat. He's feeling miserable and all you think about is your stomach."

Napoli walked across the street and bought two dogs and a soda.

"I think better on a full stomach," he said. Yellow mustard splattered his jacket.

The Deputy Medical Examiner was waiting outside of the morgue. "Mr. Beverly. I'm Robert Johnson, Deputy Medical Examiner. I assisted your investigators Thompson and Clayton on the Koch inquiry a while back."

"Yes. Thank you for helping me today," said Sam.

Dr. Johnson led the three men down a corridor which grew progressively colder. "It's understandably cold in here, Mr. Beverly," Johnson added as they arrived in front of a viewing window. An attendant on the other side uncovered the body. Sam gasped. He stood gazing at his wife's face. He began crying. Dr. Johnson signaled for the attendant to close the window blinds.

"I'm so sorry, Mr. Beverly. Please follow me. I have to show you a report and, sadly, we need to do some paperwork," said Dr.

Johnson.

Sam was dazed. He followed Dr. Johnson and the other two men, not knowing or caring where they were headed. Dr. Johnson's office was very simple, almost stark, for a New York City bureaucrat. Sam sat at a conference table with Farrago and Napoli on either side.

"Mr. Beverly. The preliminary autopsy report is in. We haven't totally ruled out suicide, but I'm afraid this is a homicide. Mrs. Beverly died from a combination of alcohol and a drug overdose. The medication was lorazepam.

"The lab report showed the wine bottle had a residue of the drug on both the inside and outside of the bottle. Taken in small quantities there might be a small reaction, but I suggest in this case, someone had spiked the wine with enough of the drug to bring on an anaphylactic reaction. In this case, the wine was tainted with haloperidol, a dangerous antipsychotic drug."

"Napoli found Valium on your wife's nightstand. Only one pill was missing. The toxicology report shows little Valium. Valium and lorazepam are both benzodiazepines. Valium stays in the body much longer and it would have shown in a greater quantity. The detectives found absolutely no trace of lorazepam in the apartment."

"Damn. I told you the guys who bugged Beverly's apartment were in a hurry to clean up. They took the garbage, but forgot the wine bottle," said Napoli with a look a smug pleasure.

The three men talked with Dr. Johnson for over an hour when Napoli said, "We have another stop at Midtown South."

"Dr. Johnson, I can't complete these forms since I haven't spoken with my daughter. She has a strong personality and will expect me to wait. I'll contact a funeral home as soon as I hear from her. She probably has tried to reach me, but I've been…well, you understand. I'll telephone her from the police precinct."

Dr. Johnson placed the file on the corner of his desk. "I'll have copies of the paperwork waiting. Take the preliminary report. We can't release your wife's body just yet. Since we had reason to believe Mrs. Beverly died under questionable circumstances, the law requires an autopsy. I don't have the official report. We also removed a number of organs to do a thorough toxicology report.

You'll need to sign a request if you want the organs returned."

"This is all sounding a bit gruesome to me," said Sam.

"Gruesome? Not really. You want to get to the bottom of your wife's death, don't you?" asked Napoli.

"Of course, I do."

"Really, Mr. Beverly? Why didn't you tell us about the other photographs?" asked Napoli.

Sam looked at Farrago and Johnson and said, "Why don't you tell me, Napoli?" Sam's dislike for the detective had reached the surface.

"If you knew about the so-called photographs, why didn't you tell me?"

"Why didn't you tell us?"

"This is turning into a pissing contest," said Farrago. "Tell us what you know, Napoli."

"I don't have all the details. Your wife and Vikki Ambrose were lovers. Their lawyer informed us Mr. and Mrs. Ambrose fought over the photos. Mr. Ambrose broke a chair."

"We were both blind-sided, I guess," said Sam. "I called my wife when I found the package of photos in the mailbox. I was angry and confused. I'm working on a top secret investigation, and my first thought was blackmail."

"And what do you think now?" asked Farrago.

"I believe they were sending me a warning that got out of control. The person and people behind this are trying to discredit me. I don't believe murder was in the cards."

"So, why didn't you tell us about the pictures?" asked Napoli again.

"I still haven't shown them to my boss, the Inspector General. It's not the pictures. It's the investigation."

"Mr. Beverly. You are a lucky man in this case. I could still charge you with obstruction of justice in the investigation of your wife's death. But what good would it do?" asked Napoli. Mr. Ambrose surrendered four of the photos, but he said there's a fifth photo. Do you have the photos in your possession?" asked Farrago.

"No. They're in my safe at Headquarters."

"I need them. That's not a request. I want those photos," said

Napoli. "Don't force me to get a court order. It becomes messy and the press is sure to get wind of your predicament. Right now it stays in this room."

Farrago nodded agreement, but Dr. Johnson did not.

"I will go along with what you are telling us, Detective Napoli, as long as I'm not involved in a further investigation."

"You are involved, Dr. Johnson. I'm trying to do a bit of damage control. That's all," replied Napoli.

"I'm not going to release your wife's body now, for sure. Once I feel confident this mess isn't going to blow back on me, I'll call you. Until then, I've changed my finding to 'inclusive and pending.'"

Sam tossed the file back on Dr. Johnson's desk. "No sense me taking this. I've got to get out of here," said Sam. He was weary. He opened the door and looked back at the three men. He scowled and walked out. Sam wandered the maze of corridors in the ME building. He finally found a door leading to the main entrance and the street.

"Take me to the Hotel Roosevelt," Sam told the cab driver.

⁂

Sam arrived home in Fredericksburg on Friday afternoon. The last thing he did before flying home was meet Tom Ambrose. Tom was angry.

"I'm filing for divorce," Tom said. "Why didn't we realize what was going on? I called my daughter in New Jersey. She's pregnant. Can you imagine how this could hurt her?"

"I'm just as distraught as you, Tom," Sam said.

"Here's what you don't know. Vikki was with Grace earlier in the evening Grace died. Grace wanted the both of them to clear out. Go to L.A. Grace told Vikki the pictures weren't about them. Someone is blackmailing you," explained Tom.

"Maybe she was right. Maybe it is blackmail. But why send the photographs to you? Sam asked. "I received a call telling me the photographs were in my mailbox. The caller said he would call back. I haven't heard from him since. I feel certain this wasn't blackmail. It was intimidation. Someone wants me to stop my investigation."

"About what?" asked Tom.

"I can't tell you. It's all classified."

"My wife was drugged, heavily sedated, in that nut house of a hospital. She's acting crazy. And you can't tell me?"

"What else do you know, Tom?"

"Vikki ran out of the apartment during the argument with Grace. Late that night, early the next morning, Vikki can't remember. She decided to return to apologize to Grace. Vikki saw two men unlock the door to Grace's apartment. A tall guy and shorter man. They had a key," said Tom.

"What did Vikki do?"

"She hid at the far end of the corridor until they left. Then she went in. The bedroom light was on. Vikki found Grace's body slumped over the edge of the bed. 'I called to Grace,' Vikki told me. 'When I couldn't wake her up, I checked her pulse. Grace wasn't breathing,' she insisted. It was awful for Vikki."

"Why didn't she call the police?" asked Sam

"Vikki panicked. Her immediate reaction was that Grace had committed suicide. Then Vikki thought about the two guys she saw. Maybe it was murder. All Vikki wanted to do was run…and she did."

"Have you told all of this to Napoli?" asked Sam.

"I have," said Tom.

Napoli…that son of a bitch. I am a suspect.

Sam expected Rachael to be home when he returned to Fredericksburg from Manhattan. There was a lot he needed to explain. He wanted to be there for her. He waited impatiently There was no answer at her dormitory room. Sam walked through the house. On the dining room table was an envelope with a letter inside from Rachael. Without knowing the entire sequence of events, Rachael blamed Sam for her mother's death. Rachael accused Sam of neglecting his marriage. 'You always placed your career ahead of us. That's all you care about,' she wrote.

Where is this coming from? Sam read the letter over and over. "I want my personal things and clothes. I don't want to live in that house with you. Do not call or try to contact me. I will attend the funeral or memorial, if you have time to plan one. I will never speak to you again." The letter was unsigned.

Sam was devastated. At a time when he needed the most precious thing in his life, Rachael was gone.

Chapter 18

Spring 1977 was a chaotic time for Sam Beverly and the GAO team. Now, Dakota Putnam was about to add to the frenzy.

"Okay, okay…hold on; I'm coming," shouted David Clayton as he rolled out of bed, wakened by insistent pounding on his door. David pulled on a pair of jogging shorts and stumbled toward the kitchen. The clock read 6:00 a.m. *Who the hell pounds on a guy's door at six in the morning?* He looked through the security peephole. It was Dakota.

"What the hell," he called out as he removed the security chain and opened the door. "For God's sake, Dakota, what's so important? You've got a key."

"What good is a key, if you have the door chained?"

"You could have called," said David, pulling Dakota inside the apartment.

"The other evening you told me to avoid calling. You thought the phone was tapped. Give me a break."

"I'm sorry. Sit down. I'll make some coffee. I hate to say this, but you look beat. What's wrong?"

"I've been working overtime, scrambling," said Dakota.

"All right. Calm down. Take a deep breath. What's so important?"

"This wire service report came across my desk." Dakota unfold two continuous sheets of perforated paper and handed them to David.

"Help me out. Tell me what this is about. I've had a couple of bad days myself and yesterday was a topper."

Dakota gave David a severe look.

"Get back to the wire service report," he said.

"I remember the trip you made to Long Island. The one you didn't want to talk about."

"And?"

"A college professor. A guy named Nagle…"

"Matthew Nagle?" David asked.

"Yes. He freelanced a story for a Long Island weekly. The wire services picked up on it last night. Here's the gist: Nagle claims the government had a Nazi scientist on its payroll."

"What?" David began to read the wire service report.

"According to Nagle, the guy's a veterinarian or maybe a virologist."

"Oh, my God! What has he done?" David dropped the report on the table in disbelief.

"I know you and Jack Thompson were on Long Island. You talked with the guy."

"How do you know so much? You didn't get that information from me," David responded.

"I have my own sources," Dakota said.

"What? Tell me you're double dipping for the CIA."

"Forget the CIA. I called Nagle's home."

"In the middle of the night?"

"I wasn't the only caller. Anyway, his wife answered the phone. She is really pissed off. Some guy from the State Department threatened a lawsuit, if Nagle didn't print a retraction."

"Nagle's wife blames you two guys, you and Jack, for getting her husband involved in what she called a life-threatening mess. Is Nagle's story accurate?"

"I can't go into it. You know that."

"Nagle claims he wrote the story after his friend and family disappeared." Dakota picked up the wire service report. "The guy's name is Portavani. He was a subcontractor at the DOA facility on Plum Island. Nagle doesn't name either you or Jack Thompson. But, and it's a big but, he claims the General Accounting Office is investigating allegations."

"Come on, Dakota. You know damn well, we're working on a task force inquiry. It's a wild goose chase. These charges came up in the '60's. We don't have a thing." With that, David put two coffee mugs on the table next to a jar of instant coffee. "The water's boiled. Help yourself. No milk. Sorry."

"You don't know anything else? Bullshit. Liz Nagle got a call from Justice. They want to interview her husband."

"Hey, hold on. I'm telling you, no one else from Justice is involved."

"Maybe you three ought to get your act together." Dakota sipped the coffee. "I hate instant coffee." Dakota slid the mug across the table to David.

"There's nothing to the story, Dakota. Nagle is upset and angry. Some crazies tried to run him off the road. He chased them on his motorcycle and ended up in the hospital."

"That's crap, David, and you know it."

"It doesn't matter," said David. He shrugged his shoulders in dismay. "Nagle has opened a can of worms. He's out there all alone. Jack warned him. His wife begged him not to get involved. So what does he do? Just the opposite. I've got to get hold of Jack. He knows a cop on Long Island. Nagle needs police protection and the Feds won't touch this thing."

David called Jack and arranged for a meeting at the Justice Department.

"I'll meet you at ten thirty," said Jack. "What's up?"

"I'll tell you when I see you. Have you spoken with Sam?" asked David.

"No. I'd call Sam, but he won't answer the phone. He's taking this thing hard."

"His wife's dead. How would you take it?" asked David.

"You mean if my wife were dead? Give me a second. Let me think."

"This is serious, Jack."

Dakota overheard David. "Taking what hard?" she asked.

"Gotta go, Jack. Ten thirty. Your office. Is it alright if I bring Dakota Putnam along?"

David's request stunned Dakota. *Why the hell is he bringing me into it? David knows Jack dislikes me after Watergate.*

"Okay. Thanks. We'll be there," David said.

"What's going on with Sam Beverly and why the hell are you taking me to a meeting with Jack Thompson?" Dakota got up from the table and began to pace. "You do this to me all the time,

David." She clenched her teeth.

"Sam's wife died last Tuesday. Grace and Sam separated a while back. She wanted a divorce."

"I didn't know she was dead. I'm sorry."

"The FBI and NYPD are trying to keep the case under wraps. It's bizarre. All I know is she died and the medical examiner is withholding the findings."

"She was living in Manhattan?"

"Yes. It's more complicated, but I don't have all the details. Her body was cremated. Sam brought the ashes home to Fredericksburg. For now, Jack and I will have to keep working on the investigation. Sam's on bereavement leave. Jack's in charge."

Jack Thompson did not want to be in charge of anything at this point in his life. The responsibility of substituting for Sam Beverly was unexpected and never considered when he came on board. Jack got the call over the weekend.

"I'm not asking you to take on all Jack's duties. This INS inquiry…the Congresswoman is pushing the Inspector General for a report; even something preliminary. This thing is dragging on too long. Damn it, Thompson. Make something up if you must, but get her something." The Attorney General pounded his fist on the table. Jack could hear something crash. "Listen, Jack. You and Clayton are moving to the GAO building. That request came from upstairs."

"Upstairs?" Jack asked.

"Jack, please just go along with me on this. You don't want to be back in the basement."

That was a threat. "No, sir. No, I don't."

"Looking forward to reading your report, Jack."

Jack dreaded going to work on Monday morning. He didn't know what to expect.

"Morning, Mac," said Jack as he approached the recently installed security checkpoint in the lobby of the Justice Department building.

"Yes, sir, Mr. Thompson. It's a great day. What brings you in so early?"

"Work, Mac. I'm looking forward to retirement."

"Yes, sir. Me, too." said the burly security officer, getting up and walking around his desk and into the lobby. "There's an FBI agent waiting for you."

"Where?"

"Around the corner by the elevators. I told her you usually arrived around ten. She insisted on waiting."

"Thanks, Mac."

"Something else, Mr. Thompson. When the agent signed in, she…"

"She?"

"Yes, sir. Agent Lou-Ann Stokes. I checked her credentials. Well, she told me your name and office location wasn't on the lobby directory. I walked over and took a look. Sure enough. It's gone." Mac walked to the directory and pointed to the empty space.

"The cabinet is locked, Mac."

"Yes, sir. Personnel has the keys. Just too much happening around here. And no one tells me a thing. Last Friday, just before I punched out, a guy from maintenance tells me the basement is quarantined."

"Quarantined?"

"So I stuck around. About fifteen or twenty minutes later, a half dozen trucks pull up. They post their own security at the two elevators to the basement. Tape a quarantine notice on the wall.

"I was pissed. I'm the shift sergeant and the captain didn't tell me. I called him. He swears he wasn't told. I called maintenance. Burt told me these guys are cleaning dust spores and moving old boxes out of the basement."

"Thanks, Mac. I'll find Agent Stokes. Never keep a lady or an FBI agent waiting."

Had Mac stuck around a few minutes more, he would have seen all the action. A crew of ten men dressed in civilian clothes moved quickly through the Justice Department lobby. They gathered at the two basement elevators. With rehearsed precision, they slipped into white paper coveralls and biohazard masks. Their leader, Sergeant Bill Collins, wore a red vest. "Alpha to Beta. We are in position." He clipped the walkie-talkie to his belt and motioned for his men to ride the elevators to the basement. Beta team entered the lobby already wearing biohazard suits.

The recently formed DOD biohazard unit was on a unique mission. Biohazard containment was risky business. Sergeant Bill Collins handpicked these volunteers from Fort Detrick's fire and emergency response division.

"This way," motioned Collins, Alpha team's leader. He led them to a location not far from the cubicle Jack Thompson once called his office. The place had a distinct odor of damp cardboard and mold. "Be careful with the boxes. I have no idea what's in them. Keep the boxes in numbered order."

"'Not for nothing, Sergeant; what the hell are we doing?"

"Just get a move on it. We have our orders. They want this place spic and span."

"Who's they?" asked Clive.

"You don't want to know. Just get the job done."

"What's Trinity? The boxes are labeled 'Trinity'. That sounds religious."

"Clive, you are a pain in the ass. Why did I pick you for this unit?"

"My smile. Right?"

"Stop talking and get to work."

"The smell in here is awful. I'm getting the urge to puke," said Clive.

"Not in your mask. Stop thinking about it. Get the job done."

The sergeant looked at the inventory list. There were exactly one hundred and twelve archived cardboard boxes. Each box was labeled "Trinity," with a brief description of the contents.

"Sergeant, over here," called one of the team.

"What's the matter?"

"Over here. The two boxes on the floor. Biohazard labels. Bright orange sealing tape."

The sergeant called over the radio. "Alpha to Beta. Send down two containment bags." The sergeant was troubled. He double-checked the inventory for an overlooked box. "Bag and secure them. Don't let them out of your sight. Get them into the van. Understood?"

"Yes, Sergeant."

Collins added two boxes to the inventory, followed by a large question mark.

Six hours later, Alpha team policed the area one last time. Their work completed, Alpha team huddled in the main lobby.

"Split into two groups. Clive, take your guys to Van Four. The rest of you, follow me to Van Five. Bag your suits. No time for a washdown here. Once we arrive at Detrick, stay in the vans until I signal the washdown is ready. Change into the second set of civvies. The stuff you're wearing will be ready for pickup on Monday."

Mission accomplished, Alpha and Beta units returned to Fort Detrick early Saturday morning.

The Justice Department lobby was getting a facelift to accommodate increased security. The winding marble staircase was now mostly ornamental. Two newly-installed escalators led to the mezzanine. As Jack walked to the elevators, he found Lou-Ann Stokes sitting on a bench.

"Good morning, Agent Stokes. I wish you had called first. I'm awful about schedules. I'm always late."

"It's all right. I needed a few minutes downtime to think," Lou-Ann said.

"I've been re-assigned to your office. I looked on the directory and you don't have an office."

Jack laughed. "That's the way things go around here. You're assigned to my office. I'm assigned to the GAO. It's all screwed up. Come on upstairs. I have a coffee pot, but no milk. Sorry."

"No, thanks. I don't drink coffee."

"Oops. Sorry again," said Jack as they rode the elevator to the fourth floor.

This is going to be one of those days. There was a piece of cardboard on the elevator floor. Jack picked it up as the elevator door opened. The reverse side was bright orange with a biohazard symbol and the warning, 'Quarantine Do Not Enter.'

"This must have been left from the clean-up," said Jack.

"What is this place, Jack? What's wrong?"

Jack knew damn well what was wrong. With the exception of his so-called office, the entire floor was still being used as a storage facility for contractors' supplies.

Jack unlocked the door. "No secretary. I answer my own phone. I spend most of my time at GAO. I pick up my check at

Personnel." Jack's office remained in disarray. Jack turned to Lou-Ann. "Off the record. How is it you've been assigned to the GAO?"

"I know how I got here. I just don't know the "why" or "who." I don't know where to begin," said Lou-Ann. "This whole thing is a surprise."

"Oh, just start anyplace you want."

Lou-Ann brushed back her hair. "Here's what I know. It may sound confusing; my head is still spinning. Last Friday, I was summoned to the Deputy Director's office." Lou-Ann told Jack the unusual conversation with the Deputy:

"'Don't bother sitting down, Agent Stokes.'

"'Sir?' I felt perplexed by the Deputy Director's abruptness. Ted Anderson had a reputation for a no-nonsense style. He was downright rude."

"'Is that a question or an answer, Stokes? All I want is a straight answer.'

"'Sir. What is this all about?'

"'Stokes, have you had any dealings with the White House?'

"'No, Sir.'

"'How about Senator Javits' office?'

"'No, Sir.'

"'But you have been in contact with Sam Beverly over at the GAO…Deputy Inspector General Sam Beverly.'"

Jack interrupted Lou-Ann's story. "Wait a minute. Anderson knew you worked the meeting I had with Peterson at the Smithsonian? Sounded like an accusation." Jack poured a cup of coffee and straddled a chair. "Then what happened?"

"I told him, 'I have'. Anderson knows Beverly is conducting a GAO inquiry for the INS oversight committee."

Lou-Ann continued with her story: "'Who authorized that contact?' Anderson demanded.

"'I acted on my own. It was a brief surveillance…a Sunday afternoon.' Anderson had me on the defensive."

"'Unless you are looking for a transfer to Brazil or Argentina, don't do it again!'

"I protested. I told him, 'Sir, I can explain the nature of the surveillance'.

"'I don't want to know more. It's ridiculous. World War II ended thirty two years ago. Counterintelligence rounded up Nazis in the United States. It's time to move on. But no! Now we're looking for mysterious Nazis on the government payroll.' Anderson picked up a piece of stationery and waved it in my face.

"'Last Friday morning, I received this memorandum. Arrived by courier. Now, isn't that nice?' Anderson stood up and reached over his desk. 'Here. Read it!' Anderson shouted at me, then fell back into his seat.

"'I don't understand, Sir. It says here I'm being assigned to The General Accounting Office. Why?'

"'Congresswoman Harrington asked specifically for you. The Attorney General signed the memo.'

"I attempted to hand Anderson the memo. His hands waved like a heron taking flight. He pushed it away.

"'Keep it,' he shouted. 'One last thing, Agent Stokes.'

"'Yes, Sir.

"'If you ever go over my head again, it will be the end of your career.' Anderson began scribbling on a legal pad."

"Then what happened?" Jack asked.

"I stood there. He hadn't dismissed me. I said, 'Sir. Is there anything else?'

"Anderson looked up from his desk and asked me, 'Are you still here?'"

Lou-Ann paused as though she were reliving the moment.

"And?" Jack asked.

"What do you think? I awkwardly backed out of Anderson's office. And that's how I got here." Lou-Ann handed the memo to Jack. "Here. Read it."

Jack read the memo and said, "Crazy. I guess we're both moving to the GAO building."

Jack finished his coffee. The cardboard quarantine notice was still on his mind. "Just for the hell of it, let's take a look at the basement cleanup. I lived down there for quite a while."

"Lived in the basement?" Lou-Ann asked.

"Another story. I'm sure it will come up when David Clayton and Dakota Putnam arrive. Oh. Watch what you say around Dakota Putnam. Nothing is off the record with her."

"I'm not acquainted with Putnam."

"Just as well. Be on your guard. She's a reporter with the *Washington Post*. She's not entirely responsible for killing my career, but I got one big kick in the ass for talking with her. Watergate. Forgive me."

"I'd like to check out the basement."

"Okay. I'll call Mac." Jack called the security desk and asked Mac to meet him at the basement elevators.

"There are only two elevators to the basement on this side of the building," Jack said.

Jack and Lou-Ann met Mac in the lobby. "I've only been to the Archives section of the basement a few times," he said. "I remember the day we moved your office, Mr. Thompson. I couldn't stand that smell."

Jack laughed. "I remember."

They stepped out of the elevator. "I know the way to the Archives," said Jack.

Mac laughed. He pointed to a hallway off to the left. "That's where your office used to be."

"You had an office down here? I'd go mad," said Lou-Ann.

"I did go a bit crazy, but that's another long story. Hey, you and I should have dinner some night. We can swap stories."

Lou-Ann looked at Jack. *Surely, he has to be kidding. Dinner? I don't think so.*

The trio rounded a corner. Jack gestured for them to halt. "I don't believe it."

"What's wrong?" asked Lou-Ann.

"The Trinity files. Probably a hundred boxes or more. They were stacked over there. Rows of boxes. Maybe six feet high. They're all gone," Jack exclaimed.

"That foul odor is gone, too," said Mac.

"Wait 'til Sam and David hear about this. Sam told me he filed an interagency request to review the Trinity files."

"The cleaning guys on Friday night. I'll bet they removed the boxes," said Mac.

"Security must keep a log. Surely someone knows who moved them," said Lou-Ann.

"We do keep a log. Let's go upstairs and check it. Those boxes were classified," said Mac.

When they arrived at the security office, Mac went to the locked filing cabinet. "We keep the weekly logs in here, Mr. Thompson."

Jack walked to the cabinet.

"I don't believe this," said Mac in disbelief. "The pages for Friday have been removed. Hold on. Let me check one more thing."

Mac walked to a storage area marked Top Secret and Classified Catalog. It took him a minute. "Something is wrong, Mr. Thompson. The catalog cards for the Trinity inventory… they're gone."

"Now what do we do?"

"I don't have a clue. You're in charge," said Lou-Ann.

"I'll file a report. I can't believe this. Somebody's in for an ass-kicking. I'll get back to you, Mr. Thompson."

Chapter 19

"Hello," David called, entering the empty office. "Typical. Jack's never on time."

"I heard that," said Jack, as he and Lou-Ann entered the office.

"I recall the day we met. You haven't made much progress unpacking."

"Just as well. I'm moving."

"Really? And Agent Stokes, I didn't expect to find you here. Jack didn't tell me."

"He didn't know. I popped in on him. Speaking of surprises…" Lou-Ann handed David her transfer memo.

"Getting a little crowded, isn't it?" asked David.

"That's why I'm moving to the GAO building," said Jack.

"What? If you're moving, that means Agent Stokes is moving, too?"

"It looks like it," said Jack.

"Sounds like you have some objections to my joining the team." said Lou-Ann.

"What team?" asked David. "From my perspective, we've become fragmented, just like our investigation."

"Excuse me, folks. Since David isn't going to introduce me, I'll do the honors. I'm Dakota Putnam with the *Washington Post*."

"And with David, too." Jack added the dig since he knew Sam had warned David about becoming involved with a reporter, especially a hungry one.

"Now is that any way to greet an old friend, Jack?" asked David.

"Old friend? I don't think so. This is the first time I've met Ms. Putnam in person."

Dakota's face flushed. "Still with the Department of Justice," she said. "I thought you would resign after the screwing you got."

"So you followed up?"

"I called after the dust from Nixon's pardon settled. Rumor had it you were *persona non grata*."

"They call it the Archives."

"Now may we move on?" David was impatient to plan their next move.

"Sure, David," Jack replied.

"I understand you're in charge until Sam returns."

Jack nodded his head reluctantly. "We have to pull everything together. When Sam returns I want to have a preliminary report. He can take it from there." *Preliminary, crap. It will probably be the only report.*

"I suggest we move to the GAO as soon as possible. We need access to the situation room. Any ideas?"

"Situation room?" asked Dakota.

"Sam's idea." David stifled a laugh.

"Sam wanted a secure location for the team to work. It's just down the hall from his official office. Sam requested security cameras in the hallway. A guard is stationed there." Jack added, "Unfortunately, I don't have the combinations to access the office or the walk-in vault. Without a way in, I'm stymied."

"Who does have access?" asked Lou-Ann. Before Jack or David could respond, she added, "I'll bet Lynn Stahl has the combinations."

"You may be right. Let's head over Sam's office now," David insisted.

"Okay. You two go ahead. I'll arrange with Personnel and Security to move this stuff to GAO," said Jack.

"I'll give you a hand, Jack," said Lou-Ann.

The group split up.

While Jack was packing the contents of his desk drawers, Lou-Ann said, "I've already informed Sam. I'll share this with you. I saw Dakota Putnam leaving Erskin Young's office."

"Erskin Young? I don't recognize the name."

"Most people wouldn't. He's one of our mythical holdovers from the OSS."

"Tell me more," said Jack.

"Young's staff doesn't exist."

"Then how did you see Dakota coming out of his office?"

"Young's unit is unattached. Supposedly, Young is the coordinator for historical documents restoration."

"We don't have an historical records division. We have archivists."

"Believe me. There is an historical records restoration group."

"How do you know that?"

"Never mind how I know," said Lou-Ann. "Do you recall the Saint Lewis Archives fires back in 1973?"

"Yes. Sam asked me to find the military records for some Army Air Force flyers shot down over China during World War II. They were captured by the Japanese. Sam found a reference to a Unit 731 among Tony Portavani's records."

"Portavani?"

"The guy who worked on Plum Island and disappeared."

"Getting back to Erskin Young, he's a powerful man with a low profile."

"What makes him so powerful?"

"It's common knowledge his walk-in vault holds documents so sensitive they aren't cataloged except in Young's head. It's been said Young is the guardian for the Sunrise File."

"The Sunrise File?"

"The summary of agency operations following World War II. The rush to get scientists before the Russians snatched them. In some cases, the government altered documents, even war records. Government agencies circumvented the Nuremberg and Dachau trials. The Russians were furious."

"Are Sunrise and Operation Paperclip related?"

"Yes. I only know what I've read. One gathered the scientists. The other brought them into the country."

"Quite a twist, isn't it?"

"Twist?"

"Everyone remembers the first man in space, the moon landings. They recall the name of Werner von Braun."

"What's your point, Jack?" Lou-Ann asked.

"We remember the moon landing but not the slave laborers

who gave their lives in hidden tunnels building the first rockets. The government brought those rockets here, along with von Braun. I'm guessing the same arrangements were made for virologists and veterinarians.

How do I know this for certain? I've read documents. All classified. I could go to jail for telling you."

"We're getting into deep philosophical issues, Jack. Your argument could be applied to pharmaceutical research."

"I've read the horror stories. Patients injected with all sorts of diseases; malaria. A thousand at Dachau were executed by injection."

Jack continued, "Do we disregard research if it leads to a life-saving antibiotic or miracle drug?"

"There's the predicament. Sam was leaning toward the theory a pharmaceutical company was behind the cover-up. Drug patents…that's where the money lies."

"Cover-up? Is that what this is all about, Jack? I don't believe in conspiracy theories. Americans love them. I don't."

The answer to Lou-Ann's question was printed across Jack's face. "I'm skeptical of conspiracy theories. Since Watergate, I know conspiracies do exist."

"I'm confused. What do you mean?" asked Lou-Ann.

"Not now. We have to finish packing this mess. I want to get over to Sam's office and speak with Lynn."

"And perhaps we should confront Dakota Putnam about her meeting with Erskin Young?"

"Not yet. But watch yourself. I have a plan for dealing with Ms. Putnam."

When Jack and Lou-Ann arrived at the GAO, David was dejected.

"What took you two so long?" David sounded irritated. "I spoke with Lynn. She doesn't have the combinations. Sam didn't tell her."

"Where is she now?" asked Lou-Ann.

"She finished a phone conversation and left," said David.

While David and Jack discussed a timetable for getting back to the investigation, Lou-Ann left the office and walked down the long hallway, where she encountered Lynn.

"Lynn, we need to talk," said Lou-Ann.

"Everyone wants to talk with me. Let me guess. This is about access to Sam's room."

"That's the point, Lynn. It isn't Sam's room. The team needs it. We need to read files. I believe you know the combinations, or you know where they are stored."

"About fifteen minutes ago, I got a telephone call from the Inspector General. He wanted access to the room and the inner vault. I felt uncomfortable. There was an implied threat my job was on the line."

"It may well be. That's why it's so important we get in there."

"I can't. Sam told me not to allow anyone into the room."

"You do have the combinations. Who else would Sam trust?"

"I have them."

"Lynn, listen to me. I'm convinced someone's trying to sabotage this investigation. They'll stop at nothing. Believe me, they will hurt anyone in their way. You could be in danger. Think about Sam. Hasn't he suffered enough?"

Lynn nodded her head in agreement. "No, I don't want Sam to suffer."

"Let Sam get on with the investigation. The people we're dealing with hide in the shadows. As long as we're out in the open, they can't touch us."

"Let me call Sam, first," Lynn sobbed.

"Aren't you concerned the telephone lines are tapped? Sam and Jack think they are."

"Sam and I discussed this predicament a while ago. I have a script. Give me a chance to gain my composure."

Lynn returned to Sam's office and telephoned him. When she returned to the group she said, "I'll turn the combinations over to Jack. The room is his responsibility." She handed Jack a business envelope. "Here you go."

David, Dakota and Lou-Ann followed Jack to the security guard seated outside the room. "From now on, this will be called the 'situation room'. Got it?" Jack stepped forward, showed his ID to the guard, and punched in the numbers. The door opened. The room was untouched. "Looks like the day we left." Jack opened the walk-in vault and returned with Portavani's records. "David.

On the bottom shelf in the vault, you'll find Koch's briefcase. We never took it apart."

"And what am I supposed to be doing?" asked Dakota.

"I know one thing you won't be doing," said Jack. "And what's that?"

"You won't be writing about your little adventure with us."

"What?" Dakota walked over to Jack; invading his space.

"You heard me. This is a classified investigation. Anything you read, see or hear fall under the National Secrecies Act. I can't stop you from publishing a story you get from outside our circle. But I will have you prosecuted for any story you publish about our group."

"You can't stop me."

"I can't stop you from scooping a story from your own sources. In fact, I'd love it. You'll put the bastards who are sabotaging us on notice." Jack spoke with an authority David hadn't heard before.

"Everyone connected with this investigation may be in grave danger. Have I made myself clear, Ms. Putnam?"

Dakota was furious. She looked to David for support.

"He's right, Dakota. Somebody is pulling our chain. Sam's wife is dead. I was roughed-up. Someone attempted to bribe Jack," said David.

Lou-Ann walked over to Dakota and said, "I feel we may be dealing with more than one interest group, Dakota. Someone is watching our every move. I'm certain you're under scrutiny as well, especially your relationship with David."

"That's our business. It has nothing to do with you or the investigation," Dakota said.

"You're wrong. You no longer have a private life, Dakota. Not while this investigation is under way. Perhaps, never again. I'm warning you. Be careful."

"Dakota, what's your relationship with Erskin Young?" asked Jack.

"Relationship? I don't have a relationship with Young."

"You were seen coming out of his office."

"It goes back to a conversation I overheard. David was talking with someone he called Robert. David refused to tell me what was going on. I knew you guys were chasing Nazis. I went back to the *Post's* morgue and found some files from the '50's. There were references to Operation Paperclip. Erskin Young was one of the guys who testified about the Nazi round-up. He admitted a few Nazi war criminals had been inadvertently hired for priority government projects. The individuals in question were repatriated. Young assured the committee the scientists involved in government and industrial research were not war criminals."

"And now, we've discovered Young was less than candid. He testified under oath," said Jack.

"Dakota, how did you locate Young?" asked Lou-Ann.

It wasn't difficult. I know some old timers at the paper. They told me Young was a war hero. Operated with the Free French in the '40's. While in Germany, Young led a team searching for German biologists, doctors, anyone in the medical field connected with IG Farben. Young became an interagency legend. MacArthur brought Young to Japan around 1948. He rounded up Japanese researchers doing similar work. One of the reporters pointed me to a story about the St. Louis records fire."

"The National Personnel Records Center?" asked Jack.

"Yes. The fire was devastating. But there's more to it. One of the reporters suggested I check the files again. I found an interesting side note: Young was one of the Department of Justice attorneys assigned to cover the recovery and restoration programs. Young was in charge of a computer index for Air Force personnel. Firefighters used tremendous amounts of water to suppress the fire. The salvaged documents were transported to an aircraft plant. They went through a drying process. Other records were sent to NASA. That's where the side notes helped."

"How?" asked Lou-Ann?

"The Sunrise File."

Jack looked at Lou-Ann and said, "Are you sure? Sunrise File?" he asked.

"I'm positive."

"So how did you eventually find Young?" asked Lou-Ann.

"Young isn't listed in the Department of Justice directory. My next tactic was simple. I walked into the building. Asked to speak with Personnel. Told them I was looking for Erskin Young. A couple of minutes later, Young's office called back. I met him. He's real. Not much of a legend, if you ask me."

Lou-Ann smiled. *If only Dakota knew the extent of Young's power.*

"Did you ask him about the Sunrise File?"

"Not at first. I told Young I was writing a story on the fire and the lost records. Then I dropped the reference to the Sunrise File."

"Do you know what the Sunrise File contains?" asked Jack.

"No. Of course not. I was fishing. Young never reacted. He calmly told me the Sunrise File, or files, are a myth, pure fantasy. The interview lasted about thirty minutes. That's it."

"Did Young ever refer to Veteran's Administration claims files or payroll records?"

"No. He insisted medical records from military hospitals were destroyed. The fire created another controversy. The fire destroyed thousands of records requested by the GAO."

"He referred to a GAO investigation?" asked David.

"Yes."

"I wonder if Sam knows?" Jack was jotting notes. He hoped to meet with Sam.

"So the Sunrise File is a myth? I doubt it." Lou-Ann was skeptical.

"Lou-Ann. You follow up on the Sunrise File."

"For the moment, let's summarize what we know and finish looking at the material we already have." Jack pointed to Koch's briefcase. "We never took a close look at Koch's briefcase."

"So that's it for me?" asked Dakota.

"I guess so. At least for now. Unless of course you want to listen to more stuff you can't write about."

"No thanks, Jack. I can still cover the story, but from my own angle."

"Please, Dakota. Don't complicate this investigation."

"I won't be seeing you for our dinner date this evening, David. I'm leaving now." David knew she was steaming. *Women. Serves me right for mixing business with pleasure.*

Once Dakota left, Jack turned to the other two and said, "Well thank you, Dakota Putnam. It had to be Erskin Young who ordered the Trinity files moved. Who knows where? Erskin Young is more interested in documents destruction than preservation."

"Think we'll ever locate the Trinity files?" asked David.

"Yeah. When they find Jimmy Hoffa's body."

"Hey, you two. Get to work. Tell me about the diagram on the blackboard," said Lou-Ann.

"Sam started connecting the dots. Sam contends there is an emerging picture. Somehow, Matt Nagle's Freedom of Information request triggered a sequence of events. The names on the blackboard are key players," said Jack.

David pointed to the pictures pinned on the wall. "These two are Koch and Webster. Dead. You'll learn all about them." He continued. "Meet Dr. Walther Liechtenauer, Director of Trinity PharmoDynamics, USA. That's the best photo we have. Liechtenauer spent five years in prison for war crimes. Following his release, the good doctor became the chairman of a multinational pharmaceutical company. Rumor has it Liechtenauer is ill. He's handing the reins to Ashton Pickering."

"Pickering? Seems like I've heard that name before," said Lou-Ann.

"You have?" asked Jack.

Lou-Ann paused for a moment. "Yes. Now I remember. I was doing some PR work for the Attorney General's office. Pickering's name was on the AG's personal mailing list. I went to high school with a guy whose first name was Ashton. What a jerk."

"Look at these files. Sam was working day and night on research. I wonder if he ever went home?" asked Jack. David handed Jack Ashton Pickering's file.

Ashton Pickering: Liechtenauer's successor. Ashton is the grandson of J.J. Pickering, a Circle of Twelve disciple. Ashton's father, J.R. Pickering, is an obscure figure. Avoids the limelight. Financial advisor to Presidents and tyrants alike. A proponent of the balance of power concept. "One world power must never be stronger than another." J.J. Pickering made his fortune in World War I armaments. J.R. and his associates control the flow of Middle East oil and the futures market.

Lou-Ann pointed to the next photograph. "I recognize this guy.

That's Peterson, AKA von Leer, the man from the Smithsonian."

"We know von Leer and a Jules Smylee were involved in a scheme to purchase independent laboratories," said Jack. "Von Leer appears to have an unlimited source of money. Up until this weekend, I felt certain DOJ was about to indict him."

"What changed your mind?" asked Lou-Ann.

"The Trinity Files disappeared," said Jack. "No files. No indictments."

"And the guy with the "x" over his photo?" asked Lou-Ann.

"That's the late Jules Smylee. Committed suicide a few weeks ago."

"And the sketch. Who is it?"

"Ah. Now that is interesting. We have an unknown suspect. Sam thinks he may be a foreign national. The sketch is an FBI composite. I think Sam was close to identifying our mystery man. That was just before Grace died," said Jack.

"There have to be more players," said Lou-Ann.

"Too many coincidences."

"Sam hasn't listed Robert's name on the board," said David. "Robert is our Deep Throat. We don't have a clue as to his identity. He supplied us with files, a few names and some leads. His last contact was several weeks ago."

"Interesting. Did Robert give any hint where he was getting his information?"

"He told me he was the case manager for three German Nazis. He brought them into the country illegally. All three were on the war criminals list. He named Karl Peter Koch."

"And the others?" asked Lou-Ann.

"Good question. Robert left a package of documents at a dead drop."

David walked to the long oak table and picked up the envelope. "Here. We haven't looked at the documents. We were working with Portavani's records first," said David.

"Then let's get to it," said Lou-Ann. "Hand me the briefcase." Lou-Ann pulled a pair of latex gloves from her pocket and put them on. She emptied the briefcase on to Sam's desk. *Notes. A magazine. A couple of receipts.* "Not very much for a guy traveling on an international flight," Lou-Ann said. Then she felt the lining of the case. "David or Jack. One of you carry a knife?"

"I do," said Jack, handing it to Lou-Ann. She slit the lining. "Look at this. A passport." Lou-Ann handed it to Jack.

"Otto Bruns? David, that's the name Koch was using on the flight from London. This passport doesn't have a photograph, but it looks genuine."

"Hold on, Jack. Suppose there is an Otto Bruns? Imagine if Bruns was brought into the country illegally. Let's presume Robert was his case worker. Robert knew Bruns was hot on, say, the Dachau wanted list."

"We don't have time for suppositions, David. Let's work with what we have," said Jack.

"Hear him out, Jack," said Lou-Ann.

"Okay. Get on with it."

"Imagine Otto Bruns is in the United States. He must be important or Robert wouldn't be involved. Suppose Bruns, or someone claiming to be Otto Bruns, was the guy Portavani spotted on Plum Island. Bruns demands a new cover, or maybe out of the country to Costa Rico or Brazil, wherever. Bruns needs a passport."

"I think I'm following you on this, David," said Lou-Ann.

"Yes. Robert is no longer in the picture, or maybe he no longer wants to be associated with Operation Paperclip. Who knows? Bruns turns to Koch or his associates for help." Jack was intrigued with David's theory.

"In other words, Koch flies home using a passport issued to Bruns. Koch switched identities between South Africa and Egypt. Must have been stressful. He was in Ghana, London, and back into the United States." David walked to the wall and added Otto Bruns' name to it. As he tacked it to the wall, he said, "Bruns may still be in the U.S. That explains the passport with no photo. Koch flies in as Bruns. Bruns flies out with this passport."

"It sounds too simple," said Jack. "One problem for Bruns; he doesn't have the passport."

"Perhaps Koch's employer didn't expect him to die on the flight," said Lou-Ann.

"What gives you that idea?" asked Jack.

"I cut the lining on the other side. These two vials may give us a clue. They're still sealed." Lou-Ann handed two tan-colored glass vials to Jack. The seals were unbroken. Jack held them to the light.

"They still contain liquid," said Jack. "Bag the vials. We have to get the contents tested."

"Can we trust the FBI lab? Jack, somebody is watching us. We can't trust anyone." The worried look on Lou-Ann's face convinced Jack they needed an alternative.

"I've got it," said David. "Dr. Massri."

"Who?" asked Lou-Ann.

"Doctor Youssef Massri, the forensics specialist with the New York Medical Examiner's office. He's the exotic disease specialist who assisted with Koch's autopsy."

"David, you arrange to get these vials to Massri as soon as we're finished here."

"Now for the hard part: Portavani's journal." Jack handed the journal to David. "Review this map of Plum Island, too."

"Portavani told Nagle there were two guys on the Plum Island dock. The Asian guy. Portavani spotted them the next day at Smithaven Mall."

"You're right. So much has happened I forgot about the Asian," said Jack. "You said you challenged Robert about the Asian."

"Let me go through the dead drop envelope," David insisted. He opened the envelope. There it was. "I've got it," said David.

"What?" asked Lou-Ann.

"Here's a file labeled Unit 731. Look at this, Jack."

Jack walked around the table and looked over David's shoulder at a photograph of a man attached to a dossier. "Do you think this is the Asian Tony Portavani saw?"

David opened the folder. Sam's notes speculated the man Portavani saw on Plum Island was a Japanese virologist, Kumori Nishimura.

Unit 731 was a biological and chemical research program run by the Japanese Imperial Army during World War II. The complex was located in northeast China. The Japanese carried out bizarre medical experiments. It is rumored Allied prisoners of war, including captured

*U.S. military personnel were victims of the Japanese experiments. Program was led by General Shiro Ishi. Kumori Nishimura was the youngest member of the so-called research staff. (My inquiries have been met with resistance.) General Douglas MacArthur pardoned all but a few of the bio-weapons researchers. I suspect all records have been expunged. Note: St. Louis fire. **Immunity from war crimes.***

"Immunity from war crimes?" David sounded shocked. "How can that be, Jack?"

"I recall reading a letter. The writer's father was a prisoner of war. Just before he died, the father revealed he was intentionally infected during an experiment. The dad had to sign a waiver agreeing never to tell or he would be denied VA benefits. He was threatened with prison."

"What? The victim feared going to jail while the captors went free?"

"The son couldn't prove a damn thing."

"Look at this." Jack pointed to Sam's final notation.

Suspect several Unit 731 researchers visited U.S.; Fort Detrick.

"My God, Jack. I can't believe our government has suppressed such horrors."

"I can in a way, Lou-Ann. My uncle fought at Normandy on D-Day. I never heard him talk about the invasion. Retelling the story is just as painful as the actual experience."

"Maybe it's just as well the public doesn't know the stuff we're finding out," said David.

"How can you say that, Jack?" asked Lou-Ann.

"Even if the public had all the information, would they believe it?" asked David.

"No one will believe it until you write your novel, David." Lou-Ann chuckled.

Jack looked at Lou-Ann. "Folks will only accept the truth if they think it's fiction. Perhaps you're right. No publisher is going risk government retaliation."

"I have an idea," said Lou-Ann. "Leak the story to Dakota. She can write the novel." The trio laughed. Jack said, "Let's get serious.

We have a pile of work in front of us."

Lou-Ann was intrigued by the composite drawing of the unknown conspirator. She studied it for several minutes. "David, I'm curious." Lou-Ann walked to the wall and removed the drawing. "The guys who roughed you up outside the Mayflower… was this guy one of them?"

"He wasn't the guy who pushed me in front of the cab. He could have been driving the getaway car."

"I'm going to make a copy of this drawing. The State Department has records. There has to be someone who can put a name to this face."

David started to answer when Jack exclaimed, "Would you look at this!"

"What is it?"

"Four visas. Koch, Bruns, and a third German national. I can't make out the name. It's smudged. The INS never signed off on Koch, Bruns, or this third guy. The last visa for Nishimura looks legit."

"Who approved their entry papers?"

"Apparently, they never went through INS. They received endorsements from the State Department and the Department of Justice. Look at the official stamps." David and Lou-Ann examined the document.

Several portions were deleted or blacked-out. "Didn't you say your contact's name is Robert?" Lou-Ann pointed to the signatures beneath the respective seals.

"It can't be."

"What?"

Lou-Ann handed Koch's application back to Jack. "Take a look at the official signatures."

"I must have missed something." Jack retrieved a magnifying glass from Sam's desk. "I'm either tired or careless. I totally missed the most important clues."

"Recognize those names?" David still didn't follow.

"Erskin Young. It's his signature. He vouched for the Department of Justice background check." Jack checked the other documents. "Young signed these three."

"And who signed for the State Department?" asked David.

"William Robert Mallory. Name doesn't mean anything to me. What's your point, Lou-Ann?"

"Mallory's middle name is 'Robert'. I'll wager a week's pay Mallory is your Robert."

"How can you be so sure?" Jack was certain Lou-Ann's intuition was playing games.

"Mallory is your man. Who else would have access to these copies? He stashed them just in case of blow-back. It was an insurance policy. These guys broke the law. Mallory needed to prove he was acting on orders from higher authorities. Koch and the other two were on a wanted list back in Germany. President Truman signed an executive order. It prohibited war criminals from entering the United States."

"What about Nishimura?"

"That's another story." Jack handed David Nishimura's visa application. "Nothing. He's clean. INS processed Nishimura. Remember? This guy got a full pardon, from General MacArthur."

"I just can't believe this." David walked over to Sam's desk and slumped into a chair. Lou-Ann sat with her head propped in her hands. Jack unknotted his tie and slouched as best he could in the wooden chair. "Guys, let's call it a day." *This report will never see the light of day. No wonder Sam felt he was running up against a brick wall.*

"We have to keep a lid on this stuff. We can't afford any leaks. We have to finesse the investigation from here on in. If the wrong people find out what we've discovered, every document we want will disappear or be classified for thirty years."

The other two sat up.

"I understand, Jack."

"Lou-Ann. Are you with us on this?"

"Yes, Jack. I'm with you."

"I know we have a lot to accomplish here, but I can't continue to neglect my personal life." Jack and Lou-Ann were stunned by David's remark. "Don't look so astonished. I have a life outside of this place and so do you two. I'll take care of my assignment, but I have to run."

"You're right, David. This job takes its toll."

"I agree. You ought to know, Jack. And Sam...I can't imagine what he's going through."

"Okay. Take off, David. See you first thing Wednesday morning. The clock is ticking. I'm apprehensive. We have to tie this thing up, before someone decides to close us down." The trio looked at one another, but said nothing. There was silent agreement.

David left for parts unknown. "It's time for us to knock off work, too. Let's close shop. Meet back here on Wednesday. You take care of our mystery profile. He has to be connected to one or more of our persons of interest. Make your inquiry as vague as possible. We don't want this to become nasty. We're dealing with some powerful people."

"I understand, Jack. And you? You're so thin and pale. You need to take better care of yourself."

"Thanks." I need some new clothes, too."

"I have an idea. Let's grab some supper. I know this wonderful little place, not far from here."

"I don't know."

"Come on. It's right in the center of D.C."

Lou-Ann finally persuaded Jack to have dinner with her. They secured the situation room. Lou-Ann waited for Jack to check his mail. Lynn was working late. She told Lou-Ann that Sam had called. The FBI assured Sam the team's lines were clean.

"Please have mine checked, too."

"Okay. Jack looks awful."

"Yes. I'm forcing him to have dinner with me tonight."

Jack returned in time to hear Lynn tell Lou-Ann, "Great news! Sam will be returning to work before the end of the week."

"When?" asked Jack.

"Hopefully, Wednesday or Thursday."

Chapter 20

"How did you find this place?"

"That's a secret." Lou-Ann smiled. The restaurant was hidden behind an antique furniture gallery. Lou-Ann pointed to the far end of a meandering alley. It opened onto a secluded lush garden. "Voila. Nous viola en France."

Jack scratched his head. He always did when he was trying to come up with something witty. "I failed high school Spanish."

"That was French, Jack." They both laughed.

"We can take our time. It's slow paced, but that's exactly what we need." *Why am I saying these things? This isn't a date…hmm.*

"Good evening, Miss Stokes."

"Jack, this is Jon. Jon adds a flourishing touch to La Petite Coquette."

"Au contraire. It is you. On such a beautiful spring night, may I suggest a garden table for you and the gentleman?"

"Of course, Jon." Jon led them to a secluded table on the far side of a fountain.

"Thanks for taking pity on me."

"This isn't a mercy mission. Think of this as my contribution to the team. I'm helping you keep healthy. Shall we order some wine?"

Jack laughed. He felt comfortable with Lou-Ann. He wanted to trust her. He struggled with his suspicious nature. "Now that we're working together, you might as well hear this from me."

Lou-Ann set down the wine list and listened intently.

"I want to be straight with you. There are a couple of things you should know about me, personally. I'm a recovering alcoholic.

David kids me about coming late to work. I'm probably at an AA meeting. If it works, work it. It works for me."

Lou-Ann intently listened.

"Second, I have a difficult time trusting women. My ex-wife cheated with my best friend. She got just about everything. I have visitation rights, but the kids always seem too busy. Dakota Putnam 'outed' me in a *Washington Post* story. Dakota's story earned her a promotion. I was sent to "no man's land.""

Lou-Ann looked puzzled.

"The basement of the Justice building. It was a rough time. I slid from sadness into despair. The booze didn't help. It created a haze. Kathleen no longer loved me. She mocked me. I felt lost. I was in denial."

"Did your wife drink?"

"On occasion. We had bitter arguments. Doesn't matter now. It's over."

Lou-Ann felt a growing sense of sadness for Jack. She wasn't ready to reveal her own demons to Jack. *My mother was an abusive alcoholic. The disease destroyed my parents' marriage. I feel a bit bewildered. This guy is really complicated.* She took a sip of water. "Thanks for being honest. I've experienced a few break-ups, but I can't imagine a divorce. I'll have to earn your trust."

Jack moved on. "Enough of this gloominess. Tell me about yourself."

Lou-Ann smiled.

"Do you have a boyfriend?"

"Not exactly. I do have a special friend. He and I are married to our careers. We try to find time for an occasional dinner, but rarely a weekend escape."

Lou-Ann ordered a glass of pinot noir.

When the wine arrived, Jack lifted his water glass and proposed a toast. "To the beginning of a new friendship."

"A new friendship," Lou-Ann repeated as their glasses touched.

❧

While Jack and Lou-Ann were getting acquainted, David was pulling into his apartment complex's parking lot. He spotted Dakota's MG-B. *Now what? I'm in no mood for one of her outbursts. Wait 'til she finds out I'm going to Long Island this weekend.* David felt apprehensive as he unlocked the apartment door.

He walked in to find Dakota perched on the kitchen table. One of David's dress shirts was loosely draped over her shoulders.

"What are you doing?"

"It's my way of saying I'm sorry about my outburst this afternoon." Dakota reclined a bit. The shirt slid to the table.

David froze. "This is how you apologize? Sitting half-naked on my kitchen table?"

"Come on, David. I'm sorry."

"Do you have any idea how much that shirt costs to be laundered?"

Dakota jumped off the table. "Why, you…" She pounded on David's chest. "You are such a nerd. That's just like you. I can't stand you." Dakota ran to the bedroom and slammed the door.

"Stop behaving like a child. I was kidding. I'm thrilled. Open the door."

The door slowly opened. David and Dakota hesitated, then embraced. "I'm sorry," she whispered.

"Me, too," David echoed as they tumbled on to the bed. They laughed as Dakota playfully undressed David and they made love. Soon David was asleep, but not Dakota.

Dakota couldn't suppress her reporter's curiosity. She recalled one letter in a pile of mail she had cleared from the table and tossed on the counter. Dakota tiptoed to the kitchen and searched for the envelope. *Airline tickets? Where the hell is he going? He never told me.* She felt the Putnam temper rising. She took the envelope into the bedroom and shook David. "David, are you flying someplace, soon?"

"What?" David turned and looked at Dakota. "What's wrong?"

"This envelope. Return receipt guaranteed. Airline tickets. Correct?"

"Hold on. You have no business going through my mail."

Dakota was unmoved. She waved the envelope.

"Yes, if you must know. I'm going with the New York Delegation to New York. The delegation has been invited to what promises to be the event of the year out on Long Island. Trinity PharmoDynamics, USA. Exclusive. The place will be packed with big shots. Plus, it gives me a chance to size up the new CEO,

Ashton Pickering."

"Pickering. His picture is pinned to the situation room wall."

"That's him. A little pleasure mixed with business."

"You are so smug. You weren't going to tell me. All I deserve is a last minute phone call from the airport. 'Poor Dakota.'"

"We aren't engaged. You don't live with me. You have a key, but…"

"But you aren't in love with me." Dakota threw the envelope at David. "I'm leaving."

"That's your answer to everything, Dakota. If you can't get your way, you either rage or walk out. Well, maybe it's best if you leave. Oh, one more thing." Dakota was about to step into the shower when David dropped the bomb. "I have an interview with Jones and Rolland, a Wall Street firm."

"You what?"

"You heard me."

"And you weren't going to tell me?"

"I told Jack. That's it. I wasn't sure how you would react. Now I know."

"How would you expect me to act? I'm falling in love with a clueless geek and he tells me he may be moving to New York City."

"Falling in love? Dakota, please don't say that."

"Why not?"

"Because, I'm uncertain how I feel about us. You're so controlling. You ask my opinion, I give it. You tell me I'm wrong. Why ask me? And, if you can't get your way, you start an argument. I can't win. You have to be right all the time; even when you're wrong."

"Stop flapping your arms. You're always so animated," she taunted.

"Flapping? Animated? There you go."

"You deserve it. You're so ridiculous. There I was, sitting in my panties and you have to make a joke out of it. There's someone else." Dakota's temper gave way to tears.

"This damn investigation has me nuts. I just want out. It's a dead end. I don't want my life to turn out like Sam's and Jack's."

"Sam and Jack?"

"Sam's finished once news of Grace's death gets out. Any hint of scandal will ruin his career."

"Scandal?"

"Just forget it."

"And Jack?"

"This time next year he'll be retired."

"So that's it? And I thought we had something special." Dakota sobbed.

"We do, but I'm not ready to make a commitment. Too much is uncertain."

Dakota shuffled to the side of the bed and looked down at David. "Now what am I supposed to do?"

She read the expression on David's face. "I really hate you, David. No. I love you so much."

"Oh, Dakota. Why does everything between us have to be complicated?"

She shook her head. "I don't know."

"Damn you, Dakota. You drive me crazy."

David couldn't hold up against Dakota's sobs.

"Okay. I give in. Dakota, will you fly to New York with me?"

"You're not teasing? You're serious?" She rubbed the tears from her cheeks.

"Yes. We'll go together. I'll find someplace nice out on the Island, away from the rest of the delegation. Dakota, I know one thing for sure."

"What's that?"

"You look absolutely spectacular, standing there bare-assed naked telling me you love me."

Dakota sat on the edge of the bed and touched David's hand. He pulled her back under the sheets.

"I do love you. You must know it," she murmured.

Events weren't quite as pleasurable for Sam Beverly. Sergeant Napoli called earlier in the day and intensified Sam's anguish.

"I spoke with the ME's Office a few minutes ago, Mr. Beverly. The bottom line…it's definitely a homicide."

"Now what happens?"

"I'll be honest with you. I have a couple of leads. I wish I had something substantive. I do have description of the men who rented the unit directly above your apartment."

"What do you have? The manager and rental agent both gave me descriptions. The manager has a vivid recollection of one of the guys."

"And?"

"The manager distinctly remembers a tall man. He described him as cold-looking with a diabolical smile. Evil-like. Short hair. Mid-30's to early 40's. Close cropped hair. Neat as a pin."

"That's it?"

"No. The big guy spoke with an accent. The manager thought it might be German."

"And his accomplice?"

"A short, chubby guy. Didn't say much. The rental agent agreed."

"Did you get their names?"

"Not the big guy's. The other one signed the agreement. Gave the agent cash. He signed the agreement using the name Richard Shipe. Probably a phony. Nobody in their right mind would sign their real name."

"You never can tell. Will you check it out?"

"I'm already on it. How are you doing, Mr. Beverly? This must be difficult for you."

Sam paused. *Difficult? My wife is murdered. My daughter has disowned me. I can't eat. I have a pile of work waiting for me. My career is over. Difficult?*

"Thanks for asking, Sergeant. I'm managing." That's all Sam could muster.

"Good luck, Mr. Beverly. I promise to keep in touch."

Sam put down the phone. He lay on the couch. Sam recalled the psychiatrist's couch. Dr. Jed Nethers' practice was located in Columbia, Maryland. *The further from Washington, the better.* Sam needed to deal with his increasing sense of isolation; the growing distance from Grace. Dr. Nethers' huge leather couch made Sam feel relaxed and secure.

"I had this epiphany."

"Tell me about it, Sam."

"It started a while back. Grace and I never enjoyed an easy marriage. I always felt something was missing. I blamed myself, my career. You know how that goes."

"I'm not sure Sam. Tell me."

"Yes, an epiphany. A sudden aha! It came to me."

Dr. Nethers made a note, but didn't comment.

"One day…a midafternoon…I playfully rolled my wife on the bed as she was reading. I knew better. I caressed her. I sensed she wasn't into it. Our lovemaking had diminished. Sometimes several months passed. I told myself, 'Today would be different.'"

"Different?"

"At some point, I rolled on top of her. Turning my head, I looked at her. I wanted to kiss her. I longed for her to kiss me. Her face was turned to the wall. Her eyes were wide open. I looked into her eyes. I saw emptiness and desperation."

"Desperation?"

"Like she was thinking, 'Just do it'. I raised myself to kiss her forehead. Her eyes abruptly shifted, first at me and then away. I felt numb. I imagined she felt nothing. I knew it then."

"You knew what?"

"It was over. It was time for one of us to say goodbye. Have you ever experienced knowing it was over?"

Dr. Nethers didn't answer. He continued to jot a note.

Tonight, Sam was alone and experiencing that same empty feeling. The urn with Grace's ashes rested on the fireplace mantle. "What should I do next, Grace?"

I can't deal with all this. I dread the pressure. Facing all the questions. I dread the investigation. Look where it's taken me.

Sam knew the answer. It was time to go back to work.

Sam telephoned the Inspector General's home. The answering machine picked up. "Hi. It's Sam. I apologize for calling at this hour, but it's important. I'm returning to work in the morning. I know I have another week of leave, but I need to return to work. I'll call your office in the morning. Thanks."

Jack felt increasing pressure to bring the inquiry to closure. "Lou-Ann and David, use the day to follow up on outstanding leads."

Lou-Ann arrived early for her meeting at INS. She anticipated another stonewall. She was shuffled from one official to another. It was exasperating. Her FBI status meant nothing. This morning's appointment wasn't an interview. Jack had signed an official authorization to review INS files.

David was feeling put off at the Department of Justice. When he arrived at the security desk, Mac greeted him, "Good to see you again, Mr. Clayton."

"Thanks, Mac. How's it going?"

"Fine, thanks. I'm afraid I have bad news."

Clayton's smile turned to a frown. "What's wrong?"

"Mr. Young was called to another meeting this morning. It was an emergency. His secretary asked that you call her later today or tomorrow to reschedule."

"You know, Mac, this is some bureaucracy. It's tough pinning someone down. Seems whenever I ask for an appointment…"

"The Federal government is a maze. I can't imagine how the ordinary citizen can get any help. I see the look on their faces. They wander in here looking for assistance and I tell them they are in the wrong place."

David abruptly raised his arms shoulder height, let them fall and said, "I'm ready to give up."

Mac laughed. "Sorry for laughing, Mr. Clayton. What you said is so true it's funny."

"Not today, Mac. Today it's pathetic." David grimaced. He had several hours before his next appointment. *I wonder if my next appointment will have an emergency.*

Jack opened the door to Sam's office, stuck his head in and said, "Morning, Lynn. I'll head to the situation room."

"Jack, get in here. Where have you been? It's eleven o'clock and you didn't call in."

"I'm sorry. Calm down. I didn't know I had to call in. Lou-Ann and David aren't expected in today. I had a couple of errands to run and…"

"Close the door." Lynn stood up and pointed to Sam's private office. "Sam's back."

"Back? He didn't give me a heads-up."

"I came in early. Sam was already here. He looks awful. To

make matters worse…"

"Worse?" Jack exclaimed. "Sam needs to stay out on leave."

"Let me finish. Just about an hour ago, two FBI agents arrived, pushing an old man in a wheelchair."

"Who is he?"

"Mr. Erskin Young. Never heard of him. He runs a group at the DOJ. He must be eighty years old. I thought they had compulsory retirement."

"Never mind that. Where are they now?"

"The situation room. Mr. Young must be a powerful man. You should have seen the look on Sam's face. Sam was so pale…like he was going into shock."

"Young is a powerful man. He's an enigma. I'll bet ninety per cent of the administrators at DOJ don't know who he is.

"I'll be back later. I've got to get down there." Jack rushed to the situation room. The security guard was standing at an uncomfortable attention. His chair was gone. Jack followed the security check and punched in the combination to open the situation door. He entered the outer room. *These two must be Young's security detachment.* Jack identified himself and approached the inner office to find Sam and Young. They appeared to be arguing. Jack knocked on the door.

"Good morning, Jack. I apologize for not letting you know I'd be here this morning. It was a late decision. Not that late, apparently." Sam looked down at the man in the wheelchair. "Jack, this is Erskin Young. Mr. Young is with the DOJ. The Attorney General asked Mr. Young to drop by."

Young turned his wheelchair and looked up at Jack. "That's a lot of bullshit. I can tell you now both the Secretary and the Attorney General are unhappy about your little investigation. In fact, Beverly here has pissed off a lot of people. And you, Thompson? Wasn't the Watergate mess enough for you? I'm told you never know when to let go."

"You don't have any grievances with Jack, Mr. Young. I'm in charge here."

"Doesn't look like it." Young scratched his head in a way that looked like he was pulling out his hair. He was nearly bald. Flakes of dandruff covered his suit jacket.

"I'm an old man, Beverly. I don't have time for your bullshit. I want answers." Young pointed to the wall. "So this is your hall of fame?"

"Those are the persons of interest. The first two photographs…"

Young interrupted. "I don't care about them. It's the others. I can tell you one name you won't have to check out."

"Sir?" Jack walked to the wall.

"William Robert Mallory," Young snickered.

"Mallory? I'm lost," said Sam.

"Here we go again. Don't try to bullshit me, Beverly. You didn't come up with all this information. It would have taken years to assemble these files. Mallory! I listened to the tapes about a week ago. Your entire team…their phones were tapped."

"What's the connection with Mallory? You idiots! Mallory was my associate on Operation Paperclip. We handled the transitions. I covered all the bases. Mallory was the control. He handled a hundred or more cases INS refused to approve. Robert had to be Mallory."

"Had? You said had," Jack insisted on clarifying Young's remark.

"That's right. You haven't received calls from Mallory since the drop at the Mayflower. Correct?"

Jack and Sam looked at each other in acknowledgement.

"I can tell by the look on your faces, I'm right." Young rolled the wheelchair to the wall. "You can stop looking for Robert. He's dead." Young spoke abruptly and indifferently.

"We never knew Robert's identity. Mallory was the cosigner on the visas we examined. It was a guess." Sam tried to argue the point with Young, but he didn't have the stamina.

"Mallory died in a plane crash. And no, he wasn't assassinated. I'm sorry he's dead. I wanted to prosecute the bastard for violating the secrecy laws."

"I guess that's it?" asked Jack.

"No, that's not all. I didn't come all the way over here to tell you assholes Mallory was dead. I want answers." The entire side of Young's torso jerked up and down. He was obviously in pain and quite distracted. "How much longer is this inquiry going to take?"

"We've just touched the tip of the iceberg, Mr. Young. Quite honestly, you're under scrutiny as well."

"My point exactly. Well, boys, here's a message for you. Wind this thing up. I give you another two weeks. No subpoenas. No press releases. Beverly, get control of this team. If I were your boss, I would have canned you by now. Bereavement or no bereavement. Get your thumb out of your ass and start writing the report."

"I don't care who you are, Young. You're an old man. You lied to Congress. You've destroyed records. Now you come in here acting like a saint and telling us what to do. I don't take orders from you." Sam was angry.

"If you know what's good for your career, Beverly, you'll do as I'm telling you. By the way, you also have responsibility for your personnel. Don't you?" There was something sinister in Young's remark.

Sam paused then replied, "I'll wind it up in two, no later than three, weeks. We will be prepared to appear before a closed Congressional hearing."

"You can bet your ass on that, Beverly. And Jack, your life is chaotic. I've listened to the tapes. That ex-wife of yours…" Young pulled out a small notepad. "Ah, yes. Your wife is screwing you… and a couple of other fools, too. Quite the lady. She thinks you're a damn fool. And I think she's right."

Jack leaned over. His breath singed Young's face. "Up yours!" Jack walked into the other room. The two agents must have overheard the exchange. Jack caught them laughing.

"Dump that man, Beverly. He's headed into retirement one way or another."

"I'm in charge here."

"You are for another three weeks at the most. I'm not kidding. This isn't me talking. I could give a damn. You know damn well who's pulling the strings. You embarrass them and you will be in trouble." Young rolled his wheelchair through the doorway. He wheeled around. "One last thing. The State Department is into something big. Way beyond you, me or this foolishness about Nazis. You'll understand when you read the papers."

"What?"

"Don't let your little investigation cause any distractions." He wheeled around and said to his escorts, "Gentlemen, we have much more important things to do today." One of the agents pushed his wheelchair.

"Camp David." Young called out. "Camp David." Suddenly, the old man started to uncontrollably cough.

The second agent was carrying a black bag. "Sir, do you need oxygen?" The coughing stopped. Young fell forward in the wheel chair. He quivered and gasped.

The two agents pulled the old man from the chair and laid him on the floor. "Call for an ambulance. Get help!" shouted one of the agents.

Young died before the ambulance arrived. Jack was baffled by the entire incident, but felt no sympathy for the tyrant. *I can't feel any pity for the guy. What a bastard.* "At this rate, we won't have anyone left to investigate," Jack said.

"You're probably right."

Jack sensed Erskin Young's death marked the beginning of the end of their inquiry.

"Get hold of David and Lou-Ann. Arrange a meeting. We'd better start putting a report together."

"Sam, while you were out, I received a call from the Attorney General. He claimed to have touched base with the Secretary and the Inspector General."

"What did he tell you?"

"Young's words, as though they had talked with one another. Upstairs wants this investigation finished. A preliminary report in the next two weeks. Better yet, a summary."

"I figured." Sam shrugged his shoulders. "You know we're on to something big. That explains the pressure, the threats. Young probably sent those guys to rough you up. Young anticipated the dead drop. He listened to your calls."

"That explains it. We may be dealing with two separate competing groups."

"What gives you that idea?"

"Lou-Ann. It was her idea. I agree."

"She told me, too."

"Now we know one group…the government. Who is the other?"

"Trinity PharmoDynamics Group? Liechtenauer? The

mystery man in the composite drawing?" Sam asked.

"David and Lou-Ann are trying to tie up loose ends. There's just too much. We should pursue Trinity. It's our best lead."

"I'll head over to INS and see if I can give Lou-Ann a hand."

"And I'll attack the stack of papers and unopened mail. Thank God for Lynn."

"Camp David. What did Young mean?" asked Jack.

"Beats me."

Lynn stepped into the hall. "Excuse me. There's a call for you, Sam."

"Who is it?"

"The Attorney General. He sounds annoyed."

"Not again." Sam turned and left with Lynn.

"I'll be at INS with Lou-Ann."

When Jack arrived at INS, he was escorted to a small workroom set aside for archival searches. He found Lou-Ann deep in thought, perusing the files.

"Hey. Thought I'd stop by and give you a hand."

"Come on in. Just don't talk to me. I'm on to something."

"It's been an awful morning for me. Guess what?"

"No time, Jack. Get to the point."

"You're all business. In a nutshell…" Jack recounted his morning. "The Attorney General's after Sam, too."

Lou-Ann didn't seem to hear a thing. "I'm sorry, Jack. I got bits and pieces of your story. Take a look at what I've found." She handed Jack a legal pad with notes scribbled across the page.

"Nice. I can't read this. What did you find?"

"The records for Karl Peter Koch and Otto Bruns. Do you recall the documents the State Department issued?"

"The ones we examined last Monday?"

"Exactly. Take a look. The same papers are in these two files."

Jack looked at the signatures. "Mallory and Young. What's the connection?"

"Karl Otto Koch's application for U.S. citizenship was approved. They even have social security numbers assigned. But look at Bruns' application."

Jack read a notation on the bottom of Bruns' document. "The investigator noted Bruns may be a Nazi war criminal."

"That explains why Koch was using a forged passport on his return flight from London."

"Bruns must still be in the country. The passport without a photo ID. It was for him. He isn't a citizen. He's been here illegally. He remains a wanted Nazi."

"Koch planned to enter the U.S. using Bruns' passport. If and when Customs and Immigration ran a check, the passport would be on file. Almost the perfect plan."

"What happened to Bruns? Where is he now? Someone has to be protecting him."

Jack felt certain he knew who was shielding Bruns. "Trinity," Jack declared.

"Trinity?"

"Of course. Erskin Young's warnings. Trinity, Justice and State share mutual interests."

"A cover-up."

"The State Department and DOJ already assured Congress they had cleaned out the Nazi war criminals. That just isn't so. Erskin and Mallory lied to Congress."

"How does this information help us now? They're both dead."

"If Koch was double dipping…DOA and Trinity PharmoDynamics, USA, Bruns probably was, too."

"Our investigation has ruffled feathers."

Lou-Ann laughed. "Ruffled feathers? That's an understatement. You've been dragging muddy waters and have come up with more than one body."

"To what end?"

"Your theory, Jack. We have to turn all our efforts toward Trinity."

Chapter 21

During the spring of 1977, Trinity PharmoDynamics Group staged a number of worldwide celebrations. Trinity's dark side connections to IG Farben were behind it now. Nowhere was this more apparent than at Trinity's USA subsidiary, Trinity PharmoDynamics, USA. Dr. Liechtenauer's three-fold plan was evolving. Trinity successfully purchased a number of U.S. pharmaceutical companies. Thanks to several influential members of Congress, Trinity PharmoDynamics, USA supplied the Veterans Administration with an assortment of pharmaceutical devices. The Trinity brand, with its inverted sword logo, was becoming a household name, thanks to Ashton Pickering's aggressive marketing skills. Trinity acquired a building on Madison Avenue in Manhattan. They purchased Global Advertising and embarked on an intensive advertising campaign.

It was time to manufacture pharmaceuticals. The legal staff secured the permits. Trinity received speedy approvals, thanks to friends on the Hill. Trinity began marketing generics. Pickering monitored developments in the Middle East. Schmidt confirmed Ashton's prediction.

"You were correct, Mr. Pickering. Our assets at the DOA and FDA report their agencies have shifted resources to Rift Valley Virus research. The DOD is investing heavily in it. The military wants a vaccine that will offer immunity against several diseases."

"Researchers at our Argentina facility are close to a livestock vaccine, but not a multivirus immunization. I suggest we file for a patent," Reiter insisted.

"Patience, Reiter. We will move cautiously. Filing for a patent too soon might spark inquiries into our research program. There must be absolutely no connection to IG Farben. Is that clear, Reiter?" Pickering had a peculiarity of lowering his voice to emphasize an order. This was Reiter's first private meeting with Ashton Pickering.

A foreboding tingled through Reiter's body. Pickering frightened him. Something in the way Pickering murmured foretold evil.

"I have a plan to secure the government's research."

"All in due time, Reiter. All in due time."

Ashton Pickering recognized a growing divisiveness in the United States. Americans had lost confidence in their leaders and themselves. Cynicism and anxiety were underlining themes. *American agencies destroyed evidence of Nazi criminals residing within its borders. The newspaper exposés aroused little interest.* Extensive surveys and public opinion polls revealed Americans wanted to forget the turmoil of Vietnam and civil unrest. Some wanted a return to the opulence of the '20's. To Trinity's benefit, the public had lost interest in the horror of World War II.

Against his physicians' warnings, Dr. Liechtenauer planned every detail. At first, the extravagance made Liechtenauer uneasy. As the expenditures mounted, Kurt Strauss expressed concern. "These financial reports indicate you have spent over one hundred thousand dollars for this reception. This is so unlike you, Liechtenauer."

"Not to worry, my dear Strauss. This is to be my first and last 'hurrah'. Regrettably, I will not be attending. Look at me, Strauss. I'm a dying man. My life depends on all sorts of machines. I despise the feeding tube."

Liechtenauer's agony was evident. Weeks earlier, his physician telephoned Strauss to warn of an impending crisis. "Liechtenauer will soon be unable to speak or swallow. He refuses to eat." Strauss knew Liechtenauer's death was imminent.

Strauss rarely addressed Liechtenauer by his first name. On this occasion, it was appropriate. "Walther, spend all you want on your celebration. You have worked tirelessly for the alliance. Your event will surpass Fitzgerald's Gatsby."

"Please wheel me to the window, Strauss." Liechtenauer pointed to a huge mirror on the far wall. "On your left, Strauss.

Press the corner of the frame."

Strauss touched the frame's gilded edge. A blue hue covered the mirror, turning it into an immense window. Below was an ornate ballroom, once the mansion's grand hall. Black Knight's banners were gone. No reminders of Nazi Germany or Teutonic influence remained.

Strauss stepped back. *It must be the medication. Liechtenauer is losing his mind. Liechtenauer decorated the room with Strickland's most expensive tapestries and window coverings. All the furnishings were custom-made.*

Strauss anticipated Pickering's objections to the lavish furnishings. The entire project was underscored by cost overrides. Pickering scowled on one occasion. "Eighty-two million dollars for 35 copper bathtubs? Outrageous, Strauss."

"I understand," said Strauss.

"Has Liechtenauer placed the order?" asked Pickering.

"Yes."

"Oh, well. You will have to answer for Liechtenauer's extravagance, not me. Hand me the invoice. I'll approve it. This is the last time, Strauss," said Pickering in a nearly inaudible tone.

The celebration day arrived. Liechtenauer felt a sense of great accomplishment as he surveyed the ballroom below. *Within hours our guests will be arriving. Three hundred invitations. Only a handful of regrets.*

A Smithtown catering firm delivered food all day. The mansion's huge kitchen bustled with activity. One of the chefs supervised the finishing touches on a gigantic ice swan in the center of a champagne fountain. Hundreds of floral arrangements decorated the tables and the entrance hall. Musicians tuned their instruments.

The fourteen hundred acre Trinity estate bordered the Villages of Nissequogue and Head of the Harbor. The estate's transformation increased traffic along Route 25A bordering the Nissequogue River. Trinity received numerous complaints.

Liechtenauer called Strauss with a request. "Strauss, we need to gain community confidence. This is no time for adverse publicity. Speak with the local opinion makers."

Strauss's staff attended several coffee klatches. Trinity

PharmoDynamics, USA donated two million dollars for community improvements and recreational programs. Trinity's community relations team scheduled an open house exclusively for village residents. Finally, the makeover was complete. It was time for a gala affair reminiscent of the November 1944 celebration. Liechtenauer frequently remembered the evening.

With Germany on the brink of destruction, Liechtenauer drank champagne and cheered as four V-2's were launched at London. Liechtenauer offered the first of many toasts saluting von Braun, the mastermind directing Hitler's vengeance weapon. *What a strange turn of events between then and now. 1944 was the last time I spoke with von Braun and his Peenemunde associates. Under no circumstances could there be any link between Trinity and von Braun.*

Von Braun died in June 1977. Liechtenauer refused to allow anyone connected with Trinity to send condolences or attend NASA's memorial service. Now, it was time for Liechtenauer to make his own "final arrangements."

"Strauss, I have a few requests. In my desk is a brown envelope. Inside, you will find my will and several other documents. The Alliance has approved your role as Chief Financial Officer. I depend on you to assist Pickering. The present board of directors has been dissolved. Reiter will continue as International Director for Research. Schmidt will continue to head our legal division. Everything is in writing."

"And Berg?" asked Strauss.

"Berg has been retired." A brief smile crossed Liechtenauer's lips.

"Has he been informed? He won't like this."

"Ah. This evening, prior to Pickering's greeting, Berg will receive a letter informing him of the Alliance's decision."

Strauss knew better than to express what he was thinking. *Berg was insubordinate once too often. He'll be....* Strauss feared thinking about Berg's fate.

"It's time for my feeding," said Liechtenauer. "Enjoy the evening, Strauss. You are my most trusted ally. The Alliance has faith in your judgment." Liechtenauer's medical aide entered the room.

"It's time, Sir."

"Yes, one minute, please."

Liechtenauer raised his head and looked at Strauss. "Strauss, do you believe in God?"

Liechtenauer's question surprised Strauss. The doctor had never mentioned religion before.

"I'm not sure. At one time I believed. I imagined an orderly universe with a benevolent God."

"And now?" Liechtenauer asked.

Strauss was confounded. "I'm an old man. I see things differently. We live in a chaotic world. Do you remember Treblinka, Walther? Himmler sent me to inspect the inventories of seized possessions. I saw huge piles of women's hair, shoes, and clothes."

"I remember both I and II. Treblinka II was a model of efficiency," Liechtenauer replied.

"It wasn't a prison or concentration camp. Treblinka II was built for one purpose…to exterminate Europe's Jews," said Strauss. I stood outside one large building, watching. There was a boy, about my son's age. No more than six years old. He was naked. He ran to me. He wrapped his arms around my legs. I felt his terror. A guard pulled the child away. He looked directly into my eyes. He knew his fate."

"The boy's destiny was out of your hands, Strauss. You had your orders. The SS had a job to do."

"I saw a building with a Star of David and huge relief doors. It was the gas chamber. I watched them enter. Some refused. They were clubbed or shot. The guard shoved the boy through the entrance."

"You sound sentimental, Strauss. The ruminations of an old man."

"You may be right. I never hated Jews. I sometimes wish I had." Strauss's voice lowered to a whisper. "I stopped believing in God that day. No. I don't believe in God, nor Heaven or Hell."

"Strauss, you surprise me. Of all people, you should know good and evil are relative," said Liechtenauer.

"Why are you asking? Is it your health?" Strauss asked.

Liechtenauer lowered his head for a moment. "Thank you, Strauss. And now you must excuse us."

As Strauss entered the elevator, he turned and nodded a grim farewell to Liechtenauer. Strauss knew it would be the last time he saw the doctor.

❧

"David, this is such a wonderful inn. How did you find it?"

"The Stony Brook Yacht Club is across the way. My friends owned a gorgeous sailboat…a yacht, really. Eventually, they sold their home and set off to who knows where. That was several years ago. They were living in Saint Maarten."

"Would you ever want to do that?"

"Only with you, Dakota." David caressed her cheek and pulled her close.

A slight breeze ruffled the curtains of the open window. The bed took up most of the room. But who cared?

"I can taste the salt air from the Sound." Dakota pushed David onto his back and rubbed his chest. Soon they were making love.

The couple arrived at the Three Village Inn the night before. David convinced Dakota to dine in. The Steinway baby grand piano in the Shell Bar caught his eye. David ordered a bottle of St. Emillion.

"A bit extravagant, David," Dakota whispered.

Before he could respond, Bunty Bendleton's unique voice drifted through the room.

"La Vie en Rose. Edith Piaf."

"You know the song?"

"Know it? It's my favorite. It reminds me of my mother. She loved French, too."

And so began a romantic evening. They closed the bar.

The next morning, Dakota was first to shower. "I want to walk through the garden."

"Okay, but don't get lost. I have some calls to make. By the way, don't you have an interview with Liz Nagle?"

"Yes. I'll give her a call while you shower. Hey, don't take all day."

Dakota dialed the Nagle home. The phone rang several times before Liz Nagle answered.

"There'll be no interviews, Miss Putnam. I've had it."

"I promise not to take up a lot of your time."

"No. I can tell you this. Matt was granted a medical leave by the college. He's probably arriving at a hunting cabin upstate as we speak. I have no idea where it's located."

"Mrs. Nagle, it wasn't my intention to upset you."

"If I wasn't working, our family would be homeless, thanks to Matt. I'm sick of this whole business. Those two thugs from the Justice Department convinced me."

"Two thugs from Justice? Are you certain they were from the Justice Department?"

"Bad enough they threatened me over the phone, but to come to my home and…"

"Hold on, Mrs. Nagle. I know for a fact the General Accounting Office is conducting this investigation, not the DOJ."

"They showed me their badges and an official letter ordering me to cooperate."

"Can you describe them?"

"Of course. I'm no dummy. One guy was short, stocky, unkempt. Didn't look at all respectable. Not like I pictured an agent."

"And the other?"

"He frightened me. Tall, a conservative dresser. There was something about him. If I were superstitious, I'd say I felt the presence of the devil himself."

"Then what happened?"

"What do you think? I told them to get out. The little guy backed off, but the big one…he glowered. I felt he might hurt me or the kids."

"I'm sorry you had to go through this, Mrs. Nagle."

"I'm assuming you're not married, Miss Putnam."

"I'm not."

"Listen to me. Never marry a dreamer. Oh, their eccentricities will charm you. They're so easy to love, at first. You will regret it. Matt Nagle's mind wanders from hither to yon. He can never accept anything for what it is. He's always questioning and searching."

"I understand, Mrs. Nagle. Believe me."

"Matt talks with strangers on the street. He'd talk with a

billboard. If his nose isn't buried in a book, he's jotting a note. Wants to write the great American novel. He lives in a fantasy."

"Oh, Mrs. Nagle. Surely you love him."

"Yes. Of course I do. That's my downfall." Liz Nagle ranted for a minute more. "I thought Matt would be different than my father. Why does love have to mean sacrifice?"

"I don't know."

"Where is my knight in shining armor? I'm cursed. I shouldn't be telling you these things. Goodbye, Miss Putnam."

"Please, one last question."

"No more questions. Goodbye."

Dakota flopped into the wingback chair next to the window. She took a deep breath. *Now what do I do?*

David walked out of the bathroom, a towel wrapped around his waist. "What's the matter, Dakota?"

"Oh, nothing. I guess you're stuck with me for the rest of the day."

"No interview?"

"I called Mrs. Nagle," Dakota groaned. "She's irate. Claims two Justice Department investigators came to her home and threatened her."

"Threatened?"

"She's frightened, David.

"I assured her they weren't from Justice. She described the pair. The one character sounds like the guy you might be looking for."

"Jack had a hunch our investigation was running out of fuel. Dead suspects. Hostile witnesses. Missing documents. Where do we turn next?"

Dakota's eye motioned back toward the bed. "Oh, no you don't. It's a beautiful day. Let me show you around this cozy village."

"You must be pretty sure of yourself, David Clayton, to turn down a beautiful woman's offer." Dakota pulled David's towel and it fell to the floor. She beckoned.

"Oh, no, you don't," he giggled and darted into the bathroom.

David dressed and they walked downstairs. They each took a coffee to go and walked toward the water. As they reached dockside, David pointed to a finger of land in the distance. "That's

West Meadow Beach. My grandfather owned a summer home on the water back in the '50's. And across the way, up in the hills, that's where we will be this evening."

"It's serene." Dakota reached out for David's hand.

"Come on. I'll take you for the tour."

David drove to Setauket and into Port Jefferson Village.

"A great place to raise a family."

"Not for you, Dakota. You're a big time city girl now. Maybe a summer place out here, once you've published a couple of exposés. You thrive on the excitement."

"I could learn, David. Honest."

David quickly changed the subject. "Tonight should be awesome. A room filled with dignitaries. Maybe you'll pick up a juicy bit of gossip. I took a peek at that dress you brought. It's a…"

"Never mind, David. I bought that dress with you in mind."

The couple stopped in Port Jefferson for a quick snack, then returned to the Three Village Inn. "Well, here we are." David parked the car.

"We'd better hurry. The cocktail party starts at six thirty. I don't want to miss a thing."

Up in their room, Dakota and David dressed for the black tie event.

"Help me with this zipper, David."

"My God, Dakota."

"Stop it."

"Every guy in the room is going to be ogling your cleavage."

"I hope so. How else am I going to get any juicy scandal for a story," she chuckled.

"Forget it. Help me with this damn bow tie."

Chapter 22

The winding driveway leading to Trinity PharmoDynamics, USA headquarters was backed up to the road. A dozen or more valets were parking the assortment of automobiles.

"Just like I told you. Not a Chevrolet in the line."

"You warned me," David conceded.

A valet drove the car to a distant spot. Two security guards dressed in tuxedoes greeted them.

"Good evening, sir. May I see your invitation?" The guard checked it against the master list and smiled. "Thank you, Mr. Clayton. And Miss Putnam is accompanying you this evening."

Dakota didn't acknowledge the guard. *Perhaps he's with me, Jumbo.*

The couple was taken by the ambiance of the foyer.

"How much did all this cost, David?"

"No idea, but wait till you taste the shrimp." David pointed to the huge champagne fountain. The table next to it held platters of jumbo shrimp.

"David, good evening." David turned around when he heard the familiar voice. It was Captain Briggs.

"Good evening, Captain. I hope this will be a more congenial occasion than our last meeting."

Dakota looked puzzled. *What's this all about?*

"Captain Briggs, this is Miss Dakota Putnam."

Briggs smiled and stammered, "Nice to meet you." His eyes were fixed on Dakota's cleavage.

"Quite a collection of 'who's who,' Captain."

"David, isn't that General Garner? He's a member of the Joint Chiefs of Staff."

"Yes. Don't turn around. Right behind you is the Under Secretary of State, Bill North."

"I don't doubt it," Briggs added. "Trinity PharmoDynamics, USA is involved in a number of DOD and government contracts."

"I'm not doubting you, Captain, but how do you know?"

"The Deputy Police Commissioner coordinated security with the Long Island task force and the Secret Service. There must be two or three dozen security personnel mingling with the crowd."

"I'm anxious to meet Ashton Pickering,"

"He was here a few minutes ago. He'll return to greet the guests. Rather a shy man. I've never met him. I wish I could say I was one of the invited guests, but duty calls."

"Good seeing you again, Captain."

"It was a pleasure, Miss Putnam. As for you Clayton…" Briggs shook Clayton's hand. David understood the implication, "Stay out of trouble."

Dakota gasped.

"What is it?"

"Champagne fountains."

"The servers will be around with a glass."

"Oh, come on. Let's explore."

"I'm a bit nervous about meeting Pickering."

David stopped and looked at Dakota.

"Stop it, David."

"Stop what?"

"That pained expression on your face. You're jealous."

"There's something about you this evening, Dakota. You remind me of a woman who has wandered into a world she's only dreamt about."

"Aren't you fascinated? We're mingling with international aristocracy."

"It's a celebration, Dakota. Trinity PharmoDynamics Group runs Trinity PharmoDynamics, USA. Trinity has world-wide investments."

"Of course they do. I'll share a secret with you, even though you don't share yours with me."

"What secret?"

"Not long ago I began my own research into Trinity

PharmoDynamics Group."

"Dakota, if you use any of the Project Naomi documents, Jack will go after you."

"I didn't have to. Oh, I did get the idea from that little heart-to-heart Jack had with me. Jack Thompson doesn't control me. As long as I stay clear of your investigation, I can find my own sources."

"So what's your secret?"

"The champagne market is on a slippery slope. Everybody and his brother...the Italians, even the Americans, are bottling the bubbly. Champagne comes from one place, David. France. And the French are hurting. I'm surprised the Chinese aren't into the market."

"Will you get to the point? You're taunting me."

"Rumor has it 1977 is turning sour for the leading champagne brand. One of my sources speculates Trinity PharmoDynamics Group is stepping in."

"You mean intervening?"

"My source asserted the people behind Trinity PharmoDynamics Group, the so-called aristocracy, will bolster the market."

"I can't imagine names like Bollinger, Moet, Veuve Clicquot, Dom Perignon and Krug failing and going under."

"Neither can I. According to my source, Ashton Pickering clandestinely flew to Paris. He's a marketing genius."

"Dakota, if champagne's in trouble, either the French will cut back on world distribution to maintain the price, or force it higher."

"Or they might lower the price. Flood the market with name brands. The French need innovative marketing."

"Don't tell me. Your man Pickering created a marketing scheme?

"Remember the Valentine's basket? The one with the chocolates and the bottle of champagne? The one you gave me two days late?"

"Dakota, you have quite the imagination. I imagine the next tale you'll spin is Trinity's backers control the world's supply of oil, too," David quipped.

"David, over there. Isn't that...?"

"Yes. The Attorney General."

"Does he know you're investigating Trinity?"

"Of course he does. Jack's been under pressure to end the inquiry."

Dakota and David mingled among the guests. A gala social occasion had turned into business.

"Excuse me, Dakota. I'll be back in a minute."

"I'll wait here." Dakota paused in front of a huge tapestry.

"It's a beautiful embroidery."

Dakota turned to find a tall, slim man standing to her left. "Excuse me?"

"It's Persian. Invaluable. The windows are tinted to protect our collection from ultraviolet rays."

"Our collection?"

"I'm Ashton Pickering. I wish I could take credit for the décor. But alas, my predecessor, Walther Liechtenauer, deserves the kudos. He is a man of great taste and enormous imagination. Sadly, he will not be with us this evening."

Dakota was only half listening. She was captivated by Pickering's charm, but intuitively on guard. Pickering was a dangerous man.

"Have you been to Geneva? I'm sorry, you haven't told me your name."

"Dakota Putnam."

"The Hotel de Trois Rois on the shore of Lake Geneva has beautiful gardens. Dr. Liechtenhauer was taken in by the décor… silk draperies and ornate mirrors. Look around, Miss…it is Miss?"

"Yes. Please continue."

"Doctor Liechtenauer wanted to replicate the ambiance without pretentiousness. I'm afraid he may have gone a bit overboard. Still, we are surrounded by a huge collection of the world's finest art."

"Did Doctor Liechtenauer attend the international finance conference in Basel?"

"You follow the financial world, Miss Putnam?"

"Not exactly. I do read the *Washington Post*."

"And the *Post* mentions Dr. Liechtenauer?"

"No. An anonymous letter to the editor did. It speculated that the meeting was a sham. The author alleged the world's economies are dominated by a few powerful individuals. He specifically mentioned the Basel Meeting and, of all places, The Hotel de Trois Rois."

Pickering laughed. "Forgive me, Miss Putnam. I'm not laughing at you. I'm simply reacting to the myth."

"The myth?"

"The myth of the Circle of Twelve. Surely you can't believe that twelve men control the world's resources."

"From my perspective, myths are a way of explaining phenomena, not fantasy."

"You make it sound as though the falsehood has substance."

"Perhaps, Mr. Pickering. Legendary stories often have their basis in truth."

"Believe me, Miss Putnam, there is no Circle of Twelve, Twenty, or any number."

"I'll take your word for it, Mr. Pickering."

"I've enjoyed our little chat." Pickering turned to leave, then stopped.

"Have you visited Italy's Lake Como?"

"No."

"Trinity's international conference will be in Italy next fall. It rivals Lake Geneva, believe me. The Albergo Terminus Hotel is simple, but quite luxurious in its own way. You might enjoy it." Pickering turned to acknowledge another guest.

What is keeping David?

"Sorry to take so long, Dakota. I ran into your old flame, Bob Doyle."

"Let's leave. I hate him."

"I suspect a little passion still burns for him."

"Honestly, David. You don't believe I love you, do you?"

David skipped Dakota's response and continued. "Doyle was prancing around the Ambassador to Ghana when he saw me. "He's a pompous son of a bitch. In front of the ambassador, he starts berating Sam Beverly."

"Are you kidding?"

"Doyle said Sam was milking the inquiry."

"What?"

"He said, 'You boys are supposed to have an obsessive need to follow the money. Seems like your curiosity is leading in circles.'"

"Don't pay any attention to him, David. He's a jealous control freak. Can't you see that?"

"No, but you should know."

Dakota gave David a quick tap on his buttocks and winked. They moved to a quiet corner. Dakota related her meeting with Ashton Pickering. "You know, I think he was coming on to me."

"Who wouldn't?"

"Please, David. Enough about my cleavage."

"I think I've exhausted my interest in this gathering," David confessed.

"I agree. Shall we leave?"

"The Shell Bar awaits."

As they were leaving, Dakota caught a glimpse of a man stepping out of the shadows in the foyer.

"David, quick. The man over there."

David looked over his shoulder. "Where?"

"He's gone. I swear for a second he looked like…yes the composite drawing. I'm certain it was him."

"Follow me, but don't look suspicious."

The couple walked down a dimly lit hallway. It ended at an elevator.

"Excuse me. May I help you?" asked a security guard.

"We're lost," said Dakota.

"You won't find your way out on that elevator. It leads to the private quarters."

Dakota stepped in front of David, nearly pressing against the security guard.

"I was certain the gentleman pointed us in this direction."

"Gentleman?"

"Yes. A rather tall man. He walked down this hallway only moments ago."

"Ah. Mr. Ansgar. But I can't imagine he would send you in this direction. Few people have a key for this elevator."

"We're sorry," David professed. "My dear, next time I'll take the lead."

Dakota looked askance at David. "Yes, darling," she replied.

They returned to the foyer and waited for the valet to bring their car.

"Ansgar. So that's his name."

"Let's be cautious, Dakota. You only had a brief look at the fellow."

"David, I tell you he's your man."

Their conversation was interrupted by a nervous little man arguing with one of the valets.

"Yes, Doctor Berg. I understand. However, Mr. Pickering called just moments ago. He informed me your chauffeur is ill. One of our security people drove him to Smithtown General Hospital."

"Ill? Why wasn't I informed? What's going on?"

"Mr. Pickering told me your car would be here shortly."

Albert Berg was at his wit's end. The evening had been a catastrophe.

While Ashton Pickering greeted Trinity's guests, Berg was handed an envelope.

> *Dear Albert:*
> *A simple note of thanks for your years of service*
> *to Trinity. I regret your decision to retire.*
> *Sincerely,*
> *Ashton*

A round trip ticket to Argentina accompanied the note.

"Do you see that man facing the wall?"

David turned to see Berg pacing and talking to himself. "He's agitated."

"Doctor Berg. Your car is here." The valet appeared relieved.

Berg walked to the Lincoln Town Car.

"There he is," exclaimed Dakota.

The chauffeur walked around the car and opened the door for Berg.

"Sure looks like our man," David admitted.

"Ansgar?" The frantic little man hesitated as though he was surprised by the chauffeur.

"David, he called the chauffeur 'Ansgar.'"

The car drove off before David could write down the plate number.

"Your car is here, Mr. Clayton."

The valet opened the car door for Dakota. David looked around at the huge elegant façade. *Facades hide great secrets.* The couple drove toward the Three Village Inn.

The Lincoln Town car headed east.

"Ansgar, are you certain this is the way to Garden City? We seem to be headed in the wrong direction."

"You may be correct, Doctor Berg. I'll pull over and check my directions."

"Please do. This has been the most upsetting evening of my entire life. What else could go wrong?"

Ansgar found a spot to pull over. "I have a map in the glove compartment."

He leaned forward and opened the glove compartment. Just as Berg leaned forward, Ansgar turned and fired two rounds into Berg's chest. The startled Berg died with the look of disgust he had worn the greater part of his life.

Ansgar smiled. From his pocket, he removed a small leather case and a tattered piece of fabric. "Vriend."

"David, be careful. Look at the car ahead. It's pulling out."

"I see it."

"Isn't that the Town Car Ansgar was driving?"

"Yes"

"Let's follow it."

"Absolutely not. We aren't detectives, Dakota."

"Where's your sense of adventure?" she protested.

"The only adventure I want this evening is you." He reached across and touched her thigh.

∽

Music floated into the lobby of the Three Village Inn.

"Good evening, Mr. Clayton. Sir, you had a telephone call not fifteen minutes ago. I took the message for you."

David followed the host to the registration desk in the next room.

"Thank you."

"Very good, sir. Might I add something?"

"Of course."

"The gentleman sounded quite anxious. An urgency."

The message read:

> *"David, please call me as soon as you get this note.*
> *Jack."*

David returned to the bar. Dakota was sitting near the piano.

"What's wrong, David?"

"I have to make a call. The note's from Jack. Please order my usual. There's a pay phone down the hall."

David dialed Jack's home phone. *No answer.* The answering machine didn't pick up. *Too late to try the GAO. I'll try again in the morning.*

David returned to the bar and found Dakota singing along with two other women.

"Oh, David, I wish we could stay here forever."

"Is that the champagne talking, Dakota?"

"Oh David, somewhere along the way, a woman hurt you. You are such a cynic. Why can't you let down your guard? Try to be a tiny bit vulnerable?"

David smiled, lifted his glass "To you and me, Dakota."

"And the evening ahead."

They finished their drinks.

"Shall we?" Dakota asked as she touched the back of David's hand.

"Well, if you insist."

"I do."

As they stepped into their room, Dakota turned, pushed the door closed and the couple embraced.

In a way, Dakota is dead-on. I'm too closed. Afraid to take a gamble It's not my tendency.

Dakota placed her hands inside his jacket and pulled David as tightly as she could.

"David, forget the note." She pushed up on his shoulders and pulled his jacket off.

David soon forgot the note. They undressed and lay in bed.

"I confess, Dakota. I am afraid of true intimacy."

Dakota looked surprised. "Why?"

"I guess it's from listening to my mother and father argue. They didn't fight. They bickered constantly. It was an unhappy marriage. You can't imagine how many times I wished they would divorce. They never did."

"What happened?"

"My Dad found a girlfriend. Never knew who she was."

"Sounds familiar. I know my mother had at least one affair."

"Does marriage have to be that way?"

"I don't think so. I hope not."

"Dakota, if you stopped loving me…would you tell me?"

"Wouldn't you feel it, David?"

"I'm afraid I wouldn't."

"Afraid?"

"Rejection. I'm terrified of …" David didn't finish his thought.

Dakota moved closer. "David, I will never abandon you."

David awoke the next morning to the sound of a boat horn at the yacht club. Dakota was still sleeping. The urgency to telephone Jack returned. He carried the phone into the bathroom, closed the door and dialed Jack's Alexandria number.

"Hello."

"Jack, it's David."

"Man, I'm glad you were able to catch me. I was just on my way out to meet Lou-Ann. I'll make it quick."

"What's happened?"

"They're closing us down, David."

"What do you mean?"

"Late Friday afternoon, Erskin Young's goon squad turned up."

"Young's dead."

"That's the point. They had an order signed by the Attorney General."

"For what?"

"They ordered Sam to give them access to the situation room."

"The vault, too?"

"Everything. Remember Young's two escorts?"

"Vaguely."

"Those two headed the team. Everything is gone, David."

"Everything?"

"They dismantled the conference table and took the top. Something about fingerprints and indentations."

"I still can't figure out what's happening."

"Someone wants us closed down. They're using Young's sudden demise as a pretense."

"Of course. Grab our documents. It's a hoax."

"It's worse. Sam is resigning. He telephoned the Inspector General and the Attorney General. Orders are orders. It's a massacre, David."

"I'll meet you tomorrow morning. If we can't change flights, I'll drive through the night. See you at nine at Sam's office."

"Sam's in bad shape, David. He's finished. He's been put on indefinite leave. And his appearance before the joint Congressional Committee, it's going to be a closed session."

"How did he respond?"

"David, there isn't going to be a hearing. Sam demanded to know why."

"And?"

"The entire investigation has been classified. I'm willing to bet a month's pay, someone was scared we would dredge up more dirt."

"Dirt? Has anyone opened Young's files?"

"It doesn't matter, David. I need you here on Monday. I'll tell you more then."

David woke Dakota. "We have to return to Washington."

"What's happened?"

"It's awful. I'll try to change our airline tickets. If worse comes to worse, we'll drive."

❧

After brunch, the couple drove to Islip's MacArthur Airport.

"I'm sorry, sir. The earliest plane out is tomorrow morning."

David didn't wait for the agent to explain. He walked to the Hertz counter and extended the rental. They arrived at David's apartment late Sunday evening.

❧

When David arrived at the General Accounting Office on

Monday morning, Jack was sitting behind Lynn's desk.

"Where's Lynn?"

Jack raised his hands and cupped his eyes. "I've had it. When I arrived, Lynn was cleaning out her desk."

"Has Lynn been transferred?"

"She quit. I'm the only one who knows."

"What?"

"I'm not kidding. When I walked in, she had her personal stuff in a cardboard box.

She shouted, 'I'm out of this place.'"

"I suspected she was kind of troubled by Sam's emotional health. Remember the debate over the key and combination to the situation room?"

"I know. I think she's sweet on him. A real honest woman."

"Too late now. So what's next?"

"Next? I wanted to tell you in person. I received a threatening call from Justice over the weekend. The operation is dead in the water. 'Close it down.' The implication was clear. If I go public, they won't go after me, but your career is over. And probably everyone else connected with Project Naomi."

"I can take care of myself, Jack. Sam's through."

"And Lou-Ann? Should I jeopardize her career or put her life in danger?"

"Of course not. Do you believe it will come to that?"

"I'm convinced of it, David. I'm retiring. The Attorney General got word to me. I can take an early-out and collect my full pension, providing I'm gone by the end of the week. Hell, I won't even clean out my office…except for the my pelican."

"So this is it? It's over?"

"Oh, I don't think it's over. Sometime in the future, this entire affair will rise to the surface. But it ain't going to be me who brings it up."

"What will you do?"

Jack sighed. "I'm heading to Long Island. I'll try to see my children, if they have time for me. Kathleen's happy. She'll get a piece of my pension as long as she stays single. I can't imagine any poor sucker marrying her."

"What am I going to do?"

"I thought you were looking for work in New York."

"I'm in love with Dakota. Looks like I'm here, if I can find work."

"David, you haven't been fired. You can return to the New York Delegation just as though you never left. Believe me. No one is ever going to question you. The Department of Justice has thrown a scare into that bunch."

"Who knows?"

"I'm off, my man. Looking forward to some fishing at Jackson Hole, and maybe I'll learn to play golf." Jack pushed away from the desk and walked over to David to shake his hand.

"Take care, my man."

"Hey, hold on. I'm out of here, too."

Chapter 23

Dr. Liechtenauer died several weeks after the Trinity celebration. In accordance with Liechtenauer's request, Ansgar flew to Leipzig with Strauss to inter Liechtenauer's ashes next to his mother's plot. During the return flight, Ansgar was overcome by an emotion he had never felt; the loss of his protector. Ansgar attributed it to his lack of sleep. The sensation felt unnatural. From time to time he would doze, only to be awakened by the echo of a distinct, but familiar voice. The voice echoed from deep within the recesses of his memory.

Late spring, 1977 – The Private Library, Trinity PharmoDynamics, USA

Ansgar waited in the private library on the third floor of Trinity PharmoDynamics, USA. It was the second time he had been in the library. The last time was to listen to Fritz Schmidt read Doctor Liechtenauer's last will and testament. Ansgar was amazed to learn he was the beneficiary of Liechtenauer's vast fortune. *And what good is it to me? I live in a room no larger than a monk's cell.* His thoughts were dismissed as Ashton Pickering entered the room, accompanied by Fritz Schmidt and Kurt Strauss.

Ansgar stood and acknowledged the men. It was a matter of deference, a social courtesy. Ansgar was now worth more than both Schmidt and Strauss combined.

"Good afternoon, Ansgar. Oh, no. Please be seated. How was your journey to Liepzig?"

"It went well, sir."

"Of course you remember Fritz Schmidt, Trinity's Chief Counsel, and Kurt Strauss, our Chief Financial Officer?"

"Ansgar, at our last meeting you wished to return to Europe."

"Yes, Mr. Pickering. I would like to settle near Lake Geneva. I feel a strange compulsion to visit The Netherlands."

"You must visit Eastern Europe, as well. Prague is a beautiful, mystical city," Strauss interjected. "You must travel. This time for pleasure. You have been a loyal member of the Trinity family."

The other two men agreed.

Pickering peered over his glasses. "Ansgar, we need your assistance with one final assignment before you retire. It is a mission we three agree must be entrusted to you."

"Sir, I am weary."

"I understand. Please allow me to outline this undertaking. It involves cunning and skill."

Over the next hour, Pickering outlined the undertaking.

"Once the mission is complete, you will be flown to Switzerland on my private jet within twenty four hours. Will you be able to circumvent immigration and customs? You have my word."

Ansgar looked at the men. "I'll do it."

Chapter 24

During the three day period July 13, 14, and 15, 1977, more than one thousand people died. The New York Times lead article called it "A Night of Terror"

July 13, 1977

Roscoe Transport held contracts with a number of government agencies. Their premier client was the U.S. Army Medical Research and Material Command (MRMC) at Fort Detrick, Maryland. Roscoe's mission included the joint venture between DOA and the DOD; Fort Detrick's bioresearch laboratory. The private courier service ran a Monday and Wednesday schedule between Detrick's Blue Lab and the Department of Agriculture terminal in Greenport, Long Island. The dispatch schedule accounted for road conditions, security, and the ferry or service craft between the terminal and Plum Island. The narrow cut between the Island and mainland could be turbulent. The director insisted deliveries from Detrick arrive early in the morning to allow for delays. Contingency planning was important.

Roy Taylor, Roscoe's veteran driver, signed out his van and drove to Fort Detrick. For the last eight months, Bob Small rode shotgun with Taylor, not that Small actually carried a shotgun. Taylor and Small took turns driving the customized Chevrolet van.

Earlier in the day, the dispatcher telephoned Taylor. "Sorry for this late notice, Roy."

"What's up?"

"Bob Small just called. He's sick. Get this…"

"What?"

"The boss dropped in. Told me to call you and give you the

name of his sub."

"Shoot."

"Richard Foxworth. He'll be waiting on the corner by Blue Lab's parking lot."

"Okay. It ain't like Bob to call dispatch first. He was sick back in January. Called me. He didn't want to hang me up with a substitute."

"Not this time, Roy."

"Thanks." *A new man making the run? I'd rather drive it alone. Protocol won't permit just one driver. I might run off with a virus.* Taylor laughed.

Taylor cleared Fort Detrick's security and drove directly to the Blue Lab facility, a complex of four labs. Taylor spotted a man standing on the corner adjacent to the employee parking lot.

The two men shook hands as Foxworth climbed into the cab.

"Foxworth, Richard Foxworth," panted the affable, short, stubby man.

"Roy Taylor. We'll get acquainted later. Let's make the pick-up."

They parked in front of Blue Lab's Building One. Roy locked the van. "We use this entrance." Roy pointed the way.

"That's it on the security clearances?"

"That's it for now. We wait here. Someone will walk through those locked doors. We're standing in an airlock. Don't know much about it."

"Airlock?"

"I told you, I'm no scientist. Something about the air. It blows back inside. Germs can't get out. Here comes one of the techs." Taylor pointed to the lab worker pushing a gray lab cart.

The doors sprung open. The men could feel a rush of air into the laboratory.

"Three containers to go. I need your John Hancocks."

Taylor read the dispatch receipt. Two freeze-dried. One live.

"Say, what's with the live stuff?"

"Haven't the slightest. The order was waiting for me when I signed in. Thought it a bit unusual myself, but you know how it goes."

Taylor and Foxworth signed the dispatch receipt and dated it

Wednesday, July 13, 1977.

"This weather is oppressive."

"Sure is. Lucky us. We're driving the new custom van. It's got a special cooling system." Taylor kept the top copy of the dispatch receipt.

"Be safe. Hear it's raining on and off up north."

"Thanks."

Foxworth pushed the lab cart a few yards to the truck. Taylor unlocked and opened the rear doors. Next, he unlocked the security cage and climbed in.

"Hand them to me. Numbers two and three are freeze-dried. They go in here. Number one goes in this refrigerated compartment. Live vaccine has to stay cool in transit."

Foxworth handed the containers to Taylor, one at a time. The sealed orange Styrofoam containers were numbered and coded. The international biohazard emblem was emblazoned on every side.

"Don't look so nervous, man. They're packed tight. Look at those seals."

"Hey, it's dangerous stuff," Foxworth replied.

"I guess so. I only know what it states on the receipt. Here; look for yourself."

Foxworth beamed.

"What's the smile for?"

"You don't have to be a biologist to know this stuff is potent. Rift Valley Fever Experimental Vaccine. West Nile Disease. Anthrax. We're transporting dangerous stuff."

"It's a slam dunk. I've been doing it for years. That's why they pay us the big bucks."

"Tell me another one," Foxworth laughed.

Taylor closed and locked the cabinets. "I lock the keys in this box, along with the receipt. I keep the key in the glove compartment."

"Okay."

"I don't anticipate a problem. You need to know just in case."

Foxworth gave Taylor a casual salute and walked to the front of the van. *Taylor can't imagine the trouble he's in.* The man Roy Taylor knew as Rich Foxworth was Richard Shipe, Ansgar's partner on the Grace Beverly debacle. This was Shipe's last chance to redeem himself with Trinity and Ansgar. As the night's events unfolded, Shipe was in for a surprise.

While the van was fully equipped by 1975 DOA standards, it was due for an upgrade in August. The new standard required a military transceiver and multichannel scanner. An additional reserve gas tank was installed to extend mileage and limit stops. The van was always secured. Pit stops were done one man at a time.

"Tell me something, Roy."

"What's that?"

"I thought the Army Medical Command closed the Detrick research lab in 1969."

"What gave you that idea?"

"I read it someplace."

"The bioweapons program ended, not the medical research facility."

"What's the difference?" Shipe asked.

"Hey, I told you I'm not a scientist."

"I don't see much difference."

They pulled up to Detrick's exit security booth. Taylor handed the guard the receipt. The guard glanced at the paper and waved the van through.

"Our next stop will be a rest area. We're required to check in."

The ride was uneventful. It rained from time to time. Shipe jabbered about their cargo.

"Mind if we listen to the radio?"

"No." Shipe folded his jacket and placed it against the window. I'll nod off until you want relief."

"Great."

On a clear night, Taylor could pick up the traffic reports from New York City. Tonight there was a lot of static. *Must be the weather. It's raining in Jersey.*

Taylor made his first stop on the other side of Baltimore. Shipe waited in the locked van. Taylor made the mandatory call to Roscoe's dispatcher. Then he telephoned home.

"Honey, seems there's a power outage in parts of New York City. Please be careful."

"Everything's cool. The sub the company assigned sure ain't Bob Small. We have nothing in common. Nothing to talk about."

"You'll find something. You always do." Taylor heard her stifled laugh.

"Okay. Call you in the morning. I love you."

"I love you too, Roy."

When Taylor returned to the van, Shipe was sitting behind the wheel. The engine was running.

"I'll drive," Shipe insisted.

Taylor shrugged and climbed in. "Up to you."

Shipe rolled down the driver's side window.

"Keep the window closed. You know the rules."

"That's careless of me. Hey, hand me my clipboard."

"Sure." Taylor leaned forward to reach the clipboard.

Without warning, Shipe raised his concealed Ruger and fired one round. The bullet pierced the top of Taylor's ear and continued through his skull. The passenger side window instantly shattered. The muzzle blast was deafening. Taylor's torso fell against the door. His head perched on the broken glass. It was all over in less than twenty seconds.

Instinctively, Shipe placed the pistol in his lap, raised his hands, and cupped his ears in pain. Thunder rolled through his head. *My ears! Damn it. Look at this mess. I didn't want the window smashed.* Shipe grabbed a handful of Taylor's hair and yanked the dead man's head and body away from the door.

"Come on, sucka. Don't give me a hard time." Shipe didn't take time to check for witnesses. He shifted into first, popped the clutch and got out of there as fast as he could. He looked for the first available exit off I-95. It was an effort to keep Taylor's body upright as the van approached the toll both. Luckily, the toll taker was distracted. His radio blared, "Stay home. Stay off the streets." *What the hell is the announcer talking about?* Shipe sped away.

Shipe drove east for a few miles. He found a dirt road bordered by a large drainage ditch. *Perfect. I'll dump him here. He'll sink to the bottom. It will be a long time before they find the body, if they ever do.*

Shipe pulled the corpse from the van and dragged it to the side of the ditch. He searched through Taylor's pockets and removed their contents. With one final attempt, he pushed. The body rolled into the muddy water. Only the left arm remained above the murky surface. Shipe made one last check using his flashlight. *Shit! I forgot his wedding ring.* Sure enough, the wedding band reflected the flashlight's beam. Once again, Shipe had bungled the job. There was no time to retrieve it. Shipe had a deadline to meet. He drove back to the Turnpike.

Soon, the Turnpike traffic began to bog down. Shipe kept checking the time. It was approximately 2:00 a.m. on Thursday, July 14, when the unmarked white Chevrolet van exited the New Jersey Turnpike. Shipe took Exit 13 to the Goethals Bridge. The van crept across Staten Island toward the Verrazano Bridge. The traffic gradually thinned out. *What the hell is wrong with this radio?* Shipe pounded the dashboard. He turned the dial until he found a broadcast on WABC. The announcer, George Michael, confirmed Shipe's worst fears. There was a citywide blackout. The complete loss of communications and lighting gradually spread to the surrounding suburbs. All off-duty police were ordered to report. The lights went out at Shea Stadium. Fans at the Mets-Cubs game were safely evacuated. All five boroughs were in total darkness. Only areas serviced by Long Island Lighting had power. Con Edison officials attributed the blackout to lightning.

"Colonel. Roscoe Transit called. Their driver missed his last checkpoint call-in."

"It's probably the city blackout." Colonel Patrick O'Toole, Fort Detrick's Security Chief, opened the dispatch log. *I don't recognize the code on one of the packages.* I'll check the code book. O'Toole opened the guide book. "Holy crap," he declared. O'Toole's exclamation was an understatement. "That van is carrying a priority shipment of vaccine. The RVD vaccine was in its final stage of testing. The test had to be conducted on Plum Island. The FDA had already signaled tentative approval. The State Department demanded a quick test with final approval no later than August.

"We have to locate that service van. Get Mayor Beame on the line, pronto."

"It's useless, sir. I can't get through to the Mayor's office. The line is functioning, but I keep getting a busy signal."

"Telephone the Secretary of Defense. Tell his aide we have a DEFCON Domestic."

⁓

O'Toole wasn't a man to be kept waiting. He paced the security office. Finally, the sergeant called out, "Sir. I have the Secretary on the line."

"Mr. Secretary. We have a dire situation here."

"It must be to call a DEFCOM Domestic. My God, Colonel. What in the hell demands a DEFCOM Domestic? We've never activated a domestic alert during my tenure."

"Sir. I'll get right to it. We have a missing service van en route to Plum Island, the research facility on Long Island. The rioting in and around New York City may be the cause. Bottom line, the van is carrying three major containers, Rift Valley Fever Disease, West Nile Disease, and, of all things, anthrax."

"Not the Rift Valley experimental vaccine? You guys ship stuff like that in a service van? Any escorts?"

"No, sir. We have a contingency plan, but not for a major blackout. We have to locate the van. I can't raise anyone in the city."

"What do you suggest we do?"

"Activate a response team at Bragg. Get them into the city as quickly as possible."

"They'll have to go by chopper. The airports are closed."

"Yes, sir. My honest assessment? We are in deep shit. I wouldn't know where to begin."

"Give it a guess, Colonel."

"Bushwick. Yes, Bushwick. Roscoe's owner assured me Taylor is the best driver. Taylor was a Long Range Reconnaissance Patrol man in Vietnam. He knows his way around. He may have taken an alternative route. I'd go with Bushwick, sir."

"Bushwick it is. I'll take it from here, Colonel. I want your office locked up tight. No one in or out. Can you imagine the repercussions? Not a word of this can leak to the press. Understand? Take care of your end. Let Bragg handle the mission."

"Yes, sir. I understand."

O'Toole wasn't happy with the Secretary's closing order, but orders are orders.

⁓

Shipe crossed the Verrazano Bridge into Brooklyn. He was frightened and confused. He remained convinced he could make the rendezvous on time. *Ansgar would be waiting. There had to be some power in Manhattan. WABC continues to broadcast.* Shipe didn't know WABC's transmitter was in Lodi, New Jersey. George Michael kept broadcasting the same information over and over. Only southern Queens and parts of the Rockaways still had power.

Another call was placed to Fort Detrick from Plum Island. "Any word on the service van?"

"Not a thing. Colonel O'Toole has alerted DOD. That's all I have for you."

"Any reports from the police?"

"You have to be joking. From what we know, the NYPD is stretched to its limit. Fires burning out of control. The Fire Department and EMS can't handle the emergencies."

Hours passed before both Detrick and Plum Island suspected a potential disaster.

"We may have lost the van, Mr. Secretary."

"Can you imagine if looters get their hands on those shipping containers? They'll have no idea the danger they are in."

"That's my fear also, Mr. Secretary."

O'Toole anticipated the catastrophe.

"We're doing the best we can. Keep me updated."

The van was not lost. Shipe was caught in gridlock only a few hundred yards from his rendezvous point with Ansgar. *Trapped. Trapped in Bushwick.* Suddenly, Shipe realized his worst nightmare. A pack of looters moved along the street. They smashed windows and climbed into storefronts. The high-pitched store alarms added to the madness.

Shipe eased his way around a group of looters. Two men rushed the van. One of the rioters ran to the passenger side. The other smashed at the driver's window with a pipe. He shoved the pipe through the broken glass, striking Shipe on the side of the head. Shipe was dazed.

"Hurry up, man. Pull him out," shouted the looter holding the

277

pipe. The other man ran around the front of the van and dragged Shipe to the pavement. Shipe moaned. One final blow from the pipe ended Shipe's struggle and his life.

Ansgar anxiously waited at the rendezvous corner. The looters' fury increased. Ansgar faced a crisis. Shipe was late.

If I hide, Shipe won't find me. If I stay here, I may be killed. Ansgar felt for his pistol. The Beretta 92 held fifteen rounds with one in the chamber. *Even with the extra magazine, I can't hold off this pack. Shipe should be somewhere along Broadway.* Ansgar ducked into a doorway. A crowd was prying the chain gates off a jewelry store. It crashed onto the sidewalk. The hysterical crowd rushed in. Ansgar ran.

There in the distance, he spotted the service van, surrounded by a mob.

The van. I have to retrieve the containers. Smoke billowed from several buildings in his path. Ansgar was determined to reach the van. He darted into another doorway. From his vantage point, Ansgar saw Shipe's body on the street. Two men lifted Shipe's body and heaved it aside. Several other looters smashed at the rear doors. A short, stooped man with a limp smashed the doors with an ax.

Ansgar was forced to move again. Across the street, a gang tied a rope from their car to a huge medal security gate. As the driver pulled away the door collapsed, trapping one of the looters. They stampeded over the fallen gate, crushing the trapped man. Havoc ruled the night.

If I don't act fast, that mob will get the containers. I can't wait any longer. Ansgar reached for the Beretta and moved closer to the van. With a hellish scream, he charged the looters. The short, stooped looter turned just as Ansgar reached the rear doors. The man wielded his ax. Too late. Ansgar fired two shots. The man fell. The frenzied crowd turned on Ansgar.

"Get him," screamed a woman. She ran towards Ansgar. He fired one round. She crumpled to the ground, holding her stomach. The other looters ran for cover. Ansgar swept around, looking for another assault. The van's doors were open. The security cage gate was breached. It hung precariously. Ansgar climbed into the van. The battered keybox lay on the floor. The keys were still inside.

Ansgar unlocked the storage cabinets. The containers were still intact. The refrigerated compartment was untouched. While Ansgar focused on the containers, two looters moved silently toward the van.

I can't carry three containers and fight off this horde. He pulled out his knife and cut the seal on the first container. It contained twelve samples secured in Styrofoam. *The vaccine is my priority. I've got to secure as many of the vaccine samples as I can.* Ansgar took six vials and put them in his right jacket pocket. *Now for the other containers.* He opened the container holding the freeze-dried West Nile Virus samples. *No time. I'll take a few. I've got to get out of here.* Ansgar scrambled to open the last container. It was too late.

The hoodlum who killed Shipe returned. He caught Ansgar off guard. In haste, Ansgar placed the Beretta on the van's floor as he searched through the cabinets. The thug dropped the lead pipe and drew a switchblade. "I've got you now," he yelled.

I can't reach the pistol. The thug lunged at Ansgar. He twisted onto his back. As the thug fell to the floor, Ansgar grabbed his knife. The attacker hit the floor. Ansgar buried the knife deep in the thug's chest. The man attempted to lift himself and fell again. The knife sunk deeper. Ansgar took a deep breath just in time to find a second assailant at the van doors. He snatched the pistol and fired. *My God. Was that five or six rounds? I've lost count.* Exhausted, Ansgar had to make a decision. *Shall I stay here and open the third container or attempt an escape? Pickering wanted me to intercept the RVF vaccine. I have samples. The contingency called for destroying the West Nile samples. Anthrax was never part of the bargain. I'm out of here.*

Ansgar lay prone on the van floor. *They're out there waiting for me.* Ansgar grasped the security gate to hoist himself from the floor. All of a sudden, the heavy gate collapsed. He cried out in pain. The shock traveled through his body.

"My shoulder!" Ansgar shrieked. *Don't pass out!* he felt faint. Trapped under the heavy steel gate, Ansgar could barely move. His vision blurred. With one final burst of energy, he lifted the gate and rolled out from under. Blood trickled from his nose and mouth. He felt dampness in his ears. The slightest movement of his left arm sent waves of pain to his brain. *I'm not finished, yet.*

From a distance, he heard a warning. "Be quiet. Don't speak. Don't let the man find you." The old grey-haired woman. It was her warning each night when she put him to bed. The fires from the burning building raged. Smoke enveloped the van. Slowly and cautiously, Ansgar slid to the pavement. He clutched the Beretta tighter. His shoulder throbbed.

He crawled across the pavement towards the shooting flames and heat. Just ahead was a burning storefront. Looters returned to the van. *Go to it, shitheads. I hope you take it all.* He spotted an open doorway. The path appeared clear. *No looters. I can make it. I must.* Debris and glass littered the street. He moved cautiously. *The voice. Where are you, old woman?* "Don't make a sound. The man will find you." Ansgar grew weaker. His head hit the pavement. *My left pants leg is soaked.* The collapsed gate had punctured his femoral artery. Ansgar was bleeding out. It was only a matter of minutes. He crawled on. *The samples. I must destroy the samples.* He clawed forward. *There has to be a sewer grate. He reached out with one last effort. A grate!*

His left arm was useless. Ansgar let go of the pistol and grasped the grate. "Pull, you son of a bitch. Pull." He lay face down over the sewer grate. One by one, he smashed the vials of vaccine and dropped them into the sewer. He rolled onto his back. A bolt of pain shot through him. He pulled on his tattered jacket to open the other pocket. One by one, he smashed the rest of the glass tubes against the grate and pushed the contents into the sewer.

The voice called again. "Ansgar nacht kind."

"No. It isn't time."

"Ah, child, but it is."

Ansgar could see the old grey-haired woman emerging from the smoke.

"Vriend. Vriend. Please help me."

"Be silent. I warned you, child. Never leave your room."

"Vriend. Vriend." His plea trailed off to a sigh.

"Now will you listen? Be silent." The old woman bent over and touched Ansgar's forehead. He felt her tears on his face.

"Vriend. Vriend. Please. I want Vriend. In my pocket. I have no strength."

"Ah. Here is your friend." The woman unsnapped the leather case and handed the shredded cloth to Ansgar.

Ansgar rubbed the fabric between his fingers, then touched it to his lips. "Vriend."

❧

A chopper carrying The Special Forces Response Team from Fort Bragg touched down in Bushwick late Thursday afternoon. The governor assigned a State Police unit to assist them.

"I don't understand your governor's reluctance to call in the National Guard. Look at this destruction." Major Bill Foster had experienced urban combat in Vietnam. "This place will never recover."

"I agree. But I don't make those decisions," replied Sergeant Tim West. "We were only called in earlier today."

"The State Police and not the Guard? You guys don't have the resources or the manpower."

"We give it our best shot, Major."

"What do you have for me, Sergeant?"

"I've got good news and bad news."

"What's the good news?"

"We located your van. Completely destroyed. Stripped clean. Burned to a crisp."

West pointed to a vacant lot a few blocks up Broadway.

"Nothing left?"

"We searched the van. The perimeter, too. No sign of your containers."

"Nothing?"

"Now for the bad news."

"That wasn't the bad news?"

"No, sir. We found a body just up the street. Stretched out near a sewer grate. A male. Hard to tell his age. Lying on his back. Weirdest thing."

"What do you mean?"

"Looked like he was sleeping. Kinda peaceful."

"Crazy. Nothing surprises me."

"We found five bodies on the other side of the street. Four were shot. One was mangled. A male. He was wearing the same uniform as the first guy."

"Any emblems or badges? They worked for Roscoe Transport."

"That's them. With all this chaos, you won't get a positive ID from the ME for weeks."

"So that's it? They'll be moaning and weeping in D.C. tonight."

"Those containers must have been important. Explain something, Major."

"If I can."

"If those shipping containers were so important, why wasn't security tighter?"

Foster chuckled. "Now that's a question I'd like answered."

Sergeant West looked perplexed.

Foster looked around one last time in dismay. "Thanks for all your help, Sergeant. I'll note it in my report." Foster waved his arm and called out, "Saddle up."

The chopper blades swept garbage and debris into the air.

"One last thing. It may be important," shouted West.

"What's that?"

"The body by the sewer grate. We found broken glass in his hand. I'd wager he dumped something down the sewer before he croaked."

"Too late to check now. Last night's rain and our chopper's wash…it's gone now. Just forget about it."

"Guess so. These storm sewers all drain into Newton Creek. It's so polluted nothing could survive."

"What was that? I didn't hear you over the chopper's roar."

"Forget it. Good luck, Major."

Back at Fort Detrick, Colonel O'Toole waited for a call from Foster.

It never came. O'Toole was more irritable than usual. He hadn't slept in two days. He smelled of chain-smoked cigars.

"Colonel. There's a call for you on the secure line from the State Department."

O'Toole tore the phone from the sergeant's hand. "O'Toole here."

"Colonel. Listen closely. A decision has been made. No public health alert."

"Not alert the public? I'm not sure what that means, Mr.

Secretary."

"No reporters, O'Toole. We are not telling the public some nut may be running around with a canister of anthrax."

"Sir. The anthrax samples must be found. Anthrax will remain dormant indefinitely. I'm very concerned about the shipment of West Nile and RVD."

"And we aren't? I've been in touch with DOA and CDC. We have no experience in dealing with this stuff. The environmental conditions are ripe for a potential disaster. My people have consulted with Trinity PharmoDynamics, USA. The country isn't prepared to deal with an outbreak."

"Yes, sir. This is an emergency."

"You bet your ass it is, Colonel. Anthrax, too. Now you tell me how Abe Beame is going to react. Are you stupid, Colonel?"

"No, sir, I am not stupid. I asked an important question. We have no idea if the Rift Valley samples were dumped in the sewer system. I'm no virologist, but I'm damn sure public health officials should be alerted."

"Colonel, are you telling me how to do my job?"

"No, sir."

"Then do yours and follow orders. The incident is over. Finished. Never happened. Collect every record, any scrap of paper dealing with this event. Box whatever you have. Stamp it 'Top Secret.' I want you and those records in my office Monday morning. That's an order."

The Secretary slammed the phone down.

Trinity PharmoDynamics, USA Headquarters

"Come in, Strauss. We're waiting for Reiter and Schmidt to arrive."

Pickering appears quite composed. I wish I could say the same for Reiter and Schmidt.

"I spoke with both of them earlier. I'm afraid Reiter is a nervous wreck."

"I anticipated his reaction to the Bushwick incident. Reiter lacks patience. And Schmidt?"

"Schmidt is the plotter, Mr. Pickering. I'm certain he has at least two contingencies to present."

"He already has. We'll go with the second. Where in the world are they?"

With that, both men entered Pickering's private office.

"Sit down, you two. I'm about to place a call to Washington. I want all three of you to listen to this."

"Mr. Pickering, I'm afraid the Bushwick incident is a dramatic setback for Trinity. We have no chance for a patent," Reiter lamented.

"Reiter, calm down. We have other prospects. Please sit down."

"Mr. Pickering, I have the Secretary on line two."

"Thank you, Mrs. Falon."

"Good afternoon, Mr. Secretary. Thank you for taking my call."

"Mr. Secretary. Ah yes, Ashton. Mr. Secretary does have a nice ring to it; especially coming from you, Ashton," Louis York crowed.

"I'll have to call more often, Louis."

"We missed you at the class reunion, Ashton. Surely Trinity can function for a few days without you."

"I never seem to get a vacation."

"Ashton, you dummy. I recall Lee Iacocca's admonishment to guys like you who manage billion dollar companies, but can't manage a week's vacation."

"You're so right. Regrettably, I'm calling about business."

"Business? Nothing that will create a conflict of interest, I hope."

"Of course not, Louis. We're fraternity brothers. I would never put you in that position."

"Let's hear it."

"Trinity PharmoDynamics, USA has run into an embarrassing affair. I don't want the incident to find its way into the media before bringing it to your attention."

"Sounds gloomy, Ashton."

"One of our directors, Albert Berg…I was stunned."

"Please, Ashton, get on with it."

"Berg ran the day-to-day operations at our headquarters. During a random audit, Kurt Strauss, our Chief Financial Officer, discovered a number of irregularities with Berg's accounts."

"What type of irregularities?"

"Berg was siphoning funds for a rogue project. I'll admit it was an ingenious scheme."

"I sense there's more to this."

"The scoundrel used one of our research projects as a conduit for the funds. It goes beyond embezzlement and industrial sabotage."

"What are you proposing, Ashton?"

"With your permission, I would appreciate a meeting."

"Of course. I think it wise for you not to attend."

"Naturally, Louis. I'll send Kurt Strauss and Fritz Schmidt, our Chief Legal Counsel."

"Not even a hint of this conversation to anyone else. Understood?"

"Of course, Louis."

"Have them in my office no later than two o'clock tomorrow afternoon." *I'm enjoying this. Nice to hear Ashton squirm.*

Thank you, Louis. Please remember me to Emily and the kids." *You bastard.*

"Gentlemen. You heard the Secretary. It's time to earn the millions Trinity pays you."

"Mr. Pickering, do you want me to follow up on the Bushwick fiasco?"

"Reiter, the Bushwick events will fade away. Rest assured."

"I'll be returning to Argentina. How should our research facility proceed?"

"Anthrax."

"Anthrax, sir?"

"There's always anthrax, Reiter."

Chapter 25

Butch Wade bought a pack of Winstons at 7-Eleven and returned to his truck. He tucked the cigarettes behind the visor and pulled on to Route 112. His destination, the Coram Diner, was a hundred yards down the road. He pulled into the diner's parking lot. He parked the failing truck facing Middle Country Road. Butch was early. He was puzzled why Joe selected the diner. It was close to the Sixth Precinct. It was a busy Friday night. The parking lot was nearly filled. Feeling a bit edgy, Butch searched the parking lot for a familiar car or face.

"I know it's risky," Joe explained. "I've got the information. There's something else you should know."

Butch reached overhead for his Winstons. He'd stopped smoking just before taking a disability leave. He promised Elaine he would cut back.

"Hey. It's my only vice. I don't drink. Maybe a couple of beers on the weekend," he argued.

"It's a dirty habit you picked up in the Army," Elaine complained.

Davis "Butch" Wade was a man of extremes. Either he smoked or he didn't. He knew no moderation. That was Butch. At least, that was the old Butch before his brief but ugly stay in Pilgrim State Hospital's psych ward. The divorce came next. Elaine never wanted the divorce. It was Butch's idea. They remained close.

I can't figure out why someone wants to hurt Elaine. I've got to get to the bottom of this. He was gripped by a fear for Elaine's safety. First, he had to call in an IOU. He hated to think of his request that way. Joe Larkin was a friend. Friends never call in IOU's.

"I'll do it," Joe said reluctantly. "I owe you."

It seemed like ages ago, Joe responded to a family altercation on Jennings Avenue in Patchogue. Butch was on patrol near West Lake when he heard the 10-17 broadcast. Butch notified dispatch of his location and responded.

Joe could hear the couple yelling at one another from the street. He cautiously climbed the front porch steps of the duplex. A woman screamed. The front door was ajar. Joe didn't wait for backup. Without thought for his safety, Joe courageously pushed the door open and entered the home.

A woman was standing on a couch, rubbing her bloody hand across the white wall.

"Police," Joe shouted.

"He's in there," she screamed.

The husband stepped from the bedroom, brandishing a shotgun. He shouted at his wife. "Get off the couch!" and racked the shotgun.

The wife froze.

"She's a cheating bitch," the husband shouted. "I caught her at the bowling alley."

"You bastard. You deserved it."

"Put down the shotgun," Joe demanded.

The man stepped forward raising the weapon. Joe still hadn't drawn his service revolver.

"Put down the shotgun, man. It isn't worth it. You shoot her or me, you're going to prison for life."

"I don't give a shit," the man shouted back. He hesitated, then raised the shotgun to his shoulder.

The shotgun blast was deafening. The woman lost her balance and fell backwards to the floor. She was out cold. Across the room, the husband sprawled against the wall. The blast from Butch's twelve gauge hit the husband in the chest and face. Butch racked the shotgun again and swept the room searching for any other shooters. Suddenly, he was back in Vietnam.

"Butch," shouted Joe. "He's down."

Butch turned to Joe. "It's okay, buddy," he said and walked out on the porch. The rest is history.

Butch hadn't seen Joe Larkin in two years. He regretted

tonight's reunion.

Butch sat and waited. A Sixth Precinct sector car passed. Butch worried he'd meet one of the guys from the Sixth. Nevertheless, Joe had insisted on meeting here. *It must be the cheesecake.* Butch felt in his pants pocket for his Zippo. He'd carried the lighter for years. It was his talisman, even after he stopped smoking. Butch flipped the Zippo and lit up.

Joe Larkin arrived exactly on time. Butch flicked the cigarette out the truck window and got out. The men shook hands and walked inside. Butch pointed to a table in the rear, out of view from the main entrance. Butch ordered coffee. Joe asked for coffee and cheesecake.

"Tell me, Joe. Why meet here?"

"You know, Butch, you're all business. Never start a conversation with 'How's the family?' You get right down to business."

Joe reached into his jacket pocket and pulled out a notepad. He tore off a sheet of paper and slid it across the table. "That's it. You know I could lose my retirement if someone finds out."

"I understand. Not a word. I promise."

"I checked the file. The plates were reported stolen from a vehicle owned by Trinity PharmoDynamics, USA. The GTO was stolen, too. Briggs thinks he has a lead on the guy. His name is Charlie Ross. A small-time punk. They call him the Weasel. His girlfriend, Doris McFarlane, is an addict."

"Employed?"

"He was until about a month ago. At Trinity PharmoDynamics, USA."

"Trinity?"

"You look surprised," said Joe.

"Confused. I know about the plates but nothing else."

"Ross worked in maintenance. I called their personnel department. He quit unexpectedly. The woman I spoke with said Ross's last performance review was excellent."

"You have an address?"

"It's all there. You aren't going to believe this," said Joe.

The waitress returned with their orders. "Anything else, gentlemen?"

"Not now. Thanks, darlin," said Butch.

"Weasel and Doris live at Three Stones, not far from the Sixth."

Three Stones Village was a collection of run-down town houses and condominiums. The original developer went bankrupt. The place was known for drugs and prostitution.

Butch tapped his pack of Winstons on the table and felt for his Zippo.

Joe slowly turned his head side to side in disapproval. He said, "You look troubled, Butch."

"It's nothing. Anything else?" He lit his cigarette and placed the Zippo next to his coffee cup.

"The townhouse is leased to Weasel's sister. She's never there. Has a boyfriend in Selden. Lives with him. Want a surprise?" asked Joe.

"Surprise? No surprises."

"You see that blonde serving coffee on the far end of the counter?"

Butch tilted slightly to the left to look around Joe. "Not bad."

"That's her." said Joe.

"The sister?"

"She works here six nights a week. Starts early. Around three and works until midnight."

"Patricia Foy. Divorced. She has an order of protection against her ex, Andrew Foy. I doubt he's still around. A couple of outstanding warrants."

"Thanks, Joe. Now, how are you doing?" Butch and Joe both laughed.

"I'm okay. Waiting for my daughter to make up her mind about getting married. Long Island weddings cost a lot these days. When I got married, we rented a hall. Damn it, Butch, I'm ready for retirement. I never should have gone back on patrol. I had a cozy job in communications. Got bored. It's not like the old days. Too much politics. All I do is spend time breaking in new sergeants. They need the hours. They're on the way to detective sergeant or maybe the DA's office. It's getting me down. I wangled a few months at Headquarters. After that - it's goodbye, Joe."

"You're a good man, Joe. I'll always remember our talks about my stay at the VA."

Butch rubbed his left arm. The white phosphorous burns ended his tour in Viet Nam. That's when the nightmares began. They were on night reconnaissance. Lured into an ambush, someone tossed a "Willie Pete." Butch saw the flash. His arm and then his body burst into flames. He fell and rolled. Butch was the only survivor. He spent a month in Saigon before returning stateside to Walter Reed, and then as an outpatient at the VA in Northport.

"Thanks, Joe. Let's get out of here before someone recognizes us."

"Hey. You left your Zippo on the table."

"Damn. Thanks. One of these days I'm going to lose it."

The following day, Butch drove to Three Stone Village. He found the address; a patio home. The houses on both sides of 76 Thorn Run were in foreclosure. Plywood covered their windows. Their front doors were boarded and chained. The house at 74 Thorn Run was covered with graffiti. Butch parked up the street and waited. Around noon, Charlie and Doris drove off in a beat up '73 Impala sedan. The only traffic on Thorn Road was the mail truck. Surveillance requires patience. The couple returned around five. Butch returned at different times over the next seven days. He didn't want to blow the stakeout. Charlie and Doris followed their routine each weekday, with the exception of the weekend. They left Saturday morning and returned late Sunday evening. Butch decided Friday evening would be the time to make his move.

Butch parked the pickup in a cluster of bushes and trees on the far side of an abandoned Dumpster. He wore a black jumpsuit with deep cargo pockets. He crept through the back yard of 78 Thorn Run. He stopped and listened. Sensing it was time, he approached the house. Torn black garbage bags littered the concrete patio. A small fiberglass runabout boat rested on a trailer with two flat tires. Parts from the outboard engine lay on the ground. Butch moved silently and cautiously. Perspiration dripped off his face.

From the lowest pocket on his jumpsuit, he pulled a pair of latex gloves. Next, he covered each tennis shoe with a paper bootie. He turned the brim of his Yankees cap to the rear. Butch had killed before, in a different time and place. The domestic violence incident in Patchogue nearly drove him nuts. Tonight was different. *Breathe. Three deep breaths. Be calm. Suppress the anger.* A feeling of excitement and anticipation began to grow. Butch wanted to kill.

The back door of 76 Thorn Run had six glass panes. Butch wrapped a cloth around the butt of his pistol. He smashed the pane closest to the lock. He reached in and opened the door. Butch carefully placed the rag in a small plastic bag and slipped it into his jumpsuit. The back door opened into the kitchen. Butch un-holstered his pistol and slowly moved room to room. *The place is a dump.* Butch walked to the master bedroom. He remained vigilant. *Never take anything for granted. Anticipate the unexpected.*

"Clear," he whispered after checking each room. *Wait a minute. Was that a library book on the dresser? These two go to the library?* Butch returned to the bedroom, picked up the book and walked back to the kitchen. It was 3:20. Less than an hour left. *Why were these assholes reading Ayn Rand's ATLAS SHRUGGED?* The answer would have to wait, but not for long.

Butch rested his pistol on the kitchen table and sat down. He lit a cigarette and placed his lighter next to the .22 caliber Hi-Standard. Butch pulled what appeared to be a push button tube flashlight from his sleeve pocket. He unscrewed the lens cover and removed the bulb from the disguised silencer. Butch held the Hi-Standard in his left hand and carefully threaded the homemade silencer to the barrel. *Gently. Too quick a turn and I'll strip the flashlight's threads.* He transferred the pistol to his right hand. *A bit heavy.* During the week, Butch tried several innovations he called "cans". This was simplest. *A few freeze washers, a quarter-inch drill bit, some screws, and a piece of plastic conduit. Threading the replacement barrel required a special touch. Nice job.*

The library book intrigued Butch. He pushed it into the center of the table. There was no mistaking the sound of the blown muffler on Ross's 73 Impala as it pulled into the driveway. Butch tensed. He took one last drag on his cigarette and dropped it on the floor. Under different circumstances, the next two or three minutes would have been comical. Charlie and Doris were arguing. The key wouldn't turn. She kicked the door.

"Damn it, Charlie. I'm tired of your lousy schemes," she yelled.

"Ah, shut up," Charlie replied.

He sounds frightened. The little shit. Charlie, my boy. You ain't seen nothin' yet.

Doris raged. "I told you to ask for more money. I want out of this shithole. Now you've got the cops looking for us. You douche bag. Lifting those plates from a Trinity car. The cops are sure to connect you and Trinity." Doris backed through the front door, still waving her arms. She towered over the cowering Weasel.

Butch stepped behind the bathroom door, waiting. Charlie ducked into the master bedroom to escape Doris' ranting. Doris walked toward the kitchen and stopped.

What the hell? Glass? Is that glass on the kitchen floor?

Doris approached the kitchen with caution. "Charlie, get out here. Get out here now!" Doris shouted, then turned. Intuitively, she sensed trouble. Too late.

Butch stepped out from behind the door. His pistol was aimed directly at Doris. He raised his left hand and pressed his index finger to his lips. He tilted his head. An evil smile briefly crossed his lips.

Doris started to call out. Butch raised his hand again, placing a tight grip on her throat. He whispered "Be quiet. I want Charlie. Not you. I don't want to hurt you." He pushed Doris into a kitchen chair. The Hi-Standard pressed between her shoulder blades. Doris stiffened as though to spring from the chair. Butch pressed the pistol's barrel hard into her back. He reached to the counter, switched on the radio and turned the volume up.

"What the hell is going on, Doris?" Charlie called from the other room. Butch pressed the pistol deeper into Doris's back."

"Doris, turn that thing down," demanded Charlie as he walked into the kitchen.

Charlie did a double take and started to bolt. A stranger was standing behind Doris. "What the hell is this? Who are you?"

Butch motioned for Charlie to come into the room. Butch tossed two plastic wire ties to Charlie. "Tie her to the chair. I'm warning you; don't screw with me."

Charlie began to shake with fear.

"Pull those ties tight," Butch said. "Now go over there and sit down." Butch pointed to a chair at the far end of the table. "Sit down."

"And what if I don't," Charlie said. It was a bluff. His entire body quaked with fear.

"Just sit down. Everything will be cool. I need some answers. That's all.

"My name is Butch Wade. I want you to say my name. Say Butch Wade." Butch sounded patronizing. Charlie was confused. Doris was in shock.

Butch lowered the radio volume a bit. "One more time. Say my name."

"Go to hell," said Charlie.

"Say his name, Charlie. He's going to kill us if you don't."

Charlie looked at Doris, then at Butch. "Okay. Butch Wade."

"I want you to remember my name, Charlie. It's vital."

Charlie scoffed. "Now what?"

"The GTO. Are you insane? You lifted the plates from your employer."

"I knew it. You dumbass," Doris screamed.

"Here's what I can't figure out. Why break into a house in Bayport?"

"What house in Bayport? I don't know what you're talking about."

"You killed the owner's dog and tossed it in the pool." Butch felt his anger growing. He couldn't allow his temper to get the best of him.

"I told you. I don't know anything. I never killed any dog."

"Tell him, Charlie, or I will."

"Shut up, Doris. He's fishing."

"Someone else was with you. Right? Probably taller and quite a bit stronger. The dog's neck was broken. Dead before it hit the water," Butch sneered.

Charlie smirked.

Ever so slowly, to accentuate the motion, Butch raised the Hi-Standard and fired. The round hit Charlie in the left shoulder. The lead bullet impacted clear of an artery or vital organ. Charlie was startled and winced with pain.

"Oh, man! You shot him," cried Doris. "Tell him, Charlie."

Charlie gasped. "Ansgar. It was Ansgar."

"What? Ansgar? You're not making any sense. Who is Ansgar?"

"Ansgar. He was in charge. He killed the dog. Not me. I asked him why he did it."

"And?"

"He said it was a warning. The woman would be next."

Butch's face began turning red. He felt his blood pressure rising. "What woman?"

"The owner. I don't know her name. She'd be next. That's all." Charlie began crying, more from fear than pain.

"Ansgar. Who does he work for?"

"Please, no more. If I tell you, they'll kill me," Charlie pleaded. Blood stained his shirt.

"What about me, Butch?" Doris begged. "I'll tell you."

"Shut up!" Charlie shouted again.

"Trinity. Ansgar works for Trinity. Please don't shoot me," Doris sobbed.

"I'm not going to shoot you, Doris," Butch said. He lowered the Hi-Standard to the table, but didn't release his grip. "Trinity found out you lifted the plates when the cops called. Right?"

Charlie nodded in agreement.

"Ansgar was furious. Trinity fired Charlie," Doris said.

"We're scared. Ansgar's a killer. I never meant to hurt anybody. I was supposed to tail a couple of investigators from Washington. It was a mess. That guy who chased us on the motorcycle. It was him or us." Charlie couldn't help himself. The words came spilling out.

"And Ansgar paid you to follow those guys from Washington?"

"Not exactly. No. Somebody else. He called us. I never met him. He never told me his name."

"Don't lie to me."

"I'm not."

"One more thing. I'm fascinated. What's with this library book? You a fan of Ayn Rand?"

"No. The guy called. Said my money was in that book at the Middle Island Library. He warned me to take the money and run."

"So you took the money and the book?"

"He can't help it. He's sick," cried Doris.

Charlie twitched and ground his teeth. "I'm going to get you for this," he snarled.

"I figured you'd say something like that, Charlie."

"And I'm going to get that woman in Bayport, too. I'll get even."

"The woman in Bayport is my ex-wife."

"So what," said Charlie, as he tried to stand.

"Sit down, Charlie. Do you remember my name? I want you to say my name again." Butch enjoyed tormenting the bleeding man. "Say my name."

"Say it yourself." Charlie spit defiantly.

Butch raised the pistol and fired a second round at the bleeding wound. Charlie's head flew back with such fury the kitchen chair rocked.

"Neither of you are going to hurt anyone ever again. You're a punk, Charlie. You're both worthless."

"You kill us and the cops will get you," said Doris.

"For a robbery gone wrong? A home intrusion? A rival looking for guns, drugs and money? You won't be high on the priority list, that's for sure. One other detail."

"What's that?" asked Charlie.

"It's over for you."

Charlie laughed. Butch fired again. The shot hit Charlie's right eye. His jaw dropped open in surprise. Doris screamed in vain. No one could hear her. Butch raised his left index finger to his lips then softly said, "Be quiet."

"You promised you wouldn't shoot me," she cried.

"If that's your wish, I won't."

Butch unscrewed the silencer and placed it back in his sleeve pocket. He opened the jumpsuit and holstered the pistol.

"What are you going to do?"

Butch didn't answer. He simply motioned for Doris to be silent. He walked to the wall phone and removed the plastic cover and replaced the receiver. He turned to the stovetop. He opened the lower cabinet door. Butch found the gas line connection. He reached in and tore the line from the stove fitting. The smell of propane began to fill the cabinet. It was time to leave.

"No, please. Please. I won't tell anyone. I don't want to die." Doris struggled to get free. The harder she struggled, the deeper the plastic ties cut into her wrists, drawing blood.

Butch never looked back at Doris or Charlie or the kitchen table. He walked onto the patio. *My life will never be the same.*

With arrogant disregard, Butch followed the concrete walk to the driveway and made his way back to the pickup. He drove out of Thorn Run and down Three Stones Drive. He turned right and headed west. His mission was almost complete. A Shell station with a pay phone was across from the Coram Fire Department. Butch slowly dialed Charlie's number, then deposited one dime and a nickel. The phone rang once, twice. Butch dropped the receiver and walked away. Butch felt for his Zippo. It was gone. *I left it on the kitchen table.* Panic rushed in. *The arson squad. They'll find the lighter with my initials. My good luck Zippo.* It was too late.

The Saturday morning news broadcast: "Two Dead. Three Stones Explosion Rocks Coram Development. Three homes destroyed." A spokesman for the Coram Fire Department speculated the fire started with a gas leak at 76 Thorn Run. Twelve neighboring departments responded. The chief's office was waiting for the official arson squad report. An anonymous source in the Coroner's office told the reporter it would take several days to identify the victims. "The remains were charred beyond recognition."

Butch turned off the television and shrugged. *They aren't going to hurt Elaine. That's for sure. Now for Mr. Ansgar.* Butch felt a gnawing angst and irritability. He hadn't taken his medication since the stakeout at Ross's. *The meds turn me into a zombie.* Butch's emotions were rising to the surface. *I don't want to think.* A familiar voice echoed in his head. The demon was returning. He couldn't suppress it. Butch stepped off the houseboat onto the dock. He needed Elaine. He couldn't tell her. He couldn't involve her in a double homicide. *I need to breathe. Get out on the Bay.* Butch's skiff, *Adventure,* was docked behind the houseboat. The taste and smell of salt air were the medications Butch needed to deal with the demon. He started the outboard, untied the lines and headed out Cory Creek to the Great South Bay.

The Bay was as calm as a sheet of glass. Butch pushed the throttle wide open until he rounded the point, as though he were being chased by the voice in his head. Then he throttled back to a slow meandering speed. Finally, he cut the engine and let the boat drift back toward Patchogue. The small deck was wet from spray. It didn't matter. Butch stretched out and fell asleep. It was getting late afternoon or early evening, Butch guessed, looking at the sun. *Time to head in.* The wind blowing across the Bay from Fire Island created a chop. Whitecaps formed. Butch reached into *Adventure's* locker. He grabbed his yellow slicker. His seaman's knife fell out of the slicker's pocket on to the floorboards. Butch put it back and snapped the pocket flap. *Don't want to lose my Dad's knife.* Butch turned *Adventure* east, advanced the throttle and headed toward the Patchogue River. The outboard engine roared. The skiff pounded the waves. Butch's brain pulsed to the rhythm of *River Deep Mountain High,* over and over again.

The sun was setting as Butch motored up Corey Creek. He secured *Adventure's* lines and walked to the houseboat. The sliding glass doors were ajar. Butch cautiously stepped from the dock on the houseboat. Through the glass door, Butch could see the outline of a man with his back to the door, sitting on a bar stool at the chart table. Butch slid the door open.

"Come on in, Butch." It was Joe Larkin.

"Joe. What the hell? This is a surprise. What are you doing here? How did you get in?"

"One question at a time, buddy," said Joe. He turned on the stool to face Butch.

Butch looked perplexed.

"You're awfully trusting or careless. You left the door unlocked."

"What's going on?" Butch asked. The answer was in Joe's right hand; a P-38 pistol.

"Move away from the door, Butch." Joe motioned with a wave of the pistol.

"Is this a joke, Joe?"

"No joke, Butch."

"Are you mad?" asked Butch.

"I think we both have gone a bit crazy. Don't you agree?"

"What are you talking about?"

"The fire in Three Stones Village. It was you. 76 Thorn Run. I passed that information to you at the diner."

"You caught me, Joe. Now, what are you going to do about it?"

"You saved me the trouble of dealing with Ross and his

girlfriend," said Joe.

"It was you? You were the contact between Ross and Trinity?"

"I told you, Butch, Long Island weddings cost a lot of money. These younger guys coming on the job will make twice my retirement. Look at me. I'm a wreck. Every bone in my body hurts. I put ten years in with the Village force. I joined the county in nineteen sixty. I served my country and the good people of Suffolk. And for what? Next to nothing."

"So you sold out?"

"I prefer to think I was bought out," Joe gripped the pistol so tightly his hand trembled.

"The Headquarters assignment. You're on the joint task force. Right? You fed Trinity task force information. That's how Weasel and Doris tracked Jack and Clayton. You didn't lift Ross's address from Briggs' file. You had the information all along."

"You look stunned, buddy. One thing…I never thought Trinity would hassle Elaine. I wouldn't do that. The whole plan turned sour."

"Why the pistol? Are you planning to kill me?"

"I have no choice." His shoulders slouched.

"Why?"

"Briggs."

"What about Briggs?"

"I was curious," said Joe. "I wanted to see the fire scene. When I pulled up, Briggs was there. Arson had finished the preliminary. We walked into the kitchen. Everything was charred. The smell was awful. I saw Briggs pick it up."

"Pick what up?"

"Your lighter. Briggs spotted it on the floor next to some melted plastic. Arson missed it. Your Zippo, buddy boy. I know you. You must have planned every minute detail. I can't believe you got sloppy."

"Briggs covered for me?"

"Slipped it in his pocket."

"What makes you so sure it was my lighter?"

"The diner. Remember?"

"The diner. Right. Too many voices running around in my head."

"Not good, Butch."

"That lighter was my good luck charm."

"Well, you're in for some bad luck now, buddy."

Butch started to lower his hands.

"No way. Keep 'em high. Now reach around with your left hand and slowly, very slowly, take out your piece."

Butch pretended to look puzzled. He hesitated.

"The Colt .38. This is me, Joe. Remember?"

Butch followed Joe's order and slowly unholstered the revolver. The Colt's cylinder held six rounds. Department safety protocol called for 5 rounds with the firing pin on the empty chamber to prevent an accidental discharge. Not Butch. It was always a full six rounds.

"Don't drop it!" Joe warned.

Butch nodded he understood. *Don't drop it? There's one chance in a million the piece will discharge. What the hell.*

What the hell! and *Oh, shit!* were Butch's favorite expressions before doing something risky and foolish. Butch reached behind his back and twisted his left hand to grip the revolver. It was an awkward grasp.

"Slip your index finger through the trigger guard. Gently. Don't even think about dropping it," Joe warned.

It's my only chance. Butch brought the Colt around front and dropped it. The Colt hit the floor. Joe flinched and stepped back. The revolver didn't discharge. In that instant, Butch hollered "Oh, shit!" and lunged at Joe. Joe fired the P-38.

The bullet struck Butch's rain slicker pocket and smashed the seaman's knife into his left side. Butch gasped, "Uh." The two men struggled for the P-38. It discharged again. Joe's hold weakened. He made a loud sucking sound and collapsed. Butch clasped his side and fell on the couch.

The dockside light cast shadows through the sliding glass doors. Rays of light reflected off Joe's pooling blood. Butch moaned, "How long have I been out?"

He slid to the floor and crawled to Joe. Butch felt for a pulse. Joe was dead. Butch shook Joe's corpse and cried out, "Why?" He wanted to be angry, but all he felt was confusion and despair. Depression was setting in.

Early Sunday morning, Tom Briggs parked his station wagon near the Corey Creek Bridge. *I should be in church, not here.* He glanced in the rearview mirror. Briggs' face revealed apprehension. He locked his S&W in the glove compartment. Briggs was convinced Butch would surrender without a fight. He followed the worn narrow path to the dock. Briggs had walked this path many times after Butch's divorce. Briggs talked Butch into taking the disability pension rather than face a review board and possible dismissal from the force. Briggs' younger brother was killed in Viet Nam. Butch reminded Briggs of Ted. Ted was moody and reckless. Kind but quick-tempered.

The dock was quiet. The stillness troubled Briggs. He usually heard music coming from the houseboat. Briggs boosted himself onto the dock. Over the years, the Captain put on seventy pounds. *Next time I'll drive around.*

"Butch. It's Briggs. You home?" He called again. Briggs held the railing and stepped onto the houseboat. He looked through the sliding glass door. At first it appeared to be a shadow. He looked again. There was a body on the floor. Briggs jerked the sliding glass door. It was unlocked.

"Butch," Briggs shouted and stepped inside. A man lay in a pool of dried blood. Briggs stopped. He walked around the body, being careful not to disturb the scene. "Joe Larkin!" he exclaimed. "My God, Butch, what have you done?"

Briggs paused. He looked around. *Damn it, Tom. Don't touch a thing.* Briggs walked to the bathroom. He examined the soles of his shoes. Mud. *I've got to take them off.* He placed a towel beneath his stocking feet and precariously shuffled. Briggs retraced his steps. *I can't get rid of the mud. I can wipe away my shoe prints.* Next, Briggs stepped through the sliding glass doors. He scanned the dock for boaters. *None in sight.* Holding his shoes, Briggs stepped back onto the dock. He turned on the fresh water and flushed water across the boat's walkway and the dock. His socks were soaked, but that didn't matter. Briggs didn't want to be implicated or tied to Joe Larkin's death. *I've got to find Butch before someone discovers Larkin's body.* Briggs' next challenge was getting off the dock and up the path. He looked around one last time. *The Zippo.* Briggs took the lighter from his pocket. He held the talisman in the palm of his hand. Briggs tossed it into Corey Creek. *One more glance. All clear.* He jumped from the dock and fell. *Now that was a mistake. Look at me.* Briggs' left knee and arm were covered in mud. His wrist ached. He got up and turned around. He used his right foot to cover the impression. He climbed the path to his car. "I've got to find a phone," he said. Briggs drove to the pay phone outside the Blue Point Bar and Grille.

"Suffolk County Police dispatch. Is this an emergency?"

"I'm calling to report a body." Briggs used a handkerchief to muffle his voice.

"Please give me your name and location."

Briggs answered the dispatcher's questions. Briggs withheld his name.

"Please, I need your name."

Briggs replaced the receiver and drove away. *I've got to locate Butch.* Briggs was too late. No one could save Butch.

Butch wasn't sure how long he lay on the houseboat floor. His left side burned. He reached inside the yellow rain slicker. His shirt was soaked with blood and perspiration. He felt clammy and cold. He managed to pull himself up and get to the chest at the foot of his bed. Butch tossed the clothes on the floor. The chest had a false bottom. Beneath it was Butch's stash; a ready bag, a Colt .45 caliber ACP pistol, and his field kit. Butch painfully removed the slicker and his tee shirt. The seaman's knife had saved his life. Butch had a deep flesh wound from the bulky knife. *It isn't a bullet hole. No internal damage, but I can't go to a hospital. Too many questions. Too little time. Pressure. Apply pressure to the wound.* Butch took one of the two field dressings and pressed it against his side. He taped it and wrapped the gauze around his torso. He felt faint. He had to control the bleeding. *I've got to get out of here.*

The demon's voice returned. *Too late, Butch. You know what you have to do. Now do it.*

Butch applied a second dressing over the first and wrapped his torso again. He pulled on a shirt without buttoning it and stuck the .45 inside his waistband. The fury returned.

Uncertain how he got there, Butch was behind the wheel of

the pickup. Butch felt a sharp pain with each turn of the steering wheel. From time to time, the truck wandered onto the shoulder of the road. Butch longed for Elaine. No time for a last goodbye. *One final stop.*

Butch pulled into a parking space. The pickup faced southwest. The Sandspit Marina was a favorite parking place for lovers. Butch got out of the truck. He walked to the dock's edge and gazed into the river. Memories rushed in. Butch felt the angst taking hold again. In the distance, a pair of running lights bobbed through the chop. It was slowly returning to the shelter of the Patchogue River. *I wish I was out there.*

"Not tonight, Butch. Not tonight."

Butch turned and looked. No one was there. He climbed back in the pickup.

"It's time, Butch."

"Yes. I know." Butch rummaged through the glove compartment. *I know I have a piece of paper and a pencil in here. I've found it.*

"Butch, there's no time for a note."

"There is. Damn you. A final goodbye."

"Quickly."

Butch fumbled with the stubby pencil. He scribbled a note, folded it, and placed it in his shirt pocket behind the pack of cigarettes.

> *Dear Elaine:*
> *Please know I love you. We*
> *have hopes and expectations.*
> *Sometimes life gets in the way.*
> *Love, Butch.*

"Are you finished?"

"I'm ready," Butch replied as though someone were sitting next to him. Butch slid his hand across the tattered seat and gripped the Colt.

"What the hell."

CAST OF CHARACTERS

Karl Peter Koch: Nazi scientist. Dachau Prison on malaria experiments, 1938-1945.

Matt Nagle: Associate Professor of English at Suffolk County Community College.

Sam Beverly: Deputy Inspector General for the General Accounting Office

David Clayton: Attorney assigned General Accounting Office.

Jack Thompson: Department of Justice attorney assigned to the General Accounting Office.

Robert. The mysterious whistle blower.

Tony Portavani: Electrical contractor on Plum Island.

Liz Nagle: Matt Nagle's wife.

Joan Portavani: Tony's wife.

Hilda Koch: Tony's German girlfriend. Daughter of Frieda Koch. Niece of Karl Peter Koch.

Frieda Koch: Sister-n-law to Karl Peter Koch.

Two German goons: Attack Tony. One has SS blood tattoo on his arm.

Alice Thatcher: A British Overseas Volunteer.

Anna (Bruns) Mueller: Karl Peter Koch's lover in Germany.

George Mueller: Married Anna Mueller post WW II. Works in England for Thermos.

Otto Bruns: Anna Bruns' father. Worked in the Transportation Ministry.

Edna Bruns: Anna's mother.

Nadine: Daughter of Anna Bruns and Karl Peter Koch. Born at Steinborg, Himmler's first Lebensborn. Official name was Lebensborn card number SS 1-3128.

Abid: Iranian student. Employed at the small shop where Koch purchases a walking had and secures the burst transmitter..

Rajid: Iranian student. Pencil-thin bear and deeply set eyes. The dominant of the two men in this "cell."

General Mark Webster code name Liebling: Air Force General. Supervises a secret bioresearch project at Fort Detrick, Maryland and Plum Island.

Trinity PharmoDynamics, formerly Black Knight International.

Liechtenauer, Walther, Original director of Trinity PharmoDynamics.

Berg, Albert, Operations Director for Trinity PharmoDynamics.

Strauss, Kurt, Chief Financial Office at Trinity PharmoDynamics.

Reiter, Eric, Chief of PharmoDynamics International Research based in Argentina.

Schmidt, Fritz, Chief Legal Counsel Trinity PharmoDynamics.

 Dr. Klaus Schilling : One of the world's foremost experts on tropical diseases when he was ordered by Henirich Himmler, the head of all the Nazi concentration camps, to come out of retirement to work on a cure for malaria. Resarched.at Dachau. Hanged for war crimes.

Ansgar: Assassin.

 Vriend: Ansgar's talisman.

Richard Shipe. Ansgar's cohort.

Grace Beverly. Sam Beverly's wife.

 Rachael Beverly: Sam and Grace's daughter. Attends Mary Washington College.

 Congresswoman Elizabeth Harrington. Congressional oversight committee.

Dakota Putnam: reporter for the Washington Post.

Robert Doyle: New York delegation.
Dakota Putnam's former lover.

Captain Tom Griggs, Suffolk County PD

Kathleen Thompson: Jack Thompson's ex-wife.

Elaine Wade: sister of Jack Thompson

Davis" Butch" Wade. Elaine's ex-husband.

Hermann von Leer: AKA Eric Peterson.   represents Trinity

PharmoDynamics and the Circle of Twelve.

Circle of Twelve: A select historical group of powerful international investors.
Vikki and Tom Ambrose: The Beverly's best friends. Vikki is Grace's lover.

Patricia Foy: Charlie "Weasel" Ross's sister.

Charlie "Weasel" Ross: "clepto". Tails Jack and David.

Andraxilan: an experimental antibiotic.

Sergeant Joe Larkin: Suffolk County Police joint task force.

Doris McFarlane: Charlie "Weasel" Ross's girlfriend.

Lou-Ann Stokes: FBI agent assigned to the General Accounting Office.

Jules Smylee: committed suicide. Failed to acquire Westfield Laboratory.

Lynn Stahl: Sam Beverly's secretary.

Dennis Farrago: FBI Agent. Electronic eves dropping specialist.

Anthony Napoli: New York City Detective liaison to FBI task force.

Ashton Pickering: Liechtenauer's successor. He is the great grandson of J.J. Pickering, a Circle of Twelve disciple. Ashton's father J.R. Pickering is a little know financial advisor to Presidents and tyrants alike. He is a proponent of the balance of power concept. J.R. and his associates control the flow of Middle East oil and the futures market.
dating before World War II.

Kumori Nishimura: virologist from Unit 731. Employed by US

government in disease prevention research.

Dr. Bob Johnson: Deputy Medical Examiner for New York City.

Dr. Youssef Massri : Forensic specialist. Experience with exotic diseases.

John Evans: Colonel USAF Ret. Acting Inspector General.

Erskin Young: Erskin Young is a hold over from the OSS. He transferred to the Department of Justice after WW II. He supervised the list of priority Nazis brought into the United States. He heads the secret Department of Justice documents restorations group.
Ted Anderson: Deputy Director for Personnel at FBI in Washington, DC.

Colonel Patrick O'Toole. Security Chief at Fort Detrick.

Dr. Jed Nethers. Psychiatrist.

Jon. Owner of La Petite Coquette.

Sergeant Tim West. New York State Police.

Roy Taylor. Driver for Fort Detrick courier service.

Major Bill Foster. Special Forces Emergency Response Team.